# EXTRAORDINARY MEANS

# EXTRAORDINARY MEANS

*A Novel By*

## DONNA LEVIN

ARBOR HOUSE
*New York*

Manufactured in the United States of America

10 9 8 7 6 5 4 3 2 1

Library of Congress Cataloging in Publication Data

Levin, Donna.
Extraordinary means.

I. Title.
PS3562.E88955E9   1987      813'.54      86-32034
ISBN: 0-87795-857-2

*For*
*Michael Bernick,*
*my extraordinary husband*

## ACKNOWLEDGMENTS

I would like to thank:

Drs. Charles Bernick, Jim Bernick, and Pam Medellin for medical background; Kate O'Donnell and Mimi Studley for proofreading under enormous pressure; my entire fiction workshop; Bruce Hartford and Janet Shepard for advice and many hours on the phone; Suzanne Juergensen for her encouragement, support, and most of all, her friendship; my father, Marvin Levin, for giving me the time to write.

Finally, Gloria Loomis, Beth Vessel, and Liza Dawson for their guidance and for their faith in me.

# 1

Irreversible coma. Elaina—my mother—will tell you, I've never been anything but trouble.

I can see my body, and it wouldn't make the cover of *Vogue:* What you can see of my face (there's the tube taped to my nose) is sunken. My cheekbones stick out like little doorknobs. My arms and legs are bent up to my torso like chicken wings. My hair is lank and oily; they've cut it short just to get it out of the way. Underneath my drooping eyelids, two milky irises peer out.

Behind and around the bed is equipment that looks like it belongs in an auto assembly plant. And in my throat there's a wide blue plastic tube that leads to a large console with a clear plastic cylinder on top. Within the cylinder is a bellows that swells and then retracts with a faint *whoosh*-click. This is the respirator, without the miracle of which I would no longer be with them.

But where am I? Hovering above the bed? That's my perspective, but I have no sense of occupying space. It's been about two months since the accident, judging from bits of conversation I've picked up. At first I felt groggy, like I'd been kicked in the head with two weeks' worth of jet lag, but gradually my memory and my ability to perceive returned. I fought that; it was as if someone were trying to wake me up too early and I were clinging to the cottonballs of sleep, willing the intruder to go away. Then, you know how it is, being awake

1

didn't seem so bad. I started to put things together. I'm not dead, unless someone's wasting a lot of money on a heart monitor, but I'm not about to go anywhere for lunch, either.


Now I hear it, mingling with but still separate from the other hospital sounds (whoosh of the respirator; squeak of the gurneys; arcane, incessant dings and pings)—the *clack*. My mother's heels on the waxed hospital floor. And I feel lighter, queasy, as if I were floating closer to the ceiling.

The clacking stops in front of the nurses' station. With my new-and-improved hearing, I can follow her low-pitched, hoarse voice; now melodious, now teasing, now uncertain. She's trying to get a compliment from Nurse Pinafore, the blonde, whose pug nose my mother praises to her face but whose close-set eyes she maligns behind her back.

Then my mother swirls in, her black crepe dress rustling (she's in mourning for me already; and besides, black makes her look thinner), the double choker of pearls and the high collar emphasizing her jawline and high cheekbones. Her milk skin shows a few wrinkles, but they're hardly visible in dim light, and her thick auburn hair is swept up and lacquered in a Gibson girl that went out of style a hundred years ago—along with mothers like her who take to their beds three days a month with the curse!

She gasps as if she's never seen me like this before. She slaps her hand across her breasts, the enormous breasts that she passed on to all her daughters; her egg-shaped eyes (blue-gray, the color of the Pacific before the rain) widen even larger as she digs the tips of her sculptured nails into her cheekbones and drags them slowly down the side of her face, leaving marks like red snails' tracks. "I can't bear it!" she shrieks. "My precious child!"

Give me a break!

She's here every afternoon. Mostly she sits by my bed,

sometimes reading from the prayer book that belonged to her father, but occasionally wandering out into the hall for an interval of cheerful conversation. She knows the names of all the patients on the floor; she is the queen bee of 6-West, buzzing from room to room, delivering messages and M&M's. She swells with the illnesses of others; her concern proliferates like the blossoms of a bridal bouquet.

"Mickey Mouse would like some coffee," Daniel tells Becky and Leah when all three are there with Elaina. Daniel is my brother, twenty-two, two years younger than I. It's my fault that we never got along. An early example: When he was in kindergarten, I told the other kids that he had a second penis growing out of his behind, just like our cat Choppo's short tail. Daniel never had the wit to fight me verbally and they wouldn't let him hit me—besides, I was bigger than he was until we were teenagers.

"*Guy*," Becky laughs, drawing out the expletive, "are you suddenly a double amputee?"

"I'll get it." Leah stands. She is the youngest, the blonde teddy bear of the family: fifteen, her worried, babyish face splattered with freckles.

"I wish your father were here," Elaina sniffs, dabbing at her eyes under her mascara.

"Guy, Mouse," Becky says, blowing a bubble of sugarless grape gum while she examines the moussed quills of her chestnut hair in a pocket mirror, "you make it sound like he's dead."

"With his personality, it's hard to tell sometimes. You know I'm just kidding."

But dad did come to visit yesterday. He usually comes about once a week, and then he stands in the corner, far away from the tubes and screens and consoles, tugging at his collar and clearing his throat and generally looking as though he wants to throw up. This time, though, it had only been four days since his last visit. I don't think my family knows what it is, but I'm sure that something big is about to happen. My intuition approaches telepathy these days. Without a body, I'm not limited to the information my senses can gather; I'm aware of nuances that were too subtle for me before. Their thoughts are part of the atmosphere, like particles of light or radio waves; I feel as though I could reach out and pluck those thoughts out of the air like ripe plums, greedy and hungry girl that I am.

Meanwhile, no more headaches, menstrual cramps, constipation, eyestrain, indigestion, insomnia, sinusitis. I'm a newly popped kernel of popcorn, floating on a warm current of air.

"I'll be right back," Leah says.

"Lots of cream, please," Elaina tells her.

"Beam me down a Snickers," Becky says, removing her gum from her mouth and wrapping it in a shred of binder paper.

"Nothing for me, thanks," Daniel says.

Becky and Leah both go to Alta Vista High. I'm still remembered there, by some of the teachers that have been there forever. A couple of them even taught—or tried to teach— Elaina. They always remember the troubled ones. Aren't the troubled ones, the dark ones sulking outside the circle, more memorable in the end than the light and cheerful ones dancing along its edge? Try to distinguish among the angelic voices in a children's choir; the one you will hear is the one singing off-key.


It's about eight o'clock in the evening. I feel lulled by the warm antiseptic air, the rhythmic *whoosh*-click of the respirator, and the purr from within its depths. In the distance I hear urgent, muffled voices.

Usually about now I sort of drowse a little. I have the feeling that as time goes by I won't do that so much; it's as if I haven't yet forgotten what it's like to be in a body, the way an infant thinks he's still part of his mother. This is a state that Dr. Gorgeous, the resident assigned to my case, has probably not read about in any medical books. My EEG is not flat, but I'm without cognitive functions—I've heard the doctors explain that to my parents thirty times at last count. The *thinking* part of my brain is gone, they say. True—that body below me feels nothing. But I'll give them cognitive functions! I never liked doctors, anyway.

I can't rest tonight. I want to see what my family is doing. They must be talking about me; I must be, at last, the center of their attention, as the gravity of my illness pulls their thoughts toward me. I need to know. I need to be with them. Maybe I'm not stuck here. Maybe if I really try . . .

I picture them all in the large, sunken living room of our house, where a wobbly-looking chandelier throws patches of dim light across the beamed ceiling. The room reminds me of a dusty old cathedral, except that it's kept carefully dusted by Lee Emma. Paddy O'Flanagan, our current cat, is sleeping on the piano that no one knows how to play. I can even see the vertical slits in the fabric of the couch, and the pieces of exposed stuffing, where Paddy has sharpened his claws.

My father is in the wing chair, one shoe propped up on the opposite knee. Daddy: a.k.a. Jonathan Silverstein, President of Silverstein, Inc. At the hospital, the ambulatory patients ask him for investment advice in the hall. But having a daughter in a coma hasn't kept him home from the office much; in fact, I've heard my mother complain that he spends more time there than before. He wishes that there were more than twenty-four hours in a day and that the excess fell between nine and five.

Becky is at his feet, her knees pressed up to her chin. Since this afternoon, she has "made up," which includes three black lines like cat's whiskers extending from each eye.

Leah perches on the arm of the chair. She wears a fuzzy blue sweater and her wispy hair is pulled back into a short ponytail, emphasizing the roundness of her face.

It's so detailed. So real. I feel as though it's happening

now, as though by an act of imagination and will—both are much stronger in me now that my spirit isn't dividing its time between self-actualization and wondering where the ladies' room is—I managed to travel to our house on Magnolia Street, materialized there. . . . A pleasant enough trip, no speed bumps or tacky billboards on this road. . . .

Elaina is standing in front of the fireplace. "This can't go on," she says. "Melissa wouldn't want to be kept alive this way."

Yes, I would. Sure I would.

Daniel, sitting on the couch, looks up at Elaina adoringly. He has brown eyes that resemble Jonathan's and tight dark blond curls. He dresses foppishly; the red silk handkerchief in his breast pocket is an affectation typical of his crowd of friends, a bunch of rich, overgrown partiers. I sometimes wonder if he's gay. "You're right, Mouse," he says.

"What's this?" Jonathan rouses himself from an in-depth study of the hemline of his pants. He looks around as if aware for the first time that there are other people in the room.

Elaina takes a deep breath. Once she's gotten Jonathan's attention, she's not about to throw it away too quickly. So she sucks in her cheeks and rolls her big eyes, but doesn't say anything.

*"Mom,"* Becky groans, on Jonathan's behalf.

"I just mean we have to make some decision," Elaina says. "It's been two months now."

"I think I know what Mouse is talking about," Daniel says.

"Oh?" Jonathan asks. The puzzlement in his voice is a sign of irritation.

"I think"—Elaina rolls her eyes again, breathing so hard that it sounds like she's going to hyperventilate or have an orgasm—"that we should tell Dr. Harding to disconnect the respirator."

Disconnect the respirator? But if they do that, what will happen to me?

And now I know that I *am* here. Up until now, all this has

been something I could have imagined. But I recognize this moment: the one you never quite reach in dreams, that wakes you just as it begins; the moment when control slips away and the possibility occurs that the universe is run by sinister forces. I can feel the texture of external reality, and how I am woven into the nap. I'm really here. And my family is talking about murdering me.

Daddy! I want to cry. Help me!

There is silence in the room. Paddy stretches and yawns.

Jonathan purses his lips and bunches his forehead. Then he looks at Elaina and says, not too loudly, clipping the words, "We are not even going to think about doing that."

"I beg your pardon?" Elaina pulls the red handkerchief from Daniel's pocket and dabs at her eyes.

"We are not going to do anything of the kind, and we are not even going to discuss it." Jonathan raises his voice a little. His shaggy black brows come down hard over his brown eyes. "Until you can find a way to ask Melissa and she tells you otherwise, no one is touching my daughter."

I know what daddy wants—to stash me in a home, the most expensive one he can find, where he'll never visit me. But so what? I wouldn't be stuck there. I'm mobile now. I got to the house tonight and I probably can do it again. This is my big chance, the chance I never would have had otherwise, to be with them invisibly and to learn about them, to understand them. If my mother will leave me alone . . . but she never could leave me alone. . . .

"It is pretty *radical*, Mom," Becky says. She flips her hair over her shoulders. "We saw a movie about this in civics. It was called *The Right to Die*. Melissa didn't leave a living will, so that means—"

"That's enough, Miss Know-It-All," Daniel snaps. "You're upsetting Mickey Mouse."

Leah presses her teeth into the tough, dead skin around her nail. Maybe she'll speak up for me—but I have the feeling that she's afraid to say anything that might be interpreted as favoring one or the other side.

Elaina twists her hands together as if she's rubbing lotion on them. "You're heartless," she tells Jonathan. A sob travels up her throat. "It's cruel to leave Melissa like this. Can't you see she's suffering, with that horrible thing stuck in her neck? And the way she jerks around?"

"That's just reflexes, Mom," Becky interrupts. "We read about that in science—"

"And those sores on her hip," Elaina weeps. *Mother always wanted me to look my best.*

Daniel puts his arms around Elaina's waist and leans his head on her breasts. I'm surprised he isn't crying too; he usually starts in pretty soon after Elaina. Instead, he glowers at Jonathan, which is the most defiance he dares to show. Elaina won't even do that. Her battles with Jonathan are more like guerrilla warfare: underground assaults, subterfuge, secret bombings that she later denies responsibility for. She usually gets her way, but maybe that's because he doesn't really care about the things she wants, like more money for the beauty shop, clothes, a new car. He almost never gets angry—but he's pissed at her now, and because of me!

"It's the end of the discussion." Jonathan stands up. Becky and Leah scamper out of his way. And he stomps out of the room, a portly gentleman juggernaut, taking the two steps to the foyer in one long stride, his wing tips hitting the hardwood floor with little slaps of finality—on his way to his study, his office-away-from-the-office, where he will close the door and no one will hear anything from him all evening, except the unintelligible half of a phone conversation.

Shadows are beginning to fill in the spaces between people. I don't want to be here anymore; it's just too depressing. And as my tenacity frays, so does my hold on the place, and I am slipping away, into darkness. The last things I see are the faces of my mother and brother and sisters, candle flames dying out.

And then the darkness dissolves, and I am back at the hospital.

I'm not positive that I can get to them again; maybe it was just a fluke. But I'm sure as hell not going to let my mother get away with this without a fight.


The next morning I concentrate on them all. *Whoosh*-click goes the respirator. I can picture it: Jonathan left for the office so early that it feels as though he didn't sleep at home. Becky and Leah have abandoned their cereal bowls on the breakfast-room table; a few lonely Cheerios are adrift on the milk. Upstairs, Elaina is motionless in sleep, her head on two pink satin pillows. Daniel is in his room watching game shows: "Win a Million," "Dreams Come True."

I know what they're doing without entirely knowing how I know it. It's not that they're so predictable, although they are to me—just like I always knew, when I came home to visit, what each one was going to say to make me want to strangle him or her. But if someone in my condition develops psychic powers, it's not surprising those powers would develop along the pathways that already exist: the connections among the people of one's childhood, that sometimes approach a psychic bond.

So before I know it, I'm there again, haunting the big old house on Magnolia Street, nestling in the cracks in the woodwork, watching Lee Emma dust.

At eleven, Elaina gets up to begin her toilette for the pilgrimage to Mt. Moriah Hospital. She powders her thighs and drenches her breasts with cologne. From that plump white body, mine was torn. Who are you, mommy, soft as a cushion and smelling like a warm bed? I love you, but can't find what I love in you. . . .

If only I could get inside her to know what she feels. I see that she is suffering: She weeps when she visits me and she has to take pills to sleep. But she was always weeping, taking pills, often over an unseen, past grief—she would say that she was mourning the death of her father, though he died when I was four. And she has flowed, too, with a troubled inner tide that sometimes took her (unwillingly?) away from us.

There were other times, too, that I can't forget, though I try: before Daniel came, when she played games with me on the floor for hours. We made trains out of the dining-room chairs, and abstract sculptures out of the good china and silver. Elaina seemed to enjoy it more than I did. And even a few years later, sometimes she parked Daniel with a baby-sitter and we went to the movies, just the two of us, where she bought me all the junk food I wanted—popcorn, ice cream sandwiches, Raisinets, and Cokes. When I was a teenager, there were a few evenings in her bedroom (God knows how I got rid of all the competition then): me draped over her dressing-room chair, the two of us discussing old movies, recalling the names of character actors, wondering whatever-became-of-what-was-his-name and debating such questions as whether Vivien Leigh was prettier than Jennifer Jones or just more exotic.

Now I watch Elaina spread the mist-blue shadow across her lids and accentuate her high cheekbones with a slash of Rose Heaven Blusher 28. She is ready. She shouts for Daniel and heads down the stairs.

Suddenly I realize that I've followed her out of the house. So I'm not limited to this place, either. Lovely!

Daniel backs his Porsche out of the driveway so Elaina won't snag her pantyhose on the hedge. And as she carefully folds herself into the car, I slip in with her. Yes, I'm definitely getting the hang of this whole spirit routine.

So we all head to the hospital. I could jump ahead and meet them there, but it's much more fun as an invisible hitch-hiker. I wish I could tell them I'm here! But that would spoil it, too. I can't wait to find out what they're going to say about me.

On Twelve Oaks Boulevard, we drive past Dmitri's

Number One, but neither Elaina nor Daniel look at it as we go by. Jonathan bought Daniel a half-interest in this pizza parlor almost a year ago, but Daniel is most likely to be there when his friends have congregated for free beer. Elaina and Daniel both know that Daniel doesn't want to corrupt his soul with ambition, the compulsion to make money; Elaina says that Daniel is like her father, the rabbi, in that and so many other admirable ways.

The Porsche slowly descends from the rarefied atmosphere of the hills to the more prosaic streets of lower Alta Vista. Alta Vista is a tiny island of a city, to the east of San Francisco Bay and surrounded on three sides by Oakland.

Elaina sighs. "This just can't go on," she says.

Daniel nods grimly.

"Your father doesn't understand."

Daniel glances at Elaina's profile. Her nose is somewhat pointed, her chin firm. Her skin makes me think of white chocolate. "I don't get how dad thinks," he grunts.

"As little as possible," Elaina replies. Pause. "Now you know I don't mean that. I love your father."

Daniel grunts again, eyes on the road.

Elaina pulls down the sun visor and examines her lips in the mirror, pressing them together, then running the tip of her nail along their fine border. "He wouldn't even talk to me this morning. Not that he'll ever talk to me." She looks out the window. "I call him at the office and I say this is Mrs. Silverstein, and his secretary says, 'Who?'" Elaina sighs. "It just breaks my heart to see Melissa this way." Her voice rises, vibrates, then cracks, like a singer reaching for a note beyond her range.

"Yeah."

"Danabable, it wasn't your fault."

But the word *fault* hangs in the stuffy air of the Porsche. Daniel presses the button to lower the automatic window.

"I wish there was something we could *do*," Elaina goes on, rubbing her hands together rather spastically.

"Well, dad says no, and I guess you need both parents' permission, don't you?"

"I don't know," Elaina says, twisting her hands even faster. "I don't know about these things."

We cross the border between Alta Vista and Oakland. Here the houses are squatter, with thin curtains at the windows and broken lawn furniture on small patches of weedy grass. Signs above the stores need painting. In Oakland there is less money for facades.

"I mean"—Elaina presses her lips together repeatedly, another tic that drives me crazy but never seems to bother Daniel—"if I want to do something like this but your father says no, does that mean that we can't? That doesn't seem fair somehow."

"I don't know," Daniel says. "I guess the doctor knows."

"A doctor should know. But a doctor isn't a lawyer."

Daniel shrugs. "We could ask a lawyer, then."

"Your father's a lawyer. Of course he doesn't practice. He doesn't need to practice, because he always does it right."

"Huh?"

"He doesn't need to *practice*, because he does it right. Don't you get it?"

"Yeah, uh-huh, that's funny."

"But we couldn't ask *him*. Not about this."

"No."

"If there was another lawyer maybe, would you mind, Danabable?" Her voice has taken on that wheedling tone that, if refused, can quickly become a whimper. Or a shriek.

"Would I mind what?" Daniel asks nervously.

"Going to see a lawyer. I'm just too stupid to do things like that, but you can handle it."

Daniel straightens. "To ask him what we can do about Melissa? Sure, I can take care of that."

Elaina leans over and kisses Daniel's hair, right above the ear. He shivers. "You are the bestest boy a Mouse ever had."

She checks herself in the mirror again, this time to smooth her lacquered hair. "We'd better not tell your father, though."

"Really. Well, you know *I* can keep a secret."

Elaina claps her hands. "You are my perfect child!"

I don't like this at all. Not one little tiny bit.


How did a nice girl like me wind up looking like the cover of *Popular Science?* Jonathan blames Daniel, though he would never say so; Grandma Rose attributes the guilt to Elaina, maybe just from habit. I am willing to suspend blame. And if you'll believe that . . .

After being bored by clerical work, failing at medical-equipment sales, and surviving four months in a travel agency with a computer from the Bronze Age, I was—yes, yes, I was finally getting it together, putting the shit in a sack, wiring this baby for sound. Through a boyfriend (okay, it was a guy I picked up in a café on Telegraph Avenue), I lucked into a job at a small Berkeley newspaper, called *Get It Right.* They couldn't afford to pay anyone with experience, so I got to learn about taking photographs and they even let me write some feature articles, relevant and boring stuff about whole-grain nutrition and why automobiles should be banned from Berkeley. But I liked it. I was already rehearsing an acceptance speech for the Pulitzer Prize.

I was also seeing someone new, the same guy I'd met on Telegraph Avenue. Norman worked for the paper, reviewing films, mostly slow-paced, brooding, foreign imports that depicted the degeneration of the middle class. He was a skinny, bearded neo-hippie, and at twenty-eight he was steeped in a *weltschmerz* I had outgrown. Norman was a Marxist who knew that the revolution was doomed, but he had taken it on as a personal mission to turn me against my own bourgeois values. He wasn't exactly who Grandma Rose would have picked out for me to date, but we were having fun together: He took me to parties where there were drugs and homosexuals and failed revolutionaries, with hallucinogenic mushrooms for dessert. After two months I still hadn't gone to bed with him, a record for me by seven weeks at least.

Then the newspaper went bankrupt. (They had rarely paid me anyway, but I wasn't too proud to let dad underwrite my apprenticeship.) Now it would be almost impossible to find another job in the same field. Why, I wondered, convinced as only a twenty-four-year-old can be that I'd permanently screwed up my life, hadn't I majored in journalism?

I moved back home so that everyone else could feel sorry for me, too. It was meant to be only temporary. I would have left again in another month or two. And this time—unlike the time I went to Europe, unlike all the other times I was between apartments or semesters or jobs—I would have stayed gone. I'm sure of it. I had taken only one tiny step backward. But one tiny step backward can make a big difference if, for example, you are standing on top of the Transamerica Pyramid.

This time, like the other times, I exercised my God-given right as oldest child to dispossess Daniel of my bedroom, the best one in the house. It isn't as large as my parents' room, but it has a view of San Francisco and the Bay that shimmers like heaven in the early morning. Becky and Leah had staked out the third floor, so Daniel was returned to the middle-of-the-hall room, which has only one window, no bath, and is still painted the ghastly shade of electric blue he insisted upon when he was sixteen.

Daniel and I were in the kitchen one evening, after I'd been home about two weeks. Jonathan was at a meeting; Elaina was lying down. Daniel was going to make her some toast (heavily buttered, her favorite), but I was going to reheat some pizza, and we started arguing about who could use the toaster oven first. Daniel wanted me to use the microwave, but I said that it made the pizza soggy.

I was drinking a screwdriver. It was the first one I'd ever

made; I'd put too much vodka in it and it tasted remotely like hair spray. You see, although I had tried to cultivate a jaded, live-fast, stay-pretty persona, Norman had provided me with my first experience with serious drugs, and I was still a neophyte in the field of substance abuse. A screwdriver sounded like the kind of cocktail that adults drink. Even the name sounded tough: a tool, a possible weapon.

Maybe the screwdriver caused our fight to escalate, because I was feeling the liquor already: that sensation like falling slowly through the air. But then, I had never been inhibited about fighting with Daniel.

He called me a failure. He said if I didn't intend this last return home to be permanent, I wouldn't have taken my old bedroom back. Well, I snapped, he was obviously *never* planning to move away from home, Mouse's boy that he was, or he wouldn't have moved into my bedroom in the first place.

Then Daniel said that if I did leave home again, it would only be because I couldn't sneak my boyfriends into the house at night—he said "boyfriend" with a sneer that made it sound like "trick." I said that it was better for *me* to have boyfriends than for *him* to have boyfriends. Then he said that I'd always hated him because Elaina liked him better.

That was when I tried to throw my drink in his face. Unfortunately, the glass was empty: The half-melted ice cubes bounced off his chest, but a few drops hit him in the eyes, and Daniel is very sensitive about getting things in his eyes. He ran screaming to the nearest sink, and I stormed upstairs to the disputed bedroom.

I had found two Percodan in the nightstand drawer, in a plastic bag closed with a green twist tie. I guessed they were Daniel's—I know he had some Percodan prescribed when he had to have root-canal work done. Suddenly I wanted to see what would happen if I took them. I popped them in my mouth as if I were swallowing the bullets that I wanted to fire at my brother. It wasn't like me to do something like that. And the funny thing is, with all the mistakes I made that I got away with, that really never hurt anyone, how such a little thing. . . .

From the conversations of people who have come to visit my body, and from doctors and nurses standing in the room (and you should hear the tacky things they say about patients when they think they're alone), I have pieced together that it was Leah who found me and discovered that she couldn't wake me up. In the chaos that followed—Becky screaming, Daniel blithering about who should drive—Elaina stayed calm. She put on her robe and helped Daniel carry me out.

Apparently I was still in the land of the marginally functional; but a little after they got me to the hospital, I went and had a stroke. Like I said, nothing but trouble.

Dr. Marcus, the first doctor on the case, explained that it was an anomaly of science that when two chemicals have the same target organ, sometimes a synergistic effect causes the body to react in unpredictable ways. In other words, such small amounts of booze and pills together shouldn't have caused a coma and he didn't have any idea why they had.

Leah tried to call Jonathan from the hospital, but couldn't reach him. Elaina remarked later that even when he's standing right next to you, Jonathan is often unreachable.


A few days have passed since Elaina's announcement. Jonathan has absented himself as usual. Becky and Leah are involved in rehearsals for *Ah, Wilderness!* at school and stay away as much as possible.

But I can be with them whenever I want. I watch Becky and Leah do their homework, and Daniel pound down the beers at Dmitri's; I'm in Elaina's purse, and on Jonathan's shoulder. I am a presence that disturbs them but that they aren't quite conscious of, like the dandruff on Jonathan's suits.

I can't let them drive me away.

But Daniel asks Elaina what lawyer he should talk to about

me, and Elaina shrugs and rolls her eyes and wrings her hands, and finally says, "Well, Martin Lindner is the only lawyer I know besides your father, but I guess he's all right, don't you think?"

It's probably just a coincidence that Martin Lindner is such a good choice. He's a prominent and active member of our congregation, Temple Sherith Shalom; he's an aggressive litigator; and Grandma Rose likes him.

Marty works in downtown Oakland, in a glassy new high rise that sprang from the ashes of pawnshops and pornographic bookstores. Marty himself is jiggly fat, and smokes cigars, or sometimes just chews on the ends of them until they look like they've been mauled by a Great Dane. His lips are thick and his chin hangs down like a pelican's and his hairline recedes so that a horseshoe of scalp extends backward from his forehead. When his name comes up in conversation, Grandma Rose says, "He certainly has been successful, hasn't he?" Marty has a son, Jeff, who is a senior at Alta Vista High.

In Marty's office, Daniel sits with one ankle resting on the opposite knee, in imitation of the way Jonathan sits. But Daniel's legs are too long and thin for it to be impressive. Especially with that red silk handkerchief lolling like an anthurium in his pocket.

"In cases like this"—Marty slobbers over his cigar—"it's assumed that the husband and wife will agree." He chuckles, looking at the chewed end. "It's not a good assumption. I've done a few divorces in my time."

Daniel gives Marty his Robert Redford half-smile. I've actually seen him practicing it. I'll admit that Daniel is pretty handsome, with that blond Semitic look.

"What you'd have to do . . ." Marty coughs. "I guess we're just speaking hypothetically here. What a couple would have to do is each get an attorney and go to court and have one of them appointed the daughter's guardian, and that one would make the decision."

The cigar has gone out. Marty sucks the end. Daniel tugs at the hem of his pant leg, which is riding up and revealing a little of his ankle.

"You know"—Marty looks down at some papers on his desk, carelessly shuffling through a few of them—"I could do something like that for one of your parents, if one of them wanted me to."

And Jonathan wanted me to go to law school! Why? To be a pimp like Marty Lindner? Marty doesn't even care whose side he's on, probably because the case will be covered in the press, and either way he can make his position sound like it's for the good of mankind, and say that he's doing this out of "deep personal conviction." I bet he's already planning to write a book about it.

"How is your mother, by the way?" Marty asks. "She's a great lady, your mother."

"Yes, I know." Daniel nods. "She's fine. In fact, she's the one. . . ." He stops.

Marty coughs. "It's such a tragedy," he says. His voice sounds like a dishwasher in its first cycle. "Who knows why these things have to happen?"

Daniel blinks. Is he thinking of our fight, of all our fights, of all the years that we weren't the loving sister and brother that Elaina said she wanted us to be?

I go back to the hospital in time for Elaina's visit. She's driven herself this time.

She stands by the bed, whimpering and dabbing the moisture from the rims of her eyes. She stares at my body. It looks like a shriveled monkey; she seems both horrified and fascinated by it. As for myself, I feel the same kind of detached sentiment toward it as I might toward a favorite dress I wore in high school; it's hard to believe that people treat it like it's *me*.

"Oh, Melissa, I know I wasn't a good mother, but I tried, I

swear I tried. I know that all this is my fault somehow. It's so unfair. I just wish I could talk to you for five minutes!"

Oh, she does, does she? If I could talk to her now, I would tell her that she is right. I would say, It *is* your fault, Mickey Mouse Mommy, for all the times you didn't get up to get me ready for school; for all the times you made fun of me, then tried to say it was just a joke; for all the things that Danny could do for you that I could have done, too, if you'd just let me!

The door creaks open; Dr. Gorgeous enters and closes the door behind him. Dr. Gorgeous is actually Drew Harding, the neurology resident. He is in his early thirties; his honey-brown hair is blown dry and feathers back, and his skin is as evenly tanned as if he had applied makeup, or turned on a rotisserie; against this tawny background, his eyes are an eerie blue and his teeth glitter an unnatural shade of white. He is a Pepsodent ad, a jock in a white coat. I wonder if it bothers Grandma Rose that I finally met a young, single doctor only after I was co-matose.

"Elaina," he murmurs; he comes up behind her, soft as a promise, in his rubber-soled shoes. He's fairly short, just about the same height as Elaina is in her heels. "You can't tear your-self apart this way." He looks at my body with genuine pity, a rare emotion in a doctor. Perhaps because he's young—but, no, I've seen the other residents and they already have a fleshy, indifferent look, a way of blinking out what they see. He's an odd one, Dr. Harding. In the mornings he examines my chart and questions the nurses about what kind of night I had, with such intensity that I believe he has ideals about medicine that might better be called fantasies.

My mother turns and throws her arms around him, weep-ing quietly onto his shoulder. He looks startled, hesitates; I ex-pect him to push her away, but instead he embraces her firmly—his eyes close and he very lightly strokes the back of her hair. Suddenly she grasps his face in her hands.

Then they kiss.

# 2

Nothing stays secret long in this family.

Almost before the engine of his Porsche was cool, Daniel had told Becky and Leah about how he went to see Marty Lindner. Daniel may be loyal to Elaina, and he loves to have secrets with her, but there's no point in having a secret if no one knows about it. I followed him up to Becky's and Leah's room, where he told them to turn the stereo down, then paraded back and forth dropping hints about "the top-secret stuff that's happening," until they indicated that he should either tell them straight out or go pluck his anchovies. Under this duress, Daniel broke down.

And this morning, Elaina told Lee Emma.

Lee Emma originally worked for Grandma Rose, and Elaina has known her for almost thirty years. Elaina has given us strict instructions never to talk about the Negro race in Lee Emma's presence, but Elaina herself seems to turn the conversation in that direction whenever possible, making odd, encompassing statements like "I think black people are really the most honest people there are."

If it weren't for Lee Emma, the family would live entirely on frozen dinners and moussaka, the one dish that Elaina will prepare. Lee Emma makes basic food: pans of chicken breasts; rice and mushroom casseroles. She freezes them and we heat them later in the microwave. So it doesn't matter that Lee Emma will no longer vacuum nor iron; neither will she polish silverware. Elaina has a cleaning service send out a young man once a week; Elaina can flirt with him while he does the heavy work. Dusting is Lee Emma's real forte, and if she runs out of other things to do, she will give a second going-over to what she dusted that morning.

While Lee Emma was dusting Elaina's dresser and Elaina was reaching for whatever makeup brush required her to get in Lee Emma's way, Elaina told her that she might have to go to court in order to "find out what to do about Melissa, since Jonathan—although I would never say anything bad about him because he's my husband—doesn't seem to understand what we should do." She added, "Please, pretty please, don't tell my mother about this."

But Elaina might as well have told the Nazis about the landing at Normandy. Lee Emma is Rose's spy, and Elaina knows it. Elaina just can't keep quiet about anything, which is why I'm so confused about her relationship with Dr. Harding. Was it just a friendly kiss? I don't think so—I saw his eyes close, I saw her cheek press against his. . . . So why hasn't there been a hint or a joking reference about the good doctor to Daniel or the girls?

Unless I've misunderstood Elaina all these years. Unless her compulsive talking was supposed to convince us that there was nothing we didn't know, to distract us from the *real* secrets.

In the meantime, there will be Grandma Rose to deal with. As soon as she hears from Lee Emma, she will drop on my mother like a cluster bomb. No advance artillery, no air-raid siren. She is heavily loaded, she is a small ball of fury, she is a compact Sherman tank. She is Grandma Rose.

She was born Rose Rosenberg, the daughter of one of the early Jewish settlers of California, who prospered because he was the first person to think of selling canned borscht in Oakland. Chaim (later Chuck) Rosenberg, Rose's father, became president of Temple Sherith Shalom, the first Reform Hebrew congregation in the East Bay, and was instrumental in

bringing Saul Miller out from Cleveland to become its rabbi in
1933. Rose and Saul were married a year later.

Grandma Rose was the perfect rebbitzin: She never missed
a service, and she knew the occupations and children's names
of every member of the congregation. She pioneered relations
between the Jewish and Gentile communities by starting an in-
terfaith book club; and during World War II, she organized
women's groups from churches and synagogues to sponsor a
local USO. She taught Sunday School for close to fifty years.
This is only a sampling; a woman like my grandmother has to
keep doing more, because she suspects that the world is always
as disappointed with her efforts as she is disappointed in the
world.

It's only three o'clock and I hear grandma coming up the
steps.

She finds Elaina in the dining room, toying with half a cup
of cold coffee. The room is stately and cool. The afternoon
sunlight enters only in dusty slices through the slats of the
shutters; Elaina hates bright light. The long rosewood table
and high-backed chairs are polished to a metallic shine;
Elaina's cat eyes glint like the Wedgwood china, stacked in the
china cabinet, that she and Jonathan received for their wedding and never use. But Elaina is the one who looks like the
guest here. Maybe that's because Rose decorated this room, as
she decorated the entire house, thereby saving Jonathan thou-
sands of dollars, which-he-never-thanked-her-for-but-that's-
okay-she-knows-he's-busy.

Rose stands over Elaina, clutching her black patent leather
purse against the side of her gray tweed jacket. She is seventy-
five, and since osteoporosis has set in, she stands four-foot-ten.
She has always tried to minimize her bosom, and encouraged
her daughters and granddaughters to do the same; she con-
siders it unladylike to have a big bust. Her eyebrows are
grayish wisps and her tissuey eyelids disappear above the sock-
ets of her eyes. Spiky lines draw inward toward her mouth,

etched by the years of disapproving. But although the bridge of her nose has sunk a little, the Rosenberg bone structure is visible still, especially in this dim light: high cheekbones, firm jaw. A sharp line marks the edges of her smoky gray irises. Her still abundant hair is dyed auburn, a shade lighter and redder than my mother's.

"*Elaina.*" She clips off the name by smacking her tongue against the roof of her mouth. "I heard something very disturbing this afternoon."

Elaina lets the coffee cup clatter against the saucer. "I swear to God, that woman can't keep a secret for two minutes. I've noticed that about some black people—well, black women especially—"

"*Elaina.*" Rose's voice is a gravelly version of my mother's. "You can't treat a husband like that."

"Why should I treat him? He's the one with the money," Elaina replies.

"*Elaina.*" Rose's head quivers. "Don't you think he knows what's best for his daughter?" It isn't just because of dad's money that Rose always agrees with him. She liked him from the beginning, when he was a studious bus-ad major at Berkeley, and first dated Alison, Elaina's older sister. Rose could smell it then—the fires of success that smoldered in him. Because she sensed his need; it resonated with some need of her own that she could never fulfill, a need beyond the desire for material goods, though bound up with that as well. When my father announced a few years later that he was leaving law practice to go into real estate, his own parents told him that he was a fool to leave a secure job for something so risky. Not Rose. She knew.

"You wouldn't find another husband like Jonathan very soon," she warns.

"You always side with him," Elaina snaps.

"That is not true." Rose clicks her tongue again. "I only side with him when he's right."

"But you always think he's right."

"Have you told him? What does he say?"

"As little as possible."

"*Elaina.*"

"No, I haven't told him. And I don't want you to, either."

"Don't you think he has something to say about his daughter?"

"She's my daughter, too!"

"That poor girl . . ." Rose's voice wavers on the edge of breaking. But I have seen Grandma Rose cry only once: on the first seder after Grandpa Saul died. "They might find a cure."

Elaina looks down into her coffee cup. "Mother, it's an *irreversible* coma."

"But they might find a cure."

"An *irreversible* coma means—"

"When I was little, everyone died of influenza. The whole neighborhood."

"This is different. Her brain—"

"And how about polio?"

Elaina looks up at her mother and her eyes are clear—I can see through them to the kaleidoscope inside her, to the elusive core that is no core, just flickering lights and fragments of colored glass. Maybe she has mourned me in some real way underneath the hysterical mourning that will continue forever. Maybe she can really believe that I'm going to heaven to be with her father and my unborn brother, the boy she miscarried between Daniel and Becky. But I can't know the truth with her. Even if I could get inside her head, it's just a Disneyland ride in there, with the truth always changing.

"They might find a cure."

Elaina reaches for the coffee and takes a slow, noisy swallow, her lips reaching far beneath the rim of the cup.

"Of course, everyone in temple will know about this by Friday night," Rose says.

"That's all you care about, isn't it?" Elaina demands triumphantly.

But Grandma Rose will fight for me. She often took care of me when I was an infant and Elaina was suffering from the longest postpartum depression in the history of Western civilization. And even later: Rose was the one who took me to the podiatrist when I had an ingrown toenail; she was the one who took me shopping for my first temple dress.

Just to make sure, I follow Grandma Rose home. Maybe if I concentrate on sending her a little mental encouragement . . . I don't know if she picks up on that or not, but as soon as she hangs up her jacket, she does call Jonathan at the office to let him know that Elaina has consulted Marty.

I can hear that Jonathan is a bit pissed. So I head back to Magnolia Street to wait for his arrival.

When Elaina has finally provoked Jonathan into fighting with her, I wonder if she doesn't feel a little like Truman did after the *Enola Gay* was too far out to call back.

They are in the kitchen. Daniel, Becky, and Leah eavesdrop from the pantry. "I told you," Jonathan says, "that we were not going to touch my daughter."

Elaina turns toward him. She is wearing ovesize rubber gloves, and an apron over her black crepe dress. She has been mixing a batch of the special night cream she uses on her face, bending over the sink, stirring it like a witch's brew.

"Your daughter. You act like *you* gave birth to her, which by the way was like trying to get an elephant through a keyhole, which you would know if you'd been there with me—"

"I was too there." Jonathan is standing by the refrigerator, his face red, like the glow of a distant forest fire, with his curly gray hair the smoke. His eyes are lined with red squiggles; his irises are the color of hot bricks.

"And the doctor wouldn't put me to sleep. I begged him, but he wouldn't give me *anything*—"

"If you'd gotten a job when I asked you to—"

"I was pregnant!"

"You were always pregnant, or thought you were pregnant, or getting over being pregnant—"

"Well!" Elaina makes the shrill sound of a calliope. "I'm sorry I'm not like one of those women who squats in a field on her lunch hour and then goes back to picking rice."

"I don't want to hear that crooked lawyer's name in this house again. I want you to promise you'll leave Melissa alone."

"When was the last time you visited her?" Elaina demands.

"I'm busy trying to support you all—and the money you spend at the beauty shop—"

Elaina waves her gloved hands in the air. *I'm sorry! I'm sorry!* I know I do everything wrong!"

For a moment Jonathan looks like a gray bear about to head for the woods. Then he changes into a rhinoceros. "You never taught the kids any discipline—"

"What was I supposed to tell them, wait until your father gets home? They'd have had to stay up past midnight!"

And so their accusations fly, volleys of arrows that have been shot so often that the points are dull. "You have to embarrass me—" "You can't look up from the *Wall Street Journal*—" Elaina has never forgotten that Jonathan would only go away for a two-day honeymoon. Jonathan has never forgotten that Elaina was late to his law-school graduation. Then there was the time Jonathan "made that remark" about Elaina's father. Then there was the time that Elaina burned the steaks for Jonathan's banker and sent out for Chicken Delight.

"Your mother told me that you had a prescription for Percodan." Jonathan's lips purse smugly. This is something new.

"I can't believe she said that! Why does she do this to me?"

"Is it true?"

Elaina pauses, tucking her lower lip between her teeth. The subject of the Percodan and how I got them arises occasionally, unexpectedly, a mole that pops its head above ground for a moment, then burrows back down into its subterranean tunnels. She protests, "No! I did not! I might have had some pills or something. I did not have any Percodan!"

"I'm not going to discuss this unless you calm down." Jonathan's voice rises from bass to tenor. His own composure is getting away from him, like a cat struggling out of his arms.

Elaina pulls off her gloves, slapping them down on the counter. "I'm tired of you blaming me about Melissa!" It is half shriek, half sob.

"I don't blame you—"

"Yes, you do, you know you do, and if you had been there—"

Jonathan puckers his lips so tightly that they turn white. He takes a step forward. His arm is going up, and at the end of his arm is a fist. Elaina gasps. Then Jonathan does a military about-face, turning his back on my mother, and marches out, his stride swift and inevitable, the swish of his arms against his suit faintly audible.

Elaina shouts after him, "I know! You wish you'd married Alison! Well, I'm sorry I can't be her!"

This final verbal blow misses him by inches, bounces off the doorjamb (where my siblings duck out of the way), then ricochets back into the kitchen. Elaina sags. She lets out a long, gurgly sigh, looks down at the floor, and rubs her finger absently under her nose. As if she'd been having this fight only for Jonathan's sake.

Behind the pantry door, Becky and Leah glance at each other. Daniel, pale and shaking, creeps out, then silently goes to put his arms around Elaina. She squeezes her eyes shut as she grips him—just like she did with Dr. Harding. What would Daniel say about his precious Mickey Mouse if he knew about *that?* I wish I could tell them, tell them all—Grandma Rose and, yes, Jonathan, too. Then he'd have some concrete proof that she's unfit to be my guardian, he could stop her from what she wants to do to me. . . . And now I wonder, is all of this guardianship business part of a scheme to get Jonathan to leave her so that she can have Dr. Harding to herself? But she loves dad. I know she does.

Becky and Leah have snuck away. In a few moments the sound of Billy Death's Head singing "Don't You Dare" trickles down, the remote percussion signaling their withdrawal. Elaina and Daniel look up at the ceiling.

I rise like a helium balloon to the third floor.

There are two bedrooms and one bath here, but Leah has for a long time slept in one of the twin beds in Becky's room. In both rooms, Becky's and Leah's common makeup covers the dressers, their records are spread on the floor, and clothes spill out of the closets. Elaina argued when the girls said that they were going to paint the ceilings black. She wanted Jonathan to tell them no, but he said he didn't care what color the ceilings were. Of course, Jonathan visits this floor rarely, while Elaina is always popping up: to pester the girls when they're here or to snoop around when they're not. Becky and Leah have hidden their diaries in places where Elaina cannot reach without ruining her nails.

Becky is sprawling on her bed; her wavy chestnut hair billows out. *"Guy!"* she exclaims.

"Bee-stunk," Leah agrees.

"And I got a tee-flest tomorrow." Becky and Leah speak a patois in which *ee-fl* or *ee-st* or sometimes a combination—*ee-stee-fl*—is inserted in the middle of a word. When spoken quickly, it is difficult for others to understand, enabling the girls to communicate privately. "How am I supposed to study for it now?"

Leah, on the other bed, is lying on her stomach, her pillow folded in half beneath her chest. Leah, the horse enthusiast, has the most athletic body of all of us: a solid, chunky frame, and broad shoulders. On her, Elaina's breasts are low-slung, but the eyes (hers are hazel) are unmistakable.

"Geometry sucks," Becky concludes. Becky is getting C's in

geometry, just like she got C's in algebra, a class that Leah is getting A's in, just like Leah gets A's in everything.

"Yeah," Leah sighs. She releases the pillow, rolls over, and stares at the poster of Billy Death's Head on the ceiling. Billy is a fey young man with orange hair and sunken cheeks—here he is represented with a metal torso and reptilian limbs.

"I mean, I think I could have done okay in algebra if I'd applied myself, but geometry is a total bitch."

Silence. Except for the music that the speakers pump into the room. Billy grunts his lyrics—"Life is fucked, baby, so don't you dare try, but death is forever, so don't you die"—between heavy thumps of the bass drum and an occasional screech of the electric guitar.

Among the parents of Becky's and Leah's schoolmates, there are no observably happy marriages, so they accept that as the norm. But when Jonathan and Elaina fight so openly, they feel vulnerable. If Jonathan and Elaina don't stay married now, then the question arises, shouldn't they have divorced sixteen years ago, the time they were separated for six months, just after Becky was born?

"Megashit!" Becky finally cries, throwing one of her notebooks on the floor. "It's all Melissa's fault!"

"Bee-stecky!"

"Well?" Becky thrusts out her chin. Her lips are outlined in black, making them look thin and severe; her lids are heavy with purple shadow above her large green-golden eyes. I think of Cleopatra. Becky has Elaina's skin, and it glows with the unblemished newness of sixteen. "Wasn't Melissa kind of shorted out? Guy, she had like about forty-seven different jobs after she got out of college. She couldn't figure out *what* she wanted to do." Becky wants to be an actress. She is halfway through her junior year of high school and already the ingenue in an O'Neill play, so the road to a transcendent success appears short and smooth. Like most teenagers, she has little sympathy for the mistakes that people make in their twenties.

"And she was always flaring with some goony older guy."
Becky wrinkles her nose. "I can't figure out why she'd want
some wheelchair case anyway. But so like that's why Mouse and
dad are so wonked out about us getting into trouble, when
*we're* megastraight."

Leah sits up. She is loyal both to me and to the truth, and
since the conflict cannot be resolved, she does not respond. Instead, she starts to chew the closest thing to a nail that remains
on her right hand and mumbles through the finger in her
mouth, "You think Mouse's right, then? About the respirator, I
mean?"

"Nah. Dad."

"Why?" Leah asks. I can see that she has debated the question, and that she invests the answer with some importance.
There is a line creasing the freckled skin between her eyes.
When she relaxes her face, a trace of the line remains. I never
noticed that before.

"I mean, I think that's what Melissa would want, just to lie
around forever."

"Guy."

"Well?" Becky smirks. "Come on, don'tcha remember how
she'd move back home and just stay in bed all day?"

Leah frowns again, looking at a flake of dead skin that
sticks up but isn't quite big enough for her to grip with her
teeth. For the past several years, we were like guests in the
same hotel: I saw her when I came home from Berkeley on
weekends, and later, during the times I moved back. We were
friendly, but our lives did not overlap; nine years is a big difference in age. Still, she must remember how I carried her on
my back and made up stories for her when she was a child and
I had "gotten stuck" baby-sitting. "I just can't believe she's
really . . ." Leah stops.

"I told you, we saw that movie in civics," Becky goes on.
"We had a really heavy discussion about it afterward." She adds
somberly, "We should both make out those living wills, you 'n'

me. It'll be like a pee-stact." Becky and Leah are always making solemn pacts about one thing or another: that they will not allow Daniel into their rooms, or that they will no longer talk to a particular girl who has snubbed Becky.

Leah nods absently. "I wish we could talk to Melissa to find out what she wants. I wish she was here now, just for a second."

Becky grunts. *"Huh.* I bet that Mouse'll get her way no matter what. Doesn't she always?"

"I just wish they wouldn't fee-stight about it!" Leah says.

Becky props her head up on her hand, grinning. "You know who Mouse's lawyer is, don'tcha?"

"Daniel said Marty Lindner—"

Becky leans forward. "And you know whose *father* he is?" she hisses.

"Yeah . . ." Leah's eyes widen as she seems to make a connection that is still inarticulate in my mind. *"Jeff* Lindner."

Jeff Lindner is a senior at Alta Vista High. He is president of the Earth Club, which he founded, a quasi-political club committed to environmental causes. Last year the club staged a march to protest the dumping of sewage in San Francisco Bay, and they regularly sponsor Saturday-afternoon litter cleanups at various local parks; Jeff usually manages to arrange some local media coverage for these projects. Jeff himself is dark-eyed and black-haired, with a purity of expression that gives his pale skin a translucent pink glow. In his junior year he set two track records, and he is much sought after by the girls of A.V., not just by the studious ones (the "cave dwellers") such as himself, but also by the "coolers," the popular girls, such as Becky. Even the "weenies," those poor girls who are always in the wrong clothes and wear last year's hairstyle, dare to fantasize about him. But he remains equally elusive to all.

"So maybe we could talk to Jeff," Becky says. "Maybe he'd talk to his dee-stad."

Leah swings her clogs against the side of the bed. "I don't see what good . . ." Then she stops. Becky is grinning at her, still with

her head propped up on her hand. Becky is luscious, over-
flowing, simmering chocolate milk. (Becky herself is self-
conscious about her body, proud of her large breasts but
obsessive about her thighs. She and Leah have invented an elaborate diet consisting primarily of cauliflower, diet soda, and home-
made nachos, which they have mathematically proven should
have them in size five jeans. The diet's failure they attribute to
water retention.)

Becky nods as she sees that Leah is beginning at last to
understand. Becky has had a "groaner" for Jeff for months
now, ever since her last boyfriend, Gary Burke, proved himself
a "total weenie" by getting thrown off the basketball team for
cheating on a history test. But Jeff . . . ah, Jeff. He is said to
have scored in the 700s on the SAT. Harvard is sometimes
mentioned. He's totally *gorjo*, and prime USDA potential *bee-
stoyfriend*.

But what about Leah? I feel drawn to her now: the softness of her skin, the wispy cloud of her hair. I touch them with
my thoughts. I am aware of the irregular shape of each freckle,
the breath that makes her chest rise and fall—it's like an ocean
hissing, and her heartbeat is a great *ba-boom*. . . .

Then there's a little blank space, and I lose myself. Like
driving through a tunnel. But now fragments of Leah's
thoughts are lying around me like the clothes that are scattered
on the floor.

And I know that Leah likes Jeff, too. She would like to
have him for herself. But she is willing to give him up. There is
something that Leah feels guilty about, but she doesn't know
what it is, and that gelatinous guilt swims around in her, waiting to attach itself to something. Let Becky have Jeff and Leah
can pay off some of the debt incurred through her unknown
crime. The problem is, now that the blow that was surely intended for Leah (as punishment for that crime) has struck me
instead, the debt has grown impossibly large.

"I'm wired with you," Leah promises Becky. I'm outside of

her now: The frown is deep between her eyes and she purses her lips a little bit, the way Jonathan does. But she feigns enthusiasm, which is all Becky wants to see. Poor Leah! I had no idea who she was before—even if she was my sister; even if I recognized myself in her sometimes, unexpectedly, like watching someone else audition for the same part in a play.

I feel a bit dizzy. How did I do what I did? It's a little scary, to tell you the truth. But having survived it, I feel stronger.

My clairvoyance is like my memory: It works better at certain times and for certain things than others. But when it works, it's like the smell of freshly baked bread, that makes you turn around instinctively to find out where it's coming from.

That's how I'm drawn to dad's office the next day. I just know that he's going to consult his own lawyer.

The headquarters of Silverstein, Inc., occupy several floors of a sleek tower on the Emeryville peninsula. Down the halls, in the cubicles and conference rooms, the fluorescent lights and Touch-tone phones and thin nylon carpeting are thinly disguised by mass-ordered bric-a-brac—dried flowers, leather-bound books, framed posters—that represent no underlying vision, only the services of a highly paid decorator.

I remember dad's first office. It wasn't even an office, just a desk at the end of the hall in a three-man law firm, where he sat looking exactly like a conscientious young man doing research, turning the pages of the heavy legal books. But underneath the white shirt, the striped tie, the button-down collar, he was dreaming his dream, humming like a nuclear plant. In the mornings I sat on the closed toilet, swinging my legs, while he stood in his underwear in front of the mirror, scraping what looked like whipped cream off his face. "I'm going to be a real-estate developer, Melissa," he told me. "The biggest in Califor-

nia. I'll have my own company. By the time you graduate high
school, I'll be ready to retire."

Now he's done it. I never doubted that he would. Photographs of his buildings cover the walls of the long corridors.
They all look alike to me—gray and oblong—but Jonathan
knows them like his children: the rent per square foot, the total
square footage, the debt service, the interest he paid on the
take-out loan. He could have retired years ago, just like he
boasted, but the making of money is just an excuse for him to
work, to give birth to these steel children that he doesn't have
to share with Elaina. Just before the structures were completed,
he would come home acting a little high, kiss Elaina, and take
us all out to dinner. Then, after the Grand Opening, he would
seem depressed. Even a 300-unit condominium complex won't
change the world.

Daniel was supposed to come into the business—at least
that's what Jonathan decided on the day of the circumcision.
But Daniel has always resisted. He has stubbornly refused to
show an aptitude for economics, accounting, or tax, and when
he dropped out of Hayward State after the first semester, I was
hopeful that Jonathan would disown him. But instead,
Jonathan embarked on Plan B: to send Daniel to the School of
Hands-On Experience. He set Daniel up in a series of small
businesses, each of which Daniel drove into bankruptcy more
rapidly than the one before. The pizza parlor is the most recent of these enterprises. Poor Dmitri Garganopoulos didn't
know what he was getting into when he let Jonathan give him
money to open a new restaurant in exchange for a half-interest
in Dmitri's Number One.

But Jonathan knows that even steel, earthquakeproof
buildings do not last forever. It may be a joke to talk about "the
family business" in Jewish families, but there is a Jewish longing to pass on the concrete achievements of one generation to
the next, and that longing survives in Jonathan, who goes to

temple once a year. Jonathan has partners, of course; he has colleagues and protégés. But he has only one son.

So Jonathan, the first and last of a dynasty, sits on his throne of reclining leather with the royal seal behind him. This is a silver *S* against a green oval background, the logo of Silverstein, Inc., a symbol that finds its way onto pens, stationery, and coffee mugs.

The lawyer has come to see him. I recognize her: She is Debbie Meyers, a.k.a. Debbie Meyers-Hoffman, graduate of Boalt, an attorney married to an attorney. She sits across the desk, a very pregnant woman in a blue denim jumper and Birkenstocks. She wears no makeup; her brown hair is in pigtails. She and her husband are also members of Sherith Shalom. Grandma Rose has said of her, "Well, she certainly got herself a successful husband, didn't she? They have a lovely home, I'm told. And she hasn't given up her career, either."

Jonathan leans forward and presses the middle of the pen with his two thumbs. He talks to Debbie as abstractly as possible; while Elaina is willing to tell the refrigerator repairman how many orgasms she had last week, Jonathan is always reluctant to talk about anything personal. "I want to research the legal rights I have as her father," he says. I am very pleased to see dad take such an interest in me.

Debbie taps her pencil against the legal pad she holds in her lap. "Could you be more specific?"

"This is all just hypothetical," Jonathan replies. Right. He takes off his black horn-rimmed reading glasses and rubs his eyes; then he purses his lips. "I wonder, if we wanted to move her to a—well, let's say there was a very comfortable home where they could take care of her. Could we do it?"

"Of course," Debbie says. "Hospitals don't like to keep chronic-care patients after they're stabilized."

Jonathan glances down. Even the word *hospital* makes him nauseous.

"What does your wife say?" Debbie asks.

Jonathan replaces his glasses to look at her. He could reply, "As little as possible," Elaina's customary rejoinder. But it would hardly fit. Then he smiles a little. His choice of Debbie has already been vindicated; knowing dad, he wanted someone who would implement his own strategies, rather than try to give him advice, but he must be pleased with her acumen. "My wife has already spoken to an attorney," he says.

"What does she want to do?"

Jonathan's face reddens. His face reddens easily, and we worry about his blood pressure, and his heart. "She wants to disconnect the respirator."

"Is she willing to go to court over this?"

"I don't know." Jonathan swivels in his chair sideways, tilts back, and puts his hands behind his head. Debbie is pragmatic, no pregnant glow here. But if Jonathan does go to court, well, what judge could rule against the pregnant woman?

"If she does, you'll have to, too."

Jonathan ruffles his curly hair with his united palms. "Of course," he says. His voice rises a little at the end.

# 3

Elaina is sitting by my bedside. The machinery gleams and pings and shines around her. The blinds are open and in the clear light all the equipment looks rather cheery and efficient: One thinks of the controls of a new airplane, or an expensive stereo system. My body is the alien creature here, shrunken and contorted, my hands drawn up like a begging puppy's.

*Whoosh*-click. *Whoosh*-click. The respirator bellows swells and then retracts. Elaina looks at it. And suddenly she seems part of the machinery, keeping me alive. The tube in my throat that breathes for me, the tube in my nose that feeds me—all of it leads to her: thick and twisted umbilical cords.

The door opens and Dr. Harding comes in. She must have heard him, but she doesn't turn around. Dr. Harding glances worriedly at the closed door behind him. And then Elaina slowly turns her misted eyes to look at him, and he drops to his knees beside her chair, letting his head fall in her lap. Elaina hesitates, hand poised above his head, then strokes his hair. He twists his head to look up at her. I can almost see his tail wag.

I know Drew; he's the kind of man who has dedicated himself so totally to medicine that he could never give himself in love. Perhaps now, having learned the earthly limits of his profession, he needs to redirect his passion. And when a man like that finally does fall in love, that love is unquestioning and unwavering; it becomes the kind of religion that would have allowed Abraham to sacrifice Isaac.

But what does he see in Elaina—the forty-two-year-old mother of four? It makes sense, really. Elaina is the archetype of female suffering, redeeming humanity with her tears. What do young women know about suffering and loss—the loss of children, or the loss of their own youth? Drew must have learned by now that he cannot heal all the sick, nor save all the dying. But perhaps he can comfort Elaina, or at least share her grief. She fills the abyss between medicine and God.

I wonder just how far this relationship has gone. Is she too holy for him to touch? Does he have scruples about adultery? I sense a rigidity that serves as the foundation for his passions, the kind of rigidity that sharply divides the world into right and wrong. Has Elaina been putting him off with protestations about loyalty to her husband? Or are they meeting in a supply closet somewhere? God, how gross! How disgusting! Can't he see what she is? How can a man be so stupid and get through medical school?

"How much longer can this go on?" Elaina murmurs, looking at me.

"I wish I could tell you," Drew says, like a prayer.

"I'll fight for her," Elaina says.

"I know you will." Drew reaches his arms across her lap. She strokes his hair again. "You'll help me."

"But how?"

"You'll testify."

Drew stands up, one leg at a time. The end of his stethoscope has fallen from his pocket; he pops it back in, then quickly smooths his feathery brown hair. "To what?" he asks.

"That there's no help for her." Her eyes are deep and blue, waters too dark to show any reflection, and the hollows of her cheeks are shadowy with grief. "That she doesn't want this."

"But how do I know?" Drew asks meekly.

"You know."

Drew looks over at me. *Whoosh*-click, goes the respirator. I almost wish that I were my old self again. I'd show him a thing or two that would make him forget about my mother. "You want to go to court, then."

"No, I don't want to go to court." Elaina gestures toward me, her upturned palm cupping the air. "But what choice do I have?"

"Your husband—"

"He'll never agree."

Drew smiles sadly. "What you must be going through," he says. Apparently he believes that Elaina loves him. She's probably convinced him that it's only her loyalty and self-sacrifice that have made her stay with her cold, unfeeling husband all these years, and that it's those same qualities that compel her now to risk her marriage for the sake of her child. Lord!

Drew looks at me, frowning like a basset hound. "We don't know that much about the brain," he says slowly. "I doubt she can feel anything, but there's still some electroenchephalographic activity there. Just because she isn't conscious, I can't guarantee that she's past pain." He sighs. "I'm a doctor," he says. "I'm supposed to believe in life at any cost."

"I'm a mother," Elaina sighs. "I believe in my children at any cost."

Of course this statement is vague enough to be meaningless, and of course Drew laps it up like a puppy drinking water from the toilet. If my body could move, it would get up to vomit.

"I'll do anything I can to help," Drew promises.

I am with Jonathan in his study that night. This is where he bivouacs. Elaina is always admonishing us: *Shssh,* your father's taking a nap; your father's on the phone; your father's watching TV. If *she* wants something from him, though, three storm troopers and an attack dog couldn't keep her out. Sometimes just the sight of a closed door is too much for her to resist, and she invades the sanctuary and pesters him until he barks at her and she goes upstairs crying to take a Valium. But she generally leaves him alone here, and he settles for the privacy that it affords. He doesn't bother to keep the door locked when he's not there: Jonathan claims to be a man without secrets, and while I am skeptical of this, I know that he's too smart to leave incriminating evidence here.

The study is on the first floor: a small room facing the dense azalea bushes of our neighbors' yard. The room is neat, but not compulsively so. A *Wall Street Journal* is folded on the reclining chair next to the desk; the desk fits into the curvature of the bay window. There is nothing particularly expensive in this room, with one exception: On the desk, just beyond the edge of the old-fashioned green blotter, lies a silver letter opener, shaped like a dagger. In the base of the letter opener is a large oval emerald, encircled by diamonds. The letter opener belonged to Abraham Silverstein, Jonathan's father, who was a jeweler. When Grandpa Abe died, Jonathan quickly sold the entire inventory of his jewelry store and, sentimental fool that he is, also disposed of his father's personal collection of *objets d'art*. Grandma Sophie didn't seem any more attached to the collection than Jonathan. Jonathan kept just this one article, the letter opener, even though it is incongruously garish here. Jonathan's only other self-indulgence is an expensive watch; he drives a Volvo, and his wardrobe is simple enough to be the cause of some quiet jokes at Silverstein, Inc.

Jonathan is looking over a subdivision map, squinting through his reading glasses, following the vein-thin blue lines the way his father once squinted through his loupe and traced the secret inner lines of diamonds. He seems not to hear the knock at first.

But the knock comes again. This time he raises his head. "Come in." Reluctantly. But it's Leah, and when he sees her, his "Hello, sweetie" contains a subtle lilt. He pushes back from the desk and pats his thigh, inviting her to sit on his lap. Leah glances doubtfully at his legs, but then obediently plumps down. Jonathan grunts. "Did you finish your English paper?" Leah is in advanced-placement English.

"Yes."

"Who was it on? Dickens?"

"Swift. Dickens is later."

"When do you get it back?"

"I don't know. Daddy . . ." Leah shifts her weight and Jonathan winces briefly. "Daddy, can't you and mom decide what to do about Melissa together?"

He frowns. When he's preoccupied with something else, it's as if I don't exist for him; he can wrap me up and shove me under the bed like a broken toy. Now Leah has dragged me out again. "I hope so, dear," he says.

"I'm scared that you and mom—"

"Mother and I are just having a little disagreement, that's all."

"But—"

"We'll work it out."

"Janice Ingersoll's parents got divorced last year."

"Fred Ingersoll never found the right career."

"I just hate to see you guys fight."

"We're not fighting, dear."

"Yes, you are."

Jonathan squirms. "You're getting a little big for your old dad."

Leah slides off his lap. For a moment she hovers next to him, like a gawky prehistoric bird, then she settles on the arm of the reclining chair. "You see, just this once I think mom's right."

"When do you get the Dickens paper back? Did I ask you that already? I can't remember."

Leah sticks a finger in her mouth. She should have known better than to appeal to him. She is too young to understand that there is no danger; the grudges that Jonathan and Elaina bear each other have aged like wine, and they become more intoxicating with each year. Or does she know it—while also knowing just how unstable the mixture of time and anger can be?

She studies Jonathan's face, as she does whenever they are alone together. I wonder if she is looking for signs of resemblance between them. There is none. Her face is molded after Elaina's, but there's an untraceable, foreign element there, too. Elaina says that Leah looks like her father. "I think we get it back next week," she says finally.

"I'm just curious—did you go talk to the instructor about the paper first?" Jonathan was always "suggesting" to me, too, that I go talk to my professors.

"Yes."

"And did it help?"

"Yes, daddy."

Jonathan purses his lips. Then his eyes shift nervously to the map on his desk: unfinished work.

"I guess you have to do that kind of thing a lot in college, huh?" Leah asks.

Now Jonathan smiles. "When I was in college, I went to see all my professors every week during their office hours. I got to know them. Then, later, they gave me recommendations for law school." He props one ankle on the opposite knee, folds his hands, and settles back. "You know, if you should decide to go to law school . . ."

Leah nods. Her eyes are blooming tropical flowers. Maybe this is what she came for, after all. Her academic skill is one thing she does share with Jonathan. She chews the dead skin around her nails while he talks. Leah wants to study psychology, and Jonathan's belief in psychology is limited to the Valium that Elaina gets from Dr. Abramowitz. But graduate school is far away; in the meantime there's tonight and many ways to avoid talking about me.

"You might want to major in economics. That's what my

mother wanted me to major in, and you know I didn't, and you know I was sorry."

That was my first major, economics. I switched to English after that, then French, and ended up in history. It certainly didn't make me any more or less qualified to breathe from a plastic tube.

"Economics," Leah echoes, just like I would have. "Yeah."

I think Leah's good grades come naturally to her, and that her good study habits (in spite of Becky's influence) emerge from a nature that is reflective and curious. But she and Becky engage in the pretense both that Jonathan's preoccupation with grades is "totally shorted out" and that Leah has gotten A's only because she'd had teachers who were "just real slackers anyway."

"Economics is a good, practical major," Jonathan emphasizes. "You wouldn't think so, would you?"

"No," Leah agrees, and the depth of the crease in her forehead testifies to her fervor. "But I'm sure you're on line, dad."

"You get to read the philosophers—Adam Smith, and Keynes. Keynes . . ." Jonathan closes his eyes briefly, and shakes his head. "Whew. Keynes is brilliant."

"Parthenogenic," Leah agrees faintly.

Jonathan gives her a puckered-lip smile. "I'm glad we talked about this," he says.


The next afternoon, Jonathan and Elaina are scheduled to meet with Famous Neurologist Number 186 at two o'clock.

Jonathan has one of his assistants working almost full-time on Project Melissa, researching miracles for sale. (Doesn't this prove he loves me? If I were a building, he would have let me go into foreclosure long ago.) This latest Famous Neurologist is from Boston. Since my case did not sound unusual enough to merit a trip, Jonathan seduced him west with the bribe-promise of a contribution to a chair in his name at the university hospital where he teaches.

Jonathan arranges to meet Famous Neurologist in the lounge after Famous has had a chance to read the charts and examine me.

Elaina doesn't show up. I'm not sure where she is. My clairvoyance sometimes runs up against these barriers; and if anyone could shield herself from my prying spiritual vision, it would be Elaina, just like she could close her bedroom door to me when I was a child. (She always scheduled her naps for the times when I needed her most. Or did I decide that I needed her as soon as she took a nap?) There may be an autonomic function that helps us hide ourselves from others, even when that other is an invisible daughter.

In the lounge on the sixth floor, there is a bank of chairs upholstered in crayon colors, alternating orange and blue. Jonathan is too big for the chair; he spills like rising dough over the arms. As he speaks, he keeps his eyes on the Picasso print on the wall (it's that corny number with the two hands clutching a bunch of flowers). Occasionally he glances over to where the lounge opens onto the hall, especially when someone passes, but he never looks directly at Famous, a dour-faced man whose thick brown toupee makes a perfect rectangle of his forehead.

Famous does his bit, telling Jonathan exactly what Jonathan's heard from every other doctor for the past two months. Doctors like to use words like *improbable* and *unlikely*. They never use the word *hopeless*. And maybe there is no one moment when a situation becomes hopeless; one gives up hope in nickels and dimes, not even noticing, until there just isn't any more left. It looks like Jonathan's hope account is a little overdrawn: There are puffy half-moons under his eyes, and the skin under his jaw is sagging as he tries to tell Famous a supposed-to-be-funny story about how his parents wanted him to be a doctor because his cousin was going to be one. "I promised myself I'd never be a *noodgy* Jewish parent like they were, but once in a while I slip up." He ends on a chuckle that sounds like a cough, and Famous smiles absently, his own thoughts probably on the flight home.

And where was Elaina? That must be the question on dad's mind as he lumbers quickly out of the lounge. It was easier to talk to Famous without her, because she would have interrupted to ask if the accident was her fault, and to flirt with Famous, and she would certainly have cried. Still, she'd said she'd be there, and Famous wanted to ask her some questions about my "response to stimuli," and about gradual observable changes in my condition, which Jonathan couldn't answer as well because he doesn't see me daily as she does.

Jonathan is just revving up speed when he gets to the elevators and almost knocks over Drew Harding, who is shooting out of an elevator and revving up pretty well himself.

"Jonathan." Drew grabs Jonathan's hand like this is a class reunion. "How are you?" With his free hand he slaps Jonathan's forearm.

Jonathan automatically starts to reply, "Just fine, thanks," but then his eyes drop to Drew's hand, still squeezing his, and he slowly looks up at Drew, whose Pepsodent smile begins to wilt around the edges. "How am I supposed to be?" he asks, pulling his hand away, then pushing past Drew into an opening elevator.

Drew looks after him, but Jonathan doesn't turn around, and the elevator swallows him. Have Elaina and Drew been together just now? I picture them on an examining table, the tissue paper making crinkly sounds under them; Elaina's black dress hiked up, her plump white legs in the air—and Drew over her, his white coat flapping like a pelican's wings.

But I'm more concerned with dad right now.

I follow him back to the office, where Valerie, his secretary, is cowering behind the word processor. Valerie is thirty, dark, obsessive, and overweight, and Jonathan is always encouraging her to work for her M.B.A. by going to school at night. When she protests that she wants to spend evenings with her children, he suggests that she hire a housekeeper.

Valerie tells him that a loan negotiation has just collapsed. Jonathan actually enjoys these crises, because he can take his act on the road: He goes into a conference room and starts with the story about how his father lost his first jewelry store during the depression, and pretty soon everyone is feeling so guilty that they're ready to lower the debt service or give up a few loan points.

But this time Chris Idlewild, Jonathan's most recent protégé, has already gone in and tried to read Jonathan's lines. And blown it. Chris is a graduate of Wharton, top 5 percent of the class, and is about as effective at loan negotiations as Daniel was at running the messenger service Jonathan bought him. him.

"The bank people left," Valerie tells Jonathan as she hastily stacks his mail according to the size of the envelopes.

Jonathan replies with a rather general comment about how a person's level of incompetence increases in direct proportion to his self-satisfaction, and goes into his office.

A few hours later, Elaina is lying facedown in bed, getting a back rub from Daniel. "Oh, that feels good," she sighs into the pillow. "Don't stop. A little lower."

Daniel's fingers dance over Elaina's soft, freckled skin; she doesn't want a back rub so much as a light tickle. He inches down the sheet as he goes. He is wearing a white linen suit with the sleeves rolled up. His face is grim.

"Danabable—"

"Hmm?"

"Do I have more wrinkles than Sheila Newhouse?" Sheila is the mother of Craig Newhouse, one of Daniel's best friends.

"You don't have any wrinkles, Mickey Mouse."

"You don't mean that."

"Yes, I do."

She reaches back to squeeze his arm. "You are such a perfect child. I know you don't mean it. But she *is* pretty wrinkled, isn't she? That's what happens if you play tennis in the sun every day for forty years."

Daniel hears the front door opening and he looks over his shoulder with a jerky motion—it's early for Jonathan to be home. Elaina grunts obliviously into the pillow while Daniel begins to knead harder and harder, watching the bedroom door over his shoulder, listening to the ascending footsteps.

A moment later Jonathan lumbers into the room. Daniel's hands leap from Elaina's back.

"Where were you today?" Jonathan demands.

"Where was I?" Elaina languidly turns her head to face him. "I was right here."

"You were supposed to be at the hospital."

"Why? I feel fine."

Daniel tucks his hands under his arms. His hands are white, with long fingers; Elaina says he has her father's hands. He stares at Elaina's back, his chin pushed down against his chest.

"You know what I'm talking about." Jonathan's thumb, pressed against the doorjamb, turns pink and then white. "The specialist."

"Oh, my God, I forgot. How awful! Can you ever forgive me?"

"How did you forget?"

"I guess because I'm stupid," Elaina says.

"I won't argue with that."

"Dad!" Daniel jumps up from the bed. "That's not very nice to say about Mickey Mouse!"

"I want to talk to you, Elaina," Jonathan says. "Alone."

Elaina winks at Daniel. "He's only a baby, he can't understand what you're saying." She moves the pillow down, shoving it under her bare, loose breasts, which can't quite be seen. Daniel edges toward the door, moving sideways, close to the wall.

"I want to talk to you now."

"I don't believe it." She smiles. Outside the window above the bed, the sun is setting, spilling rose paint over the rooftops below us and igniting the turquoise in Elaina's eyes. "Dateline Alta Vista. Hell froze over today. Film at eleven."

Daniel tries to slink past Jonathan. But Jonathan blocks the doorway with his arms, raised like the wings of the American eagle. "I bet you're on your way to work," he says.

Daniel, looking at the carpet, mumbles something unintelligible.

"No? I wonder what Dmitri's doing tonight. I wonder if he could use some help. There's lots to do in a restaurant at night."

"Yeah, I thought I'd go down there." Daniel shrugs one shoulder, then the next.

"Maybe I'll stop by later and see you there."

"Okay."

Jonathan drops one arm and Daniel slips past him, bending his narrow body as gracefully as Paddy O'Flanagan. Jonathan raises the arm again.

"Why weren't you there today?" he demands of Elaina. "I really want to know."

"I had a board meeting. B-O-R-E-D. Get it?"

"Goddamn it, I want a straight answer for once."

"Please don't swear."

"I'm waiting."

"It's not my fault about Melissa! I'm tired of you blaming me!"

"I am not blaming you."

"Yes, you are."

"I am *not*." He drops his arms, sighs, and turns away very slowly, hovering in the doorway, once again about to flee the scene of the confrontation, go downstairs, slam the door to his study, world without end.

"But sometimes," Elaina says, "I think that if you just spent a little more *time* with Melissa . . ."

Jonathan stops. "I've been working to support you all—"

"Oh, please, don't start that again," Elaina says pleasantly.

"If you ever got out of bed, you could have spent time with Melissa," Jonathan barks at her.

Elaina throws back the blanket and gets up. She is naked; her white breasts sway. "There. I'm out of bed. Want to take me dancing?" She embraces an invisible husband and begins to waltz.

Jonathan ignores her, addressing himself to the air. "I spent plenty of time with Melissa. You were the one who was always undermining everything I tried to do for her. You let her run wild. A mother's supposed to set some goddam limits. I didn't know what she was going to do from one moment to the next, I didn't know when she was going to come home pregnant just like—"

"Go ahead, say it." Elaina stops and puts her hands on her bare hips. "Pregnant just like me. It's not true and you know it."

Jonathan blinks. "Cover yourself up."

"Nothing I do is right!" Elaina wails. But she obliges, sliding back into bed, pulling up the sheet, and reaching for a piece of Kleenex in the same fluid motion. The Kleenex forms a lily to hold over her nose and mouth, and her weeping is faint and delicate.

Jonathan sighs. "All right now. Maybe we can—"

"She just did it to get your attention," Elaina says softly. "What?"

"Maybe if you'd been home for once . . . She wouldn't have done it if you had been there."

Jonathan presses his lips together. Then, *"You* were here," he says. His voice is like steam escaping. "Why didn't you stop her?"

Elaina holds her clenched fists in front of her. They tremble in the air. "I'll never forgive myself!" she shrieks.

The shriek rolls around like a plate on its rim, finally settling flat in the silent air between them.

"That's it," Jonathan says, the sound coming from low in his throat. "I'm leaving." He strides to the closet.

"Going to the office?" Elaina sniffs. "What else is new?"

"No," Jonathan says. "I'm *leaving*-leaving." He cleaves apart the solid wall of Elaina's clothes.

"What do you mean?"

"What do you think I mean?" Jonathan turns to face her. He is holding the garment bag that he uses for overnight business trips. "The doctor today wanted to know where Melissa got those Percodan."

"I don't know!" Elaina tears apart her Kleenex.

"If she hadn't had those Percodan, it wouldn't have happened." He lays the garment bag on the bed and drags down the zipper. "So there." He shakes his head—his jowls tremble—and then he bends low over the garment bag, hiding his face.

Elaina watches him, her eyes wider than usual. "You can't really leave."

He stands abruptly and turns his back to her; hanging the garment bag in the closet, he spreads its panels apart with the shoulders of a dark blue suit.

"Jonathan—"

"Just watch me."

"I know I deserve it. I know I've been a terrible wife."

The second suit goes into the bag.

"My mother always said I was going to lose you. I guess she was right."

Jonathan begins to stuff underwear and socks into the garment bag. "I guess so."

Elaina tugs a lock of hair from the Gibson girl; it falls life-lessly over her ear; there might even be a single gray strand in it. "I didn't mean what I said. I know it was my fault what happened to Melissa. I just want you to forgive me."

"And I just wish she'd had a mother who wasn't a—who wasn't deranged."

Elaina whimpers, "Just don't hate me, Jonathan, please don't hate me."

Jonathan keeps throwing socks into the bag. He's obviously planning to change his socks frequently.

"You can leave. . . ." Elaina wrings her hands. "That's okay, just don't hate me. Just tell me that you don't hate me."

Jonathan looks at her; his lips are pursed, as if he's about to blow her a kiss.

"Please!"

He zips up the bag.

"Just that, just that."

Jonathan starts for the door.

"It's okay if you go. I deserve it. I don't blame you for blaming me—I know it's my fault."

But Jonathan doesn't turn around. The garment bag thumps behind him as he drags it down the stairs.

# 4

Jonathan goes to stay at the Holiday Inn, which is next to his office building.

The hotel room is right off the assembly line, colored like a postcard. The stiff aqua-print bedspread smells of disinfectant, mildly evocative of all the strangers who have slept there. The furniture is of pale synthetic wood. Glossy pictures of prime rib, advertising the restaurant, are trifolded on the dresser. But I can tell that Jonathan feels comfortable here; it probably reminds him of one of his model apartments.

He unpacks and discovers that he's failed to take any clean shirts, which means he'll have to go back home. Unless he wants to send Valerie out tomorrow to buy him new ones. I bet that's what he'll do.

He lies on the bed in his suit and reads the *TV Guide*. He eats licorice, caramels and potato chips purchased from the newsstand. Then he starts making phone calls.

The next morning, before her daily visit to me, Elaina goes (*sans* brother Daniel) to see Marty Lindner. She's wearing rustling black crepe and black heels, and she wrings her hands prettily. She tells Marty that she's ready to file suit to be appointed my guardian. Her voice drives over a few humps as she explains that Jonathan has moved out, "over this disagree-

52

ment." Then she begs Marty not to tell Rose, who "would send the Sherith Shalom hit squad after me."

Marty assures her, with a grin that reveals the dark tobacco stains on his lower teeth, that all her communications are confidential. But I have just come from our house, where Lee Emma was in my parents' bedroom, counting the socks in the top dresser drawer.


Alta Vista High School: the locker room between class periods. The crush of bodies made sharp by the corners of books; slamming metal, shouted greetings. The girls use tiny mirrors hanging from inside locker doors to put on lipstick and comb their hair. The boys curse their instructors, their homework, and the absence of coed showers in the gym.

Jeff Lindner stands quietly by his open locker. His eyes are dark and quizzical holes in his pale face. His mouth is small and sensitive, as if the slightest undeserved hurt, not to himself but to any of God's lesser creatures, would set it trembling. But his high forehead looks as though it were carved from marble; it is dauntless, determined. He is a David; gentle warrior on the side of Right.

He is reading a note that he found wedged in one of the vents of his locker door. "Meet us on top of Grunt Hill at 3:30 if you want some valuable information. [Signed] Two Investigative Reporters."


Grunt Hill is the necessary path to the P.E. grounds. I remember hiking up it in a gym suit that smelled of sweat even when it had just come out of the dryer; I usually broke Ms. Hackett's regimental formation and was one of the last girls to straggle to the top. Now I can zap myself there instantly, simply by concentrating on the place; but I take the more pedestrian route, floating up behind Becky and Leah. I wish Old Hacksaw could see me now.

We arrive a little before 3:30.

"It's just so fee-stee-*flucked,*" Leah pants.

"De-feen-imente," Becky wheezes.

Becky and Leah came home from a rehearsal last night to find Jonathan gone and Elaina sedated for the evening. Leah keeps wondering aloud at what happened, as if by vehemence or repetition she can get the reassurance she needs that everything will be all right.

Becky leans against the fence that separates them from the deserted track field. She looks coltish in her jeans and plaid shirt. "Do you think he'll come?" she asks, still short of breath.

"Oh, sure . . ." Leah says doubtfully. "De-feen-imente. I mean, why wouldn't he?" She has pulled her hair back into a ponytail, and wisps of it circle her head like a yellow crown. The weather is warm and clear; sunlight bounces off the concrete, and the sky is like chrome.

Becky strains her long neck to see over the rim of the hill. "Shee-stee-flit, Lee-steah, it's *him.* I'm going to have a cardiac arrest." She quickly smooths her hair and then runs her hands over her shirt.

Jeff's dark head appears, followed by his broad shoulders. His breathing is only slightly heavy as he approaches them and lets his backpack slide off his shoulders. "Hi," he says.

"Did you know it was us?" Becky giggles. "Who left the note?"

Jeff glances from Leah to Becky. "No," he says. Then he shrugs, "Well, I thought maybe." The mark of a frown, like a chicken scratch, appears in his otherwise smooth forehead, mirroring Leah's chronic expression.

"We just had to talk to you in private," Becky says. "You've got to help us. Our parents have wonked out."

"Majorly," Leah agrees.

"You know how parents are." Becky giggles again. "Total

'droids." This is her term for anyone who indulges in stupid or self-defeating behavior. The term generally refers to our own or others' parents.

Jeff's frown deepens. Everyone in Alta Vista knows about the trouble that has afflicted the Silversteins, and every member of Sherith Shalom knows that Elaina has consulted Marty Lindner.

"So, like, wait till you hear this." Becky shakes her hair off her shoulders and down her back. "My mom went to see your dad today to tell him she wants to go to court for sure now."

Jeff somberly folds his arms across his chest. "I think," he says after a few moments of reflection, "that everyone should leave instructions when they turn eighteen about what they want their family to do in case this happens to them. Maybe people could fill out a form when they go to get their driver's license. It'd be like the way that you say you want to donate organs."

"How scuz," Becky observes.

"I mean," Jeff goes on, "I'm opposed to bureaucracy, but—"

"You get your driver's license when you're sixteen," Leah points out.

"When you're sixteen, then," Jeff says. "If you're old enough to drive a car, you're old enough to make these kinds of decisions. You can kill someone in a car, after all."

"God, rully," Leah says. "You know, if my sister had left a paper like that, then we'd *know* what she wanted and none of this would be happening."

"Well," Becky interrupts, "she didn't, of course, and now our dad's moved out because of it."

"Oh," Jeff says. "I'm sorry."

Leah glances reproachfully at Becky; she wanted to keep that part of it a secret. I hovered near her while she slept last night and snatches of her dreams floated up to me. They were filled with the disfigured and unwanted: children sleeping in cardboard boxes, women covered with red boils. "So what we were wondering," Leah explains to Jeff, "was if you could talk to your dad, maybe tell him what's going to happen. If my mom goes to court, we're afraid they'll really split up."

"Is it that serious?"

"'Droids," Becky grunts.

Leah speaks quickly. "But if your dad wouldn't take our mom's case, then maybe she and my dad would talk about it a little more before she could find someone else."

Or maybe the next lawyer won't be so eager to murder a poor girl who can't defend herself. I find myself hoping that the plan will work.

"I guess I could talk to him." Jeff scowls at the ground, shoving his hands in his back pockets. "Usually all my dad does is be a prostitute for corrupt power brokers. At least this is a social issue that should be litigated."

"Well, guy, I guess so," Leah replies. "But our parents . . ." She breaks off.

Jeff looks, startled, at Leah; then holds up one hand to shade the sun from her face. "I'm really sorry," he says. "That was totally callous of me. Sure, I'll talk to him."

"That would be *parthenogenic,*" Becky says. She has the heel of one boot in the chain link fence; her thumbs are hooked through her belt loops, and her pelvis is thrust slightly forward.

"I don't know what good it will do anyway. My father," Jeff says, "doesn't listen much to me."

"Well, he should," Leah says. "Guy, I thought you were on line, the way you told the mayor at that hearing that he was wonked out, you know, about the level of pollutants in the reservoir."

Jeff permits himself a modest smile. "I didn't say *that* exactly."

Leah sticks the fingers of one hand through the grimy metal of the fence. "Well, you know."

"Yeah." Jeff shrugs. Then, "Listen, I really am sorry. I do that sometimes—I forget there are people behind headlines."

"Oh, like, erase it from your mind," Becky says. "We know what you meant."

"Good." He swings his backpack over his shoulder. "It's one of those human tragedies. We have to make sure that it spurs us to action. The problem is, society hasn't caught up with technology, and if we're not careful, technology will rule us, instead of us ruling it." A faint breeze caresses his hair. "Well, I gotta take off. I promised my mom I'd do some yard work." He turns into the sun.

Leah glances at Becky, who is biting her lip. "Wait!" Leah calls.

Jeff stops to look back at them, brows raised.

"Uh . . ." Leah gropes. "We're having a party in a few weeks. Do you want to come?"

He shrugs. "Yeah, sure."

"It's going to be a parthenogenic flare," Leah promises. She ignores Becky's disapproving look, and speaks quickly. "So, like, it would be megaterrif if you came, really—"

"Yeah, okay, I'll look forward to it, then." Jeff starts toward the slope again. "And don't worry, I'll see what I can do about my dad," he calls over his shoulder.

"On line," Becky shouts back.

Becky and Leah do not speak as they watch Jeff descend. But as soon as his head has vanished, Becky snaps, "What did you say *that* for? Micky Mouse'll flip if we ask her to let us have a flare night now."

"She might say yes," Leah says meekly.

"Huh," Becky grunts. She pushes herself off the fence with the heel of her boot and picks up her book bag. "Let's spin."

Leah follows the chestnut bounce of Becky's hair. I concentrate on the frown line between her eyes and penetrate her mind: She is trying to recall the exact shape of Jeff's mouth, but it eludes her, obscured in her memory by the brightness of the sun.

Becky and Leah drive home.

Lee Emma is running a carpet sweeper over the hall rug. Lee Emma is a tall, big-boned woman with a short Afro. She has Indian blood, which explains her amaretto-colored skin, and her high cheekbones, that Elaina worries might be more striking than her own. Elaina is also somewhat less than thrilled that Lee Emma looks so much younger than her actual age, which is fifty-one. "There's a whole mess of your father's things missing," Lee Emma says as soon as the girls come in.

"Don't worry about it," Becky says.

"I don't want your mother to carry on 'cause she thinks I lost your father's socks," Lee Emma retorts. "You know how she gets."

"Rully," Leah murmurs.

"And I got to get up to you girlzes room to dust. You got to put away some of them makeup things."

"Guy, just a second then." Becky clomps up a few stairs, with Leah behind her. "Shee-stee-flit." Clomp, clomp.

"What time is your father coming home tonight?"

The girls stop. "We don't know," Leah says faintly.

"What y'all think? Eight o'clock?"

"He didn't tell us," Becky snaps.

"I got to know what time to set the microwave for. I got one of them frozen pizzas he likes."

Leah turns around. "He's coming home late," she says, her hands shaping the air into a circle to evoke an ambiguous time. "Really, really late. Like, as late as he usually comes home, but later, because he said he had an extra meeting that he doesn't usually have."

"If you say so," Lee Emma snorts. She holds the handle of the carpet sweeper like Moses leaning on his staff.

\*   \*   \*

Maybe my clairvoyance is just the cumulative result of my ability to gather information more efficiently. Or maybe it's a native instinct, the only one that survived my body. Perhaps these messages from other people were always there. Perhaps everyone gets them, but they can't hear them over the rest of the static and clatter in their brains, those overworked organs that clunk along like Model T Fords.

For me, the messages are getting stronger; or maybe I'm just learning to tune in to them, and trust them.

So that afternoon, when I get a sudden urge to go to the San Francisco International Airport, I say to myself, what the hell, let's travel.

And here I am, in the TWA terminal. Taut-faced, unseeing people stride in all directions. A child in sandals has a tantrum on the heel-marked floor. A woman in a pink wool suit is eating popcorn; a man with a huge leather suitcase knocks against her and she spills it and curses. Garbled announcements come over the P.A.

At the end of the terminal, through the window, I see the tail of an L-1011. A group of people are waiting in a semicircle for the passengers to deplane. I nestle among them, noticing dandruff, halitosis, hairs growing out of moles. I wonder how I could ever stand living in a body, dragging that oily, flatulent thing around: 130 pounds of loosely packed, lumpy flesh, like so much chicken guts in a paper sack.

A man in a navy blue blazer unhooks the rope that bars the jetway, and a stream of people begins to trickle around the corner from the plane. One of the first passengers off is Alison Winchester, my mother's older sister.

She's wearing a double-breasted mustard jacket with wide lapels and shoulder pads thicker than a quarterback's; this over a toast cashmere turtleneck sweater and a tweedy skirt that reaches midcalf, covering the tops of her eggplant Ferragamo boots with the four-inch heels. With the help of weekly visits to an aerobics class, Alison has starved her Miller-Rosenberg body down to a size four. Her hair is the pale blonde of cream sauce; and her eyes, tinted by contact lenses, are the unnatural shade of dark summer leaves.

She takes tiny steps, her shoulders inclining forward and her head tilted back; the crowd seems to part for her. She peers down her long straight nose at them, partly from myopia and partly from the same contempt that I feel for the Great Unwashed.

What's she doing here? Auntie Al hasn't made more than a biannual trip west in twenty-five years, although she talks to Grandma Rose once a week.

At baggage claim, with the help of a porter, Alison retrieves enough Louis Vuitton luggage for the touring company of *Evita* and has it all put in a cab. She gives the driver Grandma Rose's address. As they head up 101, the driver asks where Alison is from, and when she replies, "The Upper East Side," he seems eager to discuss theater and opera with her. But by the time they get to the Bay Bridge, Alison has put an end to the conversation with a few observations that make it fairly explicit that there *is* no theater or opera west of the Hudson.

Finally they arrive at the one-bedroom flat where Grandma Rose has lived for the last twenty years, since Grandpa Saul died.

Rose interrogates Alison over the intercom, finally buzzes her up, squints through the peephole in the door, then unfastens the three dead-bolt locks. "What are *you* doing here?" she demands as she opens the door, leaving the chain on.

"Motha. You might et least ect happy to see me." Alison has drained all Californese from her voice, but to protect herself from the proletarian taint of New York nasality, she has cultivated an accent uniquely hers, which moves in and out of her voice like a recalcitrant flute in a disorganized symphony. The accent echoes both Boston and the British Isles, and sometimes even lapses into the melody of North Carolina.

"Now don't be like that," Rose says, unhooking the chain. "Of course I'm thrilled to see you. It's just you scared me to death when you rang. I never answer the door—you never know who it's going to be. Why didn't you call from the airport?"

"Why should I have? I didn't want you to pick me up."

"Are you staying for long? Why didn't you tell me you were coming? I don't get to see you enough. You look well, I must say."

Alison's lips are long and disdainful, with only a shallow dent at the top; they reluctantly shape the curves of a faint smile.

They sit in Rose's living room, which is cluttered with Grandpa Saul's plaques for community service, photographs of the four grandchildren (mine is prominently displayed), and bric-a-brac from the trip that Rose and Saul took to Europe in the early Sixties. Alison keeps her elbows close to her sides; she is pressed in by the accumulations of old age, the past, reminders of what was and what is therefore forever unalterable.

"So why didn't you tell me you were coming?" Rose asks again.

"It was supposed to be . . ." Alison trails off, as if losing interest in her answer. "A surprise," she says finally.

"Are you staying here?"

"No, of cohse not, there's hardly room heyah."

"Where then? I hope you have a reservation. Everything gets so full up."

Alison rises and goes to the closet, where, one by one, she squeezes the padding of the hangers. "Yes, I do."

"I hope it's somewhere safe. Most of these hotels aren't safe now. Sometimes the bellhops break in after they know where you are and steal your bags, or even"—she clicks her tongue—"do something worse."

Alison raises her upper lip slightly. "I'm sure it will be . . . just fine." She carefully slips her jacket over the contest-winning hanger.

Rose sighs. "I am glad you're here. Maybe you can talk some sense into Elaina. She's being so stubborn."

"Elaina was always . . ." Alison shrugs, then sits again and peels off one of her boots.

"I'll tell you the truth, I'm weary of problems." Rose sighs again; Alison sighs faintly in counterpoint. Rose leans back and closes her eyes. She is tiny in her carved Victorian chair; she looks like one of those dolls made from dried apples. Sometimes I think Grandma Rose spends so much time complaining because otherwise we might really think about her life and feel sorry for her.

Suddenly she opens her eyes and leans forward again. Her gray irises glint with the dull sheen of a kitchen knife. "Now, are you going to tell me to what we owe the pleasure of this visit, my love?"

"Well . . . I wanted to see Melissa."

"Oh, Melissa." Rose shudders.

"I caun't believe it even now."

"That poor thing." Rose's hands lie still and brown-mottled on her lap; the veins are blue ridges. She raises them, looks at them as if they belonged to someone else; as if wondering, how have her hands, her tiny body, survived seventy-five years of aggravation, when I couldn't navigate through twenty-four? "Poor Melissa." If there were a God, a God Who Listens anyway, I'm sure she would offer her life for mine.

Now she studies Alison again. "But why didn't you tell me you were coming?"

"Ectually . . ." Alison massages her instep. "Jonathan asked me—"

"Jonathan?" Rose chirps excitedly. "What did Jonathan ask you?"

"Jonathan asked me to come out. I would have called you fust, but I just spoke to him last night, and it was too late. Then this mawning I was running around getting ready. Of course I had to get someone to look after the agency, and one of my models has a black eye that her boyfriend gave her, and another is in the hospital getting her stomach stapled—"

"Jonathan called you last night?" Rose interrupts. "What did he say? Why did he want you to come out?"

"Well, motha, he tawld me about the trouble with—"

"Oh, that. I tell you, I'm weary of problems. Elaina is so stubborn. She was always stubborn. It was different with you."

Alison's lips curve at the ends.

"So, tell me, what did Jonathan want?"

"He just wanted . . ."

"Yes?"

"Motha, you're going to be upseht."

"When do I get upset? What did he want?"

"He wants me . . . to tistify for him at the try-all."

"At the trial? There's going to be a trial? Oh, my God." Rose falls against the back of her chair. *"Elaina,"* she moans softly.

"Hasn't that psychiatrist done her *any* good?" Alison whispers.

Rose clicks her tongue. "I'm sure *he's* feeling fine, with what it costs. Of course Jonathan always pays for things like that."

"I'm just amazed," Alison sniffs, "that Jonathan . . ." She shrugs, and slides her foot back into the Ferragamo.

"I try to tell her." Rose waves her hand in front of her face. "Nobody wants advice." She laughs a little gurgly laugh. "I told you not to marry that Mark, didn't I?"

Alison inclines her head. After a long pause she says, "Yes, you did." Mark Winchester was the Princeton graduate that Alison was married to for three years before he decided that he was homosexual. When the divorce was final, Alison had the season tickets to the symphony, enough money to start her own modeling agency, and a list of restaurants to boycott in Greenwich Village.

"It wasn't your fault," Rose says. "You've got to have *mazel* in this life. Like Ethel Lemmon. Her husband has had two heart attacks, he still plays golf every weekend. He's going to live forever. Daddy was only sixty-two when he died."

"I know." Alison's eyelids droop.

"Sometimes you wonder what could have happened. Did I ever tell you about that lawyer who was very interested in me? Then he drove his car into the Bay one night, just because it was so foggy."

"I remember," Alison says dreamily. She takes one of the throw pillows into her lap and caresses it, her fingertips hunting for a loose thread in the embroidery. She is waiting her turn: to talk about the scarcity of straight white males in Manhattan; to express wonder at the luck of Jo Beth Hart, who married that successful accountant and travels annually to Europe. But Alison can be patient because she knows that they are settling in for a good long one.


That evening, as it gets dark, Leah drifts among the big rooms downstairs, not turning any lights on, watching instead as shadows climb the walls. Even though Jonathan was seldom home, there is a kind of space that someone leaves when he goes away for a little while that is different from the space he leaves when he goes away forever. Leah is following the empty eddies of air that are Jonathan's wake.

Becky is up on the third floor, talking on the girls' private line to Janice Ingersoll. Daniel is out with his friend Craig Newhouse.

Lee Emma has just left for the day, driving off in her Thunderbird, doubtless planning to phone Rose and confide her suspicion that Jonathan has moved out.

Elaina is not at home. I wonder whether she's with Drew.

Leah wanders into the big remodeled kitchen, with its terra-cotta-tiled counters and modern conveniences: the chrome and porcelain of coffee pots, toaster ovens, food processors, polished by Lee Emma and left to shine alone. This was the scene of my final debacle with Daniel, and I can tell that Leah is thinking of me now.

Leah always seemed so young to me: a walking diaper and potential nuisance even in her C-cup brassiere. I flaunted my makeup, nylons, boyfriends, and car, as I attained each one, and I screamed at her not to bother my dates with any patter about favored teachers and horseback riding. But in the heart of a girl like Leah, I am better than I was. She probably chooses to remember the good times, like the New Year's Eve when I was left in charge while Jonathan and Elaina went to Alta Vista High Jinks Night. The four of us played Monopoly and I made hot chocolate; then, at midnight, I led Daniel, Becky, and Leah on a pot-clanging expedition down Magnolia Street that got complaints from the neighbors the next day.

The downstairs phone rings. It's Jonathan. "Hello, dear," he says.

"Hi, daddy." Leah's voice is tight.

"How are you?" Jovial.

"Fine." I can hear the questions she wants to ask: *Where are you staying? When are you coming back?*

"How's your mother?"

"Fine."

"Good." Pause. "Funny thing happened at the office today. We were about to close a sale when the buyer said his financing had fallen through. Now this was a loan that he had said was absolutely guaranteed, so I said . . ." Jonathan continues the story, casting himself as lovable hero.

"Good for you, daddy."

He coughs. "You know, doll, your mother and I may have to go to court."

"I know, daddy."

"I don't want you kids to be under any pressure."

"Like what kind of pressure?"

"Oh . . . pressure to testify for one of us."

"Why . . . why would we have to do that?"

"You shouldn't have to, unless you want to."

"Oh."

Silence.

"What are you girls doing tonight?" Jonathan asks, with a lilt.

"Just going over to Janice's house."

"Oh?"

"To study."

"Ah."

The silence comes again. I can feel Leah swimming through it, searching for the words that will prove to Jonathan that she is who she is supposed to be.

"Okay, dear," Jonathan says. "Say hello to your mother for me."

"I will, daddy." She waits for him to hang up first.


"The way I see it," Becky says, "we just can't go *either* way."

Leah nods.

"Don't look so wonked, Lee-steah, it's not a nuclear event." Becky laughs as she fastens a purple bandanna around her forehead. "It's really banal psychology. I've read about stuff like this. We just got to be firm with them. If we say we won't take sides either way, then maybe they'll get back on line."

Leah's frown almost disappears. "We'll make a pee-stact," she says. "None of us will testify, then Mouse 'n' dad won't have any evidence and they'll just have to get back together." Leah

knows much better than this—she knows about expert witnesses and our other relatives—but why should that stop her
from hoping? Especially if Becky is so confident. "We've got to
get Daniel in on this, too."

Becky and Leah postpone their departure to Janice's.
Daniel finally returns home around seven, bearing a large gray
binder under his arm, which he puts on the dining-room table.
"I don't have time to talk to you girls," he tells his sisters when
he sees that they are waiting for him. "I'm going to the restaurant."

"What a tycoon!" Becky laughs. "King Mozzarella."

"Oh, can it," Daniel mutters.

"It'll just take a second," Leah says. "Me and Becky made a
pact that we wouldn't testify for Mouse or dad," she says. "We
want to make it a three-way . . ."

Daniel looks from Becky to Leah. They both have our
mother's eyes, large and needy and observant. Becky especially
is like a young Elaina, with her sprawling auburn hair. Each of
us sisters in our own way has tried to bully him, insisting that
he is responsible for our well-being. "I can't do that," he replies
haughtily as he opens the binder. He flicks through the index
tabs, humming faintly, as if waiting for one of the girls to ask
him what the binder is for. When neither of them does, he
goes on. "I already told Mouse I'd testify for her."

"But, guy," Leah bursts out, "what if they split *up?*"

Daniel closes the binder and heaves it under his arm.
"Well, maybe that would be for the best." But he looks a little
queasy, the way he does when he has a hangover.

"*Guy,*" Leah says.

"He just wants Mickey Mouse all to himself," Becky taunts.
"Okay, be that way. *We* have some integrity, anyway. If you
didn't have that Percodan—"

"Bee-stecky!" Leah cries.

"You think you know it all," Daniel snaps. "Well . . . well,
you don't. Now I have to go. I've got a meeting."

"Oh, a *meeting*." Becky folds her arms under her breasts. "How parthenogenic can you get."

"Some of us have more important stuff to do than go talk about boys with that dipstick Janice." Daniel mimics, "Like who's the most gee-storjo-matic at school?"

"Well, what are you going to do at your meeting, toot coke with Craig Newhouse? Yeah, like that's *rully* important. If dad knew—"

"Oh, shut up."

"Make me!"

"You *guys*," Leah says. She looks as if someone were scouring the inside of her stomach with Lysol. "Come on, don't fee-stight."

"Huh," Daniel says. He looks doubtfully at the binder under his arm. Then he mumbles, "I gotta go."


Becky and Leah are on their way to Janice's, and I am tagging along for the ride, when I hear Elaina laughing. "Asbestos Fiber" is filling Becky's Camaro with the toneless blare of a moog synthesizer, but I would recognize Elaina's laughter anywhere: She laughs like a baby, as delighted with the sound she makes as with its cause. I can follow that laughter to its source, I think, like a soldier following the red lines between the trenches.

I concentrate. And then I am traveling at high speed down familiar streets, passing somewhere near Grandma Rose's flat. I am aware of indistinct, peripheral images; it's as if scenes from my childhood are being reenacted, the past come to life again. I hang on—tentatively at first, and then more firmly—to the line of my mother's laughter . . . and land with a faint thud in Drew Harding's apartment, a veritable showplace of glass shelves, lush ferns, and futons, in a high rise overlooking Lake Merritt.

In the next room, Drew and Elaina are in bed together.

I've caught her! I zip into the bedroom; her laughter is very faint now, just a titter in her throat, as Drew tickles her. Mickey Mouse! Aha! I float above the bed, pointing a spiritual accusing finger at her. And then it occurs to me that she was calling to me with her laughter. As if to say, Melissa, you're old enough to know the truth now.

Drew, lying above the sheet, wears only jockey shorts. His body is small but perfect: deep, hairless chest; tapered legs. He looks at Elaina with obvious fascination that such a creature exists: white pudding, cherry sunrise.

Elaina has the sheet pulled up to her chin. "Stop it, short-cake." She pushes him away gently, like a kitten batting at a ball of yarn. "I'm sleepy now."

"Stay here tonight."

"I can't."

"Jonathan's gone."

She sits up, letting the sheet fall. She is wearing a pink nightie. "Who told you that?"

"You did. Elaina, please."

"I can't. My children."

"They don't need you. I need you."

"No, they do need me." Elaina wrings her hands. "Melissa needed me and I wasn't there. . . ." She dabs her eyes with the sheet, leaving a little smudge of black.

Drew touches her cheekbone gently. "Don't," he says. "Please don't. Sometimes these things just happen. It's all part of a larger plan we can't see."

"Don't try to convert me."

"I'm not trying to convert you."

Elaina sniffles. "Catholics are always doing that."

"I'm not a Catholic anymore."

"You can't stop being a Catholic—haven't you got any Kleenex? It's like dyeing your hair—the roots keep coming in."

Drew goes into the bathroom, where he finds that he is out of Kleenex. Will toilet paper do? Elaina takes it with a look of mild disgust and delicately blows her nose. "I've prayed and prayed about what to do about Melissa," she says, almost thoughtfully. "And this is the answer I got. I wish I could make Jonathan understand that."

At the name Jonathan, Drew's lips stretch as if he might gag. He hesitates. "Elaina," he says finally, "am I the first?"

"The first what, shortcake?"

"You know."

"Of course." She kisses his temple, then withdraws. "I mean, what do you think of me?"

Drew runs his hand along the ridge that is her leg, with more reverence than lust. "It's just that I wouldn't blame you, with such an unhappy marriage, a husband who brings other women home. . . ."

Elaina takes his chin in her hand. "Of course you're the first, shortcake. What we're doing is wrong. Don't you think I know that? It's only right because we love each other, and after the trial we'll be together. That will make it right." I pay special attention to the lullaby in her voice. Elaina may be crazy, but she's not stupid. She knows that if Drew thought he wasn't "the first," she would lose her balance on the tightrope she walks between mother and whore.

"What we're doing *is* wrong," Drew says glumly. "It's a sin."

Elaina smiles triumphantly. "Catholic," she says.

"Don't you believe in sin?"

"Of course!" Her face gives way to tears again—God, she can turn them on fast! The Sahara would be a garden if modern science could capture her secret. "I'm the most sinful person there is! It's my fault what happened to my own daughter! I was there and I didn't stop her. But how could I stop her? I was asleep. Why didn't she come and tell me that she was upset?" She weakly pummels Drew's chest. "Why can't you do something for her?"

"Oh, God, I wish I could."

"Well, I will," Elaina whispers hoarsely. Her hands flatten against his chest, then she lightly runs her nails against his skin, moving upward, until her hands embrace his throat. "You will, too."

Drew nods in hypnotized agreement. "The trial," he says. "We'll do what we have to do. Then we'll tell Jonathan. I feel sorry for him, Elaina!"

"He won't even notice that I'm gone," Elaina says, starting to slide out from between the sheets, "until the batteries in his electric shaver go dead."

Her little feet hit the floor and then, impulsively, she leans over to scratch behind Drew's ear. He sighs: animal satisfaction. "Are you sure you can't stay?"

"My children," she says again. "I'm a mother first. Remember that."

# 5

It's a little after ten o'clock, the same night: Daniel is sitting behind the counter at Dmitri's Number One, reading a computer magazine, or trying to—he keeps looking up. Only a few of the butcher-block tables are occupied, by couples and high-school students. Twelve Oaks Boulevard, visible through the glass facade of the restaurant, is a movie set of a small-town street at night, with phantom automobiles passing under the diffused streetlights and disappearing into darkness again. The occasional pedestrian walks by without looking inside, heedless of the comfort of salami and bell peppers within.

Daniel slides off the stool, retreating from a spot of tomato sauce on the counter, just as Dmitri comes out of the kitchen, bringing a pizza. Dmitri has straight black hair that hangs shaggily over his ears and a heavy wet moustache that grows slightly below the line of his lip. His shallow-set brown eyes are patient and watchful. He silently takes the pizza to a table where a young couple are sitting. The husband doesn't look up from his book; the wife serves him a slice and then gurgles at the baby in the high chair between them, feeding it bits of mushrooms and olives that she picks off the top of the pizza. The baby wears a white bib with the words *Alta Vista Rules* printed in red.

Daniel is checking the elbow of his white linen jacket for stains when two young men enter the restaurant. I recognize them both: Craig Newhouse and Leland Cross, Jr. Daniel moistens his lips and pushes the sleeves of his jacket higher up his arms, then stops Dmitri, who is on his way back to the kitchen, by placing a finger on his shoulder. "Listen, Dim, could you bring me and my friends a couple of beers? Dark."

"Tchure, Denny." Dmitri nods. Either Dmitri is the biggest wimp in the world or he thinks that Daniel can have him deported to Greece. Maybe Daniel has even dropped a few hints to that effect—the way he used to tell Leah that he could have her sent back to the baby farm that mom and dad rented her from.

Daniel takes a big gray binder—the same one he had on the dining-room table a little while ago—from under the counter and trots over to where Craig and Leland are scraping two cane-backed chairs away from a table. Daniel's ass sways a little when he walks. I once accused him of being Craig's lover, but Craig is definitely straight. As for Daniel, I know he's not gay, either; that was just my way of giving him a hard time. I just wish he wouldn't dress like an Italian movie director.

"Hey, Lee." Daniel thumps Leland on the back. "Good to see you. Beer's coming." He drops the binder on the table.

"I started telling Leland about the deal in the car," Craig says. Craig has delicate features, a square jaw, and a full head of wavy black hair. His nostrils are naturally flared so that he has a perpetually disdainful expression. His background is typical of Daniel's friends: a couple of years of local college, biz-ad major, then "took a leave of absence" (read dropped out). He drives a car that his parents bought him, and he still wears his senior class ring. He likes to tell stories about his favorite drunks, which he remembers poorly, and his favorite practical jokes, which he remembers in elaborate detail. He says the current Alta Vista tennis team is full of "weenies," in contrast to his own day.

"Sounds good, doesn't it?" Daniel asks Leland.

"Guess so," Leland agrees. Leland was two years behind Daniel and Craig at Alta Vista. He was then, and still is, underweight, with a sunken chest and a propensity toward black-heads. His chronic nasal congestion is a symptom of allergies and earned him the name Trumpet Nose. At Alta Vista he was a weenie that Daniel and Craig threw water balloons at when they cruised this very street on Saturday nights. But they wouldn't necessarily even remember that Leland was one of their victims. The weenies were faceless.

"You guess so!" Craig snorts. "Hey, this deal is hot."

Dmitri shuffles toward them with a tray of beers. They are silent until he skulks away. Then Craig raises his glass. "To a beautiful partnership."

Daniel, too, raises his glass. After a moment, Leland lifts his and gulps noisily.

Daniel takes a napkin and pats the ring of moisture under his beer. "The thing is, Lee," he says, "we're only telling you this because we trust you. This field is real competitive—we've got to be careful." He looks over at Craig. "Did you tell him the name of the business?"

Craig smiles lazily. "I was saving that for you."

Daniel nods. "Software-to-Go. We've already filed a DBA. Later we'll incorporate. We've developed one dynamite program already and we'll get more."

Well, well, who would have thought that Danny had it in him? I just wonder why the rest of the family hasn't heard about this venture. Still, I can understand why Daniel, even though he's doing something dad's always wanted him to do, would want to keep it secret. Dad would already be auditing the books and telling him where to buy office supplies at a discount.

"The program's called 'Wizards and Warriors,'" Craig says. "Hey, Lee, you'd buy that for your kids. I know you would."

"Dunno." Leland shrugs. He wipes his hand across his mouth. "Maybe."

"We got the program from Ansel Marsh," Daniel tells him. "You remember Ansel, from lower Alta Vista? Bright guy, though. He sold this to us so he could pay off a student loan. We wanted him to come on board as head of development, but he had other commitments."

"Wizards and Warriors" must be a computer game. I can see how that would appeal to Daniel, who has always been fascinated by magic and the occult. Elaina and Jonathan hired a magician for his sixth birthday party, and he was convinced it was real magic in spite of how I tried to enlighten him. For his own good, of course.

"What do you need me for?" Leland asks warily between squirts of nasal spray.

"It's all here," Daniel says, caressing the binder with his long white fingers and giving Leland his Robert Redford grin. "Our business plan. You might be interested in an equity position—"

"We just need some cash," Craig says, and then winces. Daniel has kicked him under the table. Craig glares at Daniel.

There's something else, that they're not telling Leland. I can tell. I could always tell when something was wrong with Daniel, something he didn't want to tell anyone—like the time Johnny Nichols up the street threatened to beat him up and Daniel was afraid to walk past his house. I poked a few holes in Johnny's bicycle tires and that took care of *him*. But right now Daniel looks like he did when he came home with the F in sociology his first semester at Hayward.

Leland takes a long slurp from his beer, snorting as he simultaneously breathes through his mouth. Then he says, "I can't help you guys."

"Hey," Craig drawls. "Wait till you've seen—"

But with a flicker of his long fingers, Daniel motions for Craig to be quiet.

"I don't need to see anything," Leland says tremulously. He holds tightly to the handle of his beer mug. "I can't get into my trust fund until I'm twenty-one, and even if I could, I wouldn't give you guys a . . . a fucking cent of it."

Craig's mouth opens. "You little weenie," he sputters, starting to rise from his chair.

Leland quickly pockets his nasal spray, jumps up, and scuttles backward toward the door. "You guys are the weenies!" he cries.

"Trumpet Nose!" Craig shouts.

"Ssshh." Daniel holds a hand up to Craig while glancing over his shoulder. Jonathan knows so many people—one of his spies could be here, chowing down a poor-boy sandwich.

"Same to you!" Leland calls. Then he backs out the door.

"Weenie," Craig mutters, resuming his seat.

Daniel watches Leland waddling past the window. Then he slides over into Leland's chair and props his chin in his hand. "I guess it is kind of poetic justice, isn't it?"

"You're being pretty romantic about all this," Craig sulks.

"I mean, we did break into his locker and put all that dirty underwear in it."

"We were kids. Besides, a little cockroach like that deserves to be squashed." Craig sips his beer, sighs. "What really hurts is that on the way over here I gave that queer-bait two lines of primo blow. He could hardly toot it, poor slob. I can't figure how a guy from such a good family turned out such a loser."

"I knew it was a long shot," Daniel says. "Leland doesn't understand business." He drums his fingers on the big gray binder. "I don't know why I even brought this—I didn't think he'd ever read it. I just thought he might want to be part of our plan, get in on the ground floor of something big like this."

I can bet that this crazy scheme was Craig's idea in the first place and that he persuaded Daniel to go along with it, just like he used to persuade him to smoke cigarettes in the boys' bathroom. He always made sure that Daniel was carrying the pack.

But Jonathan's schemes must have sounded crazy once, too. Perhaps Daniel has his own vision, something mighty and tall, like the great steel towers that rose from the landscape of his father's imagination: a chain of stores, blue marquees with SOFTWARE-TO-GO printed in white, the letters glowing on suburban evenings over the parking lots of shopping malls. The problem is that Daniel still believes in magic: that it can happen with just the right dress-for-success, corporate culture, entrepreneurial attitude.

"I wouldn't want El Nerdo as a partner anyway," Craig says. He snorts in imitation of Leland.

"Hmm." Daniel gazes at the big gray binder. "We'll just have to talk to someone else. Someone, you know, who'll have a grasp of what we're really trying to accomplish here." I can see Daniel trying to hang on to what he no longer believes: that the project is salvageable, worthwhile. There's always that time lag between knowing that you made a mistake and admitting it to yourself, and it's in that space of time that the worst mistakes are made.

"There isn't anyone else," Craig says. "There's no one else we know who's got a fucking nickel in his jeans. Times are hard. You're gonna have to hit up your pops."

Daniel shakes his head. "No way. I told you, I don't want to get him involved in this."

"Man, he's *got* megabucks."

"That's not the point."

"It's your ass," Craig says.

"You signed the loan, too." Daniel reminds him, punctuating his remark with the *thwack* of a knife.

"But I don't have any assets." Craig lifts his head. He has the air of royalty-in-exile. In spite of his father's recent departure abroad with the sixteen-year-old daughter of a co-worker, after what was easily voted Best Alta Vista Scandal of 1986, Craig is proud of being *Old A.V.* "You do." He indicates their surroundings with a languid wave of his hand; the dilapidated and far-from-fashionable Dmitri's Number One, a restaurant too proletarian for Alta Vista; an atmosphere of stained, crumpled napkins and spilled beer, redolent of white flour. No flaky croissants here. This is Daniel's kingdom; it is all he can call his own, and he can't call it his own, because his father gave it to him. Craig tilts back his chair, smiles. "Partner."

Daniel traces the grain of the table with the knife. I've figured it out now—it's so typical of Daniel and Craig. They got a business loan, maybe even from someone who knows Jonathan, and then squandered the money. First they bought a gram of cocaine for entertaining prospective clients, and then another gram because they used up the first one themselves. Daniel needed a new suit, as CEO—but then it was only fair that Craig borrow from the treasury to take Suzie Rotelli skiing. Well, isn't that what successful businesspeople do? Daniel and Craig have had too many role models for their own good, most of them from television.

How much is Daniel in debt? I wonder. I concentrate on the question.

"Twenty thousand dollars," Daniel says aloud. He looks up at Craig. "Is a lot of money."

Hey, not bad. I'm so pleased with having gotten this specific information that I forget for a moment to consider what it means. Twenty thousand dollars! That must have taken some aggressive squandering. I'd blame Craig for most of it. Craig is the kind of guy who would buy a term paper instead of writing it himself, but only if he couldn't get someone to write it for him, and usually he could. I think Daniel's starting to catch on. But it's too late if he is: The bank will go after his interest in Dmitri's, and Jonathan will finally and irrevocably know that his son is a failure.

Daniel gulps the rest of his beer quickly, as if there might be a diamond at the bottom of the glass. He took a chance; he had the faith that seems like shrewdness when things work out, stupidity when they don't. What a loving baby he was, with his pudgy face and blond curls, toddling after me. I could protect him then. Now I wish I could give him a little pat on the back. I wish I could splash a little beer in Craig's eyes.

* * *

But the sound of a knock summons me to the Holiday Inn.

Auntie Al is knocking on my father's door. When he opens it, he does not look particularly surprised to see her. He has loosened his tie; otherwise he looks as though he just came from the office (which he has)—his shirt is *always* a little rumpled, after all. He is wearing his reading glasses and he holds the room-service menu in one hand.

"Oh, dair," Alison says, with no trace of concern. "I hup I didn't weke you up."

Alison has also checked in at the Holiday Inn. I suppose that's for convenience; I know she would prefer a posh hotel in San Francisco.

"No." He stands aside. "Come in."

"What a stunning rum," Alison purrs. She sits with the clang of jewelry and crosses one twig-size ankle over the other. "Ebsolutely . . ."

Jonathan studies the menu. "They stopped serving at eleven." He glances up. The whites of his eyes are lined with red squiggles. "If I were running this hotel," he says, "I'd have twenty-four-hour room service. But just have five or six selections, all cold, or things that could be microwaved, so that you wouldn't need to have a chef on duty."

Alison takes an extra fold in one of the sleeves of her raspberry silk blouse. "I jest wented to tell you, Jenathan, if there's enything I cen do . . ."

"I appreciate you coming out," Jonathan says. "This case will be easy. You'll be back at work in no time."

"Thet's awl right," she says. "Ectually, I'm in no hurry—"

"No problem." Jonathan closes the menu with an air of finality. "Her attorney is incompetent. He just doesn't see the obvious."

What do I have to worry about, with daddy on my side? But somehow . . .

"Of *cohse*," Alison says. "I certainly hope thet I can help. If you ever need . . ." She twists her wide ivory bracelet.

I have heard so many different versions of what passed between Jonathan and Alison that I long ago gave up trying to sift from them the one immutably true story. As best I can determine, Jonathan and Alison went out a few times before he began seeing my mother—but how and why that substitution was made remains unclear. Shortly after my parents' wedding, Alison moved back east.

"Are you hungry?" Jonathan asks. "We could have a bite."

"How delateful." Alison reaches for her mushroom leather Fendi bag. "Did you know the most up to-the-minute place just uppened in San Francisco—of cohse there's bain one in New Yawk for yairs. They serve Califawnia cuisine and it's upen awl naight. Then there's a posh new club I'm daying to try, it's called Edsel's—it used to be an auto shuwroom. *Sew* San Francisco. Quaint, I main."

Jonathan has been rifling through his briefcase, which lies open on the bed. Now he looks up with the foggy-eyed expression of a man who has been traveling across a silent, inward expanse. He slowly focuses on his sister-in-law. "Let's go down to the coffee shop," he says.


Two days have passed. I've been lying low.

Daniel came to the hospital once by himself; perhaps he just needed a quiet place to think. Nurse Pinafore came in with the nurse from Kentucky to turn my body over, and I thought she was flirting with him; Daniel didn't seem to notice. Maybe women are attracted to his vulnerable look. I don't see it myself. Well, maybe a little.

Elaina disappeared a couple of times and I couldn't find her, no matter how hard I concentrated. I imagine that she was with Drew, but I got to her when she was with him before, so why not again? Her guard is up; it worries me. I'm afraid they're plotting something.

The hearing to set the trial date is today. Jonathan and Elaina are the featured guests, but I am the star: This is *In the Matter of Melissa Silverstein.*

Everyone gathers in the courtroom. The law-and-motion judge announces that because of the pressing nature of the case, the trial has been scheduled for early April, just a couple of weeks away. Jonathan puckers his lips to stop a smile; he made a lot of phone calls for *this* one.

After the hearing, Debbie Meyers and Marty Lindner try to hustle my parents out separately. Good luck. Jonathan strides up alongside my mother just as they get into the hall. "Are you sure you want to go through with this?" he croons to her in the singsongy voice he usually reserves for Leah.

"Mr. Silverstein . . ." Debbie is hanging on to Jonathan's arm, loping awkwardly to keep up with him. He seems unaware that he is dragging a pregnant woman behind him.

"If you'd visit her like I do," Elaina says tearfully, "you'd *know* this is what she wants. She's suffering so much."

Jonathan stops suddenly and Debbie bumps up against him. "This is just another crazy idea of yours," he barks at Elaina. "If I let you go through with this, you'll come crying to me in two weeks and want to know why I didn't stop you."

"Oh, that's so unfair," Elaina whimpers. "You never understood Melissa at all. She wanted so much from you that you wouldn't give her. She just needed some guidance."

Marty is patting Elaina's shoulder. "Now, now, Elaina."

Jonathan grabs my mother's arm. "You're the one who let her take those pills!" Jonathan's voice is squeaky. His face is a deep red. He trembles from the waist up, and his eyes fix on some distant object.

Daddy!

I am throbbing all around him—trying to hold him. I feel

his blood, his fury, like a geyser spurting through me, as if we both could dissolve. . . .

"Mr. Silverstein!" Debbie gasps.

"Jonathan!" Elaina cries.

But Jonathan is calm again, breathing his normal shallow breaths. "I'm fine," he says coldly. His father died of a heart attack; Jonathan wouldn't repeat his father's mistake. At least I hope not. He shakes Debbie off and strides forward, turning only to promise my mother darkly, "I'll see you in court."

Elaina comes home and takes to her bed. And it is that afternoon when Becky and Leah finally ask her if they can have a party. "What?" she cries. "You want to do what? When? Oh, God!"

She is propped up against her pink satin pillows, wearing her matching pink satin pajamas, and rubbing lotion on her hands. Becky and Leah stand at the foot of the bed, looking appropriately sheepish. "Your sister is in the hospital," she reminds them. "And I'm going to court in two weeks."

"I know, Mouse—" Leah begins.

"Your grandmother would never let me have parties. Granddad would have—that was the kind of man he was—but I didn't have any friends."

Becky and Leah shift their weight and listen with relative patience. Perhaps they feel that it's the least they can do. After all, they've already invited twenty-five kids, so Elaina has them in something of a negotiating bind, though she doesn't know it unless she's clairvoyant, too, which I sometimes think she is.

"I was very unpopular," Elaina goes on. "During fire drills, the teachers used to make me stay behind in the classroom."

Becky groans.

"Your grandmother didn't want me. When she was pregnant, she tried jumping off the refrigerator." Elaina snaps on a pair of surgical gloves. "Your Auntie Al never liked me either. I don't know why she has to stay at the same hotel your father does. It's lucky I'm not the suspicious type. You know what she used to do to me? When I was little, I was really frightened of skeletons, and she used to sneak up behind me—"

"And scream, 'It's a skeleton!'" Leah finishes.

"Wasn't that mean, though?" Elaina asks in an excited whisper. "I think she doesn't like me just because I'm her younger sister—though if she keeps lying about her age, then she'll be the younger sister. I don't care who knows that I'm forty-two." She cups her gloved hands around her mouth. "Forty-two," she announces. Then she adds, conspiratorially, "Alison is four years older than I am."

Becky and Leah nod.

"I'm glad you girls are close. That means a lot to me. I always wanted my children to be close. Sometimes I think my mother and my sister are ganging up against me, and now my own husband is taking me to court. I thank God every day that my children are standing by me. Your father upset me so much this morning—"

"Guy, he's *our* dad," Becky points out.

"That's the rumor, anyway," Elaina says. She looks at the gloves. "My hands get so dry," she says. "I think I have what Job had. Maybe I should get a bell to ring when I go down the street." She arranges the top of the sheet around her waist. "There is a little favor you could do for me," she says. "But only if you want to. I mean, I'll only ask you if you promise that you'll feel free to say no."

Becky folds her arms under her breasts. Leah bites her lip, her frown deepening.

"Well, I *am* going to court pretty soon."

They wait.

"Daniel said he'd testify for me. I guess you girls want to testify for your father."

Silence.

"I wouldn't mind if you did. I don't care if I'm not your

favorite parent—I love your father. But how he can stand to look at Melissa the way she is and see her suffer like that, how anyone can stand it—"

"We can't go to court, Mickey Mouse," Leah interrupts. "We promised that we wouldn't testify for either of you guys. We made a pact."

Elaina swings her plump legs over the side of the bed; her feet pat around in search of her slippers. "I respect that. I'm impressed with you girls. When I was your age, I was still taking a bottle. A bottle of gin, that is." She bends over to feel the small bunion on her left foot. "Now you know I think your father's right about almost everything. I mean, he's the closest thing to God since *my* father, who probably *was* God, but sometimes about Melissa he might be just a little bit wrong—"

Becky rolls her eyes at Leah.

"I *saw* that, Rebecca Sarah," Elaina says. "I'm not asking for me. I'm asking for your sister."

"Guy, Mouse," Becky says, "can we have a party or not?"

"Do you have to do it the exact weekend before the trial? Couldn't you wait until afterward? Of course, I don't know, afterward I may be in the hospital myself. Dr. Abramowitz says that this much stress isn't good for me."

"All the other mothers let the kids have parties," Becky says. "Janice Ingersoll's mother and Tracy Newhouse's. Do you want us to be unpopular just 'cause you were? Guy!"

"But I do let you have parties, it's just that I have to go to court Monday, and I'm a little nervous—"

"Guy, it's not like *you* have to do anything, like clean up."

"All right," Elaina sighs. "You can have the party."

"Well, thanks," Becky says grudgingly, and starts to slouch away, with Leah slouching after her.

"Wait! Girls?"

"*What?*" Becky halts at the door.

"I was just going to say that if you want to go visit Auntie

Al, I'll understand. She is your aunt, after all. I want you to be close to her."

"Yeah," Becky replies, "I can like totally tell that you do."


As final preparations are made, Jonathan meets with Rabbi Weiss.

Rabbi Weiss is Grandpa Saul's successor at Sherith Shalom. He's in his late fifties now, already looking toward retirement. The size of his pension and his possible longevity are of great fascination to Rose. She complains of both in private, but publicly she maintains a cordial relationship with him, and she remains prominent in temple life as the dowager rebbitzin.

Rose has accompanied Jonathan to the meeting. Driving over, she observed to him, "Daniel is so stubborn." This was her way of comforting Jonathan over his son's defection; but Jonathan did not comment, so she added, "Elaina was always like that, too. I don't know where she gets it."

Now he and Rose sit in the rabbi's study. Twenty years ago it belonged to my grandfather, and the corner of Rose's mouth twitches as she sits rigidly straight and squints at the cramped shelves of books behind the rabbi's desk. *Jewish Ethics in the Post-Watergate Era. Normative Judaism and Political Commitment.*

Grandpa Saul was rabbi at a time when the Reform movement was at its height. Jews wanted it known that they didn't all wear long beards and speak with those embarrassing accents that made chopped liver out of English. They were no different from Christians; they could move into Alta Vista and not bring the property values down. My grandfather was clean-shaven and wore a neatly folded monogrammed handkerchief in his breast pocket. He was active on the boards of the Boy Scouts, the United Way, and the Rotary Club; worked with several agencies that aided the handicapped; and was a chaplain to the fire department. His favorite project was an orphanage he founded along with several other rabbis, and the orphan's home fund-raisers were always well attended by prominent Gentiles.

Saul was available to anyone who needed him. He would drive all day to a speaking engagement for which there was no honorarium. He took calls in the middle of the night from people who wanted to borrow money. And it seemed that whenever Rose planned a couple of days' vacation, someone in the congregation died.

But Rose never complained to any of her friends. Everyone was fascinated by the rabbi; everyone would have loved to talk about his family. I think how isolated that made her—how the loneliness must have congested her lungs like the pneumonia that always threatens my body now. Only her children could be made to listen.

Rabbi Hal Weiss is of the generation that logically followed my grandfather's. Rabbi Weiss was involved in the civil-rights movement, wore a beard, and later protested the Vietnam War. In his sermons he sometimes criticizes the Israeli government. This enrages Rose, who supports everything the Israelis do, as long as Rabbi Weiss doesn't support it.

"First let me say how very sorry I am, Jonathan," the rabbi says. Rabbi Weiss looks Jewish in a someone-married-a-WASP-somewhere-way. He is fleshy and has wavy, gray-streaked blond hair (too long, in Rose's opinion), full lips, and a ruddy complexion. He's tall and broad-shouldered and wears black suits; his silhouette recalls something out of Nathaniel Hawthorne, evoking New England winters and the retributive force of a Calvinist God. "I've called you a couple of times, but you've been tied up."

Jonathan's first response, when colleagues or underlings offer him sympathy about me, is usually to change the subject, rather brusquely, but he doesn't have that option today since the subject is me. Now he smiles just enough to hint at crow's feet, and to reveal the tips of his eyeteeth. "Well, we have to see what we can do about this."

"We know you have a *very* busy schedule," Rose assures the rabbi. "We know that just appearing in court would be a hardship."

Rabbi Weiss forms a steeple with his hands.

"We just need to offer evidence that Melissa would not have wanted—" Jonathan coughs. "My—the plaintiff has the burden of proof." He taps the side of his wing tip, which is propped on the knee of his gray suit. The sole is separating from the body of the shoe. "Jewish ethics are against euthanasia," he points out. He looks like he did when he used to take us on drives and ask us math problems in the car.

"That's true," the rabbi says. "The question is, *is* this euthanasia?"

"Well, of *course* it's euthanasia," Rose says, with a big smile.

"It isn't euthanasia to withhold extraordinary means of treatment," the rabbi observes, looking at Jonathan. "A respirator is considered extraordinary means." Pause. "You say the issue in the courtroom will be what Melissa would have wanted."

"That's right."

"Of *course* it's euthanasia," Rose says, no longer smiling.

"So even if it *is* euthanasia," the rabbi says, "and even if I am morally opposed to that, which I am, then my expressing that opinion won't affect the outcome."

"Well, but if you see it, there's a psychological effect that your testimony will have," Jonathan tells him. "It works analogously, since we're speculating as to what Melissa would want, that she would be influenced by those beliefs." He coughs again, then tugs at his collar.

"Are you sure this is what Melissa would have wanted? That is what's important, isn't it?"

Jonathan sticks the tip of his finger under the side of his

shoe and then pulls it out again, making a little snapping sound. "Yes, I'm sure," he says.

And he really is. He has no doubt about what I want, and even though he's right, I know that it's not because of any sympathy or rapport between us, but because he sees what I want as an inevitable extension of what he wants for me—in spite of the fact that in life I rarely did what he wanted me to do, and then only grudgingly and half-assedly.

"Of course it's euthanasia and you're against that," Rose says to the rabbi. "They might find a cure."

"Perhaps if you and your wife could discuss this further—if you'd like to come in together—"

"The question is," Jonathan interrupts, "would you be willing to testify?"

Rabbi Weiss is silent for a moment. Jonathan keeps snapping his finger out from under the side of his shoe. "Melissa once said to me that she thought unhappy people should be put out of their misery," the rabbi says finally.

I beg your pardon?

"They might find a cure," Rose points out. "You're too young to remember, but when I was a child everyone died of influenza—"

"When did Melissa say that?" Jonathan asks, indifferently enough, but with his voice rising a little at the end.

"In our confirmation class." The rabbi raises the cover of a book on his desk, then lets the cover fall again. He pushes the book aside. "I wouldn't even mention it, but she was so emphatic about it, and I've never forgotten it."

That damn confirmation class. Now I remember. But I didn't mean what I said. I was just trying to be difficult. We were talking about euthanasia and everyone else was against it, and I felt like disagreeing.

"Heh-heh." My father makes the absent chuckling sound that he does when one of us tells him the punch line of a joke he hasn't listened to.

"Of *course* it's euthanasia," Rose says.

But this is one down for our side.

When I was a teenager, Jonathan had a rumpus room constructed in the basement. He had it in mind for me, the eldest princess, but I gave only a couple of dismal birthday parties here. Daniel made somewhat better use of it, but the room was really waiting for Becky and Leah.

At a "Beckianleah" party, the following events are likely to occur: Someone throws up in the toilet; someone else throws up in the backyard because the toilet is being used; a young person loses his or her virginity; such unforgettable libations as tequila and Dr. Pepper are served; somebody steals somebody's boyfriend; and somebody else sells marijuana at a discount price.

Then there was the time that Davy Shetland shot his brother in the leg with the .38 he had borrowed from his father's gun collection. There was the time that Jamie Newhouse had an unfortunate acid experience and went running down the street naked, screaming about his math teacher. There was the time that Kari Hoffman tried to slash her wrists in the bathroom with the razor blade she'd been using to chop her coke.

One might think that Becky and Leah would have a bad reputation among the Alta Vista gentry, but their parties are not responsible for any more than their per capita share of "unfortunate behavior."

Only one thing dents the pleasure of these evenings for my sisters: Elaina comes downstairs once or twice, usually in some gypsy-style housedress, to circulate among the guests, sample their drinks, and ask questions. "Did your mother have a face-lift? Oh, I'm sorry, that was rude, I know. You don't have to tell me if you don't want." Becky and Leah negotiate her upstairs as soon as possible, but their friends do not object to her; she listens so sympathetically to their complaints about their parents.

At this party the usual group will be in attendance. Becky and Leah have a wide range of friends, from "setters" to "cave dwellers" to "tokers." And of course Jeff Lindner is expected.

He arrives unfashionably early and reports the failure of his mission to his father. "I tried to talk to him. He just said"— Jeff hesitates—"that what was happening with your mom and dad was none of his business, or my business either. I'm really sorry. His mind is just like a fascist government. If there's anything else I can do, like calling the newspapers—I know someone at the *Alta Vista Voice*—"

For tonight, the girls tell him, they just want him "to flare at the party." But Jeff has never learned how to have a good time for the simple purpose of having a good time; he believes that every hour of his life must be dedicated to a specific productive cause. So he occupies himself by reading the backs of album covers.

By 10:30, the opening awkwardness has melted into an amorphous Party: The lights are off, and the only illumination comes from the light at the top of the stairs. A few couples have paired off on the couch; sucking noises emerge from the shadows like the nocturnal sounds of unseen jungle creatures. A few other couples are dancing to the music of Straight from Hell. The base is turned up so high that the thumping seems to come from the floor and presage an earthquake. ("Would you mind turning that down a *little?*" Elaina shouted down the stairs half an hour ago. Apparently no one heard her.)

Then there are the singles: The boys lounge around the bar, traducing the honor of Hilltop High, Alta Vista's rival school, and describing in picturesque terms the bodily injuries that the members of Hilltop's basketball team are likely to receive when next encountered. The girls have gathered around the pool table and they affect boredom, yawning and stretching, some even reclining on the table, their miniskirts bunching up almost to the waist.

And in the corner a few kids gather around the TV set, where Phil Greenley is rhythmically humping a joystick, like a maestro conducting the 1812 Overture, playing "Ground Zero," one of Daniel's video games. Two of his friends, their shirttails hanging out, stand on either side of him, cheering him on. "Partho!" "On line!"

Phil is a stout senior from lower Alta Vista, with a blotchy face, whose father works in sales and whose mother has a *job*. (Acceptable careers for Alta Vista mothers include operating boutiques or being an image consultant.) Phil will probably go to a junior college. Becky went out with him once, two years ago; it was one of her first dates, before she learned how to tell a dachshund (Beckianleah-ese for a boy who thinks with his penis) like Phil how to trash himself. But Phil did manage a kiss that night, which Becky told Leah was "just like kissing the Creature from Slime Town. Gree-stunjomatic!"

When the numbers on the TV screen pass 20,000, a cheer is raised. "Fuck that, get out of the *way*," Phil declares. He wiggles the joystick frenetically. "Watch out." *Bing, zip, zap.* Purple blobs explode, orange targets dissolve into miniature mushroom clouds. His score climbs to 22,000. Someone has turned the music down; conversations have stopped as the other kids, including Jeff, drift toward the screen. *Ping, beep, whiz*—22,850. Suddenly a preemptive strike hits his ICBM, which fizzles with a slow whine.

"Aw, shit, man, *twenty-two eight fifty*." Phil pushes a section of greasy hair out of his eyes. "I can do better than that."

"On line," Janice Ingersoll says. "I can't get up past like four hundred." Janice is a not-terribly-bright girl whose popularity has been adversely affected by her parents' recent divorce simply because, according to Becky, she hasn't used it right.

*"Guy,"* Becky mutters to Leah, "some bee-stunk party, playing a megabarf video game."

Phil swigs from the warm beer resting on top of the console. "Finger action, girls. I'm famous for it." He turns and grins up at Becky, flashing sharp yellow teeth. Then he notices Jeff, standing toward the back of the group. "Hey, Lindy," he says, "ever play this?"

For a moment it seems that Jeff has not heard. Perhaps he is thinking about the current state of the ozone layer. "No," he says.

"Wanna try?"

Phil's companions snicker.

"This bunkomatic game," Becky says. "Don't bother."

"Come on, man, we want to see how it's done."

In its quiescent state, between games, the "Ground Zero" missiles wink orangely and purplely in the darkness of the rumpus room. *Beep, ping.* The other kids murmur restlessly.

"Yeah, sure," Jeff says. He moves forward and takes the joystick from the leering Phil. "How do you start it?"

Phil presses the reset button.

Enemy warheads surround Jeff's ICBM. They attack, and his first missile dissolves.

Phil guffaws.

"Oh, nuke yourself," Leah mutters.

But Jeff's fingers close tightly on the tip of the joystick. A second round of warheads appears, but he dodges their fire and begins shooting well-aimed missiles at the floating targets. Mushroom clouds like tiny orange flowers explode all over the screen, at greater speeds. *Zap, zing, boom.* The watching crowd makes a soft, collective hum that blends with the faint hum of the video game. When Jeff occasionally misses, Phil makes asides like "I coulda got that one," until Janice Ingersoll tells him to trash his stupid mouth.

Jeff dodges and maneuvers and fires. The numbers on the screen flick upward. When they pass the 25,000 mark, Jeff suddenly raises the joystick in the air. "Here," he says to Phil, "you finish the game for me."

There is brief laughter. Phil sputters, and before he can sit down again, the final ICBM is destroyed. Its death throes sound like a whining child.

"Solid, man." One of Phil's gargoyles pats Jeff on the back.

"Parthenogenic," the other one says.

Jeff does not smile. He silently and rather absently moves through the group back toward the stereo.

Someone starts the music again—Bruce Springsteen now. A classic. Gradually couples form on the dance floor again.

Jeff watches the dancers for a moment. Then he reaches for another album and begins to read the back cover. Becky and Leah have moved closer to him, ostensibly picking up empty glasses. "Go on." Leah nudges Becky.

"Lee-steah!" Becky shakes her head so that her big purple earrings flop against her neck. "I *can't*. No way."

"Yes, you can."

"No, I can't!"

"Come on," Leah announces in a louder voice. "These are bunk notes. We've got to pick something else to put on."

She takes Becky's wrist firmly and leads her to the stereo. "What's that?" she asks Jeff.

Jeff slowly looks up from the album cover, his eyes traveling the distance between himself and the outside world. "Uh . . ." He looks down again. "Cherokee Revenge."

"They're so parthenogenic," Leah says. "Let's put that on." She takes the record from Jeff and raises the hood of the turntable. "*Guy*, we haven't even danced all night. It's bunk when it's your own flare night and you don't even get to dance 'cause you're like *waiting* on everybody."

Jeff starts as if reproached. He looks at Leah; his lips part.

Leah tenses, lowering the needle onto the record. "Guy, Becky dances so spindo to this song. I can't dance to it at all."

"*Guy*," Becky says.

"Would you like to dance?" Jeff asks her.

With an equine toss of her head, Becky replies, "Sure, I guess so." She trots out to the dance floor; Jeff follows.

And I feel Leah's sigh like a shudder inside me. She stands by the stereo and watches them. Jeff's dancing is limited to a stiff swaying of the knees, although he gradually finds the rhythm of the music. Becky alternates hopping on one foot with high jumps. This is accompanied by sudden outward thrusts of her arms and forward thrusts of her breasts. Occasionally she bends over and then straightens with a sudden jerk, flipping her wavy chestnut hair over her head.

When the music stops, Jeff takes a couple of halting steps as if to walk off the dance floor, but Becky stands on one leg, examining her nail polish, never allowing him to make eye contact. As soon as the music starts, she begins to throw out her arms and legs again.

In this fashion they dance several dances together. It seems natural for Becky to stay with him after that. She talks to him about her favorite bands, her teachers, her plans to go to UCLA and then to become a TV star. She mixes rum and coke for herself, pours diet 7-Up for him. She takes him on a tour of the backyard. She shows him various items from her childhood that are stored in the closet.

Eventually, when the dancing has stopped and the room is quiet except for the occasional grunt or sigh or protest of chastity, Becky and Jeff are seated on the couch together. Some of the kids have retired to their cars or to the cars of friends. Others huddle in the corners of the room. Two have fallen asleep on the pool table. Phil Greenley has gone home.

Leah is sitting on the stairs with Albert Sullivan, who has a megagroaner for her. He is a weenie, but she feels sorry for him.

Becky keeps talking to Jeff, though in a whisper now, balancing her tumbler on top of her legs, which are crossed to reveal a healthy section of her purple-stockinged thighs. Her ongoing chatter, to which Jeff has responded politely if tersely, has created the illusion of conversation. And it is now, in the relative seclusion of the darkened room, that her monologue veers subtly out of control. She begins to talk about me, the big sister whose presence was such an obstacle. Jeff's pale face draws her like the moon, and she talks about my tantrums, the attention I stole from her. And now more than ever, from this twilight world between life and death, I demand to be the focal point of this family. With the trial on Monday morning, Elaina has been too preoccupied even to join their party. As for Jonathan, "There's all kinds of times I want to do something that dad doesn't want me to do 'cause Melissa nuked it up. Guy," she smiles with bitter irony, "it's not like I'm a different person or anything, right? It's so *narrow-minded.*"

Jeff sighs. I wonder if he is thinking of the trail of cigar ashes that Marty leaves, to further pollute an already dirty world.

"Like the time Melissa went to Europe for the summer and then she said she wasn't going to come back?" Becky giggles. "Dad had a major heart malfunction, 'cause like the worst nuclear event ever is not finishing college. But now like he doesn't want me to go to Paris like I want to, 'cause he knows I'm more independent than she was, and he's like so scared I really wouldn't come back. It's so bunk."

*"Would* you come back?" Jeff asks.

Becky flips her hair over her shoulders. "Oh, sure. Yeah, 'cause I want to be an actress." She adds, "Of course, maybe I'd want to get into the theater in London."

Finally Jeff tells her that he promised his parents he would be home before 2:00 A.M. So they tiptoe upstairs, weaving between Albert and Leah, who watches them go up with the frown stamped between her eyes.

Becky leads Jeff through the darkened house to the front porch. And there, against the backdrop of ivy that covers the stucco, he stands under the porch light, where a couple of gnats circle in an endless holding pattern. Looking down into Becky's upturned face, he says, "Thank you for a very nice evening."

"Guy, thanks for coming."

He takes a step away, stops. It is too cold to go out into the blackness, to leave the umbrella of porch light and the nest of shrubbery. And in that moment of hesitation, the outcome becomes inevitable. Now he's been standing there too long not to say, "So would you like to get together, I don't know, sometime and maybe do something?"

"Yeah, okay," Becky shrugs. "Like maybe next Friday night, we could go see *Party High,* something like that."

"Yeah, okay." Jeff nods. "That sounds okay." More nods. "So I'll see you then." He stumbles down the first step. "I mean, I'll probably see you Monday at school."

"G'night." Becky smiles tolerantly and slowly closes the door.

# 6

The Alameda County Courthouse; a modern courtroom. It's opening day of *In the Matter of Melissa Silverstein*.

The issue before Judge Raoul Picone is who shall be appointed guardian of the incompetent (me); and the question of fact is, which of the litigants (who have each made their intentions clear in the pleadings) would best represent my interest? The judge has to determine, in other words, what I would want them to do if I could call them all around me and have my own little press conference.

Court convenes at 9:00 A.M. The court reporter is limbering up on his steno machine. The clerk is whispering into the phone on her table. There is no jury.

It's early for Elaina, who looks pale in the morning sunlight. She reminds me of a Victorian photograph: She's wearing a broad-brimmed black hat with a black net veil, and the hollows under her high cheekbones are shadows chiseled into her face. She sits at the plaintiff's table, on the side by the windows.

Jonathan is a few feet away at the defendant's table, studying one of his nails as if it were the most fascinating object to come his way in months. Debbie Meyers is next to him: She wears big pink-rimmed glasses and no makeup, but she has combed her pigtails out into a pageboy.

My parents do not look at each other. Jonathan and Elaina are like light and darkness, mystic opposites, eternally attracted but equally repelled, so that they remain suspended in the same place, holding the universe together.

Daniel sits in the gallery behind Elaina, one ankle on the opposite knee, stroking his red handkerchief, which is unfolded on his thigh.

Becky and Leah are a few rows back, squirming in their itchy wool temple dresses. They are seated next to Rose, whose head is held erect, lips fixed in a grim half-smile. The smile is partly intended for Judith Weiss, the rabbi's wife, who has insisted on attending the trial "to give the family moral support." She is seated nearby, and I think my grandmother has never been so sorry that murder is a crime in California. At least Ethel Lemmon was unable to attend: She and her long-lived husband have gone to their granddaughter's wedding in another state. The bad news is that Ethel's granddaughter is marrying an orthodontist.

Rose has placed Becky next to her, and she occasionally pinches her arm and makes a comment like "Do you want the reporters to write that you were slouching?" But whom Rose loveth, she chastises. I'm sure Leah wouldn't mind a word or two of reproach.

Alison, on the other side of Rose, is examining herself in her compact.

Finally the bailiff announces the entrance of the judge. Everyone rises. A door opens and the judge walks in, led by a fluffy white Seeing Eye dog who gives the appearance of smiling. The dog trots happily up the stairs, leading the judge to the bench, then plunks down on the floor.

Judge Picone resembles a very large infant. He has flour-white skin; small, unformed features; and he is bald except for a downy patch of brown hair in the middle of his scalp. His marbly eyes, pushed deeply into the doughy flesh that surrounds them, have small, clouded irises, as if the holes through which he might have seen the world have had cotton stuffed in them. His hands move almost constantly in a ripple of motion that flows from the swerving of his eyes; he seems to be groping for the boundaries of the world around him. "Where is my gavel?" he asks. His voice is thin, with a squeak of panic.

"Here, Your Honor." The bailiff slips it gently into the judge's hand.

The trial begins with opening statements.

Marty is first. "We submit, Your Honor, that to needlessly prolong the suffering of this unfortunate young woman would be a cruel infliction of others' wishes upon her. Therefore my client seeks to disconnect the respirator that pumps air into her lifeless, pathetic lungs, and only adds to her apparent agonies." Then he blows a lot of air about how my mother is a religious woman who wants my life to rest in God's hands.

Make me barf, why don't you?

When it's Debbie's turn, she pushes herself up from the table. Her belly under the blue denim jumper rises like a whale coming up to spout. Debbie reads from notes; her voice is whiny, abrasive, as she tells the judge that this is euthanasia, which is illegal in the absence of express written consent that follows the form prescribed by the California Natural Death Act. She actually reads part of the statute. Jonathan's expression is blank, but I know what he's thinking: that the judge probably read the statute in braille last night, and that Debbie sounds patronizing. As Debbie waddles back to her seat, I wonder if my father isn't also thinking that Debbie wasn't the best choice after all, especially since her pregnancy is lost on Judge Picone.

Jonathan motions for Debbie to move closer; he whispers in her ear. If I had been a lawyer like he wanted me to be, would he be whispering to me this afternoon? I hover near him; I want to push Debbie away—he's mine!—and Jonathan brushes his hand near his head, as if a fly were buzzing near him.

Debbie raises her hand. "Your Honor," she says, "I wish to move for a summary judgment." From the way Jonathan is studying his thumbnail again, I think this was his idea. But Judge Picone wants to see the attorneys in his chambers. Judge, dog, and attorneys retire.

I could go in with them if I wanted, but I don't. I'm too nervous. They're going to decide my life here today, and as usual I feel powerless. It isn't just dying that frightens me—not that I'm so thrilled with that. If I die . . . well, they'll never entirely forget me, but I'll become part of the past, something fixed, like Grandpa Saul's plaques in Grandma Rose's living room, a memory that means something different to each of them. Alive—even if being alive is just a body curled up in a home somewhere—then their lives will steep in me like wet tea bags. They will hear the *whoosh*-click of the respirator hissing in the darkness of their rooms before they sleep. A place will be set for me at all their celebrations, and at the moment of tasting the salmon-poached-just-perfectly or the creamiest-ice-cream-ever, they will have to remember me. I will be the question that is always asked of them: *How's Melissa, poor Melissa.* I can be my own revenge, a constant reminder that things can go wrong. That I am a casualty.

Maybe I'm not as powerless as I feel. After all, that's the kind of attitude that got me into this mess in the first place! Maybe I can make my wishes known, render up a disembodied spiritual voice that declares that I want to be left as I am, goddamn it. I concentrate—trying to think of some way to tell them—and the scene swells, as if I'm trying to break through a clear but resilient barrier.

When the lawyers come out, the judge announces that while the facts do make a strong case for summary judgment, since this is a case of first impression he is compelled to give Elaina's side a hearing. Damn it! That's another one down for our side. Well, he'll be sorry after he's had a few days to listen to *her*.

And all this legal softshoeing has taken us up to lunchtime.

\*　　\*　　\*

The first witness for the plaintiff is Dr. Drew Harding.

He walks to the stand slowly, then sits in the witness box wiping his palms on his slacks. He's traded his white coat for a navy blue blazer that intensifies the color of his eyes; they are blue demon eyes, lit from within with the fear of God.

"State your full name."

Drew recoils from Marty's cigar breath. "Drew Franklin Harding."

"And you are employed where?"

"I am a resident at Mt. Moriah Hospital in Oakland, California."

Marty continues with the preliminaries, getting the whole *shpiel* on where Drew went to school and listing more or less every Scout badge Drew ever earned. Then he has Drew identify various charts and forms and some notes he made on my condition, which Marty duly enters into evidence.

Drew avoids looking at Elaina. If only I could tell Jonathan about them. That would give him the weapon he needs.

"Dr. Harding, tell us what happened on the night of January sixth, 1987."

"I was on call that night. Miss Silverstein was brought to the emergency room suffering from . . . she was unconscious."

"And?"

Drew starts to describe the tests that were run. The tracheotomy is particularly off-putting. Jonathan squirms.

"Your diagnosis?"

"Miss Silverstein was unconscious after consuming an undetermined quantity of alcohol and the narcotic Percodan."

Jonathan and Elaina raise their heads simultaneously; in a choreographed motion, they turn and look at each other for the first time today. Then their heads droop again.

"Dr. Harding, was there anything unusual that happened during your examination of Miss Silverstein?"

Drew nods eagerly. "Yes, there was."

"If you please, doctor, would you describe that for us?"

Drew is staring rigidly into Marty's piscine eyes. But I'm sure he sees Elaina anyway as she reaches her handkerchief under her veil.

"I was alone with Miss Silverstein," Drew begins, and his hand passes over the knot in his tie. "There was a curtain drawn around her bed. I was testing her reflexes."

"And?"

He hesitates. "Miss Silverstein woke up then," he says.

"I beg your pardon?"

*"Miss Silverstein woke up,"* Drew repeats. "She had stopped breathing earlier, according to her family, but she was breathing again when—when her family brought her in."

"Did she say anything when she woke up?"

"Yes. She—she said, "'Let me go.'"

I hear the gasp in the courtroom, like a vacuum cleaner being turned on. I feel the suction of it. Or maybe that's just my own rage. Because Drew is lying. I never woke up—and if I had, I certainly wouldn't have said that!

"Objection!" Debbie is swaying on her feet. "Hearsay."

"Your Honor." Marty swivels toward the judge. "With all due respect to opposing counsel, this is not hearsay since it is offered to prove the state of mind of the incompetent."

"The state of mind . . . of the incompetent," the judge echoes. His eyes roll and he seems to be pulling this information inside his head, like ticker tape, to analyze it. Meanwhile his hands travel across the bench. "Of course," he says. "Overruled."

Debbie eases herself back into her chair. Jonathan glances at her. I've seen that look before in his chocolate browns. He's disappointed. He doesn't believe that one should make a fuss over small points, because one loses bargaining power for the big points. He was particularly emphatic about this principle when it came to dealing with IRS auditors.

"Are you sure those were Miss Silverstein's exact words, Dr. Harding?"

"Yes." Drew swallows. "I remember them because it struck me at the time as such an unusual statement."

"Could you repeat them for the court, Dr. Harding?"

Debbie starts to object; Jonathan stops her, gripping her wrist under the table.

"She said, 'Let me go.'"

Elaina sniffles. Grandma Rose makes an *uuhh* sound that only Becky and Leah can hear.

But no one could possibly believe that I said that. I pulse. I throb. I am redness and light; I am the anger of the sun; I am screaming but without a voice; my screams pass like waves of air over their indifferent heads.

How can Drew perjure himself like this? Has he convinced himself that the lie he is telling for Elaina is a noble one, in the service of a truth larger than the one that inheres in mundane facts? I knew they were up to something! It should be obvious that he's lying—but, no, I forget that others don't have my perceptive abilities. Drew's pinched expression looks like earnestness, concern, to them. Even if the judge could see, he wouldn't detect the lie lines around Drew's eyes and mouth. People's faces are becoming like braille to my spiritual fingers. But a hell of a lot of good it does me.

"Ah, yes, doctor." Marty strokes an imaginary beard on his chins, then interrupts himself with his hacking cough. "Perhaps you could enlighten us further. What happened then?"

"Miss Silverstein lost consciousness again." Perhaps Judge Picone's blindness makes him more sensitive to the warbly cadence of a lie in Drew's voice. "This time permanently."

"I beg your pardon, doctor?"

Drew's mouth opens, like a fish, emitting no sound. Finally, the bubble of silence pops and the word comes out. "Permanently."

"And what is your current diagnosis, doctor, of Miss Silverstein's condition?"

Drew moistens his lips. "The patient is in a chronic vegetative state."

"Objection!" Debbie shrieks, waving her hand; unable, because of her girth, to get to her feet quickly enough. "The witness is not here as an expert, and so asking him for his opinion is not proper."

"With all due respect to Ms. Meyers and her delicate condition—"

"My condition is not relevant, *Mr.* Lindner—"

"Counsel!" the judge squeals. As his eyes make frightened circles, he seems like a child who has been locked in a dark closet and doesn't know when he will be released. "Would counsel please refrain—"

"The respected Dr. Harding is also here in his capacity as expert witness," Marty explains unctuously. "Hence our careful laying of the foundation of his credentials at the outset of his testimony."

The judge scrunches up his pudgy cheeks. "All right then, Mr. Lindner, proceed."

"Thank you very much, Your Honor." Marty cannot resist turning toward Debbie and giving her a slight bow. That starts him hacking again. Drew rubs his pants legs, watching Marty as if he were coughing fire.

When Marty finally recovers, he asks Drew if respirators are frequently used on chronic cases such as myself, and Drew explains that such extraordinary means are usually used only over short periods of time. "Usually the family agrees . . . on the best procedure."

Then Marty asks him if I am likely to survive without the respirator.

"Some chronic vegetative patients can survive for long periods without a respirator," Drew explains, "though there is always a high danger of infection. But in my opinion there has been too much brain-stem damage for even her autonomic functions to continue."

"So in the course of nature, what *some* people might call the will of God, someone like Miss Silverstein would pass on?"

Drew nods.

"Please answer the question, doctor."

"Yes."

"And in your medical opinion," Marty concludes, with a gravelly clearing of his throat, "how did Miss Silverstein seem almost to have foreknowledge of the tragic state that was her destiny?"

"In my opinion"—Drew pulls at his tie—"she lacked the will to live."

A sob is heard. Elaina.

"And is there any chance that Miss Silverstein's condition will improve? That she will ever again be able to sing, dance, or laugh?"

"No."

"Thank you, Dr. Harding. And may I add that your tireless dedication to your noble profession is admired by all." He turns to Debbie, bows again. "Your witness." And then he struts back to his seat, no doubt pleased with how much of his examination he will be able to use in the first chapter of his book.

Debbie waddles up to Drew. "Dr. Harding," she whines, "are you saying that the incompetent actually woke up from her coma to express her wishes to you?"

"No! What I mean is, she wasn't exactly comatose yet. Just a few minutes later she suffered the stroke that caused the anoxia that caused the brain damage."

"All *right,* then." Debbie smacks her tongue against the roof of her mouth. "How do you know that by saying 'Let me go,' she wasn't referring, for example, to your hand being somewhere it shouldn't have been?"

"Well—"

"Objection!" Marty says. "Calls for opinion."

"Sustained."

"Has this ever happened to you before, doctor?"

"I'm sorry . . . I don't know—"

"That someone has just conveniently told you that they did not wish to be left in a comatose state—I mean, assuming that is what she meant?"

"Objection!" Marty sputters. "Irrelevant!"

"Overruled," the judge pipes. "Answer the question."

"No," Drew says. "This is the first time."

"Well, isn't that convenient," Debbie observes. "Isn't that an awfully big coincidence."

"Objection!" Marty repeats. "Your Honor, counsel's adolescent—"

"Sustained."

"Your *Honor*," Debbie pouts. "That's not fair."

Jonathan pushes himself away from the table; he tilts his chair back and lets it fall forward with a loud *thwack*. Debbie glances over her shoulder at him. "And why"—she turns back to Drew and continues—"didn't you discuss this *alleged* statement of Miss Silverstein's with the family before?"

There is a long pause. Drew looks down. And for a moment I think that he has leaped from the net of his lie into space; that he will be unable to answer, or that he will confess. And then he says, "I regret that now. I didn't want to upset the family, of course, and I thought they would come to a decision based on what they knew about the patient." He raises his head. "Then I realized I had a moral obligation to come forward."

Debbie looks over her shoulder at Jonathan again, with an I-told-you-so grimace. Then she says to Drew, "Just one more thing before we let you get back to your important lifesaving work"—she turns to Marty—"if I may paraphrase my *esteemed* colleague. You say that there is no hope for Miss Silverstein's condition to improve?"

"That's correct."

"Well, do you really *know* that, doctor? Is Miss Silverstein brain-dead?"

"N-no."

"In fact, her EEG shows some activity, doesn't it?"

"Yes, but—"

"But what?"

"It isn't the thinking part of her brain. It's just the part that controls—"

"Oh, *really*? Doesn't the Hippocratic oath commit you to preserving life?"

"Of course, but—"

"But?"

"But this is different," Drew says, in a voice almost too soft to hear.

"And you say there is *no* chance for her to recover?"

"Well, I guess we can never be a hundred percent certain of anything—"

"Aha!" Debbie cries, raising one finger. "And yet you just told Mr. Lindner that there was no chance. "Which *is* it, Dr. Harding?"

"I have never known," Drew says, more firmly now, "ever, in all my experiences or my reading, of anyone with this much brain damage who showed any improvement. There is no medical precedent for it."

*"Huh,"* Debbie grunts. She taps her foot for a moment, as if not sure what to do next. Then, "No further questions."

She returns to her seat, where she presses her chin against her collarbone, pouting. Drew hesitates, looking at the judge and then at Marty. Elaina is staring out the window. The judge unselfconsciously presses his malleable cheeks, creating a new face for himself. Drew keeps looking around, doubtfully. Finally the bailiff leans over to him. "You can sit down now," he says.

But as Drew stands up, I know that he is forever altered. He will have to bend his life from now on, to fit the shape of his lie. He must love Elaina forever, a flawless love, a nap without nicks or uneven threads; their guilty secret binds them together.

Jonathan turns to watch Drew walk back to his seat. My father is too smart to believe Drew's little story about me. So why can't he put together the obvious about Drew and Elaina? Perhaps Elaina's infidelity has been the one possibility he could not admit without being forced to make larger changes, involving more emotional effort than he could muster. Or perhaps his crueler strategy has been to ignore it, withholding the anger that she wants from him.

The plaintiff's next witness is none other than my beloved baby brother, Daniel.

He sashays up to the witness stand, looking long and thin in his three-piece suit with the narrow pinstripes. His shoes are black leather, shiny like licorice.

Elaina watches him, her chin raised. Her mind is closed to me, but I can imagine what she is thinking—how loved she is by Drew and Daniel, these two men who are testifying for her. And yet she must feel disappointed: because there's still one who opposes her, one whose mind is unfathomable to her— and he is the one who counts.

As soon as Daniel takes the oath, Marty rises. He pats his forehead with a handkerchief, then pulls his belt up over his potbelly. "Please state your full name."

"Daniel Jacob Silverstein."

Marty goes on to elicit a few bullshit statements from Daniel about what a tragedy this is and how much he loves me and what an agonizing decision this has been for everyone in the family.

"Mr. Silverstein, do you recall a certain day in November of 1980?"

"Yes."

"What happened on that day?"

"Missy and I went to the hospital to see our cousin, Celia Goldberg."

I remember that. Celia Goldberg was Rose's second cousin, to be precise, and she was dying of cancer, as Rose's relatives have a tendency to do. Elaina had promised Rose that she'd go visit Celia Goldberg that afternoon, but then she had to take to her bed with her period, even though she'd had her period just two weeks before. She wanted Daniel and me to go to the hospital in her place. It was my first year of college: I'd just moved to Berkeley and I'd stopped at home to pick up some more clothes.

"It was a little favor for our mother, and Missy didn't want to do it, but I said . . ."

Prick! *He* was the one who didn't want to go. I remember because he complained all the way down there about how he was missing his favorite "Star Trek" rerun. I was meeting a boyfriend later, but did I complain?

". . . that good deeds come back to us in the end."

He polishes this off with the Robert Redford grin. Sanctimonious little faggot! He's saying that I deserve to be in a coma, isn't he?

"Your Honor," Debbie whines. "Are we supposed to believe that this witness remembers—"

The judge angles his head in her direction. "I'll let Mr. Silverstein continue for the present," he says.

"Well," Daniel says, "poor cousin Celia was in sad shape."

Marty pats his forehead again. "Can you elaborate for us, Mr. Silverstein?"

"She had a tube in her nose and there was . . . a catheter going under the sheet." Daniel shudders. And his shudder takes me back. I remember feeling rather nauseous at the sight of Celia Goldberg, trapped in that shrunken body; I remember the smell of feces in the room. But it didn't seem to me that *Celia* was suffering particularly, drugged as she was; it was the nurses and the people who had to come to visit her that I felt sorry for.

"Cousin Celia tried to talk to us, but I don't think she even knew who we were. She was really out of it."

"And what was your sister's reaction to this?"

Daniel's upper lip rises slightly. "She said she would never, never, never want to be kept alive like that, under any circumstances."

I never said any such thing. All right, I *thought* it, but I never said it. I'm sure I didn't. What, can he read minds, too? Then maybe he can know what I'm thinking now. I concentrate, I beg him to tell them he didn't mean what he said— Daniel, listen to me!—but he just sits there with that prissy, concerned look in his brown eyes. And now I'm angry. I close in on him, I pummel him with my wishes . . . and suddenly he looks a little dizzy and green.

"Are you all right, Mr. Silverstein?" Marty asks.

"Yes." Daniel grips the side of the witness stand. "I'm fine now." He looks at Jonathan, as if he were the one responsible for his sudden malaise.

"Thank you, Mr. Silverstein." Marty pats his hand. "I know this was a difficult experience, but you've helped your sister here today." He turns to Debbie. "Your witness."

Debbie asks Daniel for further details about the Celia Goldberg story. She asks Daniel to guess whether I might not have changed my mind in the last six and a half years, and then has to withdraw the question after Marty's objection. Apparently she thinks the questions are more important than the answers: At least the judge will hear them and consider, for example, that even if I did say what Daniel says I said, I had plenty of time to reevaluate my position. I'm gratified to see

Jonathan shaking his head just slightly, expressing his displeasure. I was feeling jealous of Debbie. But now I know that my refusal to go to law school was self-preservation. I would have become house counsel for Silverstein, Inc., and dad would have been whispering in my ear all my life, telling me how to improve my depositions, my research, my briefs.

Debbie asks Daniel whether he ever considered that Celia Goldberg was old and decrepit, whereas I am still young. Daniel looks worried for a moment, as if the thought had never occurred to him. He doesn't answer right away, and Debbie is starting to look rather schoolteacherly smug about this, but then Daniel asks, "Have you been to the hospital, Ms. Meyers? Have you seen my sister?"

Now Debbie doesn't know what to say. There is silence in the courtroom. Even I feel subdued. I think of what I look like on that bed: body like a knotted rubber band, and the blue hollows under the eyes. Sometimes the head twists around and sometimes a moan comes out of the mouth. A person—even Daniel—could reasonably believe that disconnecting the respirator would be doing me a favor.

And I'm trying to remember. I guess I didn't just think it—I guess I *did* say to Daniel that I wouldn't want to be kept alive like Celia. That's the trouble with my memory—it's like one of those toadies who hang around Jonathan: It's eager to agree with whatever I want. But damn it, Daniel, why did *you* have to remember?

Debbie finally clears her throat. "Really, Mr. Silverstein," she asks, "can you be so very certain that what your sister said applies to her in *this* situation?"

Daniel hunches his shoulders. "Yes," he replies in a babyish voice, with a glance toward Elaina.

"Well," Debbie says huffily. And then, as if she didn't want to waste any more time on him, "No further questions."

"What time is it?" the judge asks.

"Three forty-five," the bailiff tells him.

"Three forty-five," the judge repeats. "Then we'll adjourn for the day." The judge taps the side of the bench and the bailiff hands him his cane.


Friends and reporters cluster around Jonathan and Elaina. These two groups move slowly and separately toward the courtroom doors.

Once out in the hall, Marty lights a cigar and begins to take questions. Elaina looks a bit stunned, the way she does sometimes after a little too much Valium. She links her arm through Daniel's and squeezes it tightly.

But Jonathan lumbers straight ahead, not even waiting for Debbie, who waddles behind. The reporters scurry after them, some running in front, shouting their questions aloud. "Mr. Silverstein, do you think you can save your daughter's life?" "Mr. Silverstein, will all this publicity be bad for your real-estate investment company?"

Daniel watches Jonathan's retreating back.

Still inside the courtroom, my grandmother has just risen from her seat. There is nothing but rage in her body—nothing but sinew and the rage that fires it, like God fired the first man from clay. I think Rose could shake her fist at God himself; that she could tear the courthouse down, stone by stubborn Rose-defying stone. She cannot believe that it is hopeless, because she is still making plans for when I get well, and in the meantime she must keep me alive with her rage. There is no acceptance for Rose; she mourns all our lost possibilities, our never-wases, forever, because there are so many of them. Like the young lawyer who courted her before he lost his way one night and drove his 1929 Ford into the water, right where the Bay Bridge was soon to be built. The young lawyer who would have been as successful as Jonathan.

Rose turns to leave. The courtroom is nearly empty now. But a middle-aged woman with bright orange lipstick and car-rot-red hair is standing at the end of the row of seats. Rose recognizes her as a reporter (though gossip columnist is more like it) for the *Alta Vista Voice*. She is wearing a camel hair suit and thick-soled shoes. "Mrs. Miller," she says, "I am so sorry about your granddaughter."

Rose glances to either side of her, searching futilely for another means of egress.

"How did it happen?" the woman asks.

"How did what happen?" Rose echoes, grasping the seat in front of her for support.

"This terrible coma. It's so tragic." The woman smiles— there are flecks of orange lipstick on her teeth—and now she seems older than she did at first: Her skin puckers, and new lines course through her face.

Rose takes a few steps backward. "It was an accident," she says.

"But what happened?" The woman is coming toward her, edging down the row of seats.

Grandma needs help. Where is Alison? I know: Alison is out in the hall, talking to Judy Weiss (who is trying to find out if Alison is dating anyone in New York); Alison probably would like to make her own escape. Alison can help Rose. I concentrate, and try to send her a message.

"It was an accident," Rose says again.

The woman cackles. "Now there must be more to it than *that*. Nobody just goes into a coma."

"It was an *accident*," Rose repeats, more loudly.

And then the courtroom door opens and Alison appears. "Motha," Alison says, "I naid you to help me get this spot out of my blahse."

Rose steadies herself against the seat in front of her.

"I was just asking your mother a few questions," the orange woman leers.

"Oh, dair, I'm afrayed my motha cahn't be bothered now," Alison says. She holds out her hand and Rose lets go of the chair and begins to move haltingly toward her, like a toddler taking her first steps.

The orange woman backs away. "Nobody just goes into a coma," she says.

Alison takes Rose's hand. Then she tilts her head back. Her bottle-green eyes seem momentarily to stun the reporter. But as Alison and Rose leave the courtroom, the reporter calls after them, her voice a caterwaul, "Was your granddaughter a devil worshiper? Was she into drugs?"


Becky and Leah, once at home, quickly escape to the third floor, where they peel off their supernal wool dresses. The dresses lie where they fall.

"Bee-stunk," Leah says, flinging herself on the bed. "I know they're going to get a divorce immediately. I can just like totally *tell*."

"It's mega-fucked," Becky agrees, pulling her jeans over her hips. "But what can we do about it? It's the whole 'droid generation—they just never learned to communicate." She turns sideways to look at herself in the mirror, running her hand over her thighs. "I don't think it's going to change how Jeff feels, though, do you?"

Leah picks at the edge of the Band-Aid she put on one finger after the quick of the nail started to bleed. "I just can't stand it," she says. "I can't stand it. It just can't happen. We've got to stop it."

"Well, *guy*, what can we do?" Becky bends over and brushes the back of her hair forward. "I mean, we tried."

"Can't we get them to talk? I heard Mickey Mouse say that the judge said they could still settle the case—like, if they agreed now what they wanted to do, then the trial would be over."

"Oh, come on." Becky uprights herself in one quick motion so that her hair flips back and cascades over her shoulders.

"If they were gonna talk, they would've talked light-years ago." She looks at herself in the mirror again. "God, Lee-steah, I'm a tank! I've got to lose some major tonnage before my date with Jeff!"

Leah stares at the poster of Billy Death's Head above her. His limbs are emaciated, a mere ripple of bare, blue-white muscle. "But if we could just get them in the same room, like, or the same place . . ."

Becky turns to look at her sister. She absently fluffs her hair, first on one side, then on the other. Then she smiles. "Well," she says, "if we just wanted to get them like into a neutral zone together, that would be easy. I could figure out a way to do that."


According to Becky's plan, Leah calls Jonathan at the office and asks him if he'll have dinner with her that night. From the depth of her frown line, I can tell that she is pessimistic about this request. I would be, too. Jonathan's been away from work for the entire day and there must be a long line of his subordinates ahead of her, bringing him the day's crises like hors d'oeuvres at happy hour; surely their cumulative offerings will outweigh hers.

But he says yes.

Leah tells Becky that phase one has been completed and slips out quietly, headed for the bus stop.

When she is gone, Becky marches into Elaina's room, where she requests that Elaina take her to Chez Alta Vista for dinner. Chez Alta Vista recently opened on Twelve Oaks Boulevard; it's one of those restaurants with Technicolor food and anorexia-size portions.

Elaina has already gotten into bed, leaving instructions to tell Rose, if she calls, that Elaina has a piece of toast caught in her throat and can't talk. Elaina tells Becky now that she would like nothing better than to go out for a lengthy and expensive meal, but Dr. Abramowitz insisted that she rest this evening.

Becky folds her arms under her breasts and opens fire with "All the other parents take their kids out to dinner. Just because you and dad aren't together anymore, does everyone have to think we're not a family?" She follows this up with a barrage of how my accident and the trial have affected her popularity at school, accuses Elaina of trying to make her and Leah unpopular just because *she* was, and then drops the Bomb: It isn't fair that all parental energy should be expended on the comatose daughter, leaving none for those who retain cognitive functions.

Elaina is swaying slightly. "Dr. Abramowitz gets very angry at me for putting myself under too much stress."

Becky examines the chipped purple polish on one nail. She observes almost absently, "Well, if you hadn't started this whole thing, then dad wouldn't have spun out."

Elaina gets out of bed. "Call your brother," she says. "We'll make it a family outing, at least. Where's Leah?"

"She's spun out, too," Becky says shortly. "I wouldn't be surprised if she started doing crack now. This whole thing has majorly wonked her out."


Jonathan turns off the TV after he lets Leah in. "Hello, dear." He smiles at her, but she cannot see it, because the light is behind him, darkening his face. "What do you think of your old dad's room?"

"It's nice, dad."

"Good. . . . Well . . ." He puts his hand on the back of her neck, guiding her toward the door. "Shall we get a bite?"

"Yeah." Her shoulders twitch under the pressure of his hand. "Can we go to Chez Alta Vista?"

Jonathan winces. "I was thinking we could just go to the coffee shop here," he says. Jonathan hates restaurants that involve the possibility of waiting more than two minutes for a table or more than five minutes for the food. He does not care for waitresses who encourage him to have a cocktail, nor does he have the patience to study the wine list. He does not like to have a choice of fey desserts with cute names like Chocolate Orgasm, though he does like dessert and certainly bears no ill will toward chocolate. He's obviously in a hurry to get back to the office tonight; probably to meet with Debbie Meyers about tomorrow. "Would you mind if we went to the coffee shop?"

Leah bites her lip. "I'm sorry, daddy," she says. "But would you mind, do you think—I mean, could we go to Chez Alta Vista?"

He hesitates. "All right, dear. Whatever you want."

They are silent until they get into the elevator. Jonathan locks his hands in front of his stomach. Suddenly he says, "Mom and I were married too young."

"Oh," Leah says.

"I hope you kids won't make the same mistake."

"Yes, daddy."

"She was pregnant."

I can feel the tears that could leap like circus acrobats from Leah's eyes.

But Jonathan is not looking at her. He is staring at where the light marks the numbers of the floors as they descend. "I was in law school and we needed money. But she wouldn't go to work. She said, 'I didn't get married to go to work.'"

The doors open at the lobby and Jonathan ejects out of the elevator ahead of Leah; she follows the wrinkled back of his gray suit. She catches up with him; and then, as they cross the lobby, they see Auntie Al coming out of the sundry shop, carrying a dainty paper bag.

Jonathan stops and, with a look of surprise that is unusually expressive for him, exclaims, "Alison!"

"Well, hello." Alison extends the toe of one of her cerise

leather Charles Jourdan boots out at a forty-five-degree angle. I peek inside her bag: It contains lip liner and breath mints.

Jonathan squeezes the back of Leah's neck. "We were just going to have a bite to eat. Would you like to join us?"

"You two want to be alone," Alison says.

"No, that's all right," Jonathan says. "Isn't it, dear?"

The pressure on Leah's neck increases; she almost squeals.

"I'd love to join you," Alison purrs. "I just thought . . ."

Leah has one more second in which to protest. But that might hurt Auntie Al's feelings.

"Come on," Jonathan says.

He steers Leah ahead of him toward the automatic glass doors. She takes small steps, trying to anticipate the direction of the pressure of his hand.

I zap back to the house, where Elaina is powdering her nose.

"Come *on*, Mickey Mouse," Becky insists, with a little stamp of her foot. "What's the pee-stee-floint of going if you're never gonna get ready?"

"We're going in a minute, Miss Impatient," Daniel says, jingling Elaina's car keys. "What are you expecting, a talent scout to be there?"

They leave a few minutes later. I take the high view now; I see it all: Elaina's Cutlass is winding along the curvy, tree-lined Alta Vista streets (Daniel is driving, with Becky in the back seat, chomping on sugarless bubble gum), while Jonathan's Volvo is cruising along the freeway. And my laughter surrounds them. My laughter blows in through the open windows; my laughter spews from the tail pipes; my laughter is the stubbly sound of their tires on the road.

The two automobiles park at opposite ends of the commercial section of Twelve Oaks Boulevard. And my laughter rises like steam from the sidewalk, my laughter shakes the buildings, rattles the windows, although no one can see or feel it—the suburban twilight is quiet; the sky is that drowsy, magic blue between night and day, and seems to breathe, as softly as someone drifting off to sleep. But my laughter grumbles underground; my laughter cracks the pavement so that Alison catches her heel; my laughter could be the earthquake we've all been waiting for. . . .

The two halves of the family approach each other. Daniel is prancing with his arm through Elaina's; Becky is slouching the way that annoys Rose so much. Jonathan is in the vanguard of his little group, striding like a man who is late for his appointment to lease the continent of North America from God. Leah lags behind, walking as though through a mine field.

For one final moment each side is unaware of the other's presence. And then the change comes over them, in a wave of altered motions. Elaina throws back her shoulders. Jonathan's steps are just as forceful but suddenly much shorter. Daniel's legs wobble as if he were doing the Charleston. Alison's knees reach very high with each step. Becky stumbles. Leah trudges valiantly on.

The six of them meet directly in front of Chez Alta Vista. Elaina grips Daniel's hand. "Jonathan," she says evenly.

"Elaina."

Becky blows a bubble, which quickly pops. "Hi, dad," she says. Then, "Hi, Auntie Al."

"Hi," Leah says hopefully.

"Alison," Elaina says. Her voice reaches its higher, more tremulous register.

"Elaina," Alison replies indifferently.

"Well, isn't this funny?" Elaina's voice climbs higher up the scale and then falls off the edge, into laughter. My laughter is reborn in hers. "This is just so funny. Like one of those French bedroom comedies, don't you think?" She points a dagger-red nail at Alison and then at Jonathan. "I guess you two have been seeing each other for *years*."

"*Elaina*," Jonathan says.

"Oh, please don't apologize. It's not your fault that I was too big an idiot to see it."

Alison looks across the street as if trying to see the clothes displayed in the store windows—although she would no sooner shop on Twelve Oaks Boulevard than she would let someone see her reading *People* magazine. Her bottle-green eyes are vacant.

"Elaina," Jonathan hisses. "Don't be stupid."

"So now I'm *stupid?*" she retorts.

"I just said—"

"I heard what you said."

Passersby have started to notice. They turn their heads and slow their steps. People must weave among the family members to get into the restaurant. Some of these people are acquainted with Jonathan and Elaina or with Rose. Jonathan's face has reddened and he appears to be having trouble getting air into his lungs.

"What's *really* funny is that I've lost my appetite," Elaina says. She opens her purse and looks inside. "Can't find it anywhere, nope, it's nowhere to be found. Maybe I left it in the car. I'd better go get it. Danny, do you want to come with me? You don't have to if you don't want to. I'd understand if you wanted to stay with your father and your auntie Al."

She whirls around. Her sobs have begun, and my laughter has ceased.

"Let's go," Jonathan announces, to everyone and to no one. He turns the other way and launches himself down the street.


"So, like that was a total nuclear event," Becky mutters as she and Leah settle on the living-room couch.

"Rully," Leah murmurs.

"Why did you let Auntie Al come?"

Leah lowers her eyes. Her lashes are fair and naturally long.

"Well, now, like, there's no hope, that's all."

Leah bites her lip.

"Well, guy, don't worry about it," Becky says, cracking her gum.

The living room looks as if invading Huns were camping out in a deserted château. Becky's portable tape deck and headset are on the coffee table; Leah's shoes peek out from under the couch. Elaina has crowded the mantelpiece with our school pictures; unframed, some are attached to the woodwork with masking tape.

Elaina is in the bathroom upstairs. She has been there for nearly half an hour. She has decreed that they will all sit around the living room and have tea and cookies and talk. Daniel will build a fire, and they will tell stories. Elaina recalls spending many evenings with her family this way, though Rose denies ever having had a serviceable fireplace and that Grandpa Saul was ever home in the evenings. ("He was always so busy with the congregation.")

Daniel comes into the living room with the tray of tea and cookies. He places the tray on the coffee table, then starts to arrange the logs in a pyramid, which promptly collapses.

"Mr. Boy Scout," Becky laughs.

"Oh, shut up." Daniel examines his fingers for splinters. Then he glances at Leah. "That was really stupid, you know."

"Now *you* shut up," Becky says. "You trash your mouth."

Daniel mimics Becky: "We've got to go have dinner at Chez Alta Vista, Mickey Mouse, or I'll never hold my head up again."

"Wee-statch *out,*" Becky warns. "You want me to tell Tracy Newhouse that you have a groaner for her?" She giggles. "A real big groaner, rhymes with boner . . ." She nudges Leah.

Elaina appears on the landing of the stairs and calls down

to them, "Wait for me now! I'll be right down! I'm really looking forward to this!"

Daniel crumples a sheet of newspaper into a ball and
wedges it into a gap between two logs.

"Don't let my tea get cold!" Elaina shouts, then disappears
back into her room.

"What do you think, Lee-steah?" Becky asks. "D'you think
Danny could get it up for Tracy Newhouse?"

"Dee-ston't, Bee-stecky," Leah mutters.

"Leah thinks you can," Becky laughs.

Daniel strikes a long hearth match from a box with a Santa
Claus on it. "Congratulations," he says thickly, turning his back
to her and touching the flame to the crumpled newspaper,
"you're turning into a bigger bitch than Melissa was." The fire
spreads to the newspaper, ravages it; the tips of the flames lick
the logs, but do not take root there, and in a moment the fire
exhausts itself. Daniel shivers, watching the fire die. He looks
sorry for what he said, but he keeps his face turned to the
hearth, perhaps to hide his remorse. Perhaps he thinks it un-
manly.

"*Guy,*" Leah says.

"Well, if you hadn't been such a goon about that stupid
bedroom—" Becky starts.

"Don't," Leah cries. She puts out her hand as she closes
her eyes, reaching to stop Becky, to pull her back from the
edge.

"What are you kids doing?" Elaina is coming down the
stairs. She is barefoot, in her bathrobe, and rubbing lotion on
her hands. "Are you talking about me?"

"*No,*" Becky says, adjusting her headset over her ears.

"Rebecca Sarah, could you take that headset off, do you
think, for five minutes?" Elaina asks. She settles gradually into
the wing chair. "Danabable, put some sugar in my tea, will you,
sweetheart? Oh, no, more than that." Elaina takes the cup. It
rattles against the saucer. She has to put it down to stop the

noise. "When you have your children," she says suddenly, "you don't need a husband, too." The same rattling sound that the cup made against the saucer is in her voice. Daniel titters nervously, but my sisters are silent. Elaina looks at them for a moment. "I don't want to say anything bad about your father—I want you to love your father. I don't blame him for wanting to see Alison now."

"Mouse, dad *isn't* seeing Auntie Al!" Leah cries. "You know he's not."

"You always think the best of people, Leah-loo," Elaina says. She is calm again. She raises the cup to her lips with pinkie extended, then slurps noisily. "That's a very admirable quality."

"He was just going to have dinner with *me,*" Leah insists. "And we ran into her, and she wanted to come along."

"That's the way they wanted it to look," Elaina says, raising the cup again. Everyone steels himself for another *slurp.* When it is over, Elaina sighs. "My father would tell us stories. That was the kind of man he was. Anything I asked him to do, he would do. I don't want to say anything bad about your father, but he's not like that. Well, he and Alison will be very happy together. I mean, I love my sister, and if this will make her happy, then that's what I want. I've had your father for twenty-five years—that's more happiness than anyone can take and live." *Slurp.*

Daniel pokes at the charred log. The thin sheets of ash between them crumble, sending a few sparks to die on the bottom of the fireplace.

"Damn it," Daniel mutters.

"No, it was a lovely fire," Elaina says sweetly. "A *lovely* fire."

"It wasn't even a fire!" Becky says.

"No, it was a perfect fire," Elaina says. "It was the best fire I ever saw. Really, Danabable."

The phone rings.

"I'll get it!" Becky shrieks, scrambling off the couch and heading for the phone in Jonathan's study.

"Don't pry into your father's things now," Elaina calls after her. She raises her cup but does not sip; she lets it clatter back into the saucer. "I thought just once we could sit around like a family," she says. Silence. "I need my children," she goes on. "I need to keep the ones I have left."

"God, I wonder," Leah says softly, "what Melissa would say if she could see us now."

"Mom!" Becky calls from the study. "It's for you!"

"Don't shout!" Elaina shouts. "Tell them I'll be right there."

After a particularly long slurp, she gets slowly to her feet.

In a moment, Becky shuffles back into the living room.

"Who was it?" Daniel asks sharply as Becky flings herself sideways on the sofa.

"Just Dr. Harding," Becky replies.

"Is something wrong with Melissa?" Leah asks.

Becky shakes her head. "I doubt it."


Elaina closes the door to Jonathan's study, then pads to the phone at his desk. "Hello?"

"*Elaina.*" And I can see Drew in his lakeside apartment. He is sitting on a white burlap couch, wearing a navy blue running suit. His hair is pasted onto his forehead by sweat, and his breath comes hard. He must have gone for a run around the lake; gone running through the darkness that is pitted with potholes and muggers, away from the lights of Grand Avenue and the signs of people. But he outran neither his conscience nor his passion. He has come in and called Elaina without even taking a shower.

"Drewby Darby," Elaina says affectionately. She raises Grandpa Abe's emerald letter opener while she talks, trying to balance it on its point. ("I don't want to say that your Grandpa

Abe didn't have much personality," Elaina has said, "but next to him, your father is a regular stand-up comedian.") "How are you?"

"Can you come over here?"

Elaina laughs. "I thought you knew the answer to *that*."

"I need to see you. I need to see you to know that I did the right thing today."

"It's not that I don't want to." Elaina opens one of Jonathan's drawers. She absently rifles through it, then takes out a notepad. "I have to be up so early for tomorrow, though." She starts doodling a cartoon of a dog on the notepad. She adds soothingly, "It won't be long now, Drewby Dooby."

"You don't have to stay late."

"I *can't*. My children."

"You can tell them something. Tell them you have to go to the hospital."

"They won't believe that."

"Well, then, tell them you have to go to the fucking grocery store!"

"Please don't swear."

"I'm sorry. Just come over, Elaina." Her name is encased in a sob, like a baby swaddled in a blanket.

Elaina sighs. "Oh, all right. I'll be over in half an hour or so. Will you run out and get me some of that chocolate ice cream, then? You know, the one with the pecans, *not* the almonds."

I see Drew sitting on his burlap couch. He can no longer catch his breath. He just nods, his head shaking violently, like a mechanical puppy.

Elaina hangs up. She replaces the notepad and shuts the drawer. As she ascends to the second floor, she hears Billy Death's Head singing above her: "The rich can't fly, the rich should die." Becky and Leah have taken advantage of her absence to escape.

It is an hour later when she comes down again, wearing a lacy white blouse and a full print skirt, layered with ruffles. Her cape is slung over her arm. Daniel is still in the living room, surveying another failed fire.

"Danabable, I have to go out for a little while." Elaina's voice reaches the soprano register that always signaled to me that she was lying. "Dr. Harding wants to talk to me about Melissa."

*"Melissa,"* Daniel repeats, stabbing the cool logs with the poker.

"Yes, Melissa. Your sister who is in a coma."

He looks up. "You know what they say. The squeaky wheel gets the grease." Somewhere Daniel got the idea that to be masculine you must be gruff, unfeeling.

"Daniel Jacob Silverstein! I don't believe that a son of mine is talking this way!"

Daniel turns back toward the cold hearth. There are tears swelling in his eyes, about to spill over. I know that Daniel thinks of his tendency to cry as a genetic defect and that he is ashamed. No one has ever seen Jonathan cry. Perhaps Daniel wants to confide in Elaina that he is in debt; that he has squandered, once again, Jonathan's trust, in the form of the money that Jonathan invested on his behalf. But what will Elaina think of him then? She will comfort him—does he want to be comforted? Will she comfort him because she is secretly pleased? Daniel lost Jonathan's money so efficiently, so predictably, that it's almost as if he thought that was what Jonathan wanted him to do.

Elaina hugs him from behind. Daniel grabs her wrists and begins to cry harder. The tracks of Daniel's earlier failures have worn a groove in the road to Elaina's arms. It's easy for him to travel there again. I want to reach down into him and give his insides a shake. I want to put my own arms around him, push Elaina away.

There is a picture of me right above his head. My dark

hair hangs down in straight sheets. My eyes are blank, as if I were looking into my own future and saw that it didn't exist.

"What is it, Danabable?"

"Do you have to go out?"

"I don't want to."

"I don't like that doctor," Daniel says. "He's a weenie."

Elaina frees one hand to stroke his hair. "I like to think of him as petite. Someone pushed the 'down' button on his elevator shoes, that's all."

"Why does he want to see you so late?"

"Doctors keep funny hours."

"He gives me the creeps. I bet he could have saved Melissa in the beginning if he really wanted to. He said she woke up once."

Elaina loosens her hold on him. "I'd better go."

"Mouse." Daniel sniffles. "Are you sure . . . I mean . . . are you sure this is the right thing to do?"

"Well, yes, if he says he wants to talk to me—"

"No, I mean . . ." Daniel shrugs. "I mean, like in court and all. I mean, when I was testifying, I was watching dad—"

"And there's so much of your father to watch," Elaina says, indicating Jonathan's portliness by spreading her hands. Then she adds, "I have to think of Melissa. Someone has to help her." She strokes Daniel's curls again. "Do you think I'm ever going to be the same after this?"

"But you and dad . . ." When he was eight, Daniel asked Elaina if she would get a divorce so they could live together, like one of his friends who lived alone with his divorced mother. I don't know what he thought would happen to me and Becky and Leah in that scenario. "I mean, do you think dad's pissed at me for testifying?"

"You let me handle your father," Elaina says. And then, with a final kiss to her son's still-damp cheek, she throws her cape over her shoulders and heads out into the night, on her way to meet her lover.

# 7

Court reconvenes at 10:00 A.M.

Today Elaina looks like a Spanish saint. She is still wearing black, but now a lace mantilla is draped loosely over her upswept hair. She got home very late last night, but her sins do not show on her face. I sometimes wonder if she has a picture in the attic that's getting older instead of her, except that we don't have an attic.

Drew is not in court today.

Daniel sits behind Elaina, slumped back in the chair, his long legs stretched out: a casual pose. I'm not fooled. He must have listened for her return all night, staying near the surface of sleep, awakening and then wondering what had awakened him.

The judge is absently squeezing little rolls out of the soft flesh around his jawline.

And there, among the spectators, if my metaphysical eyes don't deceive me, is Howard Posner. Seeing him—his varnished walnut skin and glossy curls—I feel a rush of something that reminds me of what it was like to be in a body. There's a pair of crutches propped up in the seat next to him, and his leg is wrapped in a cast that disappears underneath where his pant leg has been severed and hemmed just above the knee. His toes peek out from the visorlike gap in the plaster; they look brown and cold.

Must be a skiing accident. He never took *me* skiing. Too busy with his studies.

What's he doing here? I'd like to think he's come to mourn me publicly; that he misses me deeply; that he wonders if his role in my life was the pivotal one, and whether he could have saved me if instead of letting me break up with him, he had promised to leave the library an hour earlier or take me dancing once in a while. But he doesn't look particularly distressed. Neither does the freckled, athletic woman who is sitting on the other side of the crutches.

Rabbi Weiss is the final witness for the plaintiff.

Rose tried to put some indirect pressure on the rabbi. She proceeded slowly and with caution lest her motivation appear rooted in her resentment toward her husband's successor. Her fear of having that discovered tempered her actions even more than necessary, because only she knows how deep that resentment goes. She lives with it, she feels it gnaw at her intestines, so she doesn't realize how well hidden it is.

"You know," she said to her friends on the board, "my son-in-law gives very heavily to the building fund." She spoke to her adherents, people who would side with her whether she was right or wrong. But they are the older generation, those with whom she and Saul socialized. Their numbers have been reduced by death.

To Jonathan's credit, he hasn't reminded the rabbi of what a large contributor he is to the synagogue. But he must know that a rabbi never needs to be reminded of something like that.

The bailiff calls the rabbi to the stand.

The rabbi is wearing a tweed jacket and desert boots, which makes Rose cringe. He seats himself and takes off his glasses to clean them on a tissue.

Marty lays the foundation for taking him back to the confirmation class, and the rabbi duly reports how I spoke out in favor of euthanasia. "And what could be more unhappy," Marty comments, "than the state she is now in?"

Debbie objects; Marty retracts. Then he finishes with a few gag-me statements about how undervalued spiritual guidance is in the modern world, and leaves the field for Debbie.

Debbie waddles up. "Rabbi," she begins, "are you so sure that the incompetent"—I really hate it when she calls me that—"intended her remarks to be applied to this situation?"

"Objection, Your Honor," Marty says, with a confident sneer, as he rises. "The question calls for speculation."

"Sustained."

"Huh," Debbie grunts. She folds her arms; they rest on top of her swollen belly. "Would it be permissible, Your Honor, for me to ask for a few more details of the event from the witness?"

"Go ahead."

I think of that morning in the confirmation class. I had just discovered a run in my brand-new nylons. I was already in a bad mood because Marla Pollak had just told me about her new boyfriend, who was twenty-two, a *college* student. I was dating Ben Wolfe, an A.V. senior, but he was trying to grow a moustache and so far had produced only a few limp sprouts. Marla's family had a beach house in Santa Cruz, where they took Ozzie-and-Harriet vacations. Her mascara never smeared, and Miss Flack, the chemistry teacher, always asked her to demonstrate the experiments. She was my best friend, and I hated her.

That morning, the rabbi did his share of Talmud-quoting about the infinite value of life, but he was trying to put the discussion in a political context: At what point does the "good of society" outweigh personal choice? Everyone in the class was very eager to make some profound observation, and everyone made the most banal one possible: that once we give someone the power over life and death, how do we ensure that the power won't be abused? I was contemptuous of all this intellectual posturing, this talk of Hitler and medical experiments and relative values. As long as they had their friends and their parties, their beer and their parents' charge accounts, they were happy.

And so I interrupted the rabbi to blurt out what I said. Everyone stopped and looked at me; I was scowling, my hand over the run in my nylons. Perhaps I looked like I wanted someone to put me out of *my* misery. I wanted to look like that, just for that moment, anyway—I wanted to hint at some dark, unspeakable trouble.

My dark, unspeakable trouble was the eternal unattainability of everything that Marla had. Her new boyfriend sounded like a combination of Mahatma Gandhi and Peter Frampton. I imagined that she possessed his inner core, the substance of another person that made her whole.

I was determined to steal him. And I did, some months later, at one of the fast parties that Marla and I often went to together—leading him down the hall to an empty room where we did some heavy petting. It was the beginning of my Bad Reputation; Marla was understandably bitter. It was also a big disappointment: Not only did Marla's boyfriend turn out to be a *junior*-college student, he was a graduate of Hilltop High. But I punished myself for it enough, I think: What I couldn't possess in Marla Pollak's boyfriend—if for no other reason than that it didn't exist in him—I cursed myself never to possess in another man.

Now Debbie asks the rabbi, "Did Miss Silverstein get along with her coconfirmants?"

"She did," the rabbi says.

"Objection—" Marty Lindner begins.

"What I'm trying to say," Debbie snaps, "is that the incompetent was probably making some statement just to shock people."

The rabbi shakes his head. "I don't think so," he says.

"That was eight years ago," Debbie reminds him. "Don't you think people change their minds?"

"Sometimes," the rabbi says quietly.

He probably thinks my accident was really a suicide attempt that my family has hushed up. I'm sure he wishes he had taken me aside that day and asked me what was bothering me and if he could help. The same way that Howard—I hope—is blaming himself a little. That's the miracle of an accident like mine: Everyone thinks they could have saved you.

"Really, rabbi," Debbie tries, "you were speaking of mercy killing in the abstract. Do you think the incompetent was talking about herself?"

"Yes," the rabbi says. "I do."

"Well, then," Debbie huffs, "no further questions."


Marty has no more witnesses, and Judge Picone decides that there's time before lunch to call the first witness for the defense. And so my aunt Alison is called to the stand.

"State your name for the record," Debbie tells Auntie Al.

"Ehlison Marie Wenchestahr." A little smile. Alison loves the sound of her name, from which all trace of Jewishness has been erased. If indeed she let Jonathan go when she was young, that must have been why: Even if she had persuaded him to shorten his name to Silver, the taint would still have been too strong.

Debbie asks, "Ms. Winchester, do you recall an incident that occurred in July of 1981?"

"I do."

"Could you describe it for us, please?"

"My niece came to visit me in Manhattan."

Manhattan in July. The air looked as though God had just emptied his ashtray in the sky. The streets were without color, narrow corridors between the buildings, the architecture varying shades of gray: iron gray, pewter gray, steel gray, charcoal gray. I trooped after Alison, trying to mimic her walk (she took small steps because her calf-length skirt was tight around her knees) and the incline of her head. She took me to "posh boutiques" to try on "stunning outfits." The restaurants we ate at were "up-to-the-minute." And at night, having a drink at the Top of the Park, the city was distilled into constellations of colored lights, and Alison could charm them into dancing for her.

It was on one of those nights that she mentioned that I might want to come live in New York after I graduated from college. I might enjoy working in fashion, she said. I don't think that was my vocation (God knows what was; I'm not sure now that it was journalism, either), but sometimes I wish I'd taken her up on the offer.

"Aha." Debbie gleefully rubs her hands over her belly. "Your niece came to visit you, you say. And what did you do together?"

"We went to severahl museums, including the MOMA."

"The MOMA?"

Alison regards Debbie with a look of splendid pity. "The Museum of Modern Ahrt. On West Fifty-theird."

"And what did you see there?"

"We saw severahl things, ectually. One of the exhibits was a photo essay about World War Two."

*The Holocaust.* That's what the exhibit was called—but Alison knows better than to use such a Jew word.

"And some of the photos were quite graphic," Alison goes on. "While we were discussing the Germans"—Alison won't say *Nazis*—"my niece very clearly stated that she did not believe in euthanasia."

"Objection!" Marty sputters, rising quickly. "It has been established that this is not a question of euthanasia. My client—"

"What was *your* last witness talking about?" Debbie snaps.

"Counsel!" the judge exclaims. His hands search along the edge of the bench while his eyes roll up, almost disappearing into the back of his head. "Will this testimony become relevant?" he asks Debbie.

"It will, Your Honor, if you'll just give me—"

"Please continue then."

Auntie Al glances up at Judge Picone. She looks rather pained by the gaucheness of the proceedings, but she goes on. "My niece and I didn't stay on the subject of euthanasia. We went to the Café Europa before the theatahr and discussed modern medical techniques. I had just read an article about gene splicing in *Smithsonian,* how it was being used to find new ways to cure diseases. My niece said she thought that everything possible should be done to keep a person alive, because of the rapid advehncement of technology."

Alison has a short, staccato laugh that she laughs now: a cold, mirthless laugh that holds a great deal of disdain and contempt and, with its tiny measure of self-pity, immunizes her against the pity of others. "My niece had a great respect for doctors. I think she wanted to marry one."

I try to remember the conversation. I don't; so I'm suspicious that it never happened. But you never know. I do remember the Café Europa: a basement restaurant on West Fiftieth, with wine racks and fake vines covering the walls. The tables were so close that I could feel the thigh of the man sitting next to me.

I couldn't stop thinking about the Holocaust exhibit. The photographs were grayer than the city: bodies in a pile— naked, protuberant eyes, stubby teeth. They made me feel guilty for living, guilty for my petty grievances against the world. But that's why we comfortable and assimilated American Jews keep obsessing over those photographs, why we cart them from city to city and hang them on our walls, store them under glass, preserve them for our unborn grandchildren. Because the people in the photographs—the withered men and the children holding the hands of doomed mothers—say: *We can forgive you for living only if you never forget us.* And the pho-

sure I did sometimes; but then, I was only four. They expect so much of us, the firstborn.

I heard how when Grandpa was first diagnosed, they had to chase my mother down the halls of Mt. Moriah with a hypodermic. Later she was calm, because she had to be, for him. She almost lived at the hospital. All I knew was that she was gone: I still link that time with the memory of her black dress rustling out the door. At night I would sneak one of her bathrobes to bed with me, cover myself with it, breathe in her scent.

She was—I'm shocked to realize it now—about the same age I was when I popped the magic Percs. I know how she felt now. Inside she was hollow, a vacuum that sucked up all the water and air. She wanted to die with her father, and she was afraid she would die without him. Sometimes she hugged Daniel and me as if she were trying to take us back into her body; she would squeeze us until we cried. But then she seemed to want to fling us away. We did not understand her grief and we could not alleviate it. We may have been links to the future, her father's immortality—what difference does that make when your daddy is dying?

And if her father was in pain, he should have something to ease it. Just as she always needed something for the pain. A drink. A tranqulilizer. A new man to give her compliments. And another new man when the old one's compliments could no longer be believed.

"Are you implying that my client wanted to practice euthanasia on her own father?" Marty demands of Alison.

Elaina has bent over the plaintiff's table in a sad but graceful black arc. Her shoulders tremble. Behind her, Daniel raises his arms, hesitantly, his hands spreading out like a rabbi pronouncing a benediction—but afraid to touch her.

"I object to this," Debbie whines from her seat, thrusting her brown pumps forward impatiently. "I fail to see—"

"Ah, but, Your Honor," Marty says, his flabby smile directed at Debbie, "counsel was allowed to raise the issue on direct, so I must be allowed to pursue it on cross."

"That's right," the judge chirps, nodding. "You can answer the question."

Auntie Al looks up at the judge, then back at Marty. Her lip curls at Marty's paunch, the stray stubble on his face that his razor missed. Then, slowly, she replies, "I mairly state what heppened."

Auntie Al is like all the women in this family: Once she's decided to fight for something, she'll never back down, never doubt the truth or virtue of her fight. Does she think that I, too, have a chance at recovery? Perhaps she thought of me as the daughter she would have had with Jonathan, had not his overachieving sperm been intercepted by my mother's obstreperous egg. Maybe she meant it when she invited me to live in New York.

"Thank you, *Ms.* Winchester," Marty says.

Marty sits down with a huff of air. Elaina slowly turns her head toward him, her eyes big and wet.

After lunch, Debbie calls her next witness: Howard Posner. So Howard is testifying for Jonathan!

He stands, and his freckled girlfriend helps him wedge the crutches under his armpits.

I met Howard in my sophomore year at Berkeley, while I was recuperating from a very bad affair. Howard was getting a doctorate in history, and he was a T.A. for my history class; his dissertation dealt with the role of an obscure village in the French Revolution. To Rose, who had met Marla Pollak's boyfriend once, and referred to him alternately as a "hood" and a "thug" (he wore T-shirts with the names of rock bands on them and he smoked Marlboros), Howard was the Messiah, come at last to Alta Vista.

Jonathan approved of Howard's scholarship, but was condescending about his interest in something so impractical. Howard's only future was in academia, and Jonathan's mission was to convince Howard that he should apply himself to something more worthwhile, like commodities exchange.

But I regret to say that I continued to play out with Howard the same doomed scenario that had begun the day in confirmation class that I vowed to seduce Marla Pollak's boyfriend. However diverse their backgrounds or varied their ambitions, all of the men I was involved with had something in common, something more essential than the dark coloring that always attracted me: an inner world that I couldn't enter, where they would retreat whenever it was convenient. What that world contained was surely different for each, but from the outside it looked very much the same to me.

Howard finally hobbles to the witness stand. The bailiff props the crutches against the side and Howard straightens them so they will be more symmetrical. Howard wears thick glasses, but with sporty tortoiseshell frames. His large, deep-set brown eyes are ringed with dense lashes. He was always the handsomest guy in the library. And, oh, how I wanted to drag him out of there! How I wanted him to think that I was more important than Robespierre! I thought it was because I was in love with him—and I was; he was the love of my life—but our relationship was so much like mountain climbing: trying to prove myself, trying to prove *something,* and always short of breath and reaching higher and feeling how precarious my hold was.

"Mr. Posner," Debbie begins, "you were on intimate terms with Miss Silverstein?"

Howard grunts affirmation. "I guess she was my girlfriend."

So he *guesses,* does he? But I shouldn't be surprised. Howard is equivocal about everything that happens in the twentieth century.

"You 'guess,' Mr. Posner?" Debbie asks.

"Yeah." Howard looks around uncomfortably. He's not used to doing poorly on tests.

"How long have you known Miss Silverstein?"

"Four years. I hadn't seen her in a while."

"Would you say you knew her well?"

Howard nods vigorously.

"Please answer the question for the record."

"Yes, I knew her well," Howard says, much too loudly. This is followed by an involuntary, embarrassed titter through the gallery. Behind his glasses, Howard's dark eyes shift nervously over the courtroom.

"So," Debbie begins, drawing out the word, "you probably shared personal secrets, isn't that right?"

"All the time," Howard says.

Like hell we did. I had to hit him over the head with a baseball bat to get his attention, and even then it was iffy. Hardly conducive to sharing personal secrets.

"You knew about her habits, her routine?"

"I certainly did."

"And what would you say Miss Silverstein's favorite activity was?"

Howard leans forward to announce loudly, "Sleeping."

The room seems to tilt.

"What exactly do you mean by that?"

"Melissa never wanted to get up in the morning."

Marty stands. "Objection, Your Honor."

"Your Honor," Debbie whines, "I don't see how I'm supposed to question my witness if counsel keeps interrupting!"

I feel disoriented. I don't want to look at Rose, but I see her anyway: head erect, that half-smile still carved into her face. I don't know if she's finding a way to rationalize this last pronouncement of Howard's, or if she's figured out now that he and I slept together. She was always warning me about "having relations," as she called it. "Most of the girls don't do that anymore." And then she would add the final caveat: "He'll know what you're like then." She will assume that sleeping with Howard is the reason I lost him, which at the time she seemed to interpret as a personal attack.

Damn! My memory is tainted enough without this. Now she's been embarrassed in front of Judy Weiss and the world. She can't *noodge* me anymore, but couldn't Debbie have had a little more consideration? What did she hope to accomplish with this trivial testimony?

The judge sucks in his marshmallow cheeks and then blows out air. "Is there a point to this line of questioning?" he asks Debbie.

"There is," she says.

"Then continue."

"Did the incompetent ever say anything to you about her sleeping patterns?"

"Yes, she did. She once said that her idea of heaven would be to be able to stay in bed forever."

Well, it's true, I did say that. I should have known better than to think that Howard the Historian would misquote me. But I didn't mean I wanted to be *comatose*, for God's sake.

"Your Honor . . ."—Marty stands—"are we to believe that Miss Silverstein intended a statement such as that to be applied to *this* tragic situation?"

"Let the facts speak for themselves," Debbie snaps. She rests her hand on her belly. "Mr. Posner, wasn't there something else?"

Howard takes off his glasses, rubs his eyes. "Uh . . ."

Debbie is waiting for something. Howard looks up at her, frightened, confused. What's wrong? I move close to Howard—I remember what it was like to see his dark head on the pillow in the morning, and for the first time I feel nostalgic for my body and all it enabled me to do and feel. I think of Howard retreating to the high ground of his mind, and me longing to invade that inner territory, pining like Alice to get into Wonderland.

And suddenly I have a vision. A vision that I know is real. I see Howard in Debbie's office, and as if I were reading subtitles at a foreign movie, I know that he came to see her. He asked to be allowed to testify; he wanted to plead for my life. "We meant so much to each other," I hear him say, and I even see tears in his eyes. Debbie expected him to repeat his emotional outburst on the stand. That would have had more power than any quote from me. Debbie didn't know—perhaps Howard didn't know either—that he couldn't do it in front of all these people any more than he could do it in front of me.

"Your Honor," Marty says, "are you going to allow counsel to lead the witness in this fashion?"

Judge Picone searches his cheek with his fingers. "No," he says. "Of course not."

Debbie looks at Howard another moment, then sighs. "No further questions," she says.

Marty declines to cross-examine Howard, which is a good choice on his part: It serves to make Howard's testimony seem even more superfluous.

The bailiff helps Howard with his crutches and Howard starts the long hobble back to his seat, swinging the crutches forward and then dragging his casted leg in an arc behind. Ah, Howard. It makes me regret . . . But I could be like Rose if I'm not careful.

At her seat, Debbie sulks. Jonathan is looking down, pressing an extra chin out of his neck and staring at scribbled-on yellow papers. His face is red. He knows that Howard's testimony was as lame as his leg, and shed an air of frivolity over the case.

"Does the defense intend to present more witnesses?" the judge asks.

Debbie stands clumsily. "Your Honor, if I could have just a moment to confer with my client . . ."

"Just a moment, then."

The moment stretches on. Debbie whispers fiercely.

Jonathan disagrees, with short, brisk movements of his head. Debbie nods and clicks her tongue. Jonathan sighs.

"Your Honor," Debbie says, rising again, "I would like to call to the stand my client, Jonathan Silverstein."

"Objection," Marty says. "The plaintiff was not timely notified that the defendant planned to testify."

"Your Honor," Debbie whines. "We appeal to your discretionary power in this matter. The plaintiff—"

"All right, Your Honor," Marty interrupts. He is twirling a pencil between his fingers and he smiles at Debbie. "The plaintiff will agree to let Mr. Silverstein testify, if my client is also allowed to testify."

Elaina tugs on Marty's sleeve. He shakes her off. I move closer, drawn to her, curious. She presses her lips together, and then again, almost convulsively; perhaps considering the possibilities.

The judge scrunches up his face, considering; dimples pop into his cheeks and chin. "All right, counsel," he says. "If the parties will agree, then I'm willing."

Jonathan gets up slowly and lumbers to the witness stand. The bailiff swears him in.

"Mr. Silverstein," Debbie begins, "this is an unusual position for a father to be in, is it not?"

"Yes," Jonathan answers.

"Could you share with us your specific reasons for believing that Mrs. Silverstein is wrong in her assessment of your daughter's wishes?"

Jonathan lets out a hissing sound, and it seems as if a thin white smoke is coming from everywhere: his ears, his nostrils, his mouth. "My wife has a series of misguided ideas," he says.

"Could you elaborate?"

Jonathan purses his lips. He looks sorry that he ever agreed to this. At the moment, the humiliation probably seems worse than letting me die. "She's been in therapy for years," he says. "Though what good it's done—"

"I'm sorry—we can't hear—"

"She's *crazy*," he blurts. "She never spent enough time with Melissa to have any idea what she would want. She never got out of bed long enough. Melissa used to complain to me about that. *I* was the one who raised those kids."

Elaina is shaking. Any minute now I expect her to rise from her seat and scream at my father. I can't figure out why she doesn't. Maybe she's taken extra Valium today. But she is controlled in a way I never thought possible. I have to know what she is feeling. I move close to her again. Her eyes are twirling, like the blue pinwheels she used to buy for us at the park. She pulls me in—or do I force my way? I can hear the throbbing of her heartbeat; it is dark, with distant, soft blinking lights. I feel her blood surging; the wash of it over me. I feel pain, pressure. . . .

And then I'm out again, on the courtroom's cold, dirty floor, feeling bloody and exhausted. Wondering exactly what just happened. The fluorescent lights sting me; the noises around me are harsh, indistinguishable, like horns honking. I still know nothing.

"Nothing makes her happy," Jonathan is saying. "Nothing is ever enough for her." His voice is thick, and there is a strange look of pleasure on his face. It's as if he's forgotten where he is—as if something has risen up in him and over-powered him, and he has surrendered to the vindictive ecstasy of it, even knowing that a moment from now he will regret the fleeting pleasure.

Debbie is glaring at Jonathan. Both her hands cover her belly, as if to protect her child from him. Jonathan looks up at her, and suddenly I see Daniel: He has that same startled expression Daniel would have when he was little and knew he'd gotten caught doing something wrong but wasn't sure what it was.

Debbie turns away abruptly. "Your witness," she says coldly.

Marty approaches the stand. "Mr. Silverstein, when was the last time you visited your daughter?"

"Last night," Jonathan replies promptly.

"And do you visit your daughter often?"

"Objection!" Debbie cries, waving her hand. "Beyond the scope of the direct."

"Ms. Meyers," Judge Picone observes, as his eyes make wide, uneven circles, "I allowed you to call this witness without adequate notice to the plaintiff."

"Huh," Debbie grunts, slouching back in her seat. "It's not fair," she mutters softly.

"Answer the question," the judge instructs.

Jonathan tugs at his collar. "About twice a week."

"Isn't it more like once a week?" Marty presses.

"Maybe."

"And isn't it true that you are no longer living in the home? And isn't it true that you left the home once before?"

"That was sixteen years ago."

Elaina starts to cry at last, bowing her head over her gloved hand.

"And isn't it true that you have sometimes . . . enjoyed the company of other women?"

"*No*," Jonathan barks. His eyelids seem to compress around his irises so that all we can see is the brick redness, rimmed in red. He's probably wondering whether he can use his contacts in Sacramento to get Marty disbarred. Or murdered.

"But you are quite certain that you know what your daughter wants."

"Yes, I am," Jonathan snaps.

"And can you say *what* makes you so certain?" Marty asks. "Can you tell the court how you and your daughter scaled the pinnacles of understanding? Can you put into words the unique nature of this special intimacy?"

Jonathan can hardly speak. He glares at Marty, who's been

getting specks of saliva on Jonathan's tie. Perhaps while my father has been sitting at the defendant's table next to Debbie, listening to all this testimony over the last two days, he has begun to realize that he had only a crude understanding of me, from the outside; perhaps it has even occurred to him that when he shoved me like that broken toy under the bed of his mind, I went on living and thinking about things in which he had no interest. I know that my moods and impulses were no more comprehensible to him than Elaina's are. But Jonathan has made a conscious choice: to decide that this is what I want. He knows that in order to accomplish what he wishes, he cannot allow any doubts to infiltrate his mind. "I just know," he barks.

"No further questions."

Jonathan stomps down from the witness stand. And now it's Elaina's turn.

Her journey to the stand is a ballet of wobbling heels and dabbing at eyes.

"Mrs. Silverstein, isn't it an unusual request for a mother to want to be the instrument of her daughter's death?"

"I . . . I suppose so." She glances about her with modest fear, eyes big and blank as white china plates. She wrings her hands.

"You realize, Mrs. Silverstein"—Marty pats his forehead with his handkerchief—"that the issue here is not what *you* think is best for your daughter, but what decision Miss Silverstein would make for herself?"

"Do you think *I* want this?" Elaina replies. "I don't want this at all. But I know it's what she would want." She looks around the courtroom, and focuses on Debbie. "I carried her in my body for nine months," she announces. "Am I supposed to let her suffer like this? For ten years, twenty years? When there's no hope she'll ever be anything but—but—but what she is now?" She is speaking low, urgently, and her voice is melodious, a ballad played by a saxophone. "I couldn't fight this hard," she adds, raising her chin, "if it was just for me."

"Thank you, Mrs. Silverstein," Marty says. "We can all appreciate what a tremendous strain—"

But Elaina looks up at him, her smoothly arched brows raised, and he stops.

As Marty sits down, Debbie sighs. "No questions, Your Honor."

"Is that it?" Judge Picone asks. "No more witnesses?" His quivering eyes jerk up toward the ceiling. "Then counsel will present their closing statements so that I can retire to consider my decision."

Closing statements are brief. Marty opens with a nineteenth-century poem, intoning, "Wrap thou the mantle of death like a dear companion's gentle caress about thy shoulders," and concludes with "Let us pray for the wisdom to help this young woman. Let us pray that the beacon of wisdom will shine through the mists of ignorance."

Then Debbie speaks grimly of setting a precedent that would allow children to kill their aged parents, or doctors to withhold treatment from political undesirables. "Unless the state protects life without judgment as to its value or quality," she predicts, "that judgment may be made by those who may be less competent than those whose lives they seek to end."

Judge Picone says that he will notify the parties of his decision tomorrow morning.

There is a rawness in the air. I can feel it; it hurts for everyone to breathe. The crowd—family, reporters, friends— moving into the hall is quieter than it was the day before.

Daniel is the first to slip away, to the men's room. While Elaina and Jonathan were testifying, he looked as though he might start to cry. But he didn't. I don't think he wants even Elaina to see him cry again.

Becky and Leah walk out of the courtroom together. They do not speak. They join the largely silent procession toward the elevators. As they move, they join hands.

Rose walks alone. Her half-smile is still fixed in place. Her lips are chapped and dry. Everything is changed for her forever. The few pleasures remaining to her in her final years— quiet gossip over the bridge table, some harmless bragging about her grandchildren that may require a little exaggeration—are over now. She is too old by many years to move away and start over; and yet she will be the subject of speculation and pity for the rest of her life. She will be encased and isolated in it. From now on, she must be wary of her friends, wondering what they say about her.

Then, up ahead, she sees Jonathan and Alison together. "You did what you had to do," Alison is telling him.

"I don't care what anyone thinks," Jonathan replies shortly.

"I only meant—" Alison breaks off. "I mean, Elaina . . ." She shrugs and looks down.

Rose glances behind her. Howard is swinging his crutches toward her. Rose openly studies the freckled girl who is helping him along. Rose's granddaughter was easily replaced.

She turns back to where Jonathan and Alison are still walking together, Alison taking quick little steps to keep up with Jonathan's longer stride. Rose follows them, but she does not interrupt.

The next day everyone gathers in the courtroom, very early.

I'm nervous and I drift outside. I feel a tug to the hospital: Someone is thinking about me, rather strongly.

I pop over to Mt. Moriah. And I see Drew standing in the

hospital corridor. His eyes are bloodshot. He checks his watch. He knows that court is in session. I try to guess from his face what went on between him and Elaina last night, but the messages I get are jumbled, fragmentary—the woman with the inoperable tumor in 245C seems to be on his mind, and then the eggs he couldn't eat that morning. He pushes back his blown-dry hair. His work is suffering, that's clear. Huh! He hopes Elaina will win, so they can put the trial behind them. But he'd have to be there with the pulmonologist when they disconnect. . . . How does he expect to do that and live happily ever after with her?

He hears his name called over the P.A. and looks up at the ceiling, as if it were the voice of God.

I go back to the courthouse. Everyone is still waiting and seems as nervous as I am. The clerk busies herself writing and whispering into her phone, avoiding the look of any of my relatives. The bailiff keeps moving, wandering toward the judge's chambers, wandering toward the courtroom doors, peering through the portholelike windows there. The court reporter cracks his knuckles. Reporters in the gallery buzz among themselves, laughing nervously. Judy Weiss, a birdlike woman with frizzy dark hair, has seated herself next to my grandmother and offers her a piece of Kleenex.

Elaina is wearing her false eyelashes today. Loose strands of her auburn hair are curled into ringlets on her forehead.

Jonathan looks as though he hasn't slept much: There are bags under his eyes. His shirt is wrinkled.

Finally the judge is led in by his smiling white dog. He slowly settles himself on the bench, fussing for a few moments with the folds of his robes.

"This was a difficult decision," he begins. His voice is squeakier than usual. "As you know, the purpose is not to determine who is the more fit parent, and no such judgment on my part is implied. Rather, I had to decide which party's intentions most likely represent the incompetent's wishes, and it is not for us to judge the wisdom of what her decision would be, if she could speak for herself. It would appear that the incompetent made several conflicting statements at different times."

I'm so nervous that I feel as though I have to struggle to maintain consciousness. It's almost like choking. As I strain, pushing against the atmosphere, I notice that a stack of papers on the clerk's table rustles. There is no draft. The clerk slaps her hand down on the pile.

"However, listening to the testimony, a relatively clear picture of Miss Silverstein has emerged in my mind. She would seem to have been a sensitive, if troubled, young woman."

Oh, yeah? Who does this guy think he is? How can he claim to know me when I'm only beginning to know myself?

"A woman who would not have wanted extraordinary means taken to prolong her life when there is no hope for recovery. Indeed, I can't believe that under any circumstances she would have wanted to survive in the pitiful state she is now in. . . ."

But it's not pitiful at all. If only I could tell them . . . It's light and lovely, it's freedom. . . .

"Therefore," the judge says, "I find in favor of the plaintiff, Elaina Miller Silverstein." He feels for his gavel. The bailiff reaches over and puts it in his hand. Judge Picone touches it lightly on the bench. "Let it be so entered."

Elaina starts to cry. Leah lets out a little squeak.

They can't do this to me. Daddy daddy daddy. Mommy mommy mommy.

# 8

But daddy will save me. As long as he is alive, perhaps I need never worry. Who cares if he doesn't love me in that special and inexpressible way that I want? He does what I need him to do: He files an appeal against Judge Picone's decision. The Supreme Court agrees to hear the case on a special writ, bypassing the appellate level. Pending the outcome of the appeal, Elaina is prevented from pulling the ol' plugaroo, since that would render the subject of the appeal moot, to say the least.

Marty Lindner (may he get lung cancer and end up connected to his own respirator) files a motion requesting, "in the interests of equity, that the appeal be expedited forthwith." It seems that the hospital, too, is eager to unload me, so that another, more deserving patient can have that bed.

"I always said your father was very appealing," Elaina says to Daniel.

Daniel is sitting on her bed. Elaina is rubbing lotion on her hands, the repetitive motions unusually brisk. Paddy O'Flanagan is curled in the valley between her outstretched legs. "I don't want to say anything bad about him," Elaina goes on, "but he just can't let me win an argument. He doesn't think about Melissa." She stops to pat Daniel's hand. "Don't feel bad, Danabable. It wasn't your fault."

"I know," Daniel says sullenly.

"Promise me you don't feel bad."

"I don't."

"Really?"

"Really."

"I feel better then. If you mean it."

"Hmm." Daniel strokes Paddy's back. "Mickey Mouse," he asks, "do you remember how many Percodan the dentist gave me when I had the abscessed tooth? I was sure I'd taken them all."

"Your grandmother said to me, 'If you hadn't started this in the first place, Jonathan wouldn't need to appeal.'" Elaina sighs and reaches for a jar on the nightstand. "How about these, cucumber eye pads. They're guaranteed to make you look like a young salad." She opens the jar and fingers one of the linen pads. "You know," she says, "I just feel so terrible about how this is tearing the whole family up. And all the money your father is spending, and of course he has to pay for my lawyer, too."

"He does?"

"Oh, I know, it's terrible. I could be like Sheila Newhouse or Paula Meyers and open one of those little stores that sell bronze jelly beans or antique croissants—now that's really doing something *productive,* and I think your father always wanted me to do that. But I'm just not that way. I was always worried about you kids. I wanted to be here when you got home from school."

Daniel is looking at Elaina as if he is trying to fathom her—not as mother, but as woman, the only woman he can be close to. I think I'm beginning to understand my brother: It seems to me that his sexuality has been compressed, reshaped into an attraction to women in the abstract that is stirred by women on TV, or in magazine ads, with flat bellies and plastic complexions. A real woman might have expectations that are even more unmeetable than Elaina's.

I've heard Elaina tell him, "You're too young for all that. People don't get married so young anymore. Wait till you're thirty, or forty. I was much too young to get married, and look what happened to me. I mean, I love your father more than life itself, but . . ." But.

Now she asks him, "What time is it, Danabable?"

"Eleven-thirty."

"I guess I should get up," she sighs. "I hate to move when Paddy O' is so comfortable, but I want to go visit your sister before I see Dr. Abramowitz. Sometimes I feel as if Melissa knows when I get there late, and then I feel even more guilty about everything. But some days it's so hard for me to get going. You know, I think your father was always sorry he married me instead of Alison. Oh, yes, she would have been a better wife. I don't know if she would have been a better mother—I don't think Alison ever really wanted children. I always did want children, and you all just fell out of me like little presents. They were easier deliveries than Federal Express. But I want you to like Alison, whatever happens."

"Mouse," Daniel says, "how could dad have been having an affair with Auntie Al? I mean, when he goes out of town on business, he never goes to New York, he always goes to Atlanta or Florida or Texas."

"That's where he *says* he goes," Elaina points out. "Of course, if anyone could be in two places at once, it would be your father. But Danabable, you do think I'm right about Melissa, don't you?"

"Of course, Mickey Mouse."

I think he does. The way my body is now, emaciated, curled next to the heaving machine, there is nothing he can do for me. I remember when Goodyear Blimp, our gray cat, was run over by a car: how Daniel sobbed, trying to pick up the broken body. Death itself is so unreal: It would be as if I moved away and didn't write. Though I think he would miss me.

"If only there was something else we could do," Elaina says.

Daniel looks up at her wonderingly. "What else could we do, Mouse?" he asks.

"Well, I don't know." Elaina spreads out her hands. "I don't know about these things."

"There's nothing else we can do." Daniel straightens. "We have to be strong, and patient." He pats Elaina's hand protectively.

"Danabable, you are so handsome and so perfect," Elaina says, stroking his curls above the ear. "Since I have you, I have everything." She leans forward and kisses his sideburn. Then, keeping her head near his and her hands lightly on his arms, she whispers hoarsely, "But you know what? If I had the nerve, I would pull that plug myself."

"Gee, Mouse, I don't see how you could do that."

"I couldn't. Or maybe I could, for Melissa's sake. But it would be for everyone else's sake, too. This is tearing your grandmother apart. And what if your father wins his appeal? We'd all have to go back to court. I don't think I could stand that. Dr. Abramowitz says I'm overstressed. I could have a nervous breakdown." She lies back on the pile of pillows behind her and reaches for a Kleenex. "Your father wouldn't like that—that would cost him a lot of money. And who would take care of you kids?"

"Mouse, you're not going to have a nervous breakdown," Daniel says. But he looks doubtful.

"Well, I'd better get up." Elaina sighs again. "Dr. Abramowitz gets so upset when I'm late. Poor man, I feel sorry for him, he's so sensitive. I tell him he shouldn't take things so seriously. He seems to be doing better these days, though."

She throws back the covers. She looks unusually sleek in her pink satin pajamas. Disturbed, Paddy O'Flanagan sleepily raises his lupine head. Elaina scratches the cat's neck. "Wouldn't you like to be a cat? His biggest problem is that he doesn't know where he's going to take his next nap. It takes him all day to decide, and that tires him out, so he has to take another nap."

Daniel absently scratches the other side of Paddy's extended neck. I remember another cat in our series of live-ins and visitors: Sylvester Silverstein, the black cat we had for a short time when Daniel was five. Sylvester started hiding under the china cabinet, meowing loudly. Finally Elaina took him to the vet, who told her that the cat had leukemia. Later she had him put to sleep. She came home and told us that she had given Sylvester away to a friendly man who wanted a cat for his own children—then she went upstairs, where she said kaddish.

"The trouble is," Elaina observed when she thought we were old enough to learn the truth, "cats don't live as long as people."

Daniel especially mourned the deaths that seemed to occur in such rapid succession, ashamed of his tears but shedding them anyway.

Paddy stretches and yawns a little cat yawn. "Look at him," Elaina smiles as Paddy leaps past Daniel to the floor. "Now he has to eat. He's so busy, we should get him a secretary, don't you think?" Another sigh. "Poor Melissa. I feel guilty every time I'm not thinking about her. I swear, I wish I could pull that plug myself."

Friday night is Becky's date with Jeff Lindner.

She is running down the stairs almost before the Ford Granada Jeff borrowed from his mother has stopped in front of the house; and before he can get out of the car, she is rapping on the window of the passenger side. She doesn't want Jeff to come inside, where Elaina might pounce on him.

Becky stands under the streetlamp, waiting, while Jeff gets out to open the door for her. The front of her hair is moussed and sticks up straight like a porcupine's quills. She wears a brown suede minidress with fringe on the bottom, and a purple bandanna around her forehead, evoking an Indian squaw's outfit. The effect is completed by the two purple stripes she has painted across her cheeks.

Jeff takes her to the movies. About halfway through, he stretches and then lets his arm drop over the back of Becky's seat. Becky slouches down so that her neck is against his arm. She does not slip her hand into his—but I think that's because her fingers are sticky from the buttered popcorn.

Afterward, he offers to take her home or over to Twelve Oaks Boulevard for ice cream. "Yeah, sure, we could do that," Becky agrees. "Or we could take a drive up to the Hills."

Jeff hesitates. "The Hills"—sometimes known as Make-Out Mountains or Herpes Heights—are an area above Alta Vista that borders Contra Costa County and has several miles of fairly deserted winding roads. The parking areas on these roads attract high-school students, especially on weekend nights. The "tokies" and "crackers" who go there give the area the risqué ambience that makes it a fashionable recreation spot for the more upright students as well. Kids sit in cars and smoke cigarettes (even Becky has been known to light up here, although she doesn't inhale) and check out the kids in the other cars, carefully observing who is wearing what and who is doing what and with whom. Until now, Jeff has been up there only during the day, on one of the cleanup trips that he organizes for his Earth Club, to pick up the litter of those same coolers and tokies and crackers. It seems politically incorrect for him to go there at night. "If you really want to," he agrees finally.

Becky really wants to; so they park, according to her instructions, on a precipice large enough for only one car, and therefore isolated. The hill overlooks lower Alta Vista and Oakland and the Bay; the multicolored lights below them look like Elaina's jewelry box emptied onto smoked glass. The Bay Bridge is a fey necklace dripping from the crown of San Francisco. The Ford Granada seems like a space capsule perched on top of the world.

"My folks are just such 'droids," Becky sighs. "It's mega-fucked, really, what's going down now. I mean, I'm humiliated just going to *school*. It's like your parents were getting divorced and it was on TV."

Jeff does not reply immediately. It is very difficult for Becky to wait out the silence; silences are rare in our family, and there is some anxiety associated with them. But she must know that Jeff needs time and silence in order to weigh the significance of his words, to seek the purest truth he can express. "Some of the stuff my dad does makes me really angry," he says at last.

Becky clicks her tongue in sympathy. "Does he want you to be a lawyer, too?" she asks.

"I don't know."

She smiles. "I like lawyers."

"Hmm." Jeff taps the steering wheel with his first two fingers. "I—I want to clean things up."

"That's parthenogenic," Becky says. "Really."

"I want to make a difference," Jeff says. He keeps tapping the steering wheel while he looks through the windshield at the city and the Bay. "I'm not going to pretend that it's all unselfish. I want some glory for what I do." He pauses, but still does not look at her. "I hope that doesn't sound shallow."

"No," Becky says, snuggling against the upholstery. The car smells of Jeff's mother's cigarettes. "I don't think so at all."

"I don't want to be like my dad, though—he's a prostitute."

"I was thinking," Becky says, sliding lower in the seat. "I might want to join the Earth Club."

"Someday," Jeff begins slowly, "I might want to run for office. I think if we had more tax incentives, that would get to people like my dad. Pollution causes most of the evils of the world, when you think about it, like cancer, and birth defects. I think it might even be too much sugar in our diet that makes people aggressive, and that's what causes war—or it doesn't help, anyway. Course, you can't be a single-issue candidate."

"Guy, no."

Now Jeff thumps his fist against the dashboard. His arm, revealed by his short-sleeved sports shirt, is pale, but swells with a large bicep. I can tell that Becky longs to touch it, to feel the masculine softness of his skin. To feel both his arms around her. "I know you have to make compromises," Jeff is saying. "You gotta play the game." He shakes his head. "But God, I hate it. Like kissing up to the administration just so we can use the bulletin boards and the school buses and stuff like that."

"Shit, the 'droids," Becky sighs. "They are so dee-scuz sometimes."

"I'm really sorry about your sister," Jeff says suddenly. "I mean, I don't know if I've really said that before."

"Yeah, you have," Becky sighs. "I mean, thanks." She absently covers her mouth with a section of her hair. The evocation of my name, especially by someone outside the family, seems to arouse a mild sense of guilt in her: After all, Leah broods over my condition, while Becky tries to think of it as little as possible. I know Becky wishes to disassociate herself from me—she rationalizes that this happened to me because I made mistakes that she can easily avoid; and indeed, she has the singularity of purpose that I lacked when I was in a body. But I remember—and she might, too—what happened the first week after she got her driver's license and her new Camaro: She was driving to Sacramento and turned off on Highway 17 by mistake. Within minutes, she was lost in Richmond. One lane, one moment of inattention, and so many miles astray.

"And I'm really sorry I couldn't get my father to get out of it," Jeff goes on. "I just don't understand him at all." Another long silence. Becky twists the bangles on her arms and bites her lip to keep from speaking. "When I was a kid, it seemed like he wanted to really make a contribution—you know, do something positive." His delicate mouth contorts as if he's bitten into sour fruit. "Now all he cares about is being a famous trial attorney."

Becky sighs again, but prettily—a softer, more romantic version of the sigh that has come down to her from Rose through Elaina. "That's all right," she says. "It's not *your* fault." She turns her face toward him, her full, burgundy lips parted. I know she wants to kiss him—his own small mouth looks so soft. She must long to stroke his head and feel the bristling of his hair against her palm. She must long to be different from Elaina and separate from her. I feel her reaching over the abyss.

Jeff moves his head slightly away from her. "Well." His voice is thick. "I'd better get you back. My parents have asked me to be home before one." He turns the key in the ignition; the car shakes like a blender and makes a noise like a death rattle, but then it starts.

When they pull up in front of our house on Magnolia Street, Jeff gets out to circle around the car and open Becky's door. Then they climb the stairs together, rising into the circle of light and honeysuckle that surrounds the porch. As they climb, Becky's hand is dangling and then it brushes against Jeff's own dangling hand, and as their fingers gradually intertwine, I'm sure it seems to him as though he reached out to hold it himself.

"I had fun tonight," Becky says.

"So did I," Jeff replies.

Becky braces her knees and rotates her pelvis forward. Her breasts sway under Jeff's chin; the floral scent of her shampoo mingles with the honeysuckle and her own faint musky odor. And I am there, too, in the scent of her, and my laughter is the tinkle of Elaina's wind chimes above the porch.

I can hear Jeff's heartbeat—it pounds as hard as if he's just run the entire track field. He looks away from Becky, puzzled, as if trying to separate himself from whatever he is feeling, to analyze it.

Too late. He looks down into Becky's golden-green eyes, and the wailing of a distant cat shoots through the night as he leans down and kisses her; her lips are chapped, but soft and giving beneath his own, and Becky's arms, thin and strong, circle his neck, pressing him close to her.

She releases him suddenly, with a giggle, her hand groping for the doorknob. "I guess I'd better go in now." Giggle.

Jeff nods. "Next week." He looks surprised at what he is saying. "We'll go out again."

"Oh . . . Okay." She opens the door, backs into the foyer. "G'night now." And blows him a kiss.

Jeff waits until the door closes again. He hesitates, as if he has left something unfinished. Then he starts down the stairs, hands in his pockets. At the bottom of the stairs, he stops again. It seems that there is something nagging at him, like a tiny pebble in one of his running shoes. For several moments he stands there in the dark, as if trying to trace the source of this unease.

Finally he crosses the street, toward the car. If he turned around he would see her: the tiny yellow-haired figure watching from the third floor, like a captive princess from a tower window.

It is a couple of hours after Becky's return when Craig Newhouse stops his Mercedes 300E in the same place on Magnolia Street where Jeff's car was parked. The passenger door opens and Daniel's head appears, nearer to the seat of the car than to the roof. His head extends a little farther, like a turtle's coming out of its shell, and then he pukes into the gutter.

When he is finished, he grasps the door handle and pulls himself up. He raises his arm as if to wipe the sleeve of his linen suit across his mouth, but stops. "You got a rag or something?"

"Here." Craig reaches behind the seat, where he grabs a towel that he throws to Daniel. Probably Craig keeps it there for occasions such as this. Craig's nostrils are a little more flared than usual. He is just as drunk as Daniel, but *he* won't throw up until he reaches the privacy of his own bathroom.

"I feel better now," Daniel says (although no one asked), tossing the rag behind the seat.

"Huh," Craig grunts. "It was pretty embarrassing, having to take Suzie home like that."

"Sorry I spoiled your fun," Daniel says.

I've figured out that they, too, have just come back from the Hills. I'm getting vague impressions of Daniel's thoughts, dark fragments, like a dream I can partly remember. There are the barely recognizable outlines of Daniel and Craig—one in the front seat and one in the back—and two shadowy young women with them. The women are faceless to me because they were faceless to Daniel and Craig. But Craig must have been with Suzie Rotelli. She goes to Hilltop High, so it's no wonder he doesn't want anyone to know about their liaison; he likes these women to whom he feels so vastly superior. I think of his father, traveling with Lizzie Goldsmith, Alta Vista jailbait.

Daniel drank too much to dilute his self-disgust. Elaina has always said that men have to "get it" somewhere; Daniel must be confused by his apparent need to get it and the unpleasantness that surrounds the getting of it. The women in the back seat of Craig's Mercedes are the opposite of the ones in the magazine ads, but they are no more personal.

"Just keep it together on Sunday," Craig says. "We don't want anything to go wrong."

"Listen," Daniel says, too loudly, "I'm the one up shit creek. You can count on me."

"I put some bucks down this garbage chute, too."

"Yeah. Everything Grandma Newhouse left you."

Craig's shoulders jerk. He turns toward Daniel; I see his head in dark profile. "Just keep it together."

Daniel grips the door handle and starts to ease himself out of the car. "I'll see ya," he says. "Sunday." I'm sure he doesn't need to look at Craig to see the flared nostrils, the stinging eyes—but I'm glad to see his back turned anyway.

As he passes behind the car, Daniel steadies himself by putting his hand on the trunk; the exhaust fumes swirl around his pants as Craig starts the engine. Daniel crosses the street, placing his feet on the pavement with more than usual care, then he climbs the stairs, stumbling forward once, but grabbing the banister before he falls.

Inside, he tiptoes past Elaina's room. Her door is slightly ajar and her Mickey Mouse smell of sleep and powder and perfume fills the hall. Through the crack in the door, Daniel can see only a tumble of sheets and a lump that must be part of her body.

I follow him into his room, where he lies down with his hands behind his head. Daniel is still settled in the middle blue bedroom, the poorly lit one with the single window and the ghastly blue walls. The issue of the bedroom has, of course, become unmentionable. It would be too great a show of callousness, too blatant a recognition of reality, if he or anyone else suggested that he move back into my bedroom, which now sits empty with the door closed. By overdosing I have, in a sense, locked him in his room.

I float above him. He looks through me, sadly, at the blue ceiling. Obviously, he knows that his dissipation can't go on forever. He probably just wanted a little time to play before he undertook the unending seriousness of Jonathan's adulthood. But by the time Daniel realized that his latent abilities—whatever they might be—were beginning to atrophy, the habit of partying had become a need, programmed into him as surely as Ansel Marsh programmed the instructions into "Wizards and Warriors."

After a few minutes he gets up and very quietly leaves the house again. Now that's curious. I'd better tag along.

He backs his Porsche down the driveway. I have one of my little clairvoyant flashes, and I know that we're heading toward the hospital, but I don't know why. Is he feeling some regret about me? I'm feeling some regret about him. I guess I didn't have to break his toy truck and pretend it was an accident. I guess I didn't have to call him Danny Pencilprick in front of his friends. I didn't have to see him as my enemy, my replacement—there might have been room for both of us on the second floor. And maybe Daniel is sorry for the times he ran to tell on me when we were little, and his snideness to me when we were grown. Maybe Daniel is sorry, as I am now, that neither of us tried a little harder to be friends.

The only hospital door open at this hour is the emergency entrance, an island of light in the gloomy parking lot. A security guard stands near the automatic glass doors. An ambulance is parked in the driveway, next to the wheelchair ramp. At the moment two paramedics are bringing in an empty stretcher. Daniel slips in ahead of them.

Jonathan has arranged (through a business contact who knows the chairman of the Mt. Moriah board) that the entire family should have twenty-four-hour visiting privileges. Still, it's almost as if Daniel doesn't want to be seen. He edges along the quiet corridors. I understand. He's ashamed of the affection he does feel for me, just like I'm a little ashamed of my growing tenderness for him. That's why he's come to see me so late: He doesn't want anyone to know that he's been here.

His shoes slide quietly along the waxy floor. He passes the nurses' station, where the two nurses are huddled over a report; then he slips into my room.

He does not turn on the light. Instead he sits in the chair

by my bed. *Whoosh* goes the respirator, then *click*. There is a
screen above my bed, monitoring my heartbeat, and a single
bleeping light flashes across it at regular intervals, like a video
game before you put money in.

Daniel pulls the chair closer, then leans over and brushes
the lank dark hair off my forehead. *Whoosh*-click. *Whoosh*-click.
His face is near mine. His breath comes faster now—it is moist
and smells sourly of bourbon. For a moment I think he is about
to squeeze his mouth between the respirator tube and the
nasogastric tube, and kiss the cracked lips in the white face of
my body. But he doesn't move. From above I see his tight dark
blond curls. And I feel uneasy—as if something were pulling
me down; as if I had substance, when I know I don't. . . .

Daniel raises his head and turns toward the respirator
now. He looks closely at the various dials, pointing a finger at
them, apparently trying to figure them out. He looks puzzled.

Then he drops to his knees. In the dark he looks like a big,
unruly dog. I hear his hands slap against the floor as he moves
around, groping for . . . for . . . the plug! Has he lost his mind?
The crazy faggot! Help! Help! I scream but I cannot scream—
that withered, useless body can't do anything. But I can feel it
like a rope around my throat—Daniel's hand feeling along the
floor, Daniel's hand gripping the heavy cord . . . Help! My
crazy brother's trying to kill me! Help! Help!

EEEEEEEEEEEEEEEEEEEEEEEEEEEEEEEE . . .

The cardiac alarm goes off. Daniel rolls back on his
haunches with a little yelp as there are running feet and
squeaking wheels in the hall—and then the door swings open
to reveal the team of nurses and technicians with their "crash
cart," loaded with their bottles and needles, ready to keep me
alive. Their shadows stretch across the room, carved into the
long rectangle of light that extends from the doorway. And
Daniel slowly gets to his feet, brushing off his suit, like a little
boy who's been playing in the dirt.

There was no cardiac arrest—I set that alarm off. I moved

it. They'll never get rid of me now—I'm stronger than any of them!


Daniel came up with some stupid story about being forced to come to the hospital late at night so that Elaina wouldn't be upset by his visit, and how he dropped something behind my bed and was looking for it when the alarm suddenly and inexplicably went off. No one believes it—but no one does anything about it, either. Well, what did I expect? That they would throw him in jail?

Still, everyone's wondering if Danny's rowboat isn't displacing a little too much water these days. "What was he doing at the hospital at that hour?" Rose asks Alison.

"I *like* Daniel," Alison insists. "It's just that he's . . ." And she shrugs and looks down.

"But what was he doing at the hospital at that hour?" Rose asks again.

"Daniel's such a handsome boy," Alison says. "But sometimes I think . . ."

"It's very odd," Rose concludes. "I find it very puzzling, don't you?"

The chief of neurology complains to the hospital administrator about the abuse of visiting privileges. The hospital administrator contacts Jonathan to apologize for the lack of supervision on the floor.

Daniel went into his room early this morning, where he has remained throughout the day. I pop in on him; he is standing in front of the bookshelves he attached to the wall with metal brackets. His hooked index finger scans the colorful bindings of his paperback sci-fi collection. The covers of these books display breastplated women with inhumanly long hair, battling reptilian creatures with bulging eyes. On the lower shelf is a row of hardcover books, with pristine dust jackets promising the secrets to *Instant Phenomenal Success; Profit from Your Neighbor's Bankruptcy; Make Money While You Sleep.*

One floor above, Becky and Leah are getting ready to go to Janice Ingersoll's. Becky has already told Leah about her date with Jeff; now she wants to relive the experience with Janice. The three girls will apply an abstruse method of analysis to every word and gesture of Jeff's that Becky can recall; their thesis surely will be that Jeff is tortured by love.

"Shouldn't we go talk to Daniel?" Leah asks. "He seems really wonked out."

"He's wonked out, all right," Becky agrees with a snort. She leans closer to her dressing-table mirror to separate her lashes with the point of a safety pin. "I think we'd better let him fly solo for a while."

As for me, I want to test my new power. It doesn't surprise me that I set off the cardiac alarm. I felt something like this coming for a while; it just took Daniel's attack to bring it out. I suppose I should be grateful.

I have a theory about what's happening. I should have died, but I didn't—I'm caught between being in a body and the "next world," if there is one—so the normal progression has been diverted. I'm discovering a dimension in between, like a secret passageway in an old house. Or like Becky taking the wrong turnoff from the freeway: The two paths are so close, but the destinations lie in opposite directions.

Anyway, I think I can move small objects now if I try hard enough. That isn't such a big step beyond being able to read minds or send mental messages—and for once I'm not going to lose interest in a project before I see it through. Look out! Today the Silverstein family, tomorrow the world! Maybe there are others like me—maybe the disembodied spirits of misunderstood daughters are causing tidal waves in Hawaii and monsoons in Japan. Because we're really pissed off.

Leah is sitting on her bed, stroking the muzzle of her stuffed horse, Melanie. Named for Melanie Klein.

Becky drops her upper body toward the floor, then straightens in a swift motion, whipping her head back, sending her hair flying in an arc above her. "Let's spin, Lee-steah," she orders. "Where's the Viral Epidemic album? We might want to hear some tunes. Guy, you're not going to bring the *horsey*, are you?"

Leah puts Melanie on the pillow.

"I'd better not go to the Earth Club meeting *this* week, do you think?" Becky is trotting out the door; Leah follows. "I think it'll be just too totally obvious, like I was chasing him or something."

On top of Becky's dressing table is a napkin that Jeff made notes on during the party. Becky rescued it before Lee Emma went down to clean. Can I move it?

I concentrate. *Move, move.* Jeff writes in a small, back-slanted hand, with thick strokes. Almost illegible. The napkin trembles. I am straining with the effort. I feel a bit winded.

But the napkin is rising. Slowly—but it *is* rising, and faster now, high in the air!

I did it! Drumroll, please! Let's hear it for me!

What to do with it now? I notice that Leah's bottom drawer is open a crack. I don't know if I can open a drawer at the same time I'm "holding" the napkin, but we'll worry about that later. First, try this. I concentrate, and the napkin slides into the drawer. Easy! What a talented girl I am! This is going to be fun.

I pop into Elaina's room. She's at the hospital now.

When I was a kid, finding Elaina's room empty was like winning one of those contests where they set you loose in a toy store. Her makeup tray is an artist's palette; her perfume bottles are shaped like Victorian ladies and gleam like crystal; her scarves flutter from the tie rack in the closet like the flags of the United Nations.

I think of pulling out all the drawers and emptying them

onto the floor. She'd know who did it, all right. She always said I was a slob.

But I have a better idea. I'm going to levitate her lipstick and write on the mirror. When they were first married, Elaina would leave messages for Jonathan on the bathroom mirror, sometimes writing with his shaving cream. Maybe she'll get the reference. I'll write something spooky, but not too direct—not *Don't let them pull the plug on me* (she doesn't care what I want), but maybe *Carry me with you,* which she claims was the oft-repeated demand of my childhood. She'll probably find some way to rationalize the message: accuse Becky or even Lee Emma of a sick joke. I do want to be careful about being found out, but I'm sure everyone will suspect everyone else of some pretty bizarre behavior before they consider the possibility that I'm here. Still—Elaina will *know* who wrote it. Maybe it will give her enough of a scare that she'll back off.

I concentrate on one of her lipsticks. The gold case trembles. This is easier each time!

The lipstick vibrates. I concentrate harder. Come on—up! Up!

But nothing happens.

Come on!

The lipstick rolls off the dresser onto the floor.

That's it. I can't move it. I'm exhausted from trying. If I try any harder, I'll fade out, I think. Damn.

If I were in a body, I would cry.


When Elaina came home, she saw the lipstick on the floor, calmly picked it up, and replaced it on the dresser. I felt so discouraged that I went back to the hospital, where I spent the night brooding.

Rose and Alison have come to see me this morning. Rose looks at me and shakes her head. "That rabbi," she says. "What a memory! I don't believe that Melissa would have said such a thing, do you?"

"Of cohse not."

"And his wife had to come to the trial. What makes him think she would have said that, then, would you tell me?"

"Thet Judy Weiss, her hair—" Alison breaks off.

Rose sits by my bed and opens her purse. She has brought a photograph of me and Howard, taken at a New Year's Eve party. I'd forgotten that I gave her a copy of that; she probably keeps a candle burning under it. She holds it up. "Look at this, Melissa," she coos. "Remember this?" She waits. My body is in a "sleep cycle"—the eyes are closed and the limbs motionless—and it doesn't respond. Not that it would anyway. Though when my body's "awake" it sometimes moves and Rose has often been convinced that I was just about to come out of my long nap. "Melissa!" Rose says, more sharply. "Don't you want to see the picture? Well, I'll just leave it here, then." She puts it on top of the respirator.

Poor Grandma Rose! If I could just lift the photograph off the respirator, then she'd know that I can hear her. I'm sure that neither she nor Alison would tell anyone about what they saw—they wouldn't want people to think they're crazy.

The photo is unframed, so it can't weigh any more than the napkin on Becky's dresser, and I had no trouble with that. I was ready to give up after last night, but that was my problem with learning to speak French and to use the travel-agency computer and to develop photographs, right? Everything takes a little practice.

"Motha," Alison says as she clicks shut her compact, "we ken't do eny more heah."

Rose sighs. "I just can't give up hoping."

I concentrate. I concentrate real hard, really I do, but nothing happens.

Shit. I *am* a failure.

Alison is insisting that Rose let her take her out for a quaint Sunday brunch, the best that Alta Vista has to offer, which isn't much, in Alison's opinion.

Rose says that Chez Alta Vista serves Sunday brunch, with wonderful eggs.

"Are you sure you want to go there?" Alison asks.

"Don't you want to go there?"

"Ef you do."

"Don't you?"

"Do you?"

They are leaving the room. As the door swings closed behind them, the photograph rises.

I wasn't even trying that time! I watch it hover in the air for a moment and then drift slowly down again. What was it? A delayed reaction?

I think about last night in Elaina's room. I felt as though I were up against a barrier, a resistance—the invisible equivalent of Elaina's prohibition "Don't play with my things." I felt that same resistance when Rose and Alison were here; but when they left, it decreased.

Maybe there's an equation. I have so much strength, or energy, to perform these little feats, but what I have to overcome is not only the inertia of the object but a counterenergy that comes from other people. Rose and Alison wouldn't want to see a photograph fly through the air. Without even being conscious of it, they resist that happening; if they had been more susceptible to the idea, I might have been able to pull it off. No wonder I couldn't lift Elaina's lipstick! She didn't even have to be there to stop me. She's stronger against me than anyone else. She's on to my tricks.

But I'm getting stronger—so if I keep working at it, who knows what I'll be able to do? Now I feel restless, eager to try something else. My telepathy clues me that Rose and Alison went to Chez Alta Vista after all, and I hop on over to join them there.

Rose is nudging with her fork at scrambled eggs and chicken livers. "They're not as good as they were when I had them before."

"Ef you don't laike them, send them back," Alison says. She is rearranging pieces of fruit salad on her plate.

"I don't want to send them back," Rose says. "But they're not as good as they were when I had them before."

I hover between Alison and her plate. During one of the long stretches in which she and Rose are surveying the restaurant, studying the other diners, I slip some of the fruit off Alison's plate, hiding sections of orange and cubes of pineapple under the napkin that covers the breadbasket, which neither Rose nor Alison has touched. When Alison looks down at her plate again, her Perrier-bottle eyes widen in dread. She thinks she's eaten the missing fruit. There's no other explanation for it. Which confirms one more attribute of my power: People will try, and try very hard, to find an explanation for whatever I do.

This is very exciting. I pop back home to see what trouble I can stir up there. First I put all the girls' Billy Death's Head albums into the Mutual Assured Destruction slipcovers. Then I stash Becky's gold-sequined halter top in the laundry hamper. I can't wait to see what she'll do after Lee Emma gets to it with a jug of Clorox.

I want to try something in Elaina's room again. But as I'm drifting downstairs, I see Daniel coming out of his room wearing his tennis outfit. I forgot; he and Craig are planning to crash the Rutherford-Nichols wedding this afternoon, so that they can talk to J. B. Nichols, the father of the bride, and ask him to invest in Software-to-Go. While I was feeling sorry for myself at the hospital last night, I overheard Daniel and Craig discussing their plans over the phone; I picked up the conversation just like I had my own little CB radio.

I think I'll go along with him.

*     *     *

The dining room and reception hall of the Alta Vista Country Club (affectionately known as "the A.V.") are closed today, but the tennis courts are open. Daniel and Craig head straight for the locker room, where they change from their tennis garb into dark suits.

Once changed, they slip easily into the reception hall, which is packed with close to 300 people and nearly as many floral arrangements. One wall of the room is glass, overlooking the pool, smooth as plastic, also closed for the day. A large white banner slung from the ceiling of the hall proclaims, "Blair and Bobby 1987."

Daniel and Craig help themselves to champagne, then gravitate toward the food table. Behind them a four-piece band is playing "I've Got You Under My Skin." Blair Nichols is dancing with her father. I drift off to check out her wedding dress; tiers of white lace flare out as she twirls around, and the brim of her white straw hat flutters.

When I catch up, Craig is swiping a cracker through some sienna-colored dip in a silver bowl. The food on the table glistens with the unnatural brightness of a magazine ad. The ice-blue of oysters, the palest pink of prawns. Salmon mousse shaped like a salmon, Jell-O molds shaped like wedding bells. Fried wonton, dolmas, chicken with pineapple and cashews, paella. A baron of beef, a turkey, a ham. Trifle, rice pudding, flan, tarts covered with slices of kiwi. The cake is five tiers of pink icing roses and ribbons draped over cream frosting. "The International Buffet," Craig sneers. "This is so fucking nouveau riche." He bites the dip off the cracker, then wedges the uneaten half back into the dip, where it sticks up like the sail of a boat. "Things have really gone downhill here since Armando left."

"There he is." The song has ended, and Daniel has spotted J. B. Nichols, leaving the dance floor.

"Don't worry," Craig murmurs. "He'll never know. It's always the women who send out the invites."

J. B. Nichols wears a white dinner jacket with a purple rose boutonniere. He is tall enough to be visible above the guests that surround him, who also seem to give him a little distance. He is sixty now, an athletic man with abundant white hair and tanned, deeply lined skin. He made his money manufacturing airline parts, but just how he got so many lucrative contracts is a subject of some interesting speculation. Especially since J.B. is usually accompanied by two extremely tall and largely built "business associates."

Daniel and Craig stare at him as he glides to the bar, where he holds out his hand and receives a glass. Then he turns and, after a moment, focuses on Daniel and Craig. He starts coming toward them. The nearer he gets, the more stiffly they stand.

"Hello, boys," he greets them cheerfully.

I see Daniel frown a little. Daniel likes to get caught at things; it relieves his sense of guilt. He's probably glad that the cardiac alarm went off. Maybe he would have found some other way of stopping himself if I hadn't beaten him to it.

"Hey." Craig clinks his glass against J.B.'s. "Just the man we wanted to see."

"To offer our congratulations," Daniel says quickly.

"Right, right," Craig agrees. "Congrats. I've known Blair for years, and—"

"And she's a really wonderful girl. A beautiful bride."

The band starts playing "Our Love Is Here to Stay."

Craig says, "You know, I bet you don't want to talk business today."

J.B. has been regarding Craig and my brother with the look of a tolerant vulture. His eyes are the murky color that has no name between blue and green and brown; it was the color I would get from mixing too many Play-Doh shades together. "Not at all, boys," he says. "Let's talk business."

"We've got our own business now," Daniel says, "and we could really use some advice—"

"Well, more than advice, really . . ." Daniel elbows Craig. "I mean, we've made some mistakes."

"But we've learned a lot," Daniel interrupts. "We know it's important to learn from your mistakes."

J.B. gulps his Bushmills. "Your dad could probably give you some good advice," he says to Daniel. "Probably wouldn't charge anything."

"We need to recapitalize," Craig explains with an indifferent shrug.

J.B. looks at them for a moment. "I bet you do," he says finally. "Tell you what, boys. You spend a couple more years walking the beat—you know, scrub a little shit off the floor with a toothbrush—then we'll talk some more."

"We haven't really told you the details," Daniel points out.

"Hey, we can't keep this offer open," Craig says, with his most unctuous smile. "I don't think this opportunity will be around much longer."

"Boy," J.B. retorts, "there's more to running a business than balling your secretary during lunch. Got it? Now I've got some real guests that I gotta talk to. My daughter's married today." A smile suddenly gives him a new face: The deep crow's feet and long, yellowish teeth make him look like someone's grandfather. He turns away, raising his Bushmills.

Daniel and Craig silently watch him go.

"We'd better get out of here," Daniel mutters finally.

"No way," Craig retorts. "That asshole. Who the fuck does he think he is? You know what? A century ago *his* family was probably stealing chickens while mine was hanging out with the Saxe-Coburgs."

*Our* family was probably pulling up potatoes in the Ukraine. I'm wondering if I could splash some of Craig's champagne onto his turquoise contact lenses.

I can see from Daniel's face that he isn't thrilled by Craig's

remark, either. But Craig isn't looking at Daniel; he is surveying the line of single women who hover near the dance floor.
"The least we can do is meet some ladies," he says. "We can
take a drive. Drown our sorrows."

Daniel is looking ill.

"*Hola!*" Johnny Nichols is swaggering toward them. His
face is ruddy from alcohol and a recent trip to Sun Valley; he is
carrying a glass of champagne. "*Qué pasa, muchachos?* Long time
no laid eyes." He leans over to rest his free hand on the table; it
lands in a bowl of fruit salad. "Oh, Lordy," he giggles. "Look
what I do."

Daniel offers him his red handkerchief.

"Thanks, Dan." Johnny hiccups as he wipes off his palm.
"Can't believe the twat is getting married. Wonder if Bobby boy
knows she's had herpes since she was twelve."

"He must," Craig observes. "Everyone else does."

"Before that, she was a nice kid." Johnny winks. Daniel
and Craig look at each other. "There's my man Binko. We've
got some biz." He winks again. "Either of you want a real
pretty new cassette deck, I can get you one cheap."

He's off. Daniel stares glumly into his fluted glass. I'm sure
he's thinking about Dmitri's. But if Craig has business on his
mind, he's still trying not to let it ruin his day. "I wonder if
Ginny Holloway is a virgin," he muses as he studies the long-
legged blonde dancing in the blue dress. The band has started
playing "I Get a Kick out of You."

Daniel sips his champagne. I remember the last night I was
in a body, how I threw a drink at him, or tried to. I suddenly
want to do it again, like I owe him one, since the glass was
empty that night. And let's not forget his stunt in my hospital
room! What if I gave his arm a little jiggle? Could I do it?

As he raises his arm and tilts his head back, I concentrate.
Yes! His arm jerks just as if someone gave it a little push. (And
someone did, of course.) A gulp or two of the champagne drib-

bles from the rim of Daniel's glass down his chin and then onto his shirt.

"What did you do that for?" he demands of Craig.

"Do what for?" Craig looks at him impatiently.

Craig has been standing two feet away from Daniel, but Daniel would have seen Craig only as a convex blur through the rim of his glass. Daniel—like Alison—is looking for a logical explanation for what happened. "You have a really *sick* sense of humor," Daniel says.

"Oh, I do, do I?"

"Yes, you do, and you've got a lot of stupid ideas. Like coming here in the first place. And not only that, but I told you in the beginning that we were undercapitalized."

"Well, la-de-fucking-da, listen to Mr. Businessman. Mr. *Forbes* Magazine."

"At least my family's had to *work* for what we have."

"Mr. Fortune Five Hundred. Like you take off for the coal mines every day."

"That's not the point. You—you don't understand anything, and what's more, you're a—"—Daniel's forehead puckers into that babyish expression of his—"a weenie."

Craig lunges at Daniel. Daniel steps back, but Craig grabs the lapels of Daniel's suit and Daniel thrusts his hands out, pushing him away—and I concentrate on the cashew chicken salad and it flies up and there isn't time to aim it but it lands exactly on top of Craig's head.

I hear gasps and shrieks and see that people are looking now. But it happened so quickly that no one could really see the cashew chicken salad sail through the air all by itself.

I think Daniel thinks he did it. He looks so guilty. Well, he probably *wishes* he'd done it.

Craig stands with eyes closed and fists clenched as a piece of bell pepper drips from his hair to his shoulder.

"I'm *ending* this partnership," Daniel announces.

The band has stopped playing. The other guests have fallen silent and stand watching.

"What's the trouble, boys?"

Two of J.B.'s "business associates" have appeared. One is white, the other black—but each is approximately six-foot-four and could lift a small giraffe with one hand.

Craig opens his eyes and now a slimy chunk of chicken falls from his head to his tie, leaving a brown smear on his nose.

"There's no trouble, sir," Daniel says. "We were just leaving."

But the two tall gentlemen follow close behind as my brother and his erstwhile friend slink out.

That night, with a great deal of concentration (enough to make me almost dizzy), I am once again able to track down Elaina at Drew's. I've often guessed that she was at his apartment, but her resistance to my powers is such that I couldn't even transport myself there when I tried.

Tonight I've made it. There she is, sitting up in Drew's bed, wearing his bathrobe and leafing through *TV Guide*. An ice bucket on the nightstand holds a bottle of champagne. "There's been a lot of things misplaced at our house lately," Elaina observes, dog-earing a page and putting the *Guide* down on the nightstand next to the ice bucket. "I wonder if Paddy O'Flanagan has turned into a kleptocatiac."

Drew lies with his head in Elaina's lap. He pulls the belt of her bathrobe—his bathrobe—across his upper lip, like a navy blue moustache, and breathes deeply, as if to see if the robe smells like her yet. "We'll leave California," he says. "We'll go back east, stay with my family. I'll start a practice there. You can bring the girls. I'll be a good father to them. And it's time Daniel was on his own."

I guess he's just lost it completely. Wonked out, as my sisters would say. A few months ago he was such a fanatic doctor—is that kind of passion always a source of madness?

Elaina doesn't laugh at his idea. "What about Melissa?"

"Let it go. Let Jonathan deal with her."

Elaina sighs. She skims the fair hair on Drew's arm with the tip of her sculpted nail. "I wish I could, but if we left together *now,* don't you see, it would make your testimony sort of . . . oh, I don't know, you'll have to help me—what's the word I'm looking for?"

"Suspicious?" Drew asks. Under his tan, he's looking a little green.

"That's the word," Elaina says.

"So we have to stick it out to the end," Drew says grimly. "All right." He stares at the ceiling as if looking for a burning cross. Then, "Elaina, why *did* Daniel go to the hospital in the middle of the night?"

Elaina sips from her glass of champagne. "I think he likes the mashed potatoes at the cafeteria."

"No, seriously."

"To get his blood pressure checked?"

Drew sighs.

Elaina sets her glass down, then scratches Drew's chest. "You know what, peewee doll?"

"What?"

"Oh, it's nothing. I just had this funny dream last night."

"What was it?"

"I dreamed that Melissa . . . well . . . I can't say it. I'm superstitious."

Drew turns his head and looks at her. "You mean that she . . ."

Elaina nods. She takes Drew's chin in one hand, squeezes. "You are so cute," she says. Then she scratches behind his ear, and he closes his eyes. I have the fantasy of picking up the bottle of champagne and cracking it over her head. But I wouldn't do it even if I could. I wouldn't stoop to it. "Just think," she purrs. "It wouldn't matter what you said then. We could put all of this behind us. And poor Melissa wouldn't be suffering anymore."

Drew opens his eyes. They are wide and pale blue. His pupils are tiny and his gaze is fixed, as if he were dead.

"And poor Melissa wouldn't be suffering anymore." She leans closer to him, murmuring. "That's what you're supposed to do, keep her from suffering." She leans closer still, bites his ear. His face contorts in pain, then in pleasure.

When they start to kiss, I feel what in the vocabulary of the body would be described as terminal nausea. Yuck. I want to split. But I wish I could get dad to see this!

And when I think of dad, I realize that he's at the office, planning his appeal. I decide to join him there.

If you were to drive down Highway 80, you would see the Silverstein Building stippled with lights. The density of lighted windows is greatest near Jonathan's office, representing the M.B.A.'s and J.D.'s who work in proximity to it, and who dream of one day being chosen crown prince by the heirless monarch. As if they can emulate my father merely by keeping his hours.

But it's Sunday night and there aren't even many syc-ophants to keep Jonathan company. In his corner suite, the buzz of the fluorescent lights is faintly audible, and Jonathan labors under their greenish glow. His lips are puckered lovingly close to his pocket Norelco. (He has a habit of dictating reminders to himself on this miniature tape recorder; when I was talking to him, he sometimes whipped it out to say something like "Talk to Gold Coast Savings about refinancing the Pinecrest Apartments.") Right now he is dictating a letter to the dean of the medical school that Drew attended.

Jonathan has replaced Debbie Meyers (who went into labor

the day after Judge Picone's verdict) with Arthur McGee, a San Francisco attorney who specializes in appeals and is working on the constitutional angle: the right of privacy and equal protection. Jonathan doesn't disapprove of this tactic, but he also has other ideas, which I've heard him discuss with Arthur. Jonathan is investigating Drew's past, looking for a history of instability. He has learned from interviewing other emergency-room staff that Drew was alone with me for about twenty minutes, during which time I might possibly have awakened. Still, should the case be remanded for a retrial, he'll have the opportunity to impeach Drew as a witness, and he hopes that he can find some motive for Drew to have lied.

I'll give it to him. I ruffle daddy's black-and-gray curls—he always liked to have his head scratched—though all he feels is a tickle, and he pushes his pen through his hair without looking up.

Now I concentrate. I let myself become the message. *Go see the doctor. Go see him now.* If I can get dad to go over there now, he'll catch Elaina and Drew in the act. I can't get to Elaina directly, but maybe I can do it through the back door, as it were.

*Go see Drew. Go see Dr. Harding.* Jonathan is already suspicious of Drew in a vague, unsettled way, and that will help me, I'm sure. *Dr. Harding, Dr. Harding.* Strange images are passing through me: daddy pushing me on the swing at Lake Merritt Park so that the daytime moon was under my knees—and the cobwebby hotel in Barcelona across from the train station, where Howard and I fought about whether to leave a day early. *Daddy, daddy, daddy. Go see Drew.*

Suddenly Jonathan shoves his chair away from his desk, and I know that I've finally gotten through to him.

I move like thought. I am back in Drew's apartment, and I see that Elaina has just left. Damn! Damn! How did she get away from me? MEWS—Mother's Early Warning System. She dressed hastily, for I notice her panties are under the couch.

She must have tossed them there during the pregame warm-up.

I pop outside, where I see her slipping into her Cutlass. In a few moments she is cruising down Lakeside Drive while Jonathan's Volvo passes her, going in the other direction. All they would be able to see of each other are two blurred yellow lights.


When Drew's intercom buzzes, he immediately pushes the button to unlock the downstairs door. I'm sure he begged Elaina to spend the night; he probably hopes she's relented and come back after making him suffer the appropriate length of time. He doesn't seem to notice that the tread coming down the hall is too heavy and the knock is too sharp, and he flings open the door.

"Jonathan!" Drew exclaims, his voice high and squeaky. He forces the register down. "Good to see you." He is wearing his underwear and a silk kimono, which is open to reveal his smooth chest, and he fumbles, trying to close the kimono with one hand while he pumps my father's hand with the other. "Come in."

Jonathan enters silently and plunks down on the burlap sofa. There is a box of See's candy on the coffee table, which Drew had put out for Elaina, and Jonathan quickly pops a whole one into his mouth.

"Glad you didn't come any earlier, Jon," Drew says, perching on a barstool. "I just got back from the gym. Had a good workout." He flexes one arm. "Haven't had time to take a shower. Can I get you a drink?"

Jonathan stares at the box of candy as if studying a chessboard. Then his hand darts out and grabs another piece.

"Can I get you a drink?" Drew asks again.

"No, thank you."

Drew's eyelids are fluttering. "If you don't mind, I'm going to have a quick one." He slides off the barstool, belting his kimono, then pads into the kitchen, which is separated from the living room by a counter. "You know, old man," he says, "I hope you're not angry that I testified for Elaina. Had to do what I thought was right, you know." He unscrews a bottle of Glenfiddich and pours some into a shot glass.

"Right." Jonathan is weighing a third piece of chocolate in his palm. "I wanted to talk to you about that."

"Shoot, Jon." Drew resumes his seat on the barstool and raises the shot glass. "Here's to better times, hmm?" He knocks off the shot in one gulp and coughs. "I really like it straight— how about you?"

Jonathan purses his lips while he chews. "I don't drink much," he says finally. "It keeps me from thinking clearly."

"Right. Of course. Neither do I." In spite of Drew's repeated insistence that Elaina confront Jonathan with the details of their affair, he doesn't look too thrilled with the idea of telling Jonathan himself. Maybe he thinks Jonathan has been outside all evening, waiting for Elaina to leave. I'm sure he wishes Jonathan would get this over with.

But Jonathan seems determined to make him wait. After sucking some chocolate off a finger, he looks up and asks, "Where's your bathroom?"

"Right in here!" Drew gestures and, with arms outstretched, leads the way through the bedroom, where the tepid champagne still sits on the nightstand. Then he returns to the living room, where he begins to pace. He stops and looks down at his hands. They are trembling. What could be worse for a doctor? He presses his hands together, harder and harder, until they look numb. Then he bounds into the kitchen and unscrews the top of the Glenfiddich.

Alone with Drew, I feel my energy rise. Self-hatred has corroded him, made him vulnerable. I feel as if I could do anything.

As soon as he turns his back to the living room, I go to

work. I concentrate on Elaina's panties, pushing them out from under the sofa in little spurts. It isn't hard. Now they're lying on the carpet, half-under the coffee table.

Then with one big *oomph,* I lift them up and drop them next to the candy box—just in time, for I feel the resistance rising as Jonathan lumbers back from the bathroom. He plops down on the sofa again and reaches for piece number four, his fingers touching the chocolate before he sees the panties. It's just a white nylon pair, with a rather worn elastic band, but you aren't married to someone for twenty-five years without being able immediately to recognize their underwear.

He picks them up by the band. Drew is coming back from the kitchen, and Jonathan looks up into the glassy, terrified blueness of his eyes. Drew stops, tries to say something; only garbled sounds come from his throat, like a tape recording played very slowly.

Jonathan's face is red. His heavy black brows come together hard. "Things are clearer to me now," he says. He stands, and drops the panties into the wide, square pocket of his gray chalkstripe suit.

"I—" Drew manages to say. He holds out the arm with the shot glass. "I can't imagine—I can't understand—"

Jonathan is lumbering past him, with his nothing-can-distract-me walk. "Wait, Jonathan," Drew squeaks.

But Drew should know better. God knows I do. When Jonathan has started the Walk, nothing can stop him. He's gone.

Jonathan only pauses with his hand on the door. "You've practiced your last day of medicine," he says.

# 9

Alison has never been in Jonathan's office before. And there's a flicker of something on her face, a bitter downturning of the mouth, as she follows Valerie down the hall, which is lined with the glassed-in offices of the junior executives. (The glass allows Jonathan to check up on everyone whenever he strolls to the bathroom.) Alison frowns at Valerie's broad behind as they go past faceless heads locked in front of VDTs, past clicking printers, past ringing phones and half-drunk cups of coffee, all the way to the corner suite.

"Hi, Al." Jonathan is poring over a large volume of statutes.

"Please." Alison motions for him not to get up as she sits.

"Hmm." Jonathan turns the page of the book without looking up. "I wanted to ask you if you could stay in town for a while," he mutters as he squints through his reading glasses and traces a line with one finger.

"Ah." Alison tilts her head.

"I need you to testify again."

"But . . ."

He glances up. "There's going to be a retrial soon."

"Of cohse." But Alison could go back to New York and then return, so she must believe that this invitation has larger meaning. I, too, am suspicious.

Jonathan slams the heavy book shut. He jerks his neck as if

184

trying to wrench it from his collar. "That damn doctor," he declares. "I'm going to have his ass in a sling."

"Relly?" One of Alison's brows forms a parabola. "Why?"

"He lied about Melissa."

"I've never laiked thet doctor," Alison sniffs. "He's just so . . . What meks you think he lied?"

Jonathan's arm falls like the blade of a guillotine on a pile of papers. "I just know, that's all," he says. His eyes are like bullets.

"I thought there might be some raison. I thought maybe you thought . . ." Alison shrugs and looks down.

"He botched up Melissa's case." Jonathan rises and paces behind his desk. "She might still be all right if it weren't for that— shmuck. I talked to the chairman of the hospital board this morning, told him if he wanted to keep his accreditation—"

"I understand how you fale," Alison says in a monotone. But does she? I think I understand Alison now: She believes in love but cannot feel it; a simple incapacity, just like some people happen to be color-blind. But she doesn't know she can't feel it, any more than the color-blind person can conceive of the color red. She only knows that people are given to a set of behaviors that, observed from the outside, constitute loving relationships. These behaviors include putting roses on an American Express Gold Card, surprise trips to Paris, and appearing in public with one light hand on the beloved's arm. So consider Alison's tragedy: She needs to be loved as much as anyone, and she needs the real thing—no imitation with a pirated designer label will do. Her need is what gives her that anorexic look, as much as her starvation diet. "But I hope you don't think Elaina . . ."

Jonathan does not reply. He keeps pacing. Why doesn't he denounce Elaina for the adulteress she is? I am confused by the way his brows are pressed together, the anger that seems to be more than just anger. Is he hurt, ashamed? Why should he care? It's only Elaina's body, dad—that's worthless! But maybe this discovery has started him wondering about earlier years, made him unable to deny suspicions he's had in the past. Maybe it has made him wonder about many things that shouldn't be wondered about. Perhaps even now he is struggling to find some way to reassure himself that this is Elaina's first affair. The stress of what happened to me, the trial, something like that. "How's your business?" he asks Alison.

"Well . . ." Alison laughs joylessly. "I'm in a . . . very competitive fee-ald. You knuw, I always hoped Melissa might—"

"May I make a suggestion?" Jonathan, standing behind his chair, squeezes its leather upholstery. He seems to relax a little, his face regaining its normal, puttyish color. "Have you thought about combining a catering service with the modeling? You could call it Messes and Dresses. What do you think?"

"I don't know much about catering," Alison replies. This surely isn't what she wants to hear, and I doubt she's listening as Jonathan goes on to describe how he taught himself about land syndication. Alison has always been proud of being an independent woman, but after twenty-five years she probably feels she's proved her point. She could move the agency to California; or she could sell it. If there were a reason.

Jonathan is pacing again. "Then in the late Sixties I saw a piece of raw land in Shasta County—"

Alison interrupts. "About Elaina and thet doctor . . ."

Jonathan stops and looks at her, as if surprised to see her there. After a moment he asks, "How's your mother?"

"She's . . ." The laugh again, bitter and violent, like tin cans dragged behind a car. "My mother thinks vary highly of you, you knuw. I sometimes think she wishes she'd married you herself." As Alison's laugh passes through me, rattling me like wind through a venetian blind, I absorb her thoughts: that *it almost worked out* between her and Jonathan—but then it didn't, because he was weak and Elaina was an opportunist, and quick.

I watch Alison's Ferragamo bob up and down and I wonder at the little turns of all our lives, the wrong exits off the freeway and the tiny steps off the ledges of tall buildings. The two Percodan in a nightstand drawer. I know Alison thinks that letting Jonathan go was the pivotal mistake of her life. But the actors have reassembled. And I just bet she's thinking she can rectify that mistake.

That evening, Jeff calls our house. In the kitchen, Daniel answers the phone.

"This is Jeff Lindner," Jeff says. "May I speak to Becky, please?"

"Did you try *her* number?"

"There was no answer."

"Then she's not here," Daniel says gruffly. Becky and Leah are at a rehearsal.

"What time do you expect her back?"

"Who is this?"

"Jeff Lindner," Jeff repeats patiently.

"Am I supposed to know who you are?" Daniel probably imagines someone like the video-game champion, a beefy boy in a leather vest, with pimply skin and greasy hair. Daniel worries that Becky might be a bit of a tramp; I heard him say once that she was too young to go out with boys who have their own cars. I think he wants to protect her, regrets that he couldn't protect another sister of his who shall remain nameless.

"My father . . ."—Jeff hesitates—"is Martin Lindner."

"Oh." This does nothing to raise Daniel's opinion of Jeff.

"Would you give Becky a message for me?" Jeff asks, a little less patiently.

"Huh."

"Tell her I'll pick her up Friday at seven," Jeff says.

"Yeah." Daniel wraps the phone cord, like *tefillin*, around his arm. "Listen," he begins, "my sister is only sixteen, you know."

"Yes," Jeff says, "I know."

"Yeah, okay," Daniel says. "Okay, I'll give her the message."

Daniel finds the phone pad: Elaina used it to prop up Paddy's water dish. He hunts for a pencil, finally locating one that rolled under the refrigerator. I am wondering if I can repeat what I accomplished with Jonathan last night, and sort of scramble Daniel's thoughts so that he writes down the wrong message. Like what? Well, what if he told Becky that Jeff was coming on Saturday instead?

I concentrate. *Saturday, Saturday, Saturday.* I'm just feeling mischievous; Jeff will arrive unexpectedly on Friday night and Becky will have the avocado pack on her face or the mayonnaise treatment in her hair.

*Jeff will be here* . . . Daniel writes. "Saturday," he says aloud, and then looks startled to hear himself speak. *Saturday,* he writes.

That wasn't hard. An insignificant message doesn't meet with much resistance. If confronted with the mistake, I wouldn't be surprised if Daniel insisted that Jeff actually told him Saturday.

The phone rings again, and Daniel picks it up while he is affixing the message above the phone with the Scotch tape he found in the paper-bag bin. "Daniel?"

"Oh, hi, grandma," Daniel says. (At least we aren't one of those families that has special names for the grandparents, like "Mia and Dada," or "Nanny and Bud.")

"Is your mother there?"

"No, grandma."

"Are you sure?"

Daniel looks at the ceiling. In fact, Elaina is in bed, eating the toast that Daniel brought her a few minutes before, but she left specific instructions not to be disturbed if Rose called. "I'm sure, grandma."

"Where is she?"

"She's . . . she's getting her nails done."

"So late at night?"

"It's a special place that's open late."

"I've never heard of such a thing." Pause. "I don't see how she can do that at a time like this, do you?"

"A time like what?"

"You know what I mean."

"I'll tell her you called," Daniel says hopefully.

"Have you been to the hospital lately?"

"No, grandma."

"Are you still going in the middle of the night?"

"No, grandma."

"What were you doing there so late?"

"I . . . I wanted to see Melissa."

"So late?"

"Dad said we could go whenever we wanted."

"But so late?"

"Why *not*?" he counters. "Listen, grandma, I can't talk now, I've got some quiche in the microwave. It's going to be radioactive if I don't take it out."

"Well, then, go," Rose tells him.

"I'll talk to you later," he says.

"Fine."

"Goodbye."

"Goodbye."

"Goodbye."

He waits for her to hang up, but she sits silent on the line. He can hear her breathing, and hear Elaina's breaths, on the extension, in between Rose's. Finally he puts the receiver down.

"Danabable!" comes the shriek from upstairs. "Who was that?"

"Grandma Rose!" Daniel shouts.

"I can't hear you!"

"Grandma Rose!"

"Don't shout!"

Daniel sighs and heads upstairs. I hop on his shoulder and go up with him.

Just as we get to Elaina's bedroom—she is propped against her pillows, applying glue to a crack in one of her nails—the phone rings again.

"Do you want me to get that?" Daniel offers, reaching for the blue Princess phone on her nightstand. "It might be grandma again."

"Uh . . ." Elaina studies her nail. Then, "No, wait, no." She stops him, placing her hand on his wrist just as he touches the receiver. "I think I'll get it this time." She picks up the phone in the middle of its second ring. "Hello?" Her eyes dart back and forth. "Oh, hi, Paula," she says after a moment.

This just confirms my suspicion that Elaina is a little clairvoyant herself. Because the caller is actually Dr. Drew.

Daniel has stretched out on the foot of the bed, head propped on one elbow.

"Just a second, *Paula*," Elaina says. She covers the mouthpiece with her hand. "Danabable, perfect child, would you make me some more toast?"

Daniel looks at the plate, where the slices he just brought her remain untouched, the butter soaking into the blackened surface that Elaina prefers.

"I let these get cold," she explains.

Daniel frowns at the mouthpiece of the phone. He glances back at the toast. "You know, Mouse," he says, eyes averted, "I was about to go out."

"Really? Where are you going?"

"Uh . . . Dmitri's."

"Then never mind, it's all right."

There is a long pause between Daniel and Elaina. "It's all right," she says again.

"Good," Daniel says, rising. "I don't know when I'll be home."

Elaina watches him sashay out of her room and start down the stairs before she uncovers the mouthpiece again. "Hello, peewee doll," she says.

"Elaina." On the phone, Drew is fairly wheezing. "He knows."

"Whose nose is that, dear?"

"Elaina, Jonathan knows about us."

Elaina drops her nail glue into the tray on her nightstand. "Well, he's so nosy," she says, but her voice sounds as though it's coming from rather far away.

"What are we going to do?" Drew pleads. "I didn't go to the hospital today. I was afraid to. I called in sick." So much for Drew's plans to declare his love for Elaina to the world! I almost feel sorry for him; I know what it is to look inward and not find the extraordinary virtues you hoped were there.

"If you were sick," Elaina says, still in that faraway voice, while she stares at herself in the mirror over the dressing table across the room, her eyes wide and motionless, "then a hospital would be a good place to go, don't you think?"

"You've got to come over here, so we can talk."

"Oh, gosh." Elaina raises the finger with the mended nail. "Oh, gee. You know, peewee doll, I don't think I can do that. See, I just had a little accident. I hurt my hand."

"My God, are you all right?"

"Oh, yes, yes, don't worry about me."

"Come over tomorrow then. Soon."

"No, peewee doll, I don't think so."

"What do you mean?"

"I mean, I think . . . I don't think . . . oh, God, I can't say it."

"Elaina," Drew cries, panicked, "I have to see you!"

"You're better off without me." Elaina sniffles. "I always hurt the people I love the most."

"I'll kill myself!" Drew cries.

"Peewee doll," Elaina says, her voice warmer now, "you're making me feel so guilty."

"Elaina—"

"We can't be selfish. We have to think of Melissa first. Do you know what this will do to our case?"

Of all the low-down hypocritical excuses. If she came up with anything but that, I could stand it.

On the other end of the line, Drew swallows.

"It's only temporary," Elaina croons. "But you mustn't say anything to anyone. We're in this together, to help Melissa."

Drew is taking deep, slow breaths.

"Everything we've done is to help Melissa. That's what makes it all right, don't you see that?"

"You . . . you're right, Elaina."

"Try to imagine how a mother feels." She caresses him with her words, the way she would stroke Paddy O'Flanagan's fur. "If you-know-who can prove anything about us, then poor Melissa could be stuck like this forever. Would you want that?"

"N-no."

"We know what Melissa would want, don't we?" Elaina rocks back and forth. "When she's safe, and taken care of, then it won't matter who knows. Then we can think of ourselves."

I know what she's telling him. I should be angry, and I guess I am, but her lullaby voice is so soothing, so reassuring— like syrup over pancakes. I soak it in.


The steady, insistent yapping of our neighbors' poodle draws me down to Jonathan's study. Daniel has slipped in here; he is sitting in the captain's chair at Jonathan's desk, looking out the window to the neighbors'—the Grimbys'—side yard.

The Grimbys' house is white stucco, with pillars in front and grillwork over the windows. This is the predominant architectural style of Alta Vista, evoking the antebellum South.

Daniel absently strokes the green blotter on Jonathan's desk. The study has not been disturbed since Jonathan left. Lee Emma has dusted more relentlessly than before, and the odor of furniture polish, that Daniel associates with Jonathan, makes our father seem almost present. Besides Grandpa Abe's letter opener, there are a few ornaments on the desk and bookshelf: figures of coral and jade, inlaid boxes. These are gifts from Jonathan's protégés, brought back from their vacations. Most of the gifts remain in the trunk of Jonathan's Volvo; they will probably be there when he trades in the car. Jonathan disapproves of vacations anyway.

There is also a picture of the four of us, taken ten years ago: Posed by a photographer, we are pressed too close together, our smiles propped up as if by invisible toothpicks and our arms bent at unnatural angles. But none of Daniel's offerings—monogrammed pens, pencil holders, leather appointment books—have ever made it this far. Several years ago Daniel stopped giving Jonathan presents. On Hanukkah and Father's Day, he shakes Jonathan's hand and offers good wishes in what is meant to be a hearty, manly voice.

Now Daniel picks up an ivory figure of an elderly Chinese monarch: It is a white king, a stray from an ancient chess set. Half the pieces were lost when we moved, years ago, from Berkeley to Alta Vista. (Elaina was in charge of packing.) Jonathan let Daniel and me play with the chess set when we were little. I remember one time we hid the pieces around the family apartment complex where we lived—the bishop behind the garbage can, and the rook in the drainpipe—in preparation for a game of treasure hunt.

Suddenly I know that Daniel is remembering this, too. I see his image, almost identical to mine, of the unworking fountain in the lobby of the apartment complex; both of us can remember the stone base, but the shape of the upper tier is lost. As the two images merge—like two negatives pushed together—I feel a pounding, like a heartbeat, that grows louder and louder, and I realize that I am in Daniel's mind.

And so as he sets down the white king and picks up the silver-and-emerald letter opener, I know that he is remembering how he once took the letter opener from Jonathan's desk so he could play "warriors." When Jonathan found out, he spanked Daniel—one swift blow to the rear—one of the few times he ever hit any of us. It was dangerous, Jonathan said, and Daniel must never touch Grandpa Abe's letter opener again. Ever since, Daniel has admired its sinister gleam from a safe distance.

But now there is no one here to see. Daniel barely touches the handle with the tips of his fingers and slowly turns it on its side, watching the diamonds that encircle the emerald shoot out beams of light. *How much is it worth?* I hear him think. Easily $20,000—probably more. Enough to pay back the Bay City Bank. And who would know? Who could prove it? Lee Emma might be held responsible, or Elaina. And if Jonathan really wanted it, he would have taken it with him when he moved out—for surely he is never coming back.

I should tell Daniel not to do it. I don't know if he'd listen or not—a lot depends on how much he wants to listen. But he listened to Elaina, and she almost got him to kill me. So why should I help him anyway? I don't know. Because here, in his mind, it feels warm and cozy, like snuggling under the covers in the morning. Because here, in his mind, I think of him sobbing as he tried to pick Goodyear Blimp, the dying cat, up off the road.

Daniel raises the letter opener and balances it on its tip, twirling it slowly. I hear it sing in the sweet contralto of Elaina's voice: *Take me, take me.* I wait. Daniel's hearbeat is getting louder, faster, like the drums of an approaching army. It's too hot in here now. I want out.

Suddenly Daniel lets the letter opener fall on the blotter. The moment has passed, and he's safe, with no help from me. I slip out of his mind, feeling as though I'm gasping for air.

Daniel looks up at the ceiling. Soon Elaina will start calling for him again. There's a look almost of hatred on his face. I can see that he wants to escape, but I know he doesn't want to see Craig, and I have a feeling he doesn't want to see any of his other friends, either. His other friends will only offer him beer and cocaine, and tell him stories of sexual conquests and feats of tanning on the beaches of Maui and Puerto Vallarta.

But he refolds his red handkerchief and gets up to leave. Where is he going? I have a guess, anyway: Dmitri's Number One. Daniel doesn't like to lie to Elaina.

Later that evening I feel drawn to the hospital; I have the presentiment that my body might be getting sick. Call me a hypochondriac—but let's face it, I'm not exactly at fighting weight these days.

The first thing I see when I arrive at Mt. Moriah is Drew, slinking along the corridor in his squeaky white shoes.

In the pocket of his white coat is a syringe and a bottle. Demerol.

Aha. There's something seductive about murder. I almost feel aroused. Elaina is the one with the real power over Drew, but remember that he met me under inauspicious circumstances. If things had been different . . .

When he reaches my room, Drew turns and gives the night nurses a sickly version of his Pepsodent smile. "Gotta check on Melissa Silverstein," he says. They look at him. One is a bleached blonde, very fat, and the other is tall and jointy, with a wide mouth. The tall one is leaning over the fat blonde, who is filling out a report.

"You know," Drew goes on, his hands behind his back, pressing against the door, "she needs to be checked on a lot."

"Sure, doctor," the fat nurse says. "Do you need any help?"

"No! No!" Drew whips his head quickly from side to side. "I'd prefer not to be disturbed."

"Whatever you say, doctor," the fat one says, raising one eyebrow in the direction of the other nurse.

Drew enters and closes the door carefully behind him. He approaches my bed slowly. I can hear his breathing; it is slow and regular, but scratchy, like the *whoosh* in the *whoosh*-click of the respirator.

In his presence I feel my powers increase. His mind doesn't resist me—it collaborates. It feels soft as a sponge. I can see the thirst for disaster on his smooth, open face.

He pokes the needle into the bottle of Demerol and turns it upside down, tilting his head up to the light. There is a layer of perspiration like shattered glass on his forehead. He slowly retracts the plunger of the syringe.

That's when my IV bottle starts to vibrate.

At first Drew doesn't seem to notice; he just bites his lip, as if his body knew that something was wrong but his mind was still ignoring it. But when the IV bottle detaches itself from its holder and makes a little circle, he gasps, and the syringe and the Demerol fall from his hands.

The IV is motionless now. Drew shakes his head as if trying to cast the image from his mind. He's probably afraid he's going crazy, but I think he's been worried about that for a while now. He takes a breath, and it seems that he's hanging on to the edge of reality, still thinking of the job he has to do. He reaches down for the syringe and bottle, which hasn't broken. But before he can get to them, I snatch them up. It's not hard for me at all, and it's getting easier by the moment. It's as if the more I do with him, the more he wants. The syringe rises and makes little jabs at him. Drew backs away, his mouth clamping silently open and shut.

By this time I've got the bed rocking like a hobbyhorse, as much as I can without pulling out any of the tubes. I raise up the blanket—exposing my knobby, curled-up frame—and let it hover in the air. Next to the bed is a vase of roses that Jonathan sent and I raise it up and twirl it around and then the flowers rise out of the vase and flatten out and circle like a merry-go-round, a technical feat that makes me feel rather proud.

Drew retreats toward the window—but as soon as his back touches it, I rattle the blinds and send the drapes flying out. He jumps up and bounds away, his eyes like blue Frisbees, a scream snuffed out in his throat.

I wish I could muster up a deep, hollow, ghostlike laugh, but audio effects are a bit beyond me. Still, it's an adequate show. I bet I could even do the laugh with a little practice. Did he think he could mess with a Silverstein, a Miller? I'm still my mother's daughter, and my father's, too—dead or alive or in between—and we may be crazy but we know how to get things done. Little fool! Don't you see who I am? I'm not just some dipstick college girl anymore. I'm Melissa Silverstein! I'll stop you all, all of you—none of you will ever hurt me again!

When the nurses come to check on Drew a little later, they find him kneeling by my bed, muttering to himself and fingering the IV line as if it were a string of rosary beads.

The next day, the chief of hospital administration explains to Jonathan that the medical and moral pressures of the trial have caused Drew to become overly tired.

"Bullshit," Jonathan says.

The chief further assures Jonathan that Drew has been suspended from his staff position, and he apologizes for the vase that Drew broke.

But Jonathan isn't satisfied.

So that afternoon, Jonathan's on the phone talking to his Mt. Moriah connection. "Bert," he says as he tilts back his chair.

"About this Dr. Harding. I want him before a medical review board."

That's a problem, Jonathan's friend tells him, because the hospital wants it known only that Dr. Harding is taking a leave of absence for medical reasons. Mt. Moriah is already hurting from the publicity they've gotten over my case. "We're not overlooking his incompetence," Bert quaveringly assures him. "We just want to wait a while, till things sort of die down, you see, and then if we haul Harding's ass over the coals, it won't get so much press coverage."

Jonathan bites his fingernail. "Maybe we can have Harding committed," he says, as if to himself. "That would render him incompetent as a witness." Daddy's really getting out the big guns. I love it. Maybe he'll have Drew kidnapped or murdered. *I* certainly wouldn't lose any sleep over that, especially since I don't sleep. But I'd be even happier if I thought Jonathan's anger were all because of me, and had nothing to do with Drew's affair with Elaina. I think he's crazy if he cares what she does. But even I'll admit that Elaina warned him about this. She said that if he neglected her too much, she would have to look elsewhere for attention. Maybe—just maybe—Jonathan feels that he's a little bit at fault, too. He's often seemed to regard her with the indifferent respect he has for valuable art: something essentially useless, which is appreciating below the prime rate.

I hover next to Jonathan's ear, then nestle in the receiver. My awareness spills out and down the phone lines. And now I'm picking up a conversation between Daniel and Craig—just like I did a few nights ago, while I was brooding at the hospital.

"We've got to *do* something," I hear Daniel say.

"What you mean *we*, kemosabe?" Craig replies.

I can see Daniel at the pay phone at Dmitri's Number One. He must be feeling desperate if he called Craig. I wish daddy could hear them talking, too.

"Next week they'll be coming to cart away the pizza ovens," Daniel is saying. "Dmitri is going to choke on his pepperoni."

"Yeah, well, I'm going skiing with Suzie," Craig replies. I don't see where Craig is, but probably at home.

"Wait just a second, Bert," Jonathan says.

Bert obediently hushes up in the middle of his explanation of why committing Drew Harding to a mental institution might cause people to ask questions.

Jonathan moistens his lips. He stares out the window at the freeway. He's hearing the conversation, too! How did I do it? Perhaps the wishes of people like me are a physical force, like gravity or entropy. Or like radio waves: You can use them, once you know they're there.

"You didn't want pops to find out about the loan," Craig snorts, "but he's going to find out now."

"Don't you want to come help me plead with his friend, the banker?" Daniel has managed a joking tone. "Maybe he'll let me trade my virtue for an extension."

"I don't think your virtue's worth twenty thousand," Craig says.

"Hey—"—Daniel's joviality is sounding more like sarcasm—"we could offer him yours." He adds, "Just show me how to use a little of that Newhouse charm."

"After the other night, I show you how to use my toilet."

On the other end of the phone, Daniel says nothing. Jonathan is staring hard at the freeway.

"I gotta go, Dan." Craig's voice again. "It's been real. See ya."

"Is everything all right?" Bert asks my father. He hasn't heard any of Daniel's conversation. Why should he? My wish was directed at Jonathan. Maybe in the state I'm in, the boundary between wishes and actions starts to dissolve. That's the really frightening idea. I always knew that my powers would become greater the longer I stayed here, but I'm starting to feel like Alta Vista's answer to Typhoid Mary.

Jonathan tilts his chair forward again. "Fine, Bert," he replies. He waits a moment, not saying anything, but Daniel and Craig have hung up. Jonathan says, "Bert, I'll get back to you."

After he hangs up, Jonathan sits forward in the chair, legs outstretched, staring out the window at the Emeryville Flats. This is a muddy area between Highway 80 and the Bay, where kids from Berkeley make driftwood sculptures, often tearing down existing sculptures for their material. At the moment, rising from the assorted trash, there are a scarecrow and a peace sign and a wheelchair with a banner protesting the treatment of Vietnam veterans.

Jonathan looks so lonely now, his hands pressed between his knees. In the world he can always get what he wants; with his family it's something else. I anticipate what will happen: He will confront Daniel. There will be a scene, at least as much of a scene as Jonathan will permit himself. And then he'll withdraw, and Daniel will watch the wrinkled back of dad's suit getting smaller, knowing that the remaining filament of trust between them is severed.

I know the sadness of watching the back of dad's gray suit disappear. I know that Daniel tried.

But the one power that even I will never have is to be able to undo the past.

# 10

Rose inclines her head to regard Elaina. "I was just on my way out."

"I won't hold you up then," Elaina says, sitting down.

Two feathers of peacock-blue eyeshadow are spread across Rose's lids. Elaina has observed both that Rose's hairdo usually lasts three weeks and that Rose does not seem to perspire.

"Don't you have time for a cup of coffee?" Elaina wheedles. "You never have time for me."

"My book club is discussing the new Isaac Bashevis Singer," Rose says. "It's my turn to make the presentation. We meet at eleven-thirty."

"Oh, of course, the book club," Elaina says. She crosses her legs; one of her black high heels bobs up and down. Rose is wearing an almost identical pair. "My husband and your favorite daughter are . . . dating."

"What are you talking about?"

"They're having an affair."

"Don't be ridiculous," Rose says, looking at her watch. She adds, "I wouldn't blame him if he did have an affair. Men do these kinds of things. Especially when provoked."

Elaina bends over to pull a bag out of her stocking. "Maybe it's not too late to have me aborted, mother. I'll get you a clothes hanger."

"Elaina." But Rose sinks into her carved-back chair now,

like a slowly deflating balloon. "You have to be good to a husband, that's all I'm saying. You have to put up with a lot."

"But you and daddy—"

"You girls don't know everything that went on," Rose says
darkly. "I protected you from most of it."

"I'm just afraid of Jonathan spreading lies about *me*,"
Elaina says, smoothing the side of her Gibson girl.

"What would he say about you that wasn't true?"

"Well, I don't know." Elaina uncrosses and then recrosses
her legs; one of her garters (Elaina says pantyhose are un-
feminine) peeks out from under the hem of her skirt. "He
might just tell you something to make you mad at me."

"Like what?"

"He would tell you *I'm* having an affair," Elaina bursts out.
"But just to cover up, because *he's* having an affair. With Alison."

Rose clicks her tongue. "Well, are you?"

"Am I what?"

"Having an affair?"

Elaina makes wide circles with her eyes, adding to the con-
cert of convulsive movements that usually accompany her lies
to her mother. "Of course not!" she says finally.

"Then why would he say so?"

"To cover up, because he's having an affair."

"You're being ridiculous." Rose's black high heel bobs up
and down in a rhythm slightly crisper than Elaina's. "I told
daddy," she says, "that he was spoiling you. That you wouldn't
be able to adjust to marriage. But he never listened to me. No
one wants advice, have you noticed that?"

Elaina tugs the hem of her dress over the garter. Grandpa
Saul is the one subject that sometimes silences her.

"All the time he spent reading to you. All the presents he
bought you. *That* we could hardly afford. Now look. He's gone
and I'm left to deal with all the crises, and there's always one
crisis after another."

"Daddy took care of all of us," Elaina murmurs.

"Huh," Rose snorts. "He took care of the congregation. They always came first."

"It wasn't his fault that he got sick."

"Ethel Lemmon's husband is eighty. He still plays golf on Saturdays."

Elaina's twitches are gradually subsiding, like bathwater after the bather has departed. She holds on to her knees and looks down.

"Do you remember that red velvet dress you wanted when you were in high school, with the rhinestones?" Rose echoes Alison's harsh, humorless laugh. "Daddy was ready to write the check. I stopped him just in time. Did you need that dress? He was always ready to buy you things you didn't need. You wanted a new dress every week. I never heard of anything so ridiculous. Rhinestones. On a high-school girl."

Elaina sits almost motionless now.

"Daddy couldn't manage money at all. He spent like a sailor and then he wouldn't ask the congregation for more money. Do you know how much life insurance he had? Not very much, let me tell you."

Elaina swallows and nods.

"I don't think daddy believed he was ever going to die. Well, he was mistaken about that. You'd think he would have asked the congregation for more money, wouldn't you? Have you ever noticed how people who like to spend it don't have it? Except Jonathan—he's not like that." Rose sighs and her thin lips curve slightly upward at the ends. "He's always been so generous."

Elaina clears her throat. Then she dabs at one eye with her handkerchief. She always says that her father was like God to her. Is she wondering how God can die?

"Well, I have to go now," Rose announces. She stands up quickly. "I'm late as it is."

"Oh, that's right," Elaina says tremulously. "The bookclub.

Those sweet, intelligent ladies. You must give them my love. I'll walk out with you." She gets up and tugs her tight black dress down over her girdled hips as she stands. Rose narrows her eyes at the sight of those hips, and Elaina sucks in her stomach and passes her hand over her belly.

At the top of the outside stairs, Elaina reaches for her mother. "Let me take your arm."

"I'm not *that* old." Rose laughs nervously as she pulls away.

"Please," Elaina says.

"It's not necessary," Rose snaps. Her arms flail as she steps back from Elaina, and she teeters for a moment before taking a step down and regaining her balance, the weight of her purse acting as ballast.

"All right," Elaina sniffs. "I just want to help my mother, that's all."

"Huh," Rose snorts, beginning her descent. She holds on to the banister rather tightly and takes the steps slowly.

Elaina descends next to her; her body almost but not quite touching Rose's.

As I see them starting down the stairs, I get inspired. Maybe I can send a zap Elaina's way, and break the heel off one of her shoes. She'll stumble a little—that'd be fun to watch. It's worth a try, anyway. Right now—as the two of them are taking, in unison, the third step down . . . right now . . . *Break . . . break . . .* This time it's going to work, I'm going to get her, I just know it!

But it isn't Elaina whose heel snaps off, it isn't Elaina who falls forward, putting out her hands for protection, whose knees and nylons scrape against the brick—it's Rose, my little grandmother, who gives a cry, while Elaina screams; Rose whose tiny body goes rippling down the stairs. I try to stop her fall, to hold her up with my thoughts, but her own weight pulls her down.

\*　　\*　　\*

Of course it's my fault. Elaina deflected the blow; it ricocheted off her and struck Rose. But how could I know that would happen? It's Elaina's fault, too—you'd think she'd take something that was meant for her once in a while! She'd want me to feel guilty, but I won't. Or not very much, anyway.

Thank God, Rose isn't hurt too badly. She landed twisted at the bottom of the stairs, but she just sprained her shoulder. That and a few scrapes. Rose is all sinew and muscle; she can take a fall like that and almost bounce. That doesn't let me off the hook, I know.

Rose and Elaina are at the emergency room at Mt. Moriah; the doctor is taping Rose's shoulder. "If only I hadn't bent over to get the newspaper!" Rose moans, which is the way she remembers that it happened. "I saw that newspaper on the steps and I said to myself, 'Get it later,' but no, I had to get it then, and I tripped over it, and that's when I broke the heel."

Elaina holds Rose around the waist as the doctor buckles the sling. Rose does not resist her embrace. But then Rose winces, and the doctor, who was once in Rose's Sunday School class, asks, "Do you want some medication? A little something for the pain?"

"It's not that serious, is it?" Rose demands.

By the time Rose is sent home, it's after three o'clock. In my mother's Cutlass, she fastens the shoulder harness, letting out a little cry as the belt crosses her body.

"If only I hadn't bent down to get that newspaper," she says, five times or more, while they are driving home. Then she moves on to "And of course it had to happen the day of my book presentation. I had some things to say about that Singer. It's nothing but sex, sex, sex. I don't see how he won the Nobel Prize, do you?"

Elaina drives slowly, with unusual concentration.

"I'm going to have to stay home now," Rose says. "I can't get around at all like this, I can't even get dressed by myself. Three weeks, the doctor said. Isn't that what he said, three weeks? I'll lose my mind. Of course when Ethel Lemmon broke her hip, her daughter came to stay with her. Alison will probably be going back to New York soon. I won't see her for another two years, if I'm still here."

"You have me," Elaina says.

"Huh." Rose lowers the window. "You know, Alison has been so successful with that modeling agency of hers. You never wanted to do anything like that, I guess, though, did you?"

Back at Rose's apartment, Elaina arranges pillows on the studio couch that Rose uses as a bed, and offers to make tea. It's funny how Elaina can sometimes come through when someone is sick. She was like that with us, too. She would move the portable TV into our rooms and make us peanut butter sandwiches, which she told us had magical healing properties.

"You know what I've decided?" Rose says. She is propped up on the pillows, lying still against the pain; she barely moves her lips when she speaks. "It's all luck in this life, that's what it is. Ethel Lemmon, I knew her when she was young. She was nothing to look at, just plain *mees*. But she married this shy boy—he was too shy to ask anyone else out—and then he went on to be a big success in the furniture business. You remember going to Lemmon's when you were little? We bought everything there, because they belonged to the congregation. You know Harry Lemmon sold those stores for millions when he retired. He's eighty, he still plays golf on Saturdays."

"His only son was killed in that plane crash," Elaina points out.

"He didn't let that bother him," Rose says.

Elaina tries to fluff the pillows, but Rose grimaces. "Do you have to reach under there like that? . . . Melissa, I thought she would be smarter. She had that wonderful boyfriend, that Posner boy. Whatever happened to him?"

"He testified for Jonathan."

"That isn't what I meant. Melissa . . ."— She starts to turn toward Elaina and then clenches her teeth—"I thought she was going to turn out so well."

Elaina offers Rose a Valium from her personal supply, aspirin, a leg massage. Rose refuses each one in turn. Elaina sits on the edge of the bed. "I'll stay with you tonight, mother."

Rose turns her head as far away as the pain allows. "Don't you think you've done enough?"

"But I can't leave you here like this," Elaina says. "What if you need something?"

"I wonder where Alison is," Rose says.

"You'd like Alison to come stay with you, wouldn't you?"

"She probably tried to call while we were at the hospital."

"Would you like me to call her?"

"She'd probably want to come over."

Elaina tries to call Alison at her hotel, but she isn't there. Until now, no one has wondered how Alison is spending her free time, but I can hear the question, unspoken, in the sound of Elaina's nails clicking absently against the phone. Rose angles her head toward Elaina; reclining as she is, the skin of her neck bunches around her slackened jaw, giving her an expression of sardonic triumph.

Well, of course, *I* know where Alison is. I can see her right now: She is standing outside of Tiffany's, with Jo Beth Hart, her old Alta Vista friend with whom she still keeps in contact. Jo Beth and her husband have recently returned from Europe; Alison probably suggested they have lunch in San Francisco so Alison could endure the exquisite torture of hearing about the poshest hotels in Venice, Lugano, and Budapest.

Now Alison is looking at the necklace in the display case: strawberry-pink tourmaline cabochons joined by diamond-studded gold links. Alison's eyes look like an underfed captive tiger's. Everything she wants is behind glass.

Back in Oakland, Rose squints at the ceiling. "Alison always tells me when she's going somewhere. She's very considerate that way. I hope nothing's happened to her. I didn't like her going to that Holiday Inn. It isn't safe."

"Maybe Becky or Leah could come stay with you," Elaina suggests.

"Maybe Becky can come," Rose says. Then, "There was a lawyer who wanted to marry me, but my father didn't think he was good enough. My father thought I should marry a rabbi. My mistake was that I always listened to my father. I know better now, but it's too late."

Here in Rose's bedroom, too, one wall is covered with family portraits. Elaina's eyes flicker over them all, then rest on the picture of Grandpa Saul.

"That lawyer, he drove into the Bay one night when it was very foggy. Everything could have been different. If it hadn't been foggy that one night. He would have been as succesful as Jonathan."

Silence. "I'll call the girls," Elaina says finally.

Becky and Leah are preparing for their Friday-night ritual of watching "Secrets," a prime-time soap opera. The program is on at nine, but now, at five, they are making the advance preparations: gathering ingredients for the ceremonial nachos they will heat in the microwave just before the show. The recipe for the nachos is their own creation, formalized after months of experimentation: It calls for three kinds of cheese, chicken, ground beef, enough sour cream to end starvation in an underdeveloped country, and guacamole mixed with mayonnaise for extra smoothness.

The Friday-evening beauty treatments are another tradition: This week it's the High-Tech Papaya Enzyme Computerized Specially Formulated Hair Reinforcer with Protein Additives. The girls' sticky heads are covered with plastic caps, and they stand at the sideboard shredding cheese and gossiping: Their conversation moves seamlessly between speculation about Jeff's previous liaisons, and predictions for the hottest romance on "Secrets."

Then the call comes from Elaina, and they are recruited for "grandma duty."

They are so relieved to hear Rose is not seriously injured that they quickly agree to help out. But after they hang up, the sacrifice seems larger than it did at first.

"Megabarf," Becky says.

"Bee-stunk," Leah agrees.

"Were's *Daniel*?" Becky whines. "How come he never has to do stuff like this?"

"Maybe he's at Dmitri's," Leah suggests.

"No way," Becky snorts. "That's, like, the last place in the universe he'd be. He's probably with Craig or one of those guys, getting ready for a megaflare night. *Guy,* I don't see why Mickey Mouse can't stay with gree-standma."

"I'll go," Leah offers.

"Are you going to take the *bus* over there?" Becky demands.

Leah won't have her driver's license for another eight months, and at the moment I imagine that she feels personally responsible for the California Vehicle Code. "I could." She hesitates.

"And take the bus *home*? After it gets *dark*? What's the pee-stee-floint?" Becky sighs, picking up a handful of shredded jack cheese and letting it flutter like yellow snow to the sideboard. "Besides, you know how grandma is. I can handle her a little better—no offense, okay? And, like, why should we *both* miss the show?"

"I'll tape it for you," Leah offers. Jonathan resisted getting a VCR—an enemy of homework—for a long time, but finally the battle cry was too loud even for him to withstand.

"It's not the same." Becky shakes her head. "I mean, like, I want to watch it *together*."

"I could take a cab," Leah says.

"Guy, it takes light-years for a cab to come," Becky says. She inserts a finger under the plastic cap and feels her wet hair. "Now that means I gotta wash this stuff out. And I have a major geometry test on Monday and this is my only night to study for it!"

But the test, I imagine, will go unprepared for, because a short while later Becky is swinging her purse over her shoulder, blowing a bubble of sugarless grape gum, and giving Leah final instructions about how to rewrap the tortilla chips and which videotape to record the show on. "And don't tape over that TV movie about incest—I might want to view it like one more time."

After Becky leaves, Leah goes upstairs to blow her hair dry. (She shampooed out her own Protein Reinforcer when Becky did, so as not to have any unfair advantage.) The fine blond wisps of Leah's hair form an electrified nimbus around her head. She pulls it back in a ponytail. Then she hears Elaina coming in the front door, and goes downstairs to meet her.

Elaina looks extremely bedraggled: One stocking has actually come loose from one of its garters and is bagging around her knee. Her mascara is smeared—black cat's paw prints under her eyes—and all that remains of her lipstick is a pale pink splotch. I think that means she's really upset; but maybe she knows that's how we measure the genuineness of her distress and allows herself dishevelment accordingly.

"Hello, Lay-around-town." Elaina strokes Leah's cheek. "Do you know what? You're the only one in the family who has freckles on her face. No, wait, my father had a few freckles on his face. I think. You look like him." She smiles drowsily. "I think I'm going upstairs and just close my eyes for a few minutes."

There is a deep frown line on Leah's forehead. "Mouse, did you take some Valium?"

"Oh, maybe a bottle or two," Elaina says. Her lids droop. "It was my fault what happened. Of course, everything is my fault."

"But grandma's going to be all right, isn't she?" I know Leah thinks the disaster that struck me was intended for her. Maybe she sees what happened to Rose as another near-miss. If so, then the threat remains, like an enemy submarine hidden in gloomy waters.

Elaina has started up the stairs. Leah follows her. "She'll never forgive me," Elaina murmurs. "She thinks it was my fault."

In the bedroom, Elaina sits on the edge of the bed and begins to cry. Leah hovers between Elaina and the door. Then, dutifully, she sits and puts her arm around her mother's shoulder. "What is it, Mouse?" she asks. "Do you want me to call Dr. Abramowitz?"

Elaina shakes her head. "I was so stupid. I did everything the wrong way."

"What do you mean?"

Elaina tucks some of Leah's hair behind her ear—the frail hairs that are too short to stay in the ponytail. "You're so pretty," she says. "You're just as pretty as Becky, but in a different way." She absently pats her cheek. "I just didn't know what else to do. I know that Melissa's suffering. You don't hate me, do you?"

"No—no, of course not, Mouse. I always thought you were right about Melissa."

Elaina grips her suddenly. "Then you'll testify for me, if we have to go back to court."

"I . . . I can't, Mouse. Becky and I promised each other, we made a pact. I can't break that."

"Of course not. I would never ask you to do that. Never. It's just that your sister needs our help."

"I know. . . ." Right after the accident, when she would come to the hospital, Leah could hardly stand to look at my body. But gradually she has made friends with it. She even told Becky that if she didn't become a psychologist, she might want to be a nurse. "But dad—"

"Your father has crazy ideas. I think he thinks I'm having an affair or something." Elaina glances at Leah and quickly laughs. "Oh, don't be silly—who'd have an affair with an old lady like me? I have as many wrinkles as Sheila Newhouse." She reaches for a Kleenex from the box on the nightstand. "Well, maybe not quite that many. But you'll *think* about testifying for me, won't you? Just think about it, that's all I'm asking. It's not for me. It's for your sister."

"Okay, Mouse."

"Would you mind getting me some water, Lay-a-hen's-egg?"

Leah goes to the bathroom. When she returns with the glass, Elaina has peeled off her dress and is getting under the covers. Then she dips into her nightstand drawer and takes a thick yellow pill out of a prescription bottle. She studies the label.

"What's that?" Leah asks.

"Oh," Elaina says, without looking up, "Percodan."

"Do you think you should be taking that, Mouse?"

Elaina puts the pill on her tongue. "I just like to think of it as a very large aspirin," she says.

"But—"

"Don't worry, Lay-a-burden-down." Elaina pulls the sheet up to her chin. Her great eyes are slowly closing. "Things like that never happen to people like me."

\*   \*   \*

Leah leaves Elaina and goes upstairs to study. She stretches out over her history book. But after a few moments, two tears spatter on the page.

Leah rarely cries. She muffles the sound, although she probably could not disturb Elaina's drugged sleep.

I have a feeling she's thinking about dad. She cares about him the most of any of us. He has already dropped hints that should "something happen between me and your mother," he will always spend weekends with his children. I know—and I'm sure Leah does, too—both that he means to spend weekends with them and that he never will. Jonathan probably has some vague ideas of taking the girls to amusement parks and buying them cotton candy. He doesn't realize that it is too late for that. He still blinks at Becky's and Leah's heavy breasts, and frowns, puzzled, at the curves of their legs in their colored tights.

I know far more about Leah than I ever could have before; in the state I'm in, I absorb bits of thoughts the way I might have unconsciously picked at crumbs on a tablecloth when I was in a body. I understand now that during the silences between her and Jonathan, she is trying to think of *that one question* she wants to ask him. If she could only think of it, and he would only answer, that would relieve forever the insecurity she feels with him.

The doorbell rings. Leah waits, as if she's expecting someone else to answer it. But no one else is home. She finds a piece of Kleenex somewhere under the colored mountain of blushes and lipsticks on top of the dresser, and slowly heads downstairs.

The bell is ringing again when she reaches the door. She opens it: Jeff Lindner is standing on the porch with his finger on the buzzer. He is wearing a gray tweed jacket with his jeans, and he carries a small bunch of red and pink carnations.

Oops. I forgot all about Jeff and the message that I changed.

"Oh, hi," Leah says. She must know that her eyes are red from crying. She tugs on her loose green T-shirt. "Like . . . I don't mean to be rude, but weren't you supposed to come *tomorrow* night?"

"I don't think so," Jeff says. "Why, is something wrong?"

Leah slips her hand behind her and gives the seat of her jeans a tug. "Well, it's bunk, but Becky isn't here."

"Oh." Jeff looks at his carnations. "I'm sorry to hear that," he says, tightly but with dignity. "I guess I'd better go. Will you tell her I came by?"

"Wait!" Leah cries as Jeff turns away. Jeff pauses and looks back at her. "Guy, I'm so rude it's *scuz*. Why don't you come in for a few minutes?"

Jeff looks doubtful. "I don't know. . . ." He glances down the stairs. "Well, maybe for a second."

Leah bites her lip as she stands back to let him enter. "I mean, Becky might be back pretty soon. She just went to sit with our grandma." She adds, "She had an accident—our grandma did."

"I'm very sorry to hear that." Jeff, stepping down into the living room, pauses at the mantelpiece to look at my picture. "I hope she's going to be all right."

"She'll be really sorry she missed you. Becky, I mean. Can you go out tomorrow instead?"

Jeff turns from the mantelpiece and Leah inhales quickly.

"I don't know," Jeff says. "My folks are having a party. I told them I'd bartend." His lip curls as if he had promised to sacrifice a virgin.

"Guy, Becky will be like—" Leah stops herself. "Hey, do you want some saccharin juice?"

Jeff hesitates. "Okay."

Leah hurries out. She stops in the guest bathroom to wash

her face and comb out her hair. Looking in the mirror, she suddenly sticks out her tongue at herself.

But when she returns to the living room with two cans of diet cola, I think she looks soft and cuddly, like a stuffed animal, with her fuzz of hair and her round cheeks and the full heart of her mouth.

Jeff takes the can, dutifully opens it, and sips. Then he looks at the label, his lips moving slightly as he reads the ingredients. "I'm sorry," he says, "I hope you won't be offended, but I can't believe people *drink* this stuff."

Leah kicks off her shoes and sits barefoot and cross-legged on the couch.

Jeff sits next to her. "It makes me think that all the big corporations are laughing at us, because even with all the consumer-protection laws, people don't try to protect them*selves*."

"Yeah," Leah sighs, opening her own can. "That's mega-true."

Pause.

"Excuse me." Jeff is looking at the cold and empty fireplace. "I know it's none of my business, but is something wrong?"

"I guess"—Leah's voice is raspy—"I'm just kind of worried about my family, you know."

Jeff nods, almost brusquely. Then he gives her arm a brotherly squeeze.

"I'll be okay." One cheek pulses. "It's just . . . it's just . . ." She stops, takes a breath, then goes on. "If we could, like, *do* something about all this—I mean what happened to Melissa— then I think I could stand it, but the way it is, it just doesn't make any sense. It's like it's all for nothing and it's just making everything else so bunk." She clenches her teeth; two tears are nestling in the corners of her eyes.

Jeff frowns, the crease in his forehead mirroring Leah's.

"We'll *make* it mean something," he says firmly after a moment. "We'll do something."

"Like what?" Leah asks.

"We'll use your sister as an example. We'll get the word out, so we can stop other families from going through this. . . ."

"If only Melissa had left a note or something," Leah muses. "Sometimes I feel that she's right here with us and she's trying to tell us what she wants, but she can't." Suddenly she sits forward. "Yeah! Wait! That's it!"

Jeff watches her expectantly.

Leah's eyes are moist and gleaming. "Remember what you said before, about how everyone should, like, register when they get their driver's license? Well, what if we just started a program at school and got everyone to fill out a questionnaire? And they'd say exactly what . . . what extraordinary means they'd want taken if this happened to them—"

"Of course!" Jeff pounds his fist on the back of the sofa. "It's perfect. It'll be like when they put the polio vaccine on the sugar cubes—you know, back in the Sixties? We'll start with Alta Vista, then get high schools all across the country." He frowns briefly. "The administration will give us lots of flak—they're so reactionary. But we'll deal with them. We'll really apply the pressure." He grins, makes a fist, and presses his other thumb against it to illustrate the point.

"Oh!" Leah cries. The tears are running down her cheeks now, but she doesn't seem to care. "We *will* do it, won't we?"

He smiles. How much hope and strength is in that smile. "Of course we will." And he reaches out and wipes one tear away.

I see Leah tense. This is Becky's boyfriend, even if he doesn't know yet that he is Becky's boyfriend. And I feel the pull on her—to get up, to walk away, at least across the room—and the weight of the need to stay just a moment longer.

Jeff brushes her hair off her forehead. His hand is trembling. And this is the moment—I can tell—when his fears have receded like a wave and when all he feels is what he feels. What he never knew before that he felt. When he is achingly aware of the connection between them, as fragile and as strong as a spider's web.

And this is the moment when God comes in, if there is a God. Because it's all timing. Like an eclipse. Everything depends on whether Leah at this moment can and will reach over her own fears. The time when Jeff can reach out is so brief. The doors are already closing. If Leah shivers, if she pushes him away, no matter how gently, then he may never be able to reach out to her again. He will never know exactly what he intended. He will think, though perhaps not consciously, that she rejected him.

And so I become Leah. I live again. Sweet sister—daughter, friend—I am her—I am you. I feel myself in her strong, young body, her teeth—my teeth—biting into our lips, her soft hands at the ends of my arms, solid, weighty flesh. . . .

And I think that Leah will remember but never understand how she let herself do it. She will remember how she pulled him close to her. She will remember his lips, so pliant, the faint roughness of his cheek, the longing for him that was like the sting of a needle in her arm. But how could she do this to Becky? She couldn't. But I can.

How luscious a body can be—once in a while, like now. I can feel the faint roughness of Jeff's cheek against Leah's—mine—and then their lips moving toward each other, driven now by a force independent of me.

Jeff holds her. His skin is soft, giving, but Leah and I can feel the layer of solid muscle underneath. He murmurs in her ear, "I don't care. It isn't Becky that I like. I like you."

Leah's voice—my voice—is husky, like the voices of all the women in our family. "Come downstairs," she says. She gets up and takes Jeff's hands, tugging on him gently. "We'll go down to the rumpus room so my mom doesn't find us."

*   *   *

For Leah it is confusing, surreal. She proceeds from moment to moment slowly, as if bouncing among clouds. She has never done more than kiss a boy before, perhaps let him feel her breasts. But I am her and I show her what to do.

Jeff is a virgin, too. And both of them share a sense that though many people have done something like this before, no one has ever done it quite this way.

Afterward they lie squeezed together on the yellow vinyl couch. That's when I leave Leah. And when I do, the recognition of what she has done seems to paralyze her. She cannot move or speak; she simply presses her nose against his warm chest.

But she is still in Jeff's arms. And could it have been like this twenty-five years ago? Did Elaina look at Jonathan like this, eyes moist with love, and touch his then-black hair in awe? "This is a nuclear event," she says at last. "I mean, Becky . . ."

Jeff sits up. His broad shoulders are a dark silhouette against the light from the streetlamp that shines through the window. "We didn't mean for it to happen. Sometimes these things just do." He takes her hand. "We have to be realistic about this," he says. "Mature."

With apparent effort, Leah sits up. "I'm shorted out by this," she says. "Becky really, really likes you. She didn't want to trash your flare night." Leah cannot speak for a moment. Then, "She was just helping our grandma and look what I did to her."

"It doesn't matter why Becky wasn't here," Jeff says with authority. He adds, with the slightest of grins, "Maybe it was fate."

"We can't see each other again."

"How can you say that?" Jeff asks. "After—I mean, after what we've done?"

"We shouldn't have." Leah shivers, and reaches for her T-shirt, lying on the floor. Her nakedness, so innocent a few moments before, makes her ashamed now. I wonder if she is thinking of me, of the rumors, and sentences broken off. *Melissa was sort of, you know.* The kids at Alta Vista have an expression for it: a thread shedder. True. I was less than perfectly discriminating.

"It was my fault," Jeff insists. "I took advantage of you." He looks puzzled again. Perhaps he is wondering at the darker nature that asserted itself in him, the desire that could overpower his restraint.

"No." Leah shakes her head. "It wasn't your fault." Even with her confused memory of the past hour, she is sensitive to the presence of ghosts, the ghosts of the living. So am I. I can feel how Elaina, sleeping two stories above, is here with us, like the heavy odor of perfume.

"We'll work it out," Jeff promises.

"I don't know," Leah says nervously. "Can't you go out with Becky again?"

Jeff frowns. It isn't his worried frown, that looks so much like Leah's—it looks more like Jonathan's angry one. "So, like, you don't care who I go out with then?"

"No!" Leah protests. "That isn't it at all!" Someone must be hurt, and that someone, Leah is used to thinking, should be Leah. But how can she tell him that? "Listen, we . . . Bunk. It's late." That's right—and by now, Becky must be on her way home from Grandma Rose's. "You'd better go."

# 11

This morning, Monday, the California Supreme Court reversed Judge Picone's decision.

I was with Dad when he got the news—by phone from Arthur McGee—and he got so excited that he raised both eyebrows at the same time.

Arthur read him the pivotal headnote:

> Where the parents are disputing custody of an incompetent child for purposes of disconnecting a life-sustaining device, because of the state's interest in preserving the life of that incompetent under the doctrine of *parens patriae,* a special burden of proof, greater than that which normally applies in civil matters, must be met by the party seeking to disconnect the life-sustaining device.

Then dad and Arthur discussed the legal aspects. Usually in a civil trial the plaintiff need only prove his case by a preponderance of the evidence. But the Court has decided that in a case such as this, since someone's life, (i.e. mine) is at issue, the burden of proof is comparable to a criminal trial, in which the facts must be proven beyond a reasonable doubt. The Court went on to hold that, as a matter of law, the plaintiff (Elaina) did not meet this burden of proof. But she's entitled, they said, to have her day in court.

So the case has been remanded for a re-trial. Arthur thinks they can get a new date set for about a month from now.

I guess I should feel that my life is saved. For starters, I doubt that Dr. Peewee Doll, a.k.a. Drew Harding, is going to be able to pull off that little story about me again.

Drew has been staying home since he was suspended from Mt. Moriah. He has started to drink; his tan has faded and his eyes are puffy. He watches soap operas, especially the ones that center around hospitals. Sometimes he talks to the television screen, trying to warn a particular dedicated young doctor on one of the programs against the mother of a patient, whom Drew thinks is trying to seduce him.

Drew often stares at the phone. He's waiting for Elaina to call. Every woman over the age of twelve recognizes the look of someone who wants to smash a poor defenseless telephone with a sledgehammer just because it isn't ringing.

I almost feel sorry for him. I'm sure he misses the hospital; he seemed happy when I first became aware of him there, in the early days after my accident. I watched him pad down the hall, bringing comfort. His white coat was his surplice and his pills were his Communion wafers. Now he stumbles around his apartment as if imaginary objects were blocking his path. Well, if he's seeing things, it's without help from me.

But even if Drew does manage to blubber his way through his testimony, dad can have Debbie ask Drew about his affair with Elaina on cross-examination, which will impeach his credibility as a witness, to say the least; so Judge Picone will never believe him this time.

And, yes, Jonathan told Arthur that he was going to retain Debbie Meyers to handle the retrial (Arthur does only appeals). Debbie is back on the job after having delivered her baby, a girl, Margaret Sanger Meyers-Hoffman. (I bet she'll bring little Maggie to the trial just so she can whip out a tit and feed her.) In spite of—or maybe because of—Debbie's previous *faux pas*, Jonathan is willing to give her a second chance. He hates to give up on people if there's any hope they still might discover for themselves Jonathan's One True Way of doing things.

He'll have to tell Debbie about Elaina's affair. I can already feel his hesitation, like a guitar string too tautly wound: He has an almost physical aversion to having his personal life made public. He has to do it though—and I'm sure he will, for my sake! After all, he certainly isn't the first Alta Vista husband who's been cuckolded. He thinks he feels the shame of it more than others, but that's only because he isn't used to feeling *anything*.

So the future looks pretty bright for *this* comatose girl. The only thing that bothers me is what happened between Leah and Jeff. I meant it for the best, I really did. I could feel how Leah cared for him—I wanted her to tell him that, and she never would have without my help. But Leah didn't want to go to bed with him. She was waiting for the proper, later time; saving herself, most likely, for a Peace Corps volunteer who was about to leave for Ethiopia. She's too psychologically minded not to blame herself for what happened—doesn't psychology teach you to blame yourself? Leah's psychology does, anyway.

Now she has one more secret to keep. All she told Becky was that Jeff came by on Friday night. Becky was furious about missing him. "It's Daniel's fault," she whined. "He's so totally wonked out, it's scuzomatic. I know he did it on purpose. What a goon!"

But when Becky saw the carnations that Leah had rescued from the coffee table and put into a vase, she purred, "That hound Jeffrey has a megagroaner for me, I can like totally tell!"

Daniel's been at Dmitri's Number One a lot lately. I'm pretty sure he went there last week, the night he almost took the letter opener. I didn't bother to check up on him after he left, but I've had a sense of his being there on several occasions since then, and not just when I overheard the conversation between him and Craig.

I wonder what the sudden attraction is. Maybe Dmitri got a new, faster-pouring spout for his draft beer. Or maybe Daniel's just drawn to the scene of the crime.

Today I decide to pop in on him. And there he is—wearing an apron, and waiting on a customer!

It's lunch "rush," which here means that about half the tables are full. There are menus sticking up in the air, smells of flour and tomato sauce, the slight tension of people waiting to eat.

I buzz after Daniel as he writes down orders. He tells the women with children that pizza dough is a source of niacin; he tells the high-school students that olives will clear up their acne. He describes to all the customers with what care the pizzas are made and how fresh the ingredients are. He encourages everyone to order salads, garlic bread, and Dmitri's baklava for dessert.

Is this a joke? Or is it part of some elaborate sting operation to convince the bank that the restaurant is profitable?

Daniel's just about made the rounds now. He delivers a large number six (mushroom, clam, and sausage), then pauses by the plate-glass window with its backward writing (DMITRI'S NUMBER ONE, it reads) to survey the crowd. Flash of silverware, slices gobbled, mothers wiping faces, red-stained napkins crumpled on plates. Daniel looks so *proud.* What's gotten into him? God, before you know it he'll be taking Jonathan's advice and passing out coupons to people in line at the Twelve Oaks movie theater: FREE SOFT DRINK WITH ONE LARGE PIZZA.

Dmitri is behind the counter. His hand flicks over a red canvas of sauce-covered dough, making patterns of the cheese, the meat, the vegetables; his dark eyes are lowered, his face intent. There are dark grease stains on his apron.

Daniel watches him for just a moment, then tucks his pad

under the strings of his apron as if he were sheathing a sword.
He starts going around to the people he's already served and
asking them if everything is all right. I hate it when he's so
nice.

I notice a man dressed all in gray, wearing a pointy gray
felt hat, passing the window. As the man enters the restaurant,
Daniel looks up and hurries over to him. "Sit anywhere you
like, sir," Daniel says, motioning to an empty table near the
door.

The man in gray places his slim, zippered briefcase on the
table, but does not sit. "Are you Daniel Silverstein?" he asks.
He speaks with a faint accent of indeterminate origin.

Daniel looks like he's not sure what the answer is. I don't
blame him. The man must be from the Bay City Bank. But
then Daniel straightens his shoulders and says, "Yes, I'm Daniel
Silverstein."

"Just the person I want to see. Can we sit down? I have a
proposition I want to discuss with you." The man removes his
gray felt hat, revealing a full head of curly, golden-red hair. He
looks younger now than he did at first, and rather elflike. Everything about him is pointy and small: His eyebrows, his nose;
even his teeth are small and pointy. He has a ruddy, mottled
complexion with darker spots like large freckles.

Daniel glances around. "It's our busy time here . . . you
know, I've got a lot of tables to take care of—"

"It'll just take a few minutes." The elf sits—or rather, he
seems to perch, his rear end only lightly touching the edge of
the chair—and motions peremptorily to the chair opposite.

Daniel sits.

"I've heard that you own the rights to some"—the Elf
breaks off with a surprisingly high-pitched giggle—"market-
viable software."

Daniel tenses. "Where did you hear that?"

"We're constantly researching the market," the Elf says as

he unzips his briefcase. The zipper sighs in response to the touch of his hand.

"But how did you hear *that*?" I can't imagine, either. Before Craig left on his open-ended ski trip, he gave Daniel his share of the rights to "Wizards and Warriors," which both of them considered worthless. Was Craig capable of a good deed at the end? I doubt it.

"Ah!" The Elf raises one finger and winks. "You'll find out that one of the keys to business success is respecting confidentiality."

At the words *business success*, I'm aware of Daniel's heart beating a little faster. I imagine that the concept is vague to him, with no dollar amount fixed to it, but that it smells like furniture polish: like Jonathan's study at home.

"My company is prepared to offer you twenty thousand for the software." The Elf raises the briefcase and lets sheaves of glossy brochures fall on the table. There are pictures of terminals and keyboards, smiling models loading floppies into disk drives. Daniel starts to reach for one of the brochures. But then his eyebrows come together in an expression of cynicism that reminds me of Jonathan. Daniel may not be very experienced, but he knows as well as I do that his software isn't worth twenty thousand: The Elf might represent a very honest company, but software is too easily imitated, or pirated, for anyone to pay such big money for it. I'm suspicious myself. I mean, isn't it an interesting coincidence that twenty thousand is exactly what Daniel needs to pay off the bank?

The Elf laughs again, as if delighted with Daniel's worry. "Oh, yes, there's a catch, my friend."

That's what Daniel was expecting. Me, too. The company is probably a front for a white-slave ring.

The Elf slips one of the brochures between Daniel's fingers. There are little tufts of golden hair on the Elf's knuckles and he is wearing a signet ring on the third finger of his right hand, engraved with a shape that resembles the human form.

I read the brochure over Daniel's shoulder. The company's called Abracadabra, and they market a series of homework aids, computer software for the student. "'From preschool to Ph.D.' is our motto," the Elf says.

"How come I've never heard of you?" Daniel asks, with that cynical look of Jonathan's.

"We've had low visibility. We've done most of our business by mail. Now we're looking to expand our marketing strategies."

"I've never even seen an ad for you guys."

"Oh," the Elf says with a disinterested wave of his hand, "we don't sell in *computer* magazines. We've targeted our market as parents of school-age children. We advertise in family publications." He leans forward and in a conspiratorial whisper adds, "That's the kind of thing you learn about in business."

Daniel puckers. Now he looks like he did when he wanted to play with one of my toys. I think I'm beginning to understand what's happened to him over the past week. He came here to escape Elaina, then started helping Dmitri, just because there was no TV to watch. And then he discovered the hard kernel of pleasure in accomplishing small, concrete tasks, like wiping tables and stacking chairs. He discovered that work was actually less fatiguing than his long search for the definitive party had been. I imagine the charm of the business unfolding for him, like one of his medieval adventure novels: the magic of recipes and the wizardry of totaling the receipts.

"What's the catch, then?" he asks.

"We're not just buying your software," the Elf says, raising one eyebrow. "We're buying *you*."

Daniel shivers.

"You have to work for us for a year," the Elf says.

"I do?" Daniel asks. He absently feels along the strap of his apron; I notice that he is not carrying the red handkerchief. "Doing what?"

The Elf is grinning. "Whatever we tell you."

Daniel looks skeptical.

The Elf giggles, rubbing his hands together. "Don't worry. You might even enjoy it. And we'll pay you, too."

"Pay me?"

"You'll be marketing software on commission. And you'll also get a draw."

"But what about my business here?" He adds, "Dmitri— my partner—really needs me."

The Elf winks. "You can work here at night."

"I don't know," Daniel mumbles. He takes a napkin and rubs at a patch of something sticky on the table.

"Do you really have a choice?"

Daniel looks up, startled. Gradually his gaze settles on the small, pale green eyes of the Elf.

Suddenly the Elf, with the deftness of a croupier, begins to gather the brochures. As he does, I notice a letter wedged between two of the brochures, near the bottom of the pile. Embossed on the top of the letter is a silver *S* against a green oval: the logo of Silverstein, Inc. Of course. I should have guessed. I suppose there really is a legitimate company called Abracadabra, but obviously Jonathan arranged this whole thing, to bail Daniel out. God! Does the man *never* give up?

Daniel is holding his breath. He must be thinking how in all the stories the worthy hero gets a chance at being rescued. Some of them pass up the chance. Others accept and it leads to their downfall, because they were tempted by the offer of something for nothing. But this offer is tied to honest work, exactly what Daniel knows he has always tried to avoid.

I know that if he sees the letter with the silver *S*, he'll never accept. He won't let Jonathan rescue him from this one. Pride, you know—I don't understand it, but men are famous for it.

And I could move that letter now, so that it's right in front of Daniel, so that he has to see it. A draft of air could dislodge it, so it'd be easy—I wouldn't be up against any resistance. Daniel seems unsure—my own nudge could push him over the edge. The Elf would have to put his pointy gray hat back on again and go his way. And even if I do nothing, in a moment Daniel is bound to see it, because the letter is under the next brochure and as the Elf slips that one back into his briefcase, the letter will be uncovered. . . .

Not if I hide it. I'll stick it to the brochure on top of it and let it go in with that.

There it goes. Daniel might be able to see a corner of the piece of paper as the Elf straightens the pile in the briefcase, but if he feels any curiosity about it, he lets it pass, along with the rest of his doubts. "All right," he says, "I'll do it."

The Elf laughs again, rubbing his hands together. "Good, good." He nods. "I'm delighted."

Daniel smiles. It isn't the Robert Redford grin at all; it's a timid, hesitant smile that wants to be trusting and isn't quite ready to be.

And that little breeze he feels in his hair is my version of a kiss. Well, give the guy a break. Let him believe he got lucky. Let him even unconsciously know what he can't let himself wholly know: that Jonathan saved him. You've got to take *some* things from your parents, and take them graciously. Let Daniel use this One Last Chance as he will. If nothing else, he'll be too busy to try to pull my plug again, and too busy to listen to Elaina trying to get him to do it. So as I watch the Elf grinning and Daniel's smile, I feel rather pleased.


Marty Lindner is trying to explain the Supreme Court decision to Elaina. "I don't understand," she says. She rocks back and forth, twisting her handkerchief. "If I won, how can I *un*win? There should be a law against that."

"Now, now, don't give up yet." Marty's chuckle gives way to a fit of coughing.

Elaina coughs too, delicately, staring at Marty's smoldering cigar. "Thank you for reassuring me." She smiles. "You're just like my father. He always reassured me. He always liked you, too. You remember him, don't you?"

Marty ignores her question. He studies the damp and mangled end of the cigar. Then he starts to tell Elaina again about the new burden of proof.

"I just don't understand these things," she repeats, closing her eyes and raising her hands as if she were throwing pizza dough in the air. "I'm too stupid."

"We need everything we've already got," Marty says, "including your medicine man." He chomps down hard on the end of the cigar, which has gone out. "*And* we have to have something more." Marty looks like a bulldog, with the cigar something that he dug up.

"What do you mean, more?" Elaina asks.

"I mean"—Marty drops the cigar in the wastebasket and gives the wastebasket a kick—"*evidence*. We need a new goddamn angle."

I concentrate on dumping the wastebasket on Marty's head, but it's too much for me. He's pissed about having the decision overturned, and I can tell that he's afraid they're going to lose this time. A book about a case he lost isn't going to sell as many copies as a book about a case he won.

"A new angle?" Elaina asks, dabbing under her lashes with her handkerchief. "I don't know what you mean. Why can't we just explain things to the judge? He seems like a nice man. He reminds me a little of my daddy."

"It doesn't matter if he does," Marty grumbles. Then he squints, and his eyes begin to disappear in the fat that surrounds them. He has gained weight since he took on this case, and he is smoking more heavily. The skin below his neck sags like a hammock and already he's fingering another cigar in the pocket of his soiled blue shirt. Elaina glances at the cigar with some distress. "How about one of your other kids—what're their names?"

"Rebecca Sarah," Elaina says haughtily, "and Leah Rachel."

"Yeah," Marty grunts. "Can't you get them to say something for us? That'd help. Couldn't hurt, anyway."

"My children have very much their own minds," Elaina muses. "You'd think they'd want to do something like this for their mother, but sometimes children are hard to understand."

"You'd better come up with something else, that's all," Marty says. "Even that doctor has lost a lot of his oomph, now that he's been fired from the hospital. . . . I dunno. Shit. Didn't she ever write poems about dying or something? Don't girls like her do that?" Marty stops to pick a fleck of tobacco from between two yellowed teeth.

"Some people think cigars are messy and smelly," Elaina observes. "But not me—I think it's a very attractive habit. So sexy." She puts her handkerchief in her purse. "I just know we're going to win. You promised me we were going to win, and you were right. I know we have this little problem now, but I bet you're going to fix it and make it all better!" She reaches out to stroke his hand. The tips of her long nails are trembling. "You're the best lawyer in the whole world!"


Jeff calls Becky that evening and sets up another date with her for this coming weekend.

Yesterday, Leah saw Jeff in the hall at school: his beloved head a black standard above the throng of students. There were two other boys with him, lowerclassmen that he tutors. Then he turned and she saw him see her—the lift of his eyebrows and the recognition that followed in his mouth. Leah started to wave to him, but then her arm stiffened. What was she afraid of? That she would end up begging him not to go out with Becky after all?

She might be wondering if Jeff is actually just a dachshund out to score. Perhaps Jeff's protests of affection were part of a larger scheme to add Becky to his list of conquests, by making himself appear innocent. He is Marty Lindner's son, after all, and even the best-intentioned children must beware of how the traits of their parents, like a lasso thrown across a generation, might rope them in and bind them to the past. In that case, Leah would want to protect Becky from Jeff. But how?

During the week Becky makes careful preparations for her date with Jeff. She steams her face daily. She drinks Diet Trim milk shakes, in addition to her regular meals. As Leah watches, I measure the depth of her frown line and sense her dread of approaching disaster increasing.

As for me, I feel less and less human as time goes by. I'm just as powerful—more so—and just as mobile as I ever was, but I don't feel as clean or as light or as pure as I did before. I feel a bit . . . logy. As if I had indigestion. Is it guilt? Maybe, in the state I'm in, whatever I do will inevitably lead to trouble. I don't see why that should be, though. Besides, look what I did for Daniel—that was a good deed, wasn't it? Doesn't that redeem me a little? But who knows how that will turn out in the end? Maybe I take too much responsibility, or give myself credit for more understanding than I actually possess.

I wonder what I'm creating out of myself. I could become like one of those monsters that are sometimes rumored to live in swamps outside of remote villages—I could be hated and feared by people who can't see me, or even give me a name.

Saturday night. "Flare night."

Jeff takes Becky for pizza at Dmitri's Number One. Becky chatters about Jeff's Earth Club, which she has just joined. "It's parthenogenic," she says. "I feel like I'm really making a *difference,* you know?" She adds, "I'm not sure I can make the next cleanup trip, though. I've got tech rehearsals for the play." She goes on to hold forth about theater, film, and television, and complains that Alta Vista High is "so regressive" that they have no video production studio.

Daniel comes over to wait on them. "Guy, like what are you doing here?" Becky wonders. "It's a Saturday night, why aren't you on snow patrol?"

Daniel was never quick with retorts. He turns to Jeff. "What can I get for you and your date, sir?" he asks.

While waiting for the pizza, Becky continues her monologue. She tells Jeff how she has decided not to let Jonathan or Elaina attend any of the upcoming performances of *Ah, Wilderness!* "Like, I already want to put a paper bag over my head most of the time I'm at school, the way everyone's blasting about this. My parents don't have to make a live appearance, too." She goes on: "I want to do some more classical work now, to broaden my range. Something like Edward Albee. I think he's gay, you know?"

She pauses when their order arrives, flipping her hair over her shoulders as Daniel silently lowers the flying-saucer pan in front of them. Jeff says, "You know, I've always been afraid of compromising myself. I think that's how politicians become corrupt. They start with something small that they think doesn't matter, and then before you know it, it's Watergate all over again."

Becky nods a perfunctory assent. As she helps herself to pizza, she giggles. "Daniel must be, like, mega-embarrassed that we've seen him pushing pepperoni."

Jeff does not reply. He lifts a slice of pizza from the metal pan; the mozzarella pulls away in narrowing threads that finally break and curl around the crust.

Jeff introduces the topics of honesty, relationships, and

human rights several times over dinner, but Becky never asks him to elaborate.

Later they drive up to the Hills. At Becky's insistence, they park Jeff's mother's Ford Granada in a less secluded spot than before, in front of the railing that was erected after Bobby Shafter rolled down the hill with a bottle of Jack Daniel's in one hand and Jennifer Merola's pantyhose in the other.

There is a steady blast of toneless noise that is the mingling of songs from the radios and tape decks of the surrounding cars. Roaming boys, carrying bottles in paper bags, lean through the open windows of the single girls' cars, trying to insinuate themselves inside.

"Guy," Becky says as she rolls down her window, "look at all the scuz faces that are out tonight." She giggles. "It's not even a full moon." She turns on the radio. "I am totally pining to hear that new Mutilated Spacemen song. I've been hooked to the transistors all day long and they just won't play it."

"Becky . . ." Jeff starts to roll up his own window.

"Don't roll up the window," Becky orders. "Somebody might want to come by and initiate some dialogue, you know?" She puts her head out of her own window again. "There's some girl in Georgie Wentworth's Corvette," she observes. "I can't see who she is—she's probably from lower A.V. But you know who I bet is here that I'd really like to find, is Janice Ingersoll. She's, like, my best friend, so it'd be terrificamente if we could say hi."

Jeff hesitates. Then, finally, he says, "Becky, I don't think we should go out—"

"Oh, there it is!" The waited-for song has begun. Becky turns up the radio until it reaches the approximate decibel level of a sonic boom. "I can't believe it—it, like, must be a sign." She snaps her fingers; her eyes are half-closed. She raises her chin so that her breasts move forward in rhythm. "Android lover, you burn my soul with your electric love," she sings along, holding the notes a little longer than the group's lead singer. "Kill me with your kisses . . . God, I love that line."

Jeff reaches over and clicks off the radio.

"*Guy,* what'd you do *that* for?"

"I have to talk to you."

"Well, guy." Becky's shoulders thud against the seat and she folds her arms under her breasts. "Go ahead then."

"I think . . . I think . . ." Jeff swallows. "I think we should start seeing other people."

"Guy, like what do you mean?"

"I've . . . I've . . ." He glances around him: Beyond the circle of moonish light from the single streetlamp, the darkness is inhabited by prowling teenagers. "I've fallen in love with someone else."

Becky's mouth opens, but she does not speak. I can feel her heart thudding, the heat of her face, the constriction of her stomach. "Like what's the big deal?" she demands. "Like we were just having a good time, right? I'm not supposed to terminate my existence, am I?" Her voice is like Billy Death's Head singing falsetto. She sucks her lower lip into her mouth, then quickly reaches over and turns the radio back on, raising the volume higher than it was before. She tries to sing along with the music while she looks out the window, away from Jeff. Her knee jostles up and down. "Guy, you act like it's a nuclear event," she mumbles. "I mean it's not like we were a major flare, we've only gone out twice. Do you think it was like a global event for me?"

"I didn't mean to . . . it's just that I wanted us to be . . . well, clear about things."

I hear the howls of the boys stumbling through the bushes on the other side of the road, looking for a place to piss out a case or two of beer. Becky is still looking out the window. Whoever Georgie Wentworth has in his Corvette has sunk down with him below view. Becky jiggles her knee as though jiggling a question in her mind, trying to worry it loose. She bites her lip and for a moment I think she's going to jump out of the car, but suddenly she turns toward Jeff and demands, "Who is it?"

"You don't know her," Jeff says. He grips the steering wheel. Then he adds, through a clenched jaw, as if speaking to himself, "I don't believe in lying. I think it corrupts you."

"Huh," Becky snorts, and her nostrils flare magnificently. "Are you guys like totally a megacouple now?"

"No." Jeff shakes his head. Then he blows air out between his lips, and I can see the outline of Marty Lindner in the shape of his face: the neck that may sag one day, the cheeks that might fatten. "I don't know what's going to happen."

"Wow," Becky says in mock awe. "Like I hope you can stand the uncertainty."

Jeff turns toward her. The frown between his eyes is like a fresh wound. "I think you're a terrific person," he says.

Becky's head jerks as if he has slapped her. Then, suddenly, she pulls on the door handle. "You can trash yourself," she says, piling out of the car in a jumble of legs. She slams the door as hard as she can and marches off; edging around Georgie Wentworth's Corvette, she heads toward the green Celica that belongs to Janice Ingersoll.

The house is dark when Becky returns. She has spent the intervening hours with Janice Ingersoll and Tracy Newhouse, who was with Janice in the Celica. Becky drank California coolers and loudly declared her groaners for almost every boy in Alta Vista, with the exception of Jeff Lindner, whom she accused of being not only a gump but a goon, and whose car she insists she left because he turned out to be such a weenie.

Janice and Tracy drop her off on Magnolia Street, and she slips into the house as quietly as possible. She waits in the foyer until her eyes adjust to the darkness, then she begins a soft climb up the stairs.

But there is one light on. Elaina's room.

"Beckaleelee? Is that you?"

"Yes, *mother*."

"Come here for a second."

*"Mow-ouse."*

"Please."

*"Guy."*

Becky places her hands on either side of the doorframe and tilts, like the Leaning Tower of Pisa, into the room.

Elaina is sitting up in bed. Her auburn hair is loose and falls just below her shoulders. The only light is from her bed-side lamp, a low-wattage bulb burning through an old-fashioned yellow shade covered with gathered material. She is wearing her surgical gloves, and a *True Confessions* magazine is open on the bed beside her.

"How was your date, cherry tart?"

"Fine," Becky says, through her nose, like a foghorn.

"What happened?"

"Nothing."

Elaina sighs and adjusts the top of the bedspread around her. "It hurts to be young sometimes."

Becky grunts. "Can I *go*, please?"

Elaina pats the bedspread. "Come here. Just for a second. I want to talk to you about something."

Becky slinks into the room, putting one leg out in a long, low step and letting the other leg drag behind her.

"Your sister really needs our help now."

Becky clicks her tongue against the roof of her mouth. She makes exaggerated circles with her eyes and lets her ban-danna'd head roll to one side. "Mouse, are you gonna start that again? I mean, doesn't it like ever occur to you that some peo-ple have their own problems?"

"Rebecca, how can you?" Elaina asks. "Your sister's in the *hospital*. She's in a *coma*. You just have to help me help her, or I don't know what's going to happen."

"Guy, what do you want *me* to do?"

"Testify for me."

Becky groans. "Guy, Mouse, haven't you got enough people already? Besides, me and Leah made a pact we wouldn't."

"Oh, that's right. I forgot." Elaina curls a lock of her hair around her finger. "Funny thing, I forgot." Pause. "I don't think you and your sister realize how important this is. We have to do something."

"We don't have to do nothing, Mouse. Why can't you just drop it? Dad's right. Why can't you just leave Mel alone?" Becky shudders. Even *she* probably thinks about the respirator at night, perhaps imagining that the winking machine with the wide plastic tube is there in her room, *whooshing* and *clicking* in the shadows. "I mean, is it just that Melissa looks so scuz now? Is that what shorts you out?"

"Rebecca, I don't believe you said that."

"Well, guy, she doesn't know how she looks. I don't see how she's hurting anyone just lying there." There is a film over Becky's eyes. "How come you always have to have your way?"

"Oh, Becky," Elaina sighs. "Someone like me just wants to be loved more than anything."

"Huh," Becky grunts.

"So it's pretty hard to be strong when you know you're making everyone hate you. It's pretty lonely, too." Suddenly, Elaina takes Becky's head in her hands and kisses her purple bandanna. "I'm sorry about Jeff, sweetheart," she says. "I'm really sorry."

Becky pulls her head away. Her chin falls against her chest.

Elaina strokes her hair. "The worst of it is now. It will get better," she croons in her lullaby voice. "He didn't appreciate you. You'll meet somebody much better. He'll always regret losing you."

Becky sighs. She does not seem to wonder how Elaina

knows what happened. Well, I guess it's pretty obvious that something is wrong, and what else could it be?

"And don't be angry at Leah. I know she loves you more than anybody."

Becky raises her head. "I *know* she does," she says slowly, in her foghorn voice.

"So don't blame her for what happened. She didn't mean it, I'm sure. I know she wouldn't hurt you for the world." Elaina puts her gloved hand under Becky's chin. "And I'm glad you girls are close. I wouldn't want to see anything happen to that."

Becky stares at Elaina. "You're shorted out, Mouse," she says. "I don't get what you're saying at all."

Elaina drops her hand. She looks down at the bedspread, carefully pulling it up around her. After a moment she says, "Well, I don't know what I was talking about either. Forget I said anything."

"I mean, are you like trying to say that Leah got together with Jeff? *Guy,*" she scoffs, "no way. It's not even feasible."

"You're right, of course. Please. Forget I said anything."

"Leah wouldn't do that!" Becky insists.

"Ssshh, please. You'll wake up your brother and sister. I know she wouldn't do that. I was mixed up. And even if she did do something like that, it wouldn't be her fault, it would be his. Men are like that. Well, not all men. I don't think your brother would do something like that, and my father wouldn't have either, although your grandmother—"

"You've just wonked out," Becky says. "And all my friends think you're weird, too." She gets up. "I'm going to bed now."

Elaina snatches at the hem of Becky's minidress. "It isn't true what I said. If you and your sister fight, it'll be my fault and I'll never forgive myself."

Becky jumps out of her reach. "Then why did you tell me?" she cries. "I hate you, Mouse! I really do!"

Becky slams the door and stomps up to the third floor.

Leah has fallen asleep, fully clothed, on top of her bed, with her French book open. A ballpoint pen has tumbled from her fingers to the valley of the binding of the book. Her mouth is open, and her blond hair is gathered in little tufts, like eiderdown.

Becky quietly sits down on the other bed. She folds her arms under her breasts and gazes at her sister.

After Becky leaves, Elaina gets up. She pads barefoot into my old room.

It's a clear night. Through the big window, one can see over the shadowy rooftops of lower Alta Vista to the shimmering lights that shape the familiar outline of San Francisco. Twinkling, distant, it makes me think of a celestial city, with the bridge a link—or a barrier—between two worlds.

This really is the best bedroom in the house. It's even bigger than the master bedroom, and it has the walk-in closet and a soft, thick carpet. Hardly worth dying for—but haven't most wars been fought over territory that seemed worthless to outsiders?

Elaina turns on the light.

The room looks the same as it did on the night they carried me out of there. The bed is even a little rumpled. It's a canopy bed, Drexel Heritage: a burgundy canopy with tiny blue flowers, and a matching bedspread and pillow shams. Rose picked it out for me. Next to the bed is the nightstand where I found the Percodan. I remember looking at them in the plastic bag, and I wonder now why Daniel put them in a bag like that, instead of leaving them in the bottle.

The books on the shelves are mostly novels that I read in high school and college. There are a few pictures of me and my friends on the dresser. One of the pictures is of me and Howard at a New Year's Eve party, the picture I gave a copy of to Rose. Why I framed it I'll never know—with my arms around him, Howard has the expression of a cat being squeezed by an overeager child.

The clothes in my closet look funereal, hanging above the scuffed shoes piled on the floor. There's a musty smell in the air, the smell of death, of defeat; the smell of something unused and abandoned.

I want to be out of here. I don't want to be reminded of who I was. I want to disassociate myself from that, to start to think of myself as something different. I would have changed, I know I would have! I just know that I was about to begin that focused, disciplined work that would have led to extraordinary achievements. If those Percodan hadn't been there . . . But my family can't know me as I would like to be. Haunting them, I become mired in their memories of me, and somehow, even without their knowing that I'm here, I have to behave as they would expect me to, and cause trouble. I wish I could bring them closer together instead of tearing them apart. But I don't know how I can do that. . . .

Elaina is going through my dresser.

She pulls out a black lace teddy I once wore in a futile attempt to distract Howard from the third quarter of the Cal-Stanford game. I'm glad she's found it. Before I started getting my meals through a nasogastric tube, I had a pretty good figure, complete with the famous Miller bustline. Why should Mickey Mouse think she's the only one with a sex life? I'm actually hoping she'll find my diaphragm—I think it's in the bottom drawer. . . .

But when she comes to the diaphragm, she passes it over quickly. Then, finished with the drawers, she moves a chair into the closet, where she stands on the tips of her little polished toenails, raising her arms so that her pink nightie reveals her dimpled thighs—and starts to go through the shoe boxes on the closet shelf.

I have to stop her. This is where I stored all my memorabilia. I was always into collecting something—postcards or matchbooks or cocktail napkins. Then I had my animal phases: ladybugs, unicorns, peacocks. There's nothing terribly incriminating in those boxes, but it's *personal*.

I try to dump the boxes on her head. There's a big pile of them, so it isn't hard to believe they'd fall over if someone started moving them around. If she were worried about their falling over, I could take advantage of that idea in her mind, and that might make me strong enough. . . .

Nothing. Can't do it. Damn! Why *not*? I can't get to her, that's all there is to it.

She opens each shoe box and rifles through the contents quickly. What's she looking for? Wait. I know. Evidence—that she can use at the trial. Of course! Oh, shit! There are some poems in there—Marty was right about girls like me—but they go all the way back to junior high, and they were mostly about sunshine and flowers and beaches. I think I'm safe.

Elaina moves the chair next to the bed and stacks a couple of books on it. Oh, God. My diary. I kept one during my first two years of college, and I wrote no dearth of maudlin, self-pitying stuff in it about how I wished I were dead and how then everyone would be sorry. I hid it, like Becky and Leah, where Elaina's sculpted nails would make it hard to reach, and where even Lee Emma doesn't dust: in the middle of the top of the bed's canopy. It's still there—a little red leather book.

Elaina gets it down. She must have found it years ago. She flips through it quickly, and turns right to November of 1981.

I said that when I met Howard I was recuperating from a bad affair. Well, during November of 1981 I was *having* the bad affair. And—I admit this reluctantly—the affair was with one Professor Willis. Thirty-five. Married. All right, so Elaina isn't the only adulteress in the family.

You know how love can be like a subtropic fever—a fever so high you start to hallucinate. So I imagined that Willie, as I liked to call him, since his first name was Cyril, who wore bow ties and smoked dark, foreign cigarettes, was charmingly ec-

centric, urbane; a modern-day Noel Coward, but more edu-
cated (although I was never blind to how badly he cut his hair).
After my fever passed, I saw him differently: He had a severe
case of naughty-boy syndrome. He would park his dented Ford
Escort five blocks from my apartment. He would cancel a date
with me because he thought the mailman might report his
movements, but then he would call me from a party, at 2:00
A.M., with his wife in the next room. It wasn't until several
years later that I fully comprehended that our affair had more
to do with his wife (who, according to him, was efficient and
frigid and who, according to campus gossip, was the youngest
woman ever tenured at Stanford) than it did with me. Willie
probably humped a new nineteen-year-old every year. Maybe
he still does.

Elaina already knows about Willie, though. I told her.
Funny, how you want to confide something like that to your
mother, even when she might use it against you later. I had to
tell her; she was the only one who could absolve me. And she
did. "Men are like coconut trees," she said. "And sometimes
one lands on your head and knocks you out."

There are some blank pages right around this time. After
Willie ended our "relationship," I kept the diary more irreg-
ularly for a while.

Elaina takes the diary over to the rolltop desk Jonathan
bought me for my twelfth birthday. She finds pen and paper.
She holds the diary open with her left hand, studying it as she
writes.

She's practicing my handwriting.

*All of my life,* she writes, *I've had a feeling that something weird
was going to happen to me. That I was destined for a sad kind of end. I
don't know what it is. But the worst thing I could imagine is being
hooked up to machines, and left to rot like an overripe tomato.*

Well, she's no Isaac Bashevis Singer, but she has captured
my style.

And I don't know how to stop her.

# 12

Sunday morning. I am summoned to the third floor of the house by the slamming of a drawer.

Leah is in bed; she must have awakened, undressed, and put herself there sometime during the night. Her eyelids flutter with the next *slam;* her eyes flash open wide, then close again; she rubs her head against the pillow.

Becky, in her short neon-purple nightie, is going through Leah's drawers just as Elaina went through mine last night.

Leah's mouth twitches and she makes a few murmuring, waking sounds. Then her eyes reopen, more slowly this time; the glaze dissolves. She turns her head toward her sister. "How . . ."—she begins groggily and cautiously—"how was your flare?"

Becky whirls on her. "I guess some people should have an idea!"

Leah slides lower under the blanket.

Becky drops to her knees and pulls open Leah's bottom drawer. She snatches something small and white from the miasma of seldom-worn T-shirts and jeans—it is Jeff's cocktail napkin from the party. She rolls back on her heels, holding it by one corner. "You tree-stee-flaitor!" she says. "You're the one who took it! I should have known!"

(Yes, when I fuck up, I do it perfectly.)

"I don't know how that got there," Leah protests; but her voice, still hoarse from sleep, sounds doubtful.

"Bee-stee-*full*-shit. Well, this is just, like, extra evidence." Becky discards the napkin on the compost heap of makeup on the dresser. Then she stares at herself in the mirror. "As if I ever could ever get a groaner going for Jee-steff anyway. He's a major weenie."

Leah pulls the sheet up over her nose and mouth. Her fingers with the bitten nails fold over the top. "What did Jeff say?"

"I guess you should know."

"Nothing happened," Leah says.

Becky narrows her eyes at Leah's reflection in the mirror.

"Or if it did, it was totally my fault."

"Huh."

"We're like never going to see each other again. He doesn't want to. I don't, either. I mean—"

"Huh," Becky cuts her off. She twists open a tube of mascara, slowly pulling out the brush. "As if I was even affected by it." She jabs the brush back into the mascara tube. "By the way," she adds, her voice suddenly thick with cruelty and pleasure, "I've decided to testify for Mickey Mouse."

Leah sits up. "But we made—" she begins.

"A pee-stee-flact? I can really like totally see how much that meant to *you*."

"But Mouse and dad—"

"Oh, who gives?" Becky retorts. "Relationships are fee-stucked anyway." She flips her hair over her shoulder, still addressing Leah's reflection. "Maybe it's just that I'm more mature than you are, Lee-steah, that I have a . . . a *longer* view of this. Like, a divorce just doesn't have global significance, that's all. So what if dad moves out? It's just another statistic. Guy, I'll be like going away to college pretty soon anyway."

Leah falls slowly backward on the bed. Her shoulders *ooomph* against the mattress.

"And you can like *forget* your rides to school," Becky says through purple nylon as she pulls her nightie over her head.

Her body is firm and white. "I don't let tree-stee-flaitors into *my* wheel box. I'm riding to school with Janice from now on."

Leah nods silently. She stares at the ceiling—but I don't think she sees the poster of Billy Death's Head. Rather, I imagine that she sees the family coming apart at last, like a handful of helium balloons released to float away into an empty sky.

The next day Elaina rises at ten. This is serious.

She shouts for Daniel, who does not respond to her call. She tries again. Finally Lee Emma marches upstairs, armed with her dustcloth, to tell Elaina that Daniel is not at home and would she please stop shouting.

"Where did he go?" Elaina asks, wringing her hands. "I need my son. I need him to take me to see my attorney. I have to be there at eleven and I'm too upset to drive."

"Maybe you're just going to have to get un-upset," Lee Emma says. She takes a random swipe at Elaina's dresser with the dustcloth and marches downstairs again.

Elaina phones Sheila Newhouse to see if Daniel is with Craig, but Sheila tells Elaina that Craig is still skiing. "Oh, Elaina, what you must be going through," Sheila says. "It's been such a long time now since Jonathan left."

"Aren't you sweet to be concerned," Elaina says. "I guess you know how hard a separation can be, from when Peter left you."

Elaina calls Dmitri's next, but Daniel isn't there either. "Tchure, I tell him, Meesis Silverstein," Dmitri promises. "I am sorry you are having heart attack."

After she hangs up, Elaina fusses for a while with a nail that is coming loose, worrying it until it almost comes off. Finally she starts getting ready.

Elaina has made me curious to know where Daniel is, so I concentrate on finding him—and land practically in his lap, like a well-aimed missile. Too bad they can't use me against the Russians.

Daniel is sitting with the Elf, in an office reception area. Above the receptionist's head are large metallic letters spelling out the name of PLASTIC AMERICAN, which is a national manufacturing firm with corporate headquarters in this pyramid-shaped San Francisco high rise.

Daniel is staring either at the metallic letters or at the receptionist, who is about twenty, with a very small chin, and a mole near her jawline. She wears earphones over her short blond hair, which is parted on the side and keeps falling over her eyes. She pushes it back, but she can't tuck it behind her ear because of the headset.

Daniel slouches down in his chair and opens the imitation-wood-grain folder on his lap. The folder contains background material on "GRADPO," an expensive piece of software that as far as I can gather is designed to take any average pot-smoking, authority-provoking, fast-driving eleventh-grader and make him obsessed with applying to college. Daniel ruffles the papers, making a flapping sound.

The Elf, whose legs barely reach the floor, is cleaning his nails with a small gold file. He glances over at Daniel and gives his high-pitched, almost-a-giggle laugh. "Don't be nervous. There's got to be a first time." Daniel looks up at him and smiles weakly.

My guess is they're waiting to see a prospective client, someone high up in the firm, a VP at least (a real VP, not one of those honorary call-'im-veepee-of-somethings); and that if the client likes the program (he must have a recalcitrant teenager at home), Daniel will follow up and get him to recommend it to his colleagues and staff.

The receptionist looks up from her console. "Okay, Mr. Silverstein, will you come with me?"

Daniel stands up, nearly dropping the folder. "Go get 'em," the Elf says, then returns to his nail file.

Daniel follows the receptionist down the hall. However nervous he may be, he seems quite distracted by the swaying of her ass under her snug yellow skirt.

"Look what I found," Elaina tells Marty. She must have driven herself to his office. According to Marty's clock, she's only forty-five minutes late for their appointment.

Marty takes the red leather book. A clump of ashes falls on the open page and he brushes them away. He reads slowly, moving his lips.

Elaina forged the entry at the bottom of a page that was only half written on, and she used a pen that wrote fuchsia ink, to match the one I used.

What's upsetting me right now is that Jonathan's going to see the whole diary. He would rarely listen to the stories that I *wanted* to tell him, so it doesn't seem fair that he should read about the parts of my life that I wanted to hide. Especially the part about Willie. Never mind that Willie was married—he was a *professor*. A girl could jeopardize her education that way, you see. Maybe he won't figure it out—I never mentioned Willie's position directly. I was a good student, at least, and I want Jonathan to have that one pristine memory of me.

"Heh-heh," Marty chuckles. "Left to rot like an overripe tomato. It's great." His chuckles break down into coughs. Finally, clearing the phlegm from his throat, he says, "This is just what we need." He smacks his lips. "Yes, just what we need."

Bastard! I'm sure he knows it's as phony as most of his teeth.

The wastebasket rattles. My fury is causing a tremor in the room. Marty feels the vibrations in his desk. "Jesus H.!" he says. "Are we having an earthquake?"

"I think it's just the wind," Elaina reassures him.

Marty's breath is shallow. "These buildings are supposed to be earthquakeproof, but I don't believe it."

Earthquake, hell. I almost feel that I could dump the
wastebasket on Marty's head, but I'd better conserve my energy.


Rose and Alison descend on Elaina that afternoon. Elaina
opens a package of fig newtons with the help of a scissors, and
persuades Lee Emma to make tea. Elaina then lays it all out on
the silver tray with the *S* engraved on it, a wedding gift from
Abe and Sophie, Jonathan's parents.

Rose is still wearing the sling, but she has managed to insert herself into a navy blue suit and powder blue blouse. She is
wearing a new pair of black heels. Alison wears a khaki
jumpsuit with epaulets, and boots with tiny gold spurs.

"You look wonderful, mother," Elaina says.

"Can you imagine how terrible I feel?" Rose asks. She reluctantly offers her cheek to be kissed. "Why did I reach down
to get that newspaper, can you tell me that?"

Alison is sitting in front of the tea and cookies. "I've been
steying with motha sence the hexident," she says. "Someone
really has to take . . ." She picks up a fig newton, sniffs it, puts
it down again. "Did you bake these yourself?" Then she laughs
her laugh.

"I'm so glad you both came over," Elaina says. She has
been fluttering around them, but she finally sits in the wing
chair. "I know we're going to have so much fun, all of us together." She lifts her cup to pour tea into it. The cup rattles
against the saucer, but I'm not doing it this time.

"Jonathan sent motha some levly flahers," Alison says with
a smirk. "Ryoses."

"Jonathan who?"

"Elaina," Rose says. She reaches for a cup, wincing as she
leans forward.

"Motha," Alison says, inclining her head, "playse let me
help yu."

"Elaina," Rose begins again, as she balances the cup and saucer on her knee, "Jonathan called me yesterday. He's very concerned. He wants me to talk to you, to *plead* with you, to listen to reason. This is your last chance."

Elaina starts spooning sugar into her tea and stirring it.

"Do you always use so much sugar?" Rose asks.

"I read an article in *W*," Alison says. "White sugar causes the brain cells to detariorate."

Elaina hits the spoon against the rim of her cup with short, rapid clinks. Simultaneously, Rose and Alison shiver. "I wish I knew where Daniel was," Elaina says absently. "I used to see more of him, or at least as much of him as there was."

"Daniel's such a nice boy," Alison says. "I just wonder sometimes if—"

"This is your last chance," Rose says. "Jonathan's not going to put up with this foolishness much longer."

"But in her diary," Elaina says, plaintively, "Melissa said—"

"What diary? What diary?" Rose chirps.

"I . . . I read Melissa's diary. I know it was wrong of me, but I thought maybe she just might have left us some kind of message there. You know, I always thought Melissa was a little psychic, just like me."

"Melissa kept a diary?" Rose demands, adjusting her sling and grimacing.

"Yes." Elaina's lower lip juts out. "I know it was wrong of me to read it, but I did, and she says very clearly that—"

"Let me see it," Rose says.

Alison, who is examining her sleeve for cat hairs, lets out a snort.

"Mr. Lindner has it."

"You're not really going to show it to the judge, are you?" Rose asks.

Alison laughs. "It's so ironic, the judge can't raid it himself. So if for some reason it looked phony—I main, if the writing wasn't quite what it should be—"

"I'm sure Melissa changed her mind later," Rose says. "And how do you know they won't find a cure? I read the other day about a woman who was in a coma for twenty-six years and just woke up one day and asked for her eyeliner."

"I've always thought it was so . . . *tacky* when diaries were read in court. And since the judge cahn't see . . ." Alison breaks off with a short laugh.

"I'm sure she changed her mind later." Rose nods. "People always change their minds, don't you think? And Jonathan was so upset. You should have heard him. I really felt sorry for him."

Alison inclines her head and looks sideways at Elaina. "I guess you end Jonathan aren't . . ." She stops.

"You're not *really* going to let everyone see her diary, are you?" Rose asks again. "I'm sure she changed her mind later."

"I dawt that Melissa would want people rayding her day-ary."

Elaina turns her cup around in its saucer. "I'm sure you're both right," she says meekly. "I'll go see Mr. Lindner and tell him I've changed my mind. I'll tell him I don't care anymore what my daughter wanted."

There is a long silence. Rose and Alison look at each other, both of them raising their eyebrows high and slowly, as if to say *Why don't we give up?* Their expressions are so identical that they look as if they're doing one of those mime exercises, pretending to be mirrors of each other.

Then Alison raises her cup of tea to her lips, sniffs it, and replaces it on the tray. "When was the lest time you washed that pot?" she asks.

"Lee Emma—"

"Oh, Lee Emma," Alison laughs. "I wish *I* hed a maid. But of cohse in New Yawk things are . . ."

Rose is looking up at the mantelpiece. "Why don't you put those photographs in some nice frames? Especially that one of Melissa—she was such a pretty girl." Pause. "It breaks my heart." She chokes a little, and with her good arm reaches into her purse for Kleenex.

Elaina stands. "Would you excuse me just a moment? I have to powder my nose."

With Elaina gone, there is another brief silence between Rose and Alison, measured by the long, noisy sips that Rose takes of her tea.

Alison is looking up at the cathedral ceiling. Finally she observes, "It's sech a beyutifil house. Too bed Elaina . . ." She shrugs.

"I'm so distressed," Rose says, trying to take a fig newton with her bad arm and wincing. "She's so unreasonable. I know there's going to be another divorce before we know it. Just what this family needs, another divorce."

Now Alison winces.

Rose bites into the fig newton. "He'll be looking for a new wife soon," she says as she chews.

Alison straightens one of her epaulets.

Rose dips her spoon into the sugar bowl, then stirs the sugar into her tea. "Look at this silver." She nods. "Jonathan's father could have given them much more of this, but he was so close with a dollar. Daddy and I couldn't afford to give gifts like this. Daddy wouldn't ask the congregation for more money." She puts the spoon in her mouth and stares at Alison with her steady gray eyes. "He won't be available long, a man like that. He's a great catch for some lucky woman, but she'll have to act fast."

Within a few hours, Jonathan learns of Elaina's new evidence from his own personal wire service, Grandma Rose. Rose also tells him that Becky plans to testify for Elaina, consoling him, "That poor little girl's just been brainwashed. Elaina's so difficult. Alison was never like that—she never even cried when she was a baby."

Jonathan won't see the diary until Debbie goes through the standard discovery procedures, but he immediately starts recruiting an army of handwriting experts who will say that the entry in question is of suspicious origin. I don't know if Jonathan thinks Elaina is capable of forgery or not—but that's hardly the point. He's a lawyer himself, after all.

Later he leaves a message for Daniel at Dmitri's Number One, asking him to come over to Silverstein, Inc., the next morning.

That night I am in Jonathan's dream. I don't just see it, I'm *in* it, and I know I'm in it, as surely as I knew that I was in the living room of our house that first night I was able to move from the hospital.

I am spectator and participant, just as I might have been in one of my own dreams, when I was still in a body and needed to dream. I see myself as a baby, wet with eyes closed, with the stubby, shriveled umbilical cord, smelling of sour milk. The dream is in the blurry, artificial colors of early television: My chest is red and my lips are purple. Rose, unseen, is asking, over and over, "Did you ever hear a baby scream so much?"

"You make more noise than the baby," Jonathan tries to shout at her, but she can't hear him.

Alison laughs. "She's certainly big for a premature baby."

"Better a fat baby than a fat adult," Jonathan says. "You're fat, fat, fat. . . ."

Jonathan is reading his constitutional-law hornbook. The print is big and looks like Hebrew. The baby is crying. I am crying. It is the middle of the night and Elaina is asleep and someone must feed me. Jonathan holds me and gives me my bottle. He is young and skinny. The baby is like a little rodent, with a large human head. Jonathan is singing to the baby. The words don't make sense, but he likes them, he sings them over and over, "Do you know the person man?"

The baby falls through his arms, crashes to the floor,

makes a hole in the floor, disappears into a blue sky that opens up beneath him.

Jonathan wakes up. I know because suddenly I am in his dark Holiday Inn room, floating above the bed. There are mysterious wet spots on Jonathan's temples and on the pillow.

Daniel arrives promptly at the requested time and makes the casual announcement "I can't stay too long." Then he sits, putting one ankle on the opposite knee. "I'm involved in a new venture"—he swings his arm out wide so he can look at his watch—"and I've got another meeting pretty soon. And then"—he sighs and shakes his head—"I've got a date tonight."

Obviously Daniel made the sale to the Plastic American exec yesterday. As for his date—which is even bigger news—I bet it's with the blond receptionist with the mole. Elaina would say natural blondes always look anemic. I guess Daniel's not going to let that stop him.

Jonathan is puckering a little, as if holding back a smile. I'm sure he's receiving progress reports from the Elf. Maybe Jonathan asked Daniel here in part so he could tell him that he was the one who sent the Elf in the first place; then he can deliver up a few parental aren't-you-glad-you-finally-listened-to-me's.

I was afraid of this. It would have been better for Daniel to see the letter in the first place. Don't tell him, dad! Jonathan wouldn't listen to me when I was in a body, but maybe he will now if I concentrate very hard. He has to! Don't get me wrong—it's not that I care about protecting Daniel. I just don't want to feel like I'm to blame for anything else.

"Are you testifying for your mother again?" Jonathan asks Daniel with fairly convincing indifference. "I'm just curious."

"I'm sorry, dad," Daniel tries to explain, "I hope you understand, but Melissa did say what she said about Celia Gold-berg, you know, and now there's this other thing, the diary—"

"You don't think she ever changed her mind." Jonathan nods, as if trying to understand a difficult legal point.

"Well . . . no. No, I don't think so." I can see that Daniel doesn't know what to do. His limbs ripple over the chair; he folds them up, but they spill over again. "I promised Mouse," he says with his confused, babyish frown.

Jonathan turns his swivel chair toward the window. After a moment he swings it back. "Do you want to tell me about . . . uh, your new venture?" he asks.

There's a gratitude in Daniel's expression that I've never seen before. "Yeah, yeah, I think I do," he says. "Real soon, dad."

Jonathan nods. I guess he *is* going to keep his part in Daniel's new job a secret. I'm glad. But I don't want to take the credit for that. I can never be certain, after all, whether it was my influence or a sensitivity that I didn't know Jonathan had.


As soon as Daniel leaves, Jonathan calls the Alta Vista High principal's office and has Leah summoned out of her al-gebra class. When she comes to the phone, he tells her that he's sending someone over to pick her up.

When Leah arrives, Jonathan is standing with his back to her, looking out the window at the Emeryville Flats. He turns around. "How about a hug for your old dad?"

Leah holds out her arms and allows the squeeze that pains the middle of her back. She is momentarily smothered by the darkness of his white shirt and gray suit. She wants him to hug her, so why does it hurt?

"I want to ask you a little favor." He sits behind the desk. When I was younger, I joked with Daniel that I was so used to seeing Jonathan behind his desk that I couldn't be sure he had a lower half. "Could you do a little favor for your old dad?"

"Uh . . ." Leah's mouth opens. "Sure."

"Here." He slaps one thigh. "Come sit on my lap."

Leah moves over to him, then eases herself down slowly, keeping one leg on the floor, trying to keep some of her weight on that.

Jonathan absently jiggles his knee, or tries to; it's hard with Leah perched there. "Mother and I . . ." He stops. "Sometimes two people . . ." Stops again.

Leah squeezes her eyes shut, as if waiting for a swift blow. She probably thinks Jonathan is going to tell her that he is about to file for divorce.

"I know this puts you in the middle a little bit," Jonathan begins. He turns his head away from her and looks out the window at the flats. There are new wooden tepees there, fashioned in the night as if by elves. "But I thought maybe you'd like to testify for me."

Leah opens her eyes. "Like what would I say?"

"Don't you want to stop mother?" Jonathan asks, as if he's encouraging a small child to eat her vegetables.

"I guess so." Leah hesitates. I think she is also feeling the weight of my presence in the family, as oppressive as it was when I was in a body, if not more so. Perhaps she is beginning to suspect that to save them all, I must be driven away. Whether that will be in time to save the marriage, she can't know. Perhaps euthanasia should be practiced on the marriage; perhaps Leah should accept its death as Jonathan should accept mine.

"Me and Becky sort of made a promise that we weren't going to do it for either of you guys," Leah says nervously. "I mean, I really hope you won't be mad. Okay, like, Becky changed her mind, but you see it's like, I mean . . ." She tucks her hair behind her ear. "I don't think I'd be very good at it anyway—I get kind of shorted out when I have to do stuff like that. I'm not like Becky—she does all that drama stuff, I always work backstage." She stops, perhaps fearful of hurting Jonathan with the reminder that Becky has taken Elaina's side.

"I think you'd be just fine," Jonathan assures her, attempting to jiggle his knee again.

"Well, like, you see, I made this promise—me and Becky made this promise, I mean—and I sort of think, like, we shouldn't, even though Becky says she's going to because, well, you see it's my fault that she's going to—she's doing it to get back at me, but I don't blame her, because if it wasn't for me—"

"I have something to say that might change your mind."

"Oh?" Leah sticks her finger in her mouth.

"Dear, are you still biting your nails?"

Leah removes her finger and rubs one of the calluses with her thumb.

Jonathan looks out over the flats again. "I think mother may have some . . . different motives for wanting to do what she wants to do."

"Oh, I see." Leah nods quickly. "Like what kind of . . . motives?"

"I think mother has a boyfriend," he says.

Leah turns her head away. The frown line divides her face into two sides of equal pain. I can hear her thoughts like a scream through a thin door. *Jonathan isn't her father.* That's the question she's always wanted to ask. The fear she's always had. Jonathan and Elaina were separated once—between Becky's and Leah's birth? And hasn't there always been some unknown, whispered—*something* about that? I feel Jonathan's hand on Leah's waist and his touch is as heavy as the rest of her life.

I wanted them to know about Elaina's affair. All of them. I didn't think; I never do.

"Oh," Leah says. She nods and just keeps on nodding while she rubs the callus on her index finger.

"I didn't want to tell you." Jonathan smiles a little, apologetically, as if he just inadvertently gave away the end of a murder mystery.

"Uh-huh." Leah is still nodding.

"So you see." Jonathan is waiting. Now Leah has a choice. She has always tried to please him, with her rows of A's and her feigned interest in real-estate development. She has tried to reassure herself all these years that Jonathan, the man she has loved from afar, which is as close as he would let her get to him, is bound to her by the duties of father. But if not, then the hole she already couldn't dig herself out of has become infinitely deep. If she doesn't do what he says now, he will have no reason to love her. Not that he has a reason to love her now, but there's always hope.

But I know something Leah doesn't know. She is Jonathan's favorite. She always has been, I realize. Oh, not that he loves her *that* much more. It's just that now I'm aware of nuances that were too subtle for me before. How could Leah know? The more Jonathan loves someone, the more he has to hide it, deep in the basement of his mind, in the trunk full of discarded objects from his own childhood, like a toy he was never allowed to play with.

"Guy, dad, yeah, I mean, I'm wired with your point of view." The finger returns to her mouth. "So I guess like if you really want me to testify, then . . ."

Jonathan starts to smile. For an instant I see Leah's face as if it were a reflection in a rippling pool, divided into numberless, shifting sections. Then suddenly she frowns and shakes her head.

"Guy, dad," she says, sliding off his lap. "Guy, dad, I guess I can't, 'cause . . . like . . . I really promised—I promised myself that I wouldn't take sides."

"Ah."

"And you see, if I did take sides, if I let myself, then I'd have to testify for . . . What I mean is, I couldn't stand to be left like Melissa is now. It's so horrible to think about—it's like you're stuck somewhere and you can't get out."

"Of course."

"So, I was really upset when Mouse said she wanted to go to court. I didn't think that was right—I thought you guys should talk about it. But still, you know, I really don't think Melissa would want to be like this, so I just can't do it." *Even for you.* "I'm sorry. I hope you won't be mad."

"Why would I be mad?" Jonathan asks, his voice rising.

"I'm really, really sorry," Leah says.

"Ah." Jonathan can barely make the sound. He pulls at his tie. Leah swallows. She looks dizzy—as if she were being carried away by a gust of wind, like a helium balloon.

# 13

I'm not at all pleased with the way things are going.

The authenticity of the diary entry doesn't seem open to serious question. Jonathan's handwriting experts have told him privately that they think I'm the author, though they're still willing to testify for him, making the most of the tail of a *G* that's a little short.

Only my mother could do this to me.

She's still immune to my powers. I've tried everything—sending mental messages to Marty to drop the case, setting fire to the diary (I thought spirits were supposed to be good at starting fires), writing Jonathan a note, and dropping a house on my mother.

Nothing works.

At first I tried to reassure myself that if Drew's story wasn't enough, then a diary entry written six years ago certainly wouldn't be. But Drew's testimony couldn't be corroborated, whereas Becky and Daniel will testify that the diary entry is in my handwriting and my phraseology, and that it reflects a state of mind consistent with my verbally expressed opinions. It's up to the judge to decide whether, as a matter of law, that is adequate evidence to give Elaina custody of me and to let her pull the plug. With everything else she's lined up, it seems like it might be.

Will she win, then? Hasn't Elaina always gotten more or less everything she's wanted? Or has she? It's hard to know,

259

because what she wants seems to shift so rapidly, like the patterns of a kaleidoscope, composed of what she wanted before, and yet altered. It's her winning that I really can't stand, even more than the idea of dying. Of course, that still frightens me. It seems so . . . permanent.

And I've been feeling weird lately. Sort of . . . *greasy*. Unattached. Slippery. Perhaps I've been weakened by my attempts to fight my mother. All my life I've found that exhausting.

And so the retrial begins.

At 8:45 A.M., the parties have gathered outside the courtroom. A sprawling but subdued crowd: the family a loose constellation with a few reporters roaming like restless space travelers among them.

Near the courtroom doors, Jonathan pulls at his tie, then jerks his neck away from his collar.

Rose is nearby; she wears her sling as if it were a diplomatic sash. Her chin is raised, but from beneath lowered eyelids she is warily looking out for the woman in orange lipstick from the *Alta Vista Voice*. Alison, sniffing at a paper cup of coffee, stands on one side of Rose, ready to fend off Ethel Lemmon or the rabbi's wife, while Becky slouches on the other. Rose plucks at the sleeve of Becky's dark wool temple dress and asks, "Are the girls wearing such high heels now?" Becky grunts. Rose adds, sullenly, "You're really sure you want to do this, I suppose." Then, a moment later, "I suppose you're absolutely certain." Pause. "How does your father feel about all this?"

At the edge of the group, Daniel is leaning against the wall with his hands in his pockets. From this distance, he surreptitiously watches Jonathan.

Drew stands off to one side. His skin looks sallow, the color of brown mustard. His hair, flat and greasy, is beginning to grow stringily onto his forehead. His hands tremble; he occasionally presses them against his sides to steady them, but then the trembling passes into his torso. He will not be asked to testify until tomorrow, since he is scheduled as the plaintiff's final witness, but I guess he just couldn't stay away. It was his chance to see Elaina, who has continued to avoid him: Marty Lindner was the one who called him to arrange to review his testimony.

Even Drew must know by now that Elaina was just using him. But like a drug addict, he remembers the pleasure of the first hit of Elaina, and he keeps chasing after the memory of that, compulsively, like a dog running after passing cars. I sense that he longs to confess his sins. But he can't do it himself; he needs help. He's like any drug addict on the way down from his drug—he can find relief only in the oblivion of a stronger drug, or death.

Leah stands on the opposite end of the group from Becky. She watches Drew with pity in her eyes; I see that she has intuited, if not all the details, at least the crucial fact of his relationship with Elaina. In her dark temple dress, Leah is Cassandra in mourning, for she knows now that it is through Dr. Harding that the revelation will come.

Elaina is in the ladies' room.

The bailiff comes to unlock the courtroom and the crowd begins to funnel inside. Everyone moves slowly and no one talks. It reminds me of a funeral.

Becky and Leah are among the last to enter. By design or coincidence, they reach the door from opposite sides at about the same time. And then, reflected in the mirror of her sister's face, Leah sees that Becky is looking at something behind Leah, something that appears to frighten her. Leah looks over her shoulder, and sees Jeff Lindner approaching them.

He wears a light gray suit, a red tie, and penny loafers. His father has already gone into the courtroom. Jeff approaches the girls at a steady jaunt, the frown deep in his forehead, but an incipient smile on his lips. He is pale this morning, and his eyebrows stand out black and thick under his high forehead. He looks a little like a young Jonathan.

Leah sees how Becky sweeps into the courtroom, flipping her hair over her shoulders and raising her chin. Leah ventures only a hesitant glance at Jeff before she bites her lip and follows after her older sister.

The blinds are up; a fragile sunlight filters through the high windows of the courtroom. At the plaintiff's table, Marty has his binder open before him. He clears his throat, making several *hawooking* sounds, while he turns the pages.

Elaina, who clacked in a couple of minutes after everyone else, sits next to him. The sunlight falls around her as if it were a lacy golden shawl. But in the sunlight and through her black net veil, I can see her age. The crinkling of her skin around her eyes, like fine white linen that needs to be ironed. And beneath that, shining through that, the outlines of her face that are eternal, incorruptible. And something else—a look of sadness. She is composed. No tears this morning.

Jeff has taken a seat near the back. Becky and Leah face forward, their necks and shoulders stiff with ignoring him.

"All rise," the bailiff commands, and the huge white dog leads Judge Picone in. The judge's brown shoes are visible beneath his robes. He stumbles on the way up to the bench.

Now it starts all over again. Marty and Debbie take out their toneless sheet music and start their shuffling, clumsy dance; I can almost hear them grunt as they verbally step on each other's feet. They accuse and retract and apologize, and accuse again.

Jonathan and Elaina sit silently. Occasionally they glance at one another, and if the other is looking, they both quickly look away.

Elaina takes the stand first. She is calm as she testifies to finding my diary on the top shelf of my closet while she was cleaning. *Cleaning?* That alone should give her away, but she is so convincing that I almost remember putting the diary there instead of on top of the canopy. Marty duly has the diary admitted into evidence.

Elaina's composure, for the moment, has spread to me. I feel lulled, hypnotized, by her voice. I start to think to myself, Would it really be so terrible to die? And suddenly I'm fascinated by the idea. I think of a roller coaster, of that sweetly agonizing moment as the car reaches the top. I think of the dark closet where Daniel and I played when we were very small.

When court recesses for lunch, Jeff follows the girls out. They take short steps, tilting forward on their too-high heels. Becky struts ahead to the ladies' room. Leah follows, but more slowly, letting the gap widen between her and her sister.

"Leah. Wait."

Leah takes a few more halting steps forward, but then she stops and turns.

"You're probably wondering why I'm here." A brief grin cracks the smooth marble of Jeff's forehead.

Leah looks around to see who might be watching—Elaina, Rose, Alison—who might then report the conversation to Becky. But then she looks back at Jeff and seems to remember that he is the one who is dangerous. "I thought," she says, not without sarcasm, "that maybe you wanted to see your dad in action. Like maybe you want to check out his courtroom style."

Jeff loses his grin and shakes his head. "I'm doing a story on the trial for the *Reporter*." Jeff is on the staff of the Alta Vista High newspaper. "I think it's time we stopped covering the football games as if they had global significance."

"Right. So instead you want to write about my parents having a nuclear war in front of the known universe," Leah retorts. "Is that why you wanted to go out with Becky in the first place? Are you planning to write like some kind of major study about what it's really like to have a sister in a coma?"

Jeff looks startled for a moment. Then he snorts, "*Huh.* It's not like some people don't act like they're too good for other people. Every time I see you in the hall, you go running the other way like I'd been exposed to plutonium."

"Well, *guy.*" Leah looks at one of her bitten nails. "You had to go and tell Becky about . . . about what happened. She's *majorly* hurt, you know."

"But I didn't tell her," Jeff insists. "Honest to God, I didn't."

"Well, guy, then." Leah notices Drew, leaning against the wall, his arms dangling limply, his head hanging, like a discarded rag doll. A few feet to the left of him, Jonathan stands in muffled conference with Debbie. Alison hovers nearby, wearing a strange smirk that is supposed to be a smile but resembles instead the expression of a hawk. And then Leah knows. Elaina.

"I've been wanting to call, to see how you are," Jeff is saying. "I was afraid to. I didn't know what you wanted."

"You could have asked," Leah points out.

Jeff's head starts to droop, but then he looks up. "I'm asking now," he says firmly.

Leah glances over her shoulder in the direction of the ladies' room. "Ask me again," she says. "But, guy, not here, and not now."


Marty's pelican lips spread into a leer as, one by one, Elaina's witnesses come forward, the evidence accumulating, making Elaina appear increasingly like Florence Nightingale and Jonathan look more and more like Josef Mengele.

Becky removes her sugarless gum before she gets on the stand. And before God, her father, and Jeff Lindner, she says that she genuinely and sincerely believes that my wish would be to die.

For me, the afternoon passes strangely, fluidly. I feel as if I were drugged. It reminds me of that last night I was at home, the first haze of the Percodan kicking in, and then the rising nausea as the Percodan and the alcohol met like two opposing waves in my bloodstream, the undertow sucking me down, and the last thought I had as I reached for the air that was disappearing forever over my head—*You finally blew it for real.* You only get so many mistakes that mommy and daddy can take care of, and this was one too many.

And now I remember. I thought of it then, as I was going under. Norman, the movie critic—the skinny, bearded, neo-hippie and failed revolutionary. *He* gave me the Percodan to keep—they weren't Daniel's at all. Norman said they were almost as good as Quaaludes, which you just couldn't get anymore—he knew someone who made pretty good Quaaludes in his darkroom, but bootleg was bootleg, and sometimes a little D76 might fall into the mixing bowl.

I looked at the Percodan in the plastic bag and there I was at home again and Daniel was a prig and the newspaper was bankrupt and then I was thinking, Why not, why not? Why not take these and see what damage I can do, make them all worry about me and be sorry for me? But never thinking I would do this, no, never this. . . . But it's too late to change that now. I'll never know if I would have gotten it together. That's all.


Court recesses at four.

Elaina prevails upon Daniel to drive her to the hospital. She still never misses a day of visiting me. You might almost think she cared. Unless she's just determined to trick Dr. Haus, the resident who replaced Drew after Drew was fired, into complimenting her beauty, or at least telling her that she doesn't look forty-two. This new resident has been a tough case; to all of her hints he remains indifferent. I wonder if she's sorry that Drew got dumped.

It's only when I get back to the hospital with her (and I follow her rather sluggishly) that I learn of a disturbing development. I have pneumonia. No wonder I've been feeling so weird.

"Why didn't you call me this afternoon?" Elaina demands of the new resident. "This is my firstborn child."

Dr. Haus is stocky, square-faced, with coarse, big-pored skin and thick wire-rimmed glasses. He is as uninterested in Elaina's grief as he is in her charms. He didn't even laugh when she asked him if he made "Haus calls." Now he runs his fingers down my nasogastric tube. "We didn't get the lab test back until just a little while ago." He seems to forget Elaina for a moment as he makes a note on a clipboard. "We're giving her antibiotics now. She should pull through."

"Thank God," Elaina says. She sounds hoarse.

Two nurses are flipping my body over, in their continuing and futile battle to rid me of bedsores. I feel a little dip as they do, like driving down a hill. I don't like this.

Elaina stares at the curled-up, bony thing on the bed. She looks a little sick. And I bet I know what she would say to me if she thought I could hear. "This is *typical*, Melissa. You could have done this three months ago and saved us all a lot of trouble. But no, you have to get pneumonia *now*."


Alison is wearing a hat that resembles a pith helmet. Very chic—but I keep thinking how Elaina would say that she looks like she's about to go lion hunting.

"I guess I'll be going back to New Yawk soon."

Jonathan flings his briefcase on top of the Holiday Inn bed, snaps it open, and rifles through it.

Alison sighs, tilts her head carefully, and tucks a section of ash-blond hair back into the hat. "I rally love running my own business, it's just thet . . ." She stops. She sees that Jonathan is not listening; she frowns, clicks her tongue, and sighs again. "Even though New Yawk is supairior in hevery way, I'd much rather live hair now. I suppose thet's becuhse—" She breaks off. "You know, your perfectly levely suit is just a teeny-weeny bit wrinkled in back. Maybe you'd laike—"

Jonathan turns around with a piece of paper in his hand. "Look." He holds up the paper. "One of my lawyers drew this up. I've got it in writing now."

Alison leans toward it, sniffs it as if it's food.

"I want you to take it to Elaina."

Alison rubs one corner of the document between her thumb and forefinger. "I don't understend."

"It's an offer. Legal. Anything she wants in the property settlement, but she has to drop this suit. You have to take this over to her now."

"Property settlement?" Alison inquires hopefully.

"Yes. In a divorce proceeding. Take it to her."

"Tonight?"

"Right now." Jonathan folds the paper and hands it to her. "If I go over there, she'll just get hysterical." He looks blank for a moment; his voice is strained, puzzled. "She hates me. I can't understand why."

Well. I got what I wanted. I've never seen dad so upset. There are red splotches in the whites of his eyes. I can almost see flecks of blood and foam on his lips. It may simply be the thought of losing. I guess he can't believe, any more than I can, that he—the man who has outwitted every Stanford Business School graduate who has come his way—is going to be felled by the *zaftig* woman whom he has placated for years simply by signing checks. It can't be that his tireless hewing and chipping away at the imaginary poverty his father taught him to fear will be for nothing. It can't be that the money he has measured his success by won't protect his children. He seems mad. And glimmering behind the madness, the dark fire in his eyes, is the realization that Elaina is not the enemy. That the enemy is life, and he cannot buy his children's safety, no matter how many towers he builds, no matter how many weekends he works. That Elaina is right: that I am dead.

"She hates me, too," Alison says indifferently, looking at the document in her lap. "I've nevah understood it. You end I—I thank we hev much more in cammon."

Jonathan is pacing next to the bed. "Get her to sign that," he says sharply. "Now."

Elaina is still at the hospital. Why doesn't she call Jonathan? He has a right to know about this.

It took me much longer than my usual *zap* to get from Mt. Moriah to the Holiday Inn, and the return trip was even more bumpy. Now there are bands of tension, like zippers, that run up and down my field of vision; they get wider as I try to concentrate on fighting this disease. I feel a choking sensation—it must be an echo of what my body is going through. I'd forgotten what a daily struggle it is just to live.

I don't want to die. I remember how I felt just after the charter plane took off to go to Brussels, taking Howard and me to Europe. We were arguing because I wanted him to play Travel Scrabble and he wanted to read—but mostly I was scared of the trip ahead: scared of oddly shaped toilets and of not being able to find places to sleep and of being arrested for something I didn't know was illegal. That's how I feel now.

But I can beat this. I'm sure. Melissa Silverstein, in a body, wouldn't have tried; she would have taken to her bed with the *Soap Opera Digest* and a tin of butter cookies. But I'm a different Melissa Silverstein at last.

Elaina sits quietly by my bed as it begins to grow dark. She does not turn on the light. *Whoosh*-click, goes the respirator. Her shadow climbs slowly up the wall, along with the shadows of the respirator and the monitor and the IV tube. The room is inhabited by ghosts. I am recalling my childhood diseases— measles, chicken pox, flu—when Elaina would read to me. No peanut butter sandwiches then; too heavy. Yes, she made soup. And I remember—how did I forget this?—the broken arm I had when I was five; how at night my skin would itch under the cast, and she would take the handle of a flyswatter to scratch underneath; how she would get into bed with me and Jonathan would call her to come upstairs but she would keep saying, "Just a minute," and then she would fall asleep, and then I would burrow next to her until I fell asleep, too.

Suddenly there is a click and the hospital room is deluged with bright, unnatural light. Alison has come in. "Becky told me you were here," she says. "Don't you want the light on?" Alison's laugh is short and harsh.

Elaina starts, and looks up at her sister, as if at a stranger. "Yes, I guess so."

Alison looks at me and then looks away. I remember, when I stayed with her in New York, how she would try to keep from looking at the hulky blind black man who stood outside of Saks Fifth Avenue with a sign around his neck that said THERE BUT FOR THE GRACE OF GOD. She knew just where he stood, so she could have avoided him completely by using the Fiftieth Street entrance, just like she could resolve not to look at me. But that would be too easy. She has to struggle with her fascination for me, someone who really *might* be too skinny. "That poor thing," she says. "I'll never get used to it, will you?"

Elaina doesn't seem to hear.

Alison stands behind Elaina's chair. I wonder if she meant it when she asked me to move to New York. I think she did. She liked me—and maybe not just because I belonged to Elaina. Maybe when she came out here a few months ago, she hadn't completely given up hope that I would get better; maybe that was even one reason why she wanted to fight on Jonathan's side. But once she saw me, she accepted the facts.

"She's sick," Elaina says faintly, "I should call Jonathan, don't you think? But it's so hard for him to deal with things like this."

"Sick? How can she be sick when she's—"

"Pneumonia."

"Oh, my God."

"Yes." Elaina tugs at the hem of her skirt. "I don't know what to do."

"Well, there's nothing you *can* do, is there?"

"There should be something I can do."

"I don't think there is." Pause. "I think you just have to wait it out."

But isn't this what Elaina wanted? Or does she just want the pleasure of yanking that cord herself? Is she afraid that I'm going to die before she can win, and cheat her out of her victory? I watch the respirator bellows—*whoosh*-click, *whoosh*-click. I can feel it now in a way I couldn't before. It's as if something's tugging at me. And then a quiver runs through my body—I see it jerk on the bed below me. As it moves, Elaina gives a little cry, starts forward in her seat, only to fall back again.

"Melissa's *always* done that," Alison observes in a monotone. "It's just reflexes." But she is hugging herself.

"I never get used to it," Elaina says. "Every time she does that, I think . . ." She shrugs and stops.

Alison looks at me again, this time holding her gaze a bit longer. "Is she really sick? Maybe it would even be better. . . ."

Elaina looks over her shoulder and glares at Alison. "How can you *say* that?"

"Huh," Alison snorts. "You're the one—"

"I know, I know." Elaina turns toward me again. "But not like this."

"Laike how, then?" Alison inquires.

Elaina says nothing. There's something on her face that I haven't seen before. I can't quite say what it is. But it reminds me of what I saw in court this morning, of something sad and eternal. It makes me think of her taking me and Daniel to the park, of my rolling down the grassy hill that led to the lake. As if that were still happening somewhere.

"I jest talked to Jonathan," Alison says finally.

"Oh? How *is* Jonathan?"

"Jest fine." Pause. "He really wants you to drep this, yew know. There isn't much time."

Elaina leans over the bed and arranges the covers around my neck for the thirtieth time at least. What, does she think I'm cold? "Marty says we're going to win," she says. "I don't know about these things."

"No, of cohse not. But Jonathan . . ."

"Yes?"

"Jonathan sehs . . . you can hev anything you want if you'll drep it now."

"Anything?" One of Elaina's stiletto-thin arched brows raises slightly.

So that's what all this was about all along! Now it makes sense! She saw this as an opportunity for a divorce on her terms. If she had divorced Jonathan on her own, he would have been able to hide away a lot of his assets. But now she's made him desperate enough to buy her off with a fair share of his millions. She wants the money so she can travel. She'll go to Monte Carlo, Martinique, Bora-Bora, Nassau, Malta—all those exotic places where Jonathan would never take her. She'll find another man to take with her, not a wimp like Drew, but not a mogul like Jonathan, either: the perfect man who can satisfy and protect her.

"Well, *almost* anything." Alison shrugs. "I'm sure. I'm sure he didn't mean . . ." She looks down.

"What's the matter?" Elaina asks. "Are you worried that I won't leave enough for the two of you?"

"Don't be silly." Alison's laugh sounds like tin cans dragged behind a car. "We talked about it for a while, he end I—we were at the hotel. . . ." Alison's tactic is to make the enemy think she's already lost. "I know he wants to take keh of yew."

Elaina tries to make fists, but her nails are too long for her hands to close properly.

"Well?" Alison asks. "I'd do it if I were you. You must want a divorce anyway, or you wouldn't . . ." She stops.

"No," Elaina says.

"I beg your pardon?"

"No."

"I don't understand. If Melissa is *sick* . . ." If Melissa is sick, then she might die anyway, so why not give in to Jonathan and get a divorce and leave the way clear for your big sister who's been single for eighteen years and from whom you stole Jonathan anyway, and who would make him a much better wife, spend his money with more style, give *lievely* parties, flirt more circumspectly with his colleagues?

"I don't understand *you*," Elaina cries, and now the wild look is in her eyes, a look I know well. "What do you think, I'm just going to *hand* him to you? He's still my husband, though nobody seems to want to remember that!"

"You're being . . ." Alison stops.

Elaina stares at her. I wait for the explosion, the rage, the pulling of hair. The tears and screams that will bring the nurses in with the sedatives that Elaina seems to enjoy so much. But it doesn't happen. The high waves in her eyes die down again. "If you say so." She smiles faintly.

And I can see, shadowing my aunt and my mother, like the ghost image on an old black-and-white TV set, the two little girls they once were. The silhouettes of those little girls pantomime the tightrope walk that they had to perform to hold up their own parents. Elaina and Alison knew early what they had to do. The only problem is that the curtain never falls on this particular circus act.

Elaina arranges the covers around my chin again. "You could do me a favor," she says, without looking at Alison. "Tell

Jonathan, when you see him—*at the hotel*—that his daughter is sick."

I'm curious to go back to the house and see what's going on. I pass familiar streets and stores; halfway there I almost turn back. I feel carsick, or whatever the equivalent is.

But I finally arrive and find Daniel, Becky, and Leah together in the living room.

Daniel is resting his forehead on the mantelpiece, gazing down at a pyramid of logs he arranged in the fireplace. Becky is drinking diet hot chocolate, with the headset of her portable tape player loose around her throat. Leah, feet on the couch, is staring over the top of *Great Expectations.* "Maybe we should give a buzz over there?" she asks.

"Mouse said she'd call if there was news," Daniel says. He crumples a sheet of newspaper and bends over to insert it between two logs, but then sighs and places it on the mantel, next to my picture.

Nobody speaks for a long time. Becky's hot chocolate is getting cold.

"Me tomorrow," Daniel says, finally. I guess he means his testimony.

"Huh," Becky says. "Well, if you still want to. I mean, I bet you could tell mom and those guys that you changed your mind."

Leah says nothing. Becky looks at her angrily, as if her silence were an accusation. "I mean," Becky says, "like, I already did it, so I guess there's nothing I can do about it now." She adds, more peevishly, "I only said like the tree-stee-fluth."

Leah nods absently. I wonder if it's occurred to her that if I die tonight, the remainder of the testimony will not be heard. That means *Drew's* testimony will not be heard—and Daniel, Becky, and Rose need not know about Elaina's affair. Because if Elaina's had one affair, then how many others. . . ?

"Guy, Lee-steah!" Becky cries. "It's not a nuclear event, is it? Tee-stell me it's on lee-stine."

"Ssshh," Daniel soothes her. "Everything's going to be all right." He straightens, and folds his hands in front of him, as Jonathan might. "We're all doing what we have to do."

Leah's head quivers. She seems not have heard anything. She lowers her eyes to the page of her book.


Elaina is still sitting up with my body at the hospital. Sometimes she breathes as though she has fallen into a light sleep, with her cheek resting on her hand; but then her elbow slips off the metal arm of the chair and she starts awake.

Elaina's presence was the strongest pull of all, and I had to come back here once again. I'm still amazed that she didn't accept Alison's offer. How mutable and elusive she is. Sometimes she is a vine growing over the trellis; sometimes she is the young flowers poking up from the earth; sometimes she is a banyan tree. I wonder if I haven't been wrong about her all along, about her motives, about so many things. The moments of strength and love that occur so unpredictably—sometimes they're like bait, taunting me with how she could be. Sometimes they're messages I uncode: "I *want* to be like this all the time, but I can't. I never grew up either. I'm only a mother because I gave birth to you. There's nothing special about that."

I will never understand her, even if I hover next to her for the rest of her life and beyond. There's only so far I can penetrate. And with the others now I wonder how much, when I have felt their thoughts, my own projections have mingled with the truth.

The nurses come in periodically to shift my position. Elaina starts awake and, bending her wrist to ease the stiffness, groggily asks them how I am doing. They shake their heads and click their tongues and say that they don't know.

If I could talk to Elaina, I could tell her that I'm going to be just fine. I'm already feeling airier. Her vigil has accomplished just what a mother's vigil is supposed to accomplish: given me strength. And with that strength my perceptions are crisp and telescopic again; I am rising up to say to my mother, You can't destroy me, no matter what you want.

She has given me strength to fight her. Whatever her motives, however they may change, I must be stronger than she is. I am.

It is a little before 3:00 A.M. Drew Harding is alone in his apartment, sitting on the sofa. He is bare-chested, wearing silver running shorts; his bare feet are propped on the coffee table, and he is gulping Courvoisier.

I traveled here with my old speed. I'm definitely back on the canvas.

Drew belches. His head tilts and his eyes roll, and I think he's about to toss 'em on the carpet—but then he balances the bottle on his knee and starts to sing "Ave Maria."

I know he doesn't want to testify tomorrow. His moral sense hasn't been completely numbed; and surely he realizes—somewhere in that stupor of his—that no lies will win Elaina.

I bet he'd love to find a way out. And I am going to answer his prayer. Can I pull it off? I've got to believe that I can. Drew has always been the easiest to influence.

I float directly above the phone on the kitchen counter. I concentrate. Nothing happens. I'm not giving up. I concentrate harder.

The phone rings. Drew jerks forward, dropping the bottle, which rolls away, leaving a brown trail of the few remaining drops of Cognac. Only one person would call him this late at night. She used to wait until Jonathan and my siblings had gone to bed, sneaking down to the kitchen; Drew could always count on her to phone when he was just falling asleep after being on call for forty-eight hours.

I concentrate. The phone rings again.

Drew is staggering to his feet now; he stubs his toe on the leg of the coffee table and moans aloud but still lurches forward—grabs the receiver and pulls the phone off the counter. "Elaina?"

"Yes, darling."

*"Elaina."* He is almost weeping.

"Ssshh. It's going to be all right now."

I concentrate on the words and Drew hears them. I don't know if someone else would hear me speaking or not, but that doesn't matter. Even Grandma Rose couldn't always tell my mother and me apart on the phone. It's the husky voice that runs in the family.

"Listen, sweetheart. We have a mission now. And you have to carry it out."

"I do?" Drew sounds eager. I thought he'd like this.

"Yes. Tomorrow, when it's time for you to take the stand, I want you to get up there and tell everyone that what you said before was a lie. Tell them that what I really said—I mean, tell them what Melissa really said was that she didn't want to die, no matter what."

"Are you sure, Elaina?"

"Yes, I'm sure. Tell them you did it for me because you were in love with me—"

"But—"

"And I wouldn't go to bed with you. You tried everything."

"But then . . ."

"You might have to go to jail for a little while. Maybe I will, too. But that's all right. It will be absolution for both of us. We'll wait for each other, then we'll be together forever and ever. We'll go back east, like we said before."

"But . . . but will they believe me?"

"You have to make them believe you. Make them believe you and I'll be your slave for life."

"Oh, Elaina," Drew sobs. "You don't have to do that."

"But I want to, dear. We'll be so happy together."

"Oh, yes," Drew blithers. A little saliva is running out of the corner of his mouth.

Well, how about *this*? I'm pretty pleased with myself, yes, indeed! But in all modesty, Drew was always easy. He'd probably be imagining a conversation about animal health with Saint Francis by now if I hadn't arranged this first.

Drew hangs up. He smiles peacefully, if somewhat drunkenly, and lurches back to the sofa, where he passes out.


During the night, my fever went down.

"Amazing recovery," Dr. Haus tells Elaina with clinical satisfaction. "Fastest turnaround I've ever seen." He smiles a flat, cheerless smile.

"Thank God." Elaina's makeup is smeared. Her dress is wrinkled, and her Gibson girl is crushed. The arm and leg that bore her weight through the night are still stiff; her wrist bends inward and she stands with her weight on the opposite foot, so she looks like a stroke victim who's been paralyzed on one side.

"Sometimes these vegetative cases show a remarkable resilience." Dr. Haus is left-handed and his hand curves like a fishhook over the clipboard as he makes notes.

"Oh, why don't you drop in a bear pit," Elaina retorts, using her good arm to hoist her purse over the higher of her shoulders and hobbling out of the room.

She takes a cab to the courthouse.


Court is scheduled to reconvene at 10:00 A.M.

Elaina is late. Marty makes eloquent apologies and Debbie starts whipping up a motion to dismiss.

But Elaina finally staggers in, still looking rather disheveled. Drew, sitting in the gallery, is the first to hear her. He recognizes her footsteps from a great distance down the hall;

he jumps, and looks over his shoulder, gripping the back of the chair in front of him.

Jonathan, perhaps, knew all along that she would come. He probably expected her to arrive just in time to keep him from winning through her default. As she enters, he turns slowly to regard her baggy nylons and crushed hairdo. He probably thinks she spent the night out with a new lover. Perhaps he even thinks she's drunk. I don't think Alison ever told him that I was sick. Now he puckers, hard and tight, as if protecting himself from something that would invade him—or guarding something that would escape. Get tough, dad! I tell him. Don't let her hurt you!

Grandma Rose looks like she wants to crawl under the nearest bridge table and put a tea towel over her head. Still, she glares at Elaina to make it clear that *she* has no part of her daughter's madness.

Elaina raises her chin. Her walk grows more steady as she moves to join Marty at the plaintiff's table.

"If it please Your Honor . . ." Marty says. He stands, his pencil forming a bridge between his thumbs, and bows slightly. "My client has arrived."

"Mrs. Silverstein." Judge Picone angles his head in her direction. "I hope you can tell us why you were late."

Elaina rises slowly and looks over at Jonathan, and once again I see that new something, as if a shard of glass had lodged in each of her expansive blue eyes. Jonathan glances at her and then shuts his own eyes, covering his nose with his cupped hands.

"I had car trouble, Your Honor." Her voice is sweetly low and melodious. "I ran out of gas."

"Why didn't you phone the court clerk?" the judge asks.

Jonathan hunches over a little farther.

"I tried, Your Honor," Elaina says. "I only had enough change to call Triple A."

The judge frowns, dimpling his doughy white cheeks.

"And why couldn't . . ." Then he stops. "Oh, never mind. Let's get on with it."

Jonathan sighs. Elaina sits down. That's it. Nobody believes her, but nobody quite holds her responsible, either. This is how she always gets out of traffic tickets. It's just how charm works, I guess. I didn't have that kind of charm, and I was always jealous that she did. And why doesn't she tell the truth? Maybe she thinks it will hurt her case if the judge thinks I could die anyway. Maybe she just enjoys lying and wants to keep in practice.

Marty smacks his lips and waves his pencil like a stripper twirling a tassle.

Daniel is the plaintiff's next-to-last witness. First we get to hear the Celia Goldberg story again. And, yes, Daniel says, he knew I kept a diary, because I threatened anyone who might read it with a violent death. No, he doesn't think this entry represents a fleeting moment of personal distress; he points out that it was written about six months after Cousin Celia's death.

I'm not angry at Daniel. He's not lying, after all; he believes what he's saying. I think of him poking at the oversize, unburnable logs in the fireplace last night, of the companionable silence between him and our sisters, and I wonder if he, at least in part, has just wanted to do the right thing all this time. Even when he tried to pull the plug that night, he might have been trying to save us all from the mess I've gotten us into since then.

And Daniel must sense, like everyone else, the coming of the earthquake: the revelation of the secret that, like the fault lines of California, will crack this fragile family apart. He doesn't know exactly how, as Leah and I do, but he knows that after today nothing will be the same again. He keeps his eyes on Marty for the most part, but once in a while he is unable to resist peeking at Jonathan. And in his quickly retracted glance, which Jonathan pretends not to see, Daniel is asking Jonathan to understand that he isn't ready to face the truth about Elaina, his Mickey Mouse mom.

During his testimony I observe the gentle rise and fall of Elaina's breasts. She must know how devastated Daniel will be if he learns about her affair. But she knows that Jonathan knows—doesn't she expect him to use that information? She knows how desperate Jonathan is—if she didn't before, then she has since yesterday, when Alison brought her his offer. I guess she's so self-destructive that she doesn't care. Or maybe she just wants to get rid of me badly enough. God, she must hate me if she's willing to let Rose find out about this. Am I that much of a threat to her? Even *now*? I can hardly believe it. Especially after the way she acted last night. Unless she really does think that this is what I want? Unless she really *is* fighting for me?

Well, if they don't find out—if Drew covers well enough—she'll have *me* to thank. I can't believe that I ended up protecting her.

Debbie cross-examines Daniel, and then he steps down.

Elaina is looking at Jonathan now. Steadily. Jonathan doesn't move his head, but I can tell that he knows she's watching him. All those times she accused him of not listening? He was listening, all right—well, most of those times anyway; he just didn't want to admit it.

Marty is looking at his notes. Drew Harding is the only name left. Marty looks up at the clock. It is 11:40.

"Your Honor," he says, "the plaintiff has one more witness. If you like, we can finish before lunch—"

"What time is it?" the judge asks shrilly, his hands groping along the bench. "What time is it? I don't know what time it is."

"Eleven-forty, Your Honor," the bailiff says as soon as the judge quiets down.

Elaina reaches for Marty, her hand on his sleeve as soft as a kitten's paw. He leans down. She whispers. Then he straightens. "I beg your pardon, Your Honor. I request instead that we do break for lunch now."

Judge Picone's eyes swerve wildly. "I do wish counsel would make up his mind."

"I'm sorry, Your Honor."

"All right," the judge says, groping for the cane that leans next to the bench. "We'll recess until one P.M."

Everyone spills out into the hallway. "We're in good shape, Elaina," Marty mutters. "They'll never refute all this evidence."

"Really?" Elaina looks up at him with a dreamy, trusting smile. I notice that she isn't even wearing her hat with the veil.

"Damn straight."

"Excuse me just a tiny second." She taps him on the sleeve and clacks away. In a moment she has overtaken Alison, who is walking toward the elevators. As she passes her, Elaina observes cheerfully, "You're certainly looking lovely today. Have you lost weight?"

Jonathan is up ahead, moving in the vanguard of the crowd, with the still-hefty Debbie waddling slightly behind him.

Elaina hurries, taking the quick, delicate steps of a young girl. "Can I talk to you?" she calls to Jonathan.

Jonathan stops. Debbie grasps his elbow and glowers at Elaina through her big glasses. Jonathan seems unaware of this; his look is foggy, indifferent, as if he didn't recognize his wife; but slowly I see the fog dissolve and the hurt shine through. "You want to talk? All right."

"Alone?" Elaina asks. She sounds a bit contrite. I don't trust her. I never trust her—but especially not when she's contrite.

Debbie moves in front of Jonathan. "Mrs. Silverstein—"

"No, that's all right, Deb," Jonathan says. "I'll talk to her." He nods to Elaina, then lumbers ahead. Elaina follows, still tak-

ing quick little steps to keep up; they break away from the
crowd and go past the elevators and around the corner of the
hallway. Finally Jonathan stops and turns, folding his hands
rather primly in front of his suit.

The noise of the crowd recedes. Jonathan and Elaina are
alone here—except for me.

"You win," Elaina says.

Jonathan's brows scrunch together. "I beg your pardon?"

"I can't do it."

"Can't do . . . what?" he asks, slowly.

"This. I can't go through with this." She gestures back toward the courtroom.

"You mean . . . you want to drop the case?"

Elaina nods. "You must have known from the beginning
that I'd never go through with it."

"Uh . . . of course," Jonathan says. "It's about time."

Elaina closes her eyes and one tear creeps from underneath a mascara-caked lash. "I don't expect you to forgive me,
but . . ." She sniffs. "But I am sorry."

Jonathan blinks and sucks in a little air through his pursed
lips. He appears to be teetering on the edge of something: as if,
from habit, he's about to forgive her. After all, if he forgives
her, he can pretend she never hurt him. But then he barks,
"You're always sorry. A hell of a lot of good it does."

"No, I'm *not* always sorry," Elaina says. "Well . . ." she
smiles a little—"I guess some people would say I'm pretty sorry
in general. But do you want to know the truth? I still think I'm
right, it's just that I can't go through with it."

Jonathan blows the air out from his puffed cheeks in little
spurts, like the chugs of a locomotive.

"And believe it or not, I really *am* sorry about the trouble I
caused," Elaina goes on. "I kept thinking that this was the right
thing to do—and you *are* a little bit stubborn, you know—but
now I just can't go through with it."

"And what brought this about?"

"I just didn't think . . . what it would be like."

Jonathan raises his eyebrows. For a moment I think he's going to put his arms around her. Then he says, "You never do," and turns away.

"Wait." Elaina tugs at his sleeve. "You have to let me take two minutes to explain. See, I felt like I could hear Melissa calling to me to help her, to let her go. But then last night I wasn't sure anymore. It was as if she'd changed her mind. I could see her fighting it."

"Fighting what?"

"Didn't Alison tell you? Melissa has pneumonia."

"Pneumonia?" Jonathan echoes. He tugs on his shirt collar. "Well, well." More tugging. "I'm sure that's nothing to worry about. It's not a big deal, is it? Can't they cure that pretty easily?"

Elaina nods. "It's clearing up already. She'll be all right. But it made me realize if I won, what we'd have to do. . . . I couldn't stand that either, I just couldn't. We'll just have to pray God takes her." A few more tears have spilled over onto her cheeks.

Jonathan says nothing. He doesn't believe in God. The annual *Index of Multiple Family Housing Starts* is the closest he gets.

"Jonathan, I really need you now."

He looks at her. Why doesn't he walk away, never look back? That's what I would do. They can never heal these wounds, no matter how much their shared past or concern for us still holds them together. No matter how used to each other they've grown, or how much nostalgia they still feel for the boy and girl they were, the boy and girl who were too young to get married. "I wish you'd thought of this three months ago."

"Me too," Elaina says, smiling and blinking her misty eyes, "but it must be for the best. Everything is, isn't it? That's what my father always told me."

Jonathan sighs. "Whatever you say, dear." And he lumbers away to tell Debbie the news.

Elaina stays behind, in the relative privacy of the empty hallway, dabbing at her eyes with her handkerchief. I feel rather odd about all this. I should be relieved. I am, I guess. But I'm disappointed, too. I guess I wanted to see Drew get up on the stand and slobber all over himself. I wanted to see how Elaina was going to weasel out of going to jail for conspiracy to commit perjury. (I had no doubt that she'd weasel out of it, but it would have been interesting to watch.) I wanted to see how Rose was going to be able to keep breathing in front of the reporters and the rabbi's wife. I wanted things to get even uglier than they already have, if that was possible. Maybe I'm a bigger bitch than Elaina ever was. I don't know. I'm a very confused disembodied young person right now.

Elaina is still composing herself when Drew Harding comes around the corner of the hallway, looking like a run-over basset hound, fairly tripping over his tongue as he shuffles toward her. She smiles at him the way she always smiles at beggars and bag ladies, at people she sees in the grocery store who are lame or disfigured. It is a generous smile. Elaina could always love the lonely and cast-off.

"I saw you with him," Drew says. "Was he mean to you? Did he make you cry?"

"No, peewee doll," Elaina says, taking another dab with her handkerchief. "I'm just crying because I'm so happy."

"I can't wait until this is over."

"Well," Elaina sighs, and puts the handkerchief in her purse. "It won't be long now."

"I know, I know," Drew interrupts, "I shouldn't be standing here with you. But I just had to tell you that since I heard your voice last night, everything's changed. I'm strong again."

"My voice?"

"It was like an angel calling me from heaven. And I had to talk to you once more, Elaina, before I do what I have to do now."

Elaina clears her throat and inserts the tips of her nails

into the flatter side of her hairdo, trying to uncrush it. "Maybe you could tell me exactly what it was that you were planning to do."

"Exactly what you told me to do, darling."

"Of course. What I told you to do." She swallows, putting her hand briefly on top of her breasts.

"Don't worry, I won't blow it." Drew pushes his limp hair from his eyes. "I'll tell everyone what Melissa *really* said"—he winks—"and about how I tried everything to seduce you but you wouldn't—"

"Yes. Hmm." Elaina glances at the wall where someone has written JUSTICE SUCKS in pencil. "You know what, dear? Everything I said last night, forget I ever said it."

Drew's mouth opens. "Forget? But what about us?"

"Don't worry about that, we'll talk about that later," Elaina says gently. "Everything's going to be just fine, I promise. You need a Snickers. Maybe a Milky Way, too. There's a vending machine next to the elevator." She is taking several quarters out of her coin purse; she presses them into his hand. She knows better, I see, than to let there be a scene right here and now. Maybe she thinks Drew is starting to have alcoholic delusions and that's why he thinks he heard her voice last night. But how calm she is! Like a wide, flat ocean; as calm and as smooth as glass. I've seen her this way before, but it always startles me. Her delicate lips form a slight smile even when her face is in repose. Her legs reach down into the earth; her head is the sun itself. She has all the answers and she always will, even if she doesn't know what they are.

And, oh, mommy, no one will ever be like you again, not on this earth or anywhere else. I do love you, and I always will, even if you are crazy.

And as I think this, Elaina looks past Drew somewhere into the air, I'm not even sure where, but it's wherever I am, and I know she's looking right at me.

# 14

It's been three days since the trial.

Marty wasn't too happy about dropping the case. At first he thought Elaina was just afraid she was going to lose, and he tried to reassure her that they would have an easy victory. Then he hinted that what she wanted to do might be illegal, even dangerous. But suddenly Elaina didn't seem as naïve about the legal system as she had in the past, and although she apologized to Marty *ad nauseam,* with much hand-wringing, for all the trouble she was putting him through, she repeated that she had simply changed her mind, and finally made it clear to him that this was all the explanation he was going to get.

Marty knew this would be bad for his book sales.

When Marty stood up and told Judge Picone that his client was withdrawing her plea, Rose gasped, and Alison, sitting next to her, dropped her lipstick on the floor. Judge Picone, though, didn't seem particularly surprised.

Jonathan, too, nodded at Debbie as if he'd known this would happen all along. Then he quickly collected his papers, glanced at his watch, and reviewed his pocket calendar, making it clear that the entire trial had just been a minor inconvenience in the hectic life of Jonathan Silverstein, Boy Real-Estate Syndicator.

And so everyone went home.

*      *      *

The next day Jonathan started making the arrangements to have me moved from Mt. Moriah. He had already researched the best chronic-care facilities in the area: There's one in Orinda, the Nature Hill Recovery Center. The brochures really make it sound lovely: landscaped grounds, Jacuzzi, friendly nutritionist and chiropractors on twenty-four-hour duty. Everything the comatose patient could want.

They're taking my body over there today, and the entire family is coming to the hospital for the Big Event. The infection is just about gone from my lungs, so with the help of a team of highly paid technicians, a portable respirator, and a special van that looks like a mobile recording studio, this should be a regular joyride.

Jonathan and Elaina arrive separately. (Jonathan is still staying at the Holiday Inn.) Elaina is actually on time, which in itself is enough to make the day go down in history. Daniel brings her, since it's a Sunday. Daniel works every weekday now; in fact, he has his very own cubicle at Abracadabra, which he has plastered with sales quotas and upbeat reminders to smile at the customer, and where he is accumulating a pile of *Wall Street Journals* on his desk. The Elf has promised him an easy rise from sales to marketing to management. But Daniel still has entrepreneurial dreams of his own: Once he has enough experience, he wants to start a computer consulting service that will go into private homes and teach people to use their personal computers. Such a business has low overhead and he can start with one employee: himself. Daniel usually goes to the office on weekends to work on this plan—make phone calls, do market research—when he isn't helping out at Dmitri's. But he is taking this Sunday off. I think he wants to see Jonathan, or maybe he even has some lingering affection for me.

I guess Elaina has adjusted to the idea of having me around. Maybe she's starting to see the good side of it: There'll be a whole new staff of doctors to flirt with; she can ask Daniel to drive her out to Orinda (she claims she gets lost whenever she drives through the Caldecott Tunnel), and maybe she can use that to wheedle Daniel away from whatever it is that's been keeping him so busy. It might not be that easy. She doesn't know yet about the girl he's been dating, the petite blond receptionist from the paper-manufacturing firm. I bet there'll be a fight or two about that when she does find out, and that'll be fun to watch. I might be able to stir things up a bit more, if I . . .

But it's hard to get psyched up for it somehow. I'm feeling kind of bored. As if the real drama is over and what am I going to do for the next ten or twenty or thirty years while they're keeping me alive with that Magic Air machine and an arsenal of miracle drugs? Okay, Elaina will be coming to visit me every day, and there's all my other relatives to keep on eye on. . . .

Rose and Alison are sitting in the lounge at the end of the hall. "I'll never get to see Melissa now, Orinda is so far away," Rose says. "I still can't drive with this arm. Elaina could take me, but she has no sense of direction. She's always so difficult." She feels the material of Alison's papaya-colored leather blouse, the one with the quarterback-size shoulder pads. "And you'll be going back to New York soon. Alone, I suppose."

God bless Grandma Rose. But enough is enough.

Of course, there's Becky and Leah to watch over. They get more interesting all the time. They've come today, too—right now they're standing outside my room. Becky has painted a purple star on her cheek. When Rose saw it she asked, "Do the girls *wear* things like that now?" Becky retorted that some of her classmates had them tattooed on their faces, and that she was thinking of doing it herself.

Becky offered Leah a ride to the hospital in her Camaro. I like to think that my near-demise put her anger at Leah into its proper context. But I think, too, from various comments she's made, that Becky is beginning to realize that nothing lasting could have come from her relationship with Jeff. He's such a *cave dweller,* after all, and he's always wonking out that somebody is going to drop a candy wrapper on the ground, as if *that* were a nuclear event. Becky feels that the world has always been somewhat polluted, and that it probably always will be. Besides, Jeff would have little in common with the movie-star friends she will have after she gets famous.

So now she stands close to Leah, softly humming "The Rich Should Die"; she looks like she's trying to think of something to say.

Leah balances on one leg; the other leg, bent to form an *L,* is propped against the wall. I see new contours in her face: Her cheekbones have emerged in just these past few months. I can read the knowledge in those lines, knowledge and decision: She is willing to carry the solitary awareness of Elaina's infidelity. If nothing else, it is a secret Leah shares with Jonathan.

And now I have a vision of the future. Like previews of coming attractions on my own private movie screen. In ten years Leah will be slimmer, the hollows of her cheeks well defined, her eyes large, clear, and enchanted. The worry lines will never fade, but they will shape her, the way Grandpa Abe could cut a diamond to give it more value. I doubt that she'll go into the Peace Corps—she's too much Elaina's daughter ever to want to live without indoor plumbing—but she might go back east to school, get a doctorate in psychology; she might do social work; she will probably have a family of her own as well. I would love to see that—for me it would be like watching one of those high-speed films of a flower opening. But the farther away I keep from her, the better it will be. I can't be too close without trying to influence her, and my intentions may be good, but she deserves to make her own mistakes and her own discoveries without me.

So what's left for me to do? I move back into my hospital

room. Jonathan and Elaina are there; somehow they ended up alone together. Jonathan is tugging at his collar and muttering about the incompetence of a hospital administration that would give a chief resident Sundays off. "No wonder they don't make a profit," he says.

Elaina is bent over me, rearranging the sheets around my neck. "How are things at the Holiday Inn?" she asks. "You must miss my cold feet and my snoring at night."

Jonathan glances around him, as if he just realized that he was alone with his wife. "Oh," he says. "Hmm." Long pause.

Elaina keeps fussing with my covers, not looking at him.

"There's one thing I wanted to ask you," Jonathan says suddenly. "About Melissa's diary."

"Yes?" Elaina asks sweetly.

"Who was Willie?"

"Willie who, dear?"

"In her diary. The one she was . . . seeing. We . . . I never met him. He sounds kind of fishy to me. I thought she might have told you about him."

Still bent over me, Elaina seems fascinated by my eyes. There are tiny white rectangles in each of my pupils, reflecting the shape of the window. She pushes the hair off my forehead. "I don't know, either, dear," she says. Her gaze moves along the tube of the respirator, from my throat to the console.

"Hmm," Jonathan grunts.

"I guess there are some things we'll never know," Elaina says, straightening up at last. "We have to live with that."

I suppose she has a point. I'm glad she didn't tell him about the prof, anyway. That was sort of nice of her.

"So what do you think, Jon-a-Man?" She turns to Jonathan now, showering blue light on him. "We don't have to make a big drama out of this, you know. You could come home."

"Huh," Jonathan says.

"You must miss Lee Emma's frozen peas."

"Mmm."

"Every night before he goes to sleep, Paddy O'Flanagan asks where his daddy is."

Jonathan puckers.

"I miss you an awful lot, Jon-a-Man."

Jonathan tugs on his collar. "Well," he says, "maybe." Pause. "Maybe."

What's this? Come on, dad! You can't forget she cheated on you, that she spends hundreds of dollars at the beauty shop every month, and wrecks a new car every year!

Or can he? Like Elaina says, I really don't understand these things. Maybe after twenty-five years, there are bonds between two people that even their children can't see. They have their secret lives as much as I do. I've been presumptuous to try to intrude on that, to think that I can know it all. I wish I could be wholly inside Jonathan's mind, so I could experience for myself what it is that might keep them together. But that's never going to happen. I have a feeling he will move back home, though. Well, good for mom and dad, but, God, I'm tired of it! I mean, isn't this where I came in?

Rose and Alison march in suddenly. Daniel follows them by a few steps; he slips into the chair next to my bed. Now the fretting about logistics begins: Where is the doctor? Where are the orderlies? Who gets to ride in the ambulance with me? Rose wants to know when was the last time my sheets were changed, and Alison wonders aloud if, in all charity, they can't put a little blusher on my cheeks.

I find it all rather irritating, and drift back out into the hall, to my sisters. Just in time to see Becky glance at Leah, then sigh, "Bee-stunkomatic, this is going to take all dee-stay."

Leah looks at her. The frown is between her eyes, but a smile is starting on her mouth. "Rully."

"If you ask me, this whole thing was fee-stucked from the start."

Leah just nods.

"Yeah," Becky goes on, thumping her rear end against the

wall. "The 'droids don't know what they're doing. Leave it to them and they always get it all shorted out."

"It's too bad," Leah says slowly, "'cause lots of other people have to like pay for their mistakes."

Pause.

"I'm sorry," Becky says.

"It was my fault."

"No, not really. I could've seen you guys were better for each other." Becky shakes her head. "I never really groaned for Jeff that much anyway. I mean, no offense, but he's so *conventional*." Pause. "It's okay if you gee-stuys want to go out and flare."

"I don't know." Leah bites her lip. So many other people dangle from the string that ties her to Jeff, and so many ghosts are trying to reincarnate themselves in her relationship with him. Perhaps it would be better for Leah to start again with someone new. Then again, there aren't many boys like Jeff, kissed with the same gentle madness as she. She knows all of this—so it's too soon for her to decide what to do.

For now at least, Leah is happy to have her sister back. The one she always cared about—like Elaina, I was always jealous of their closeness. But their relationship will have to be a little different from now on. Leah can't be the same appendage to Becky that she's always been, and she won't be quite so eager to blame herself for everything now that's she's admitted the worst possibility to herself.

Perhaps there will always be a kernel of doubt in her own mind about her paternity. The question cannot be asked, let alone answered. Even so, I don't think it will give her any more bad dreams.

Elaina comes out of my room crying. "Don't worry, girls," she says to Becky and Leah as she passes them on the way to the ladies' room. "I'll be all right. Please just stay right where you are."

Becky and Leah sigh and, with a glance at each other, tacitly decide to do precisely that.

Rose comes out of the room next. "What are you girls doing out here?"

Alison is right behind Rose. "Motha, don't you think you should set down and rest? I'll get us some coffee."

"I'll never get to see her now," Rose chirps as Alison leads her by her good arm down the hall to the lounge. "Orinda is so far away. Elaina could take me, but she . . ."

That leaves Daniel alone with Jonathan in my room. I'm curious about that—so I pop back inside.

Jonathan is peering out the window, through the blinds. "What would you do if you were running this hospital?" he asks Daniel. "Did you notice that they have two attendants in the parking lot?"

"Dad—" Daniel says.

"If I were running this hospital, I'd paint the halls a darker color that doesn't show the dirt as much. They have a new machine that lets you paint twice as fast. We've used it in some of our buildings—it looks like one of those trucks that they used to spray tear gas on campus rioters with."

"Dad . . ." Daniel starts again. "There's something I want to talk to you about."

"Of course, son."

Daniel shoves his hands into the pockets of his khaki pants. During the week he wears gray suits, herringbone or light plaids, but on weekends he sports LaCoste shirts and Topsiders. "I've got this new business thing going pretty well now."

"Really? Good for you."

"What I'm trying to say is . . ."

He breaks off. My respirator fills the room like a hissing pot. *Whoosh*-click. *Whoosh*-click. All this fuss, just so that machine can keep making that monotonous sound. My body shudders.

Jonathan is still staring out the window.

"*Dad,* I'm talking to you."

Jonathan turns to face Daniel. "I'm listening, son."

"Well, I just mean that maybe I *will* go back to school. Part-time, at night. Maybe."

I can see Jonathan struggling with the biggest smile that's been on his face since he registered his first public offering with the SEC. "Whatever you want to do, son," he says.

Daniel sighs. Well, maybe he'll learn what I never quite did: that no matter what he does, no matter how Jonathan reacts, that won't be enough. Daniel has to do it for himself.

Alison comes back in. "Janathan," she croons, "the narse said that they have sem mar equipment to set up, that it's going to be et least anothah helf en ower."

"Half an *hour*?" Jonathan chokes.

"Raylax." Alison smiles. "Wouldn't you like some coffee? Daniel, you wouldn't mind getting your father—"

"I don't want any coffee," Jonathan pouts.

"That's all right, Auntie Al," Daniel says. "I have to make a few phone calls." On his way out, he winks at dad. "Business," he explains.

*Whoosh*-click. *Whoosh*-click. How dull.

Alison glances at me, and then away, with a shiver. "You must be very heppy about this."

"Under the circumstances."

"Of course. I meant—"

"What *did* you mean?" Jonathan asks sharply. "What exactly do you *ever* mean?"

*Whoosh*-click. *Whoosh*-click. Way to go, dad.

"What I meant was . . ." Alison shrugs. "Please don't get in a huff about it." She turns, as if to go. "I'm flaying back to New Yawk tomorrow. I've truly missed Manhettan. The musayums—"

"Have a nice trip," Jonathan says.

Alison's mouth sinks into its deepest, most bitter curves.

She is practicing for the years to come. For with Alison, too, I have a sneak preview of the future: Her modeling agency will thrive. She will make all the money she ever wanted, accumulate more furs and jewelry than she can wear twice to any *posh* restaurant. She will travel to Italy for her purses and to Hong Kong for her shoes. But all the face-lifts she can afford won't erase that look of mouth sinking into chin, the face of someone who only wants what can't be had. They always said I looked like her.

Gradually, superimposed on it, I see Elaina's face, reflected in the ladies' room mirror. It is recognizably the face of Alison's sister. But Elaina is smiling and she is forever young. She is putting fresh lipstick on top of fresh lipstick with the joy of a child drawing on the walls.

Oh, mommy. You're the only one, really. The only one I don't want to leave. You're beautiful and crazy, and you make me feel crazy, but what a fountain you are! What a forest I can never finish playing in!

She leans close to the mirror and then pulls back and smooths the top of her hair. She inclines her head slightly and puckers to exaggerate the effect of her high cheekbones. Then she smiles, all girlish teeth, as if someone in her head just told a wonderful joke. As if she knew I was here, and knew what I was thinking.

She winks. I'm startled. For me? Then she puts out one finger and taps her nail against the mirror. Is she just admiring herself, or is she saying goodbye?

Because she must know that I'm not going to stick around after all. God, I don't think I ever wanted to stay like this, but I never would have admitted it as long as Elaina didn't want it, either. She must finally have realized that she had to let me choose for myself, and take a chance that I'd make the right decision in the end. That's the hardest thing for parents.

There just isn't any point to haunting them anymore. I got some of the answers I wanted, and I don't mind not knowing the rest. I could hang around for spite, but who would suffer for it in the end? Let me wish them the best and move on. Yes, I'm scared of dying, but who isn't scared of dying, or going away to college, or getting married, or any of that stuff? I'm finally more scared of what will happen to me if I stay here with them forever, unchanging.

In the distance I hear one final *whoosh*-click.

They'll be fine without me. I'm on my way.

**REGIONAL LIBRARY SERVICE**

**ATHENS AREA**

ATHENS, GEORGIA 30601